The Urbana Free Library

To renew materials call
217-367-4057

10-09

DATE DUE	
NOV 09 2009	DEC 03 2009
NOV 30 2009	
DEC 20 2009	
FEB 16 2010	

MISSING, PRESUMED WED

AN ELIZABETH PEPPERHAWK/
AVIVAH ROSEN MYSTERY

MISSING, PRESUMED WED

SHARON WILDWIND

FIVE STAR
A part of Gale, Cengage Learning

GALE
CENGAGE Learning™

Detroit • New York • San Francisco • New Haven, Conn • Waterville, Maine • London

GALE
CENGAGE Learning

Set in 11 pt. Plantin.
Printed on permanent paper.

LIBRARY OF CONGRESS CATALOGING-IN-PUBLICATION DATA

Wildwind, Sharon Grant.
   Missing, presumed wed : an Elizabeth Pepperhawk/Avivah Rosen mystery / Sharon Wildwind. — 1st ed.
     p. cm.
   ISBN-13: 978-1-59414-787-6 (alk. paper)
   ISBN-10: 1-59414-787-6 (alk. paper)
   1. Vietnam War, 1961–1975—Veterans—Fiction. 2. Murder—Investigation—Fiction. I. Title.
PR9199.4.W542M57 2009
813'.6—dc22
                                           2009016129

First Edition. First Printing: September 2009.
Published in 2009 in conjunction with Tekno Books and Ed Gorman.

Printed in the United States of America
1 2 3 4 5 6 7 13 12 11 10 09

To Ken and Jeannie, for love, a wedding, and true hope.

ACKNOWLEDGMENTS

Thanks to God for his wonderful gifts of both writing and patience.

A big thanks to the following people, who contributed huge amounts of background knowledge and assistance:

Ken Coates for his fascinating book, *North to Alaska: Fifty Years on the World's Most Remarkable Highway* (1992, McClelland & Stewart).

Jeff Augram, who helped me get a kid lost and found at the Asheville airport, circa 1974, and reminded me of a real-life juvenile officer, who became the model for Ollie Lambert.

Pam Olumoya, Sheri Gaia Chapin, Lisa Lansky, and Lonnie Cruise who were terrific supports as they read, commented, and discussed parts of the story.

Avivah Wargon, who, in addition to allowing Avivah Rosen to borrow her first name, gave me a most generous chunk of her time and reading skill.

Lee Lofland for his view of conflict of interests in small police forces and Hank Ryan for the same in relation to journalists.

Acknowledgments

Leslie Budewitz for free legal advice—for my characters, so it was okay.

Janet Bolin, Lydia Hester, Rhonda Lane, and K.B. Inglee, who knew the dos and don'ts and timings involved with tobacco suckering.

James Sterrett for military information.

Susan Wittig Albert for information about moon and strewing gardens.

My agent, Janet Benrey, terrific as always, and the people at Five Star Press, who give these characters a place to strut their hour upon the stage. Thanks to Gordon Aalborg for the editing.

My wonderful husband Ken, who not only provided his usual platinum-standard support, advice, and proofreading, but knew enough about Irish history and The Troubles to get me over the rough bits.

INTRODUCTION

In the mid-seventies, I was a member of a consciousness-raising group. Women in our group ranged from mid-twenties to mid-sixties. We met once a week to talk about how our lives were changing and how we intended to take advantage of new opportunities opening up for women.

At the time, the perceived story of women's lives ran something like this. Proper women—read straight women—centered their lives on home, hearth, and children. If they worked outside the home it was as secretaries, nurses, or teachers. Women quit work either when they married or when they became pregnant. During World War I and more so during World War II, women took on nontraditional roles to "help out" with the war effort. After the wars, they returned to their homes, and here you could choose one of two stories—either glad the men were home and they could resume their normal and proper roles, or they were as mad as hell and drifted into alcoholism, hypochondria, or illicit love affairs.

What profoundly startled me was learning that every woman in the group had, at some time, broken that perceived pattern. The older they were, the more often they had stepped outside the boundaries. Contrary to what I'd been taught, women who lived through the first three-quarters of the twentieth century drove trucks and ran farms and businesses. They had lovers. They made reproductive choices that were, at the time, both illegal and risky. They pursued lifelong careers that didn't end with pregnancy. Their whole attitude was that men might have written history, but they did so without knowing diddly-squat about what went on in women's lives.

Professional woman, stay-at-home mom, homemaker, feminist, lesbian, straight, peace activist, and veteran. In our group, labels didn't matter. What did matter was that the perceived patterns were shattering. With the changes that were happening in the early seventies, we, as women, could look forward to finally being able to get credit in our own name; to buying a house or a car without having a man's signature on the bill of sale; have a glimmer of equal access to jobs, even without pay parity; and hope that the future for our daughters would be as least as bright as for our sons.

It was fun to relive the mid-seventies with a different consciousness-raising group, the women in this book. They are most improper women, on the move in their careers and in their most intimate relationships. As Benny Kirkpatrick says, "People do go all gushy at a wedding." Sometimes, even at a wedding, women take charge of their lives, leave broken promises and false hopes behind, and learn the art of redemption.

Here comes the bride, and her attendants: revenge, deception, and murder.

CHAPTER 1

Friday, 31 May 1974, 0930 hours
Memorial Day
Asheville, North Carolina
The dispatcher's tinny voice vibrated over the ancient intercom, "Rover, pick up three."

Avivah Rosen put her finger on the long, silver switch. All it would take was a slight pressure to retort, "That's *Constable Rosen*" or, better yet, "Go to hell." She moved her finger away from the intercom button to the phone. Never antagonize a police dispatcher, the person who controlled her workday. She punched the phone button for line three. "Asheville City Police, Juvenile Division, Constable Rosen. May I help you?"

Mark Fulford's voice sounded small and breathless. "Aunt Avivah? It's Mark. I don't know how to get home. I'm hungry and thirsty, and I only have twenty-five cents left from my allowance. Is that enough to buy a hamburger?"

Avivah sat on the edge of a creaky wooden office chair. "Mark, honey, where are you?"

"At the airport, waiting for Uncle Joseph's plane."

"Where's Grandma Grace?"

"Gone. A man hit her, then he pushed her into his car and they drove away."

Sweat broke out along the elastic band at the bottom of Avivah's bra. Grace Kirkpatrick would have screamed her head off if anyone bothered her. And yet, Mark was a truthful child.

11

If he said a man hit his grandmother, that's what happened. Thank goodness the police had a substation at the airport. "Mark, do you see a policeman?"

"No."

"Do you see anyone who works at the airport?"

"There's a lady behind a counter."

"Listen carefully. Don't hang up the phone. Put the receiver down and go tell that lady there's an emergency. Ask her to come to the phone. Do it now."

A sound of the receiver banging against something hard reverberated painfully in Avivah's ear. In a moment, a woman's voice said, "This is Miss Davenport from Piedmont Airlines. Is there a problem?"

"This is Constable Rosen from Juvenile Division, Asheville City Police. The young boy with you is Mark Fulford. He's gotten separated from his grandmother. Please take Mark to the airport police office; my partner and I will meet him there. And please page Mrs. Grace Kirkpatrick."

"Grace Kirkpatrick."

"Yes, now let me speak to Mark again."

His voice was less breathless. "Hello, Aunt Avivah."

"Mark, I'm proud of you for calling me. That was exactly the right thing to do. I know your mom taught you never to go with strangers, but it's okay if you go with Miss Davenport. She'll take you to the police office. I'll be there as fast as I can."

"Okay, Aunt Avivah." He hung up.

Mark never required lengthy explanations. Point him at a task and he did it. Avivah wondered if he'd absorbed that trait by osmosis from his soon-to-be-stepfather. Ex–Green Beret Benny Kirkpatrick had always been a take-the-hill guy.

Avivah took her cap off the rack by the office door and walked down the hall, peering into empty offices. The civilian clerical staff had Memorial Day off.

She found her partner, Sergeant Oliver Lambert, wedged into a chair behind the record clerk's desk. Both the chair and Ollie looked as though they had joined the police department about the time Dwight D. Eisenhower became president. She wondered why his bulk didn't shatter the chair.

He put his hand over the receiver, "What?"

"A six-year-old possibly abandoned at the airport."

Ollie spun his chair around so that his back faced Avivah. He said, "Everything will be okay. Get a motel room. I'll be there about noon. Madge won't find out. She's visiting her sister this weekend. Love you, too." He made kissy-face noises, and hung up. The chair creaked as he stood.

Avivah turned on her heel and walked away. She liked Ollie. At least she had before she heard his side of that conversation. Behind her, Avivah heard Ollie hurrying to catch up. The sound of their boots reverberated on the old building's tiled floor.

When Ollie drew up beside Avivah, she said, "My neighbor's younger son just phoned me from the airport. He says a man forced his grandmother into a car and took off with her."

One of two officers coming through the front door said, "Morning, Deputy Dawg." The other one whistled and said, "Here, girl. Here, girl."

Avivah stared straight ahead, her eyes focused on a bronze plaque beside the front door. Pikers. She'd been jeered at by drill instructors who had been in the business before those two were born. If they thought they could intimidate her, they had another thought coming.

The policemen went past her laughing.

Claiborn Denham, the dispatcher, came out of his office by the front door. He held a piece of butcher's paper with a large, bloody bone in it. "We're having a cookout tomorrow. Thought you might like a snack." He tossed the bone at Avivah.

She stepped aside. The bone splattered against a wall and slid to the floor, leaving a red streak down the marble wainscoting. Avivah patted her flat stomach. "Thanks, Clay, but I just had a big bowl of dog chow. Couldn't eat another mouthful."

She pushed open the bronze handle on the door and went out into the small parking lot, which the police and fire departments shared.

Ollie asked, "How long are you going to put up with that?"

Avivah opened the driver's door to their patrol car. "As long as it takes."

Two elderly women in print dresses and straw hats walked past the police station. One of them pointed at her. They put their heads together and whispered.

Avivah smiled and waved to them. At least she hoped her gritted teeth resembled a smile. The women's whispered curiosity bothered her more than the officers' dog play. Specimen: police officer, female, one each, for general display, public relations, and goodwill.

Ollie fastened his seat belt. "They're sure to hire someone else to be Safety Dog by September."

Avivah started the car. "At least in the dog suit, I felt as though I made a difference. Being hugged by twenty kindergarten kids beats being shuttled back and forth every week between the back waters of Community Services and Juvenile."

Ollie's big, fleshy face looked hurt.

"I didn't mean to suggest that Juvenile wasn't important. It's just that I'm a street cop. Or I was, and want to be again."

"And I'm an overweight, over-the-hill cop who works Juvenile because he can't cut it on the street anymore?"

Avivah flipped on the cruiser's lights. She couldn't justify the siren, as much as she would like to relieve her frustration by weaving in and out of Biltmore Avenue traffic, lights and sirens blazing. "What? You want an ego boost? Want me to list your commendations and awards for youth work?"

"Not especially. I'm just in a bad mood. Hell, you're a Viet Nam veteran. That alone deserves respect."

Avivah pulled up on the bumper of a slow-moving car, hit a brief "Brrp" on the siren and enjoyed the way the driver's head jerked as he checked his rearview mirror and slid his car out of her way. "Not everyone feels that way. The Chief may think I'm the greatest public relations gimmick going, but the other constables are stuck with me, and they don't like it. At least—so far—I haven't found body fluids in my locker, and no one has tried to take me down in the evidence room."

"You say that as though that's something to be proud of."

"You haven't heard the stories I have about what happens to women cops in other cities." She glanced at him. "Where do you get off, making kissy-face noises over the phone and meeting women in motel rooms while Madge is visiting her sister?"

Ollie pursed his lips. "I was under the impression that the secretaries' restroom was a hotbed of gossip."

"Maybe it is, but conversation stops when I walk in. *The girls*—as even you refer to them—don't like me messing in *the boys'* sandbox. They're not even keen on sharing their restroom with me. I'm *persona non grata* as far as lunch invitations and sharing gossip goes."

Ollie pinched his earlobe. "Ouch. I guess I'll have to watch that girl business."

"Don't bother on my account."

"Take that chip off your shoulder for one minute and just listen. I was talking to my daughter. Those kissy-face noises were for my grandson. I'm meeting both of them in Columbia tomorrow. If you *had* heard the office gossip, you'd know that Davie was born with two fingers missing on his right hand."

Avivah stopped the "I'm sorry" before she said it. Missing fingers sounded more like an inconvenience than a tragedy, unless their absence was a marker of other problems. "Healthy otherwise?"

Ollie relaxed. "Thanks."

"For what?"

"For asking a sensible question instead of smothering me with sympathy. Yes, he's fine, except for a weird-looking hand, which he has no trouble stuffing in his mouth to suck."

"I gather you're okay with it, but Madge isn't?"

"Madge is fine. It's his other grandmother who is the problem. She can't stand any imperfection. When Davie was born, she sent out birth announcements that began, 'It is with great regret that we inform you that our grandson was born deformed.' It got worse. We got phone calls from prayer groups asking what neonatal intensive care unit Davie was in, and were we considering donating his organs."

They cleared the city limits. Avivah accelerated and let the cruiser's big engine do what it did best, run flat out on an open road. "That's stupid and rude."

"I agree. I don't know what crazy idea that woman has come up with now, but my daughter was hysterical when she phoned. She said she didn't want to talk about it on the phone, and she had to talk to me before Madge found out, because when Madge *did* find out, she was going to drive down to South Carolina and pulverize Davie's other grandmother. All I managed to get out of my daughter was that nothing was wrong with Davie."

"We seem to be up to our necks in grandmothers today."

"This kid who phoned you, you know his family?"

"We're next-door neighbors." The Fulfords were a lot more than neighbors, but she thought it best to keep it simple for now.

"His grandmother—would she think it was okay to leave a

kid alone for a few minutes while she grabbed a couple of beers?"

"Absolutely not. She takes in strays, not makes them. And she's not really his grandmother."

"Oh?"

"That is, she will be his grandmother in a week. Mark's dad was in Special Forces. He went missing in 'Nam. Mark's mom is remarrying next Saturday. The groom is my friend Benny. Grace is the groom's mother. I'm not sure if that will make her Mark's step-grandmother or grandmother-by-marriage. Not that what she's called would matter to Mark. He adores her."

Avivah closed her mouth. Too many people had an opinion about how long a wife should wait for her missing-in-action husband. Avivah didn't want to hear Ollie's opinion. She knew exactly where *she* stood. She'd watched Lorraine and Benny's hell for years. It was time to put an end to it.

All Ollie asked was, "What were Mark and his grandmother doing at the airport?"

"Grace's youngest son is flying in. She and Mark went to the airport to meet him."

"What does the boy say happened?"

"That someone hit Grace, forced her into a car, and drove away. He's a shy child, not given to making up stories."

"She have any enemies?"

"She's not even from around here. She and her husband own a farm and a hardware store in Missouri."

"She one of those frail grandmotherly types?"

"She's a politically active feminist, who is a part-time welder. Born and raised in Alaska. Helped build the Alaska Highway during World War II."

"Doesn't sound like the kind of woman who would be manhandled willingly into a car."

Avivah turned into the long road leading to the airport.

"That's what worries me."

Mark sat at a side counter in the substation. He dropped the remains of a hamburger on the paper wrap and ran to hug Avivah's leg. His hugs had always felt like little birds, gossamer and trembly. Lately, the little bird had started to grow bones. She smoothed his hair. "You okay, honey?"

He nodded, but the face that looked up at her didn't look okay. "Mark, this is my partner, Constable Lambert."

It was a long way from Mark's eyes to Ollie's face, and as Mark's gaze traveled upward, his expression grew more fearful. He'd never liked stories about giants.

"I see you like music," Ollie said, pointing to the green T-shirt Mark wore.

Mark clutched at his shirt, wrinkling it with both hands as he held it out. His words came out in a rush. "Uncle Joseph sent it to me. He's a fiddler and he travels all over Ireland. He played at this festival last year. See, there's his name."

Ollie lifted up Mark in one easy motion, and sat him on the counter so that they were almost eye-to-eye. "I like fiddle music."

Ollie leaned across the counter and tapped the constable, who was talking on the phone, on the shoulder. "Interview room free?"

The man nodded and hiked a finger toward an open door.

Mark insisted on neatly packaging the remains of his burger and drink. He deposited them in a trash can. When everyone was settled behind a closed door, Ollie said, "Mark, I want to ask you some questions, but I want your mom here when I do. Is she home right now?"

"She and Grandda Quinn went to pick up wedding stuff. They won't be back until late."

Avivah's muscles tightened. She hadn't thought about Grace Kirkpatrick's family. Grace had a husband, teenage daughter,

Benny, and two other sons, who would all have to be told that their wife or mother was missing. At least Avivah could make sure they heard the news from her instead of a stranger.

Ollie said, "Let's phone her, shall we?"

No one answered. Avivah hung up the receiver and reached for the wallet she carried in her back uniform pocket. The creased piece of paper she handed to Ollie gave her permission to take Mark and his older brother from the school grounds and make emergency medical decisions for them. "This help any?"

"It's better than nothing. You've known the family a while?"

"Four years. We were all posted to Fort Bragg. I've known Mark since he was two."

Ollie sat down across the table from Mark. "You're right, son, your mom's not home. Is it okay with you if Constable Rosen is here while I ask you questions?"

"Sure."

"If there are any questions you don't want to answer, you tell me."

"Okay."

Avivah sat at the table and opened her notebook.

"What time did you and your grandmother get to the airport this morning?"

"After breakfast."

"What did you do when you got here?"

"We parked Dad's truck in the parking lot and came inside."

A few weeks ago Benny had asked Mark and Randy to think about what they wanted to call him after he and Lorraine married. Without a ruffle, Mark had gone from "Uncle Ben" at supper to "Dad" at breakfast.

"Then what did you do?"

"We looked at this TV that tells you when planes are landing. Uncle Joseph's plane was *delayed*." Mark opened and closed his hands to show the TV was blinking.

Had Joseph Kirkpatrick's plane arrived yet? Was he wandering around the terminal frustrated that no one had met him? Avivah went to the door, opened it, and said to the constable, "Could you check on the arrival of a delayed plane out of New York?"

As she took her seat again, Ollie asked, "What did you do then?"

"Grandma Grace phoned dad. She said it would be a while before the plane landed, so we might as well go get ice cream 'cause there was no sense sitting around being bored and pinching our backsides on uncomfortable chairs."

Avivah could imagine Grace's broad midwestern twang.

"Were you going to walk or ride to get ice cream?"

"Ride."

"So you went back to the parking lot. What happened?"

Mark squirmed in his seat. He whispered, "I sat in Dad's truck and Grandma Grace fixed my seat belt. And . . . and . . ."

"Go slow, take your time."

Mark looked at the table. "She walked around the truck and this car stopped behind us. A man got out and Grandma Grace yelled at him. Then she slapped him, and he hit her back, and she kind of fell, so he stuffed her in his car, and they drove away."

When Mark sat in Benny's truck, his head wasn't visible over the seat. Avivah asked, "Mark, if you had your seat belt on, how were you able to see this?"

"In the side mirror."

Ollie Lambert leaned in closer. "What did your grandma yell at the man?"

Mark pressed his lips together. "A word I'm not supposed to say."

"How about whispering it in my ear."

Mark cupped his hands around his mouth and whispered. Mark pulled back and asked, "How come that's a bad thing to say?"

"Because it's an insult to the person's parents."

"Oh."

"Is that the first thing your grandma said?"

"Yes. The car stopped behind us, and the man got out. He said, 'Grace, I want to talk to you,' and Grandma Grace said that word."

Grace knew her abductor.

"Then what?"

"They yelled at each other some more, but I didn't hear what they said. Then he hit her and they drove off."

Avivah reached over and put her arm across Mark's shoulders. "Mark doesn't like it when adults yell. He puts his hands over his ears."

"What did you do?"

"Nothing. By the time I got out of my seat belt, they were gone. I ran and called Aunt Avivah."

"What kind of car did the man have?"

"Big. Dark blue."

"What did the man look like?"

"He was old."

Ollie stood and shuffled a few steps as though he were an old man. "That old?"

Mark put his hands to his mouth and giggled. "No."

"As old as Constable Rosen?"

"Oh, yes."

"Was he as old as me?"

"I think so. He was pretty old."

Their suspect was a middle-age man, someone about Grace's age.

"He wasn't, maybe, one of your friends' grandfather, or a

21

neighbor, or someone you've seen at the grocery store?"

Mark folded his arms. "I never saw him before in my life."

There was a knock on the door and a constable looked into the room. "Your plane from New York is due to land in ten minutes."

CHAPTER 2

Elizabeth Pepperhawk arched her neck to follow jet contrails across the sky. They were too high for Joseph's plane, and headed away from Asheville, but she could still hope. The sooner Benny corralled all of the Kirkpatricks to help with wedding preparations, the sooner she could take her own life back.

She held a string of outdoor Christmas lights, playing out a length to Benny Kirkpatrick as though he were a kite. More like a kite stuck in a tree. Green leaves concealed the upper part of his body, leaving only hips, legs, and ladder visible. Tension on the lights increased as he secured one end of it around a tree trunk.

Benny came down the ladder, carried it across the clearing, and set it up again. Pepper followed him, trailing lights behind her as she went. One ladder leg sank into softer soil near the stream bank. Pepper braced the leg with her shoulder as Benny went up the ladder. She handed the lights to him. "This is the last one." Pepper looked at the wire spiderweb overhead. "It's going to look like a fairyland."

Benny worked his way down the ladder. "You might down-play that idea."

"What? 'Drinks are served in the fairyland' might not go over too well with a bunch of Green Berets?"

"Might not."

Benny folded the ladder and laid it down. He turned his body a little away from Pepper and she knew he was checking his watch again. He looked so tired. Lately, Benny had had too many final exams. Too little sleep. Too much wedding preparation. Too large a ghost of Randall Fulford bringing Benny awake screaming most nights for the past two weeks.

Her old house might be sturdy, but Viet Nam had conditioned her to listen for sounds in the night. A year as a nurse in Viet Nam had erased any security Pepper felt growing up. Benny had said it once, "Security is only an illusion."

"Which nightmare was it last night?"

"The one where Randall is King Herod. I tried to tell him that the boys had grown up since he died, but he convinced me that they were still the same age they were when he went missing. Then he cut off their heads." He looked at his watch again.

"It's only ten minutes since the last time you looked at your watch."

"I know."

"How long has it been now?"

"Forty-five minutes."

"Forty-five minutes isn't an unreasonable time for Randy to spend sprucing up his father's memorial stone. Some families spend all of Memorial Day at the cemetery."

"*Some families* aren't a thirteen-year-old boy. I don't want him brooding, that's all. I wish he'd let me help, make it a father-and-son activity."

"It *is* a father-and-son activity."

Benny deflated as surely as if Pepper's punch had been physical. "Only I'm not the father."

"No, you're the one Randall left behind to help raise his sons."

"Thanks. You certainly know how to make a guy feel like the weight of the world rests on his shoulders."

Pepper sat down in one of several lawn chairs placed around a table made from a huge, wooden telephone wire spool. "Take it to the chaplain. You can cope and you know it."

Benny sat in another chair. He removed the kitchen towel from a tray, and poured iced tea for both of them. "There are times when coping has piss-all to recommend itself. Aw, hell, Pepper, you're right. Lorraine and I will cope, if we live through this next week. How about you? Are you *coping,* waiting for Darby to arrive?"

"Of course not. The only reason I'm not looking at my watch every five minutes is that I had to take it off or go bananas. We haven't seen each other in months."

"If Lorraine's to-do list gets any longer, you won't see him before the wedding either. I'm sorry, I had no idea it was so hard to get married. I've known courts martial that required less preparation. Why don't you and Darby just take off and come back in a week for the wedding?"

"Lorraine needs us. Believe me, as soon as we see the two of you off to—where did you say you were taking her on the honeymoon?"

Benny smiled. "Nice try. No sale."

Pepper wrinkled her nose at him. All she'd been able to worm out of him was that their honeymoon destination was special. Weren't all honeymoons special? "Right after you two are off to points unknown, Darby and I are off, too. I've got three weeks off from the hospital and we are going to use them to do nothing but enjoy ourselves."

"And meet his family."

Pepper whimpered. "And meet his family."

"You worried about that?"

"Terrified. What if they hate me?"

"They love Darby. For reasons that remain a mystery to me, you love Darby, too. People who share odd hobbies tend to club together, so they aren't going to hate you."

"Darby is not an odd hobby! And you know perfectly well

25

why I love him."

Benny pretended to shrug, but his eyes twinkled.

Pepper knew he did have a point. "What if I hate them? What if they're rednecks or something out of Tennessee Williams?"

Or worst of all, the one she didn't dare say, what if they were like her own family, so solidly conservative that they choked all life out of her.

"Then you and Darby will have to work that out." Benny stretched full out, like an old cat on his back. His T-shirt gapped above his jeans. In the gap, his burned chest looked white and ropy.

Pepper's breath caught in her throat. At times, she conveniently forgot what an errant flamethrower had done to Benny in a besieged A-camp. He was careful to keep his Viet Nam experiences in low profile, especially around Mark and Randy. After the wedding, when he moved in with Lorraine and the boys, his stepsons would see his scars all the time. Plastic surgery would only mediate the scars, but for the first time, she wondered why Benny never considered it.

Benny asked, "Is Darby going to propose?"

Pepper's heart did a little trip-hammer dance. *Mrs. Darby Baxter. Mrs. Elizabeth Baxter. Colonel Darby Baxter and his wife Pepper.* Too much caffeine, she decided, returning her iced tea to the wooden table. "What makes you ask that?"

"The kitchen isn't soundproof. I've heard the two of you on the phone; at least I've heard your half of the conversations. Do the decent thing and put that boy out of his misery."

"All I know is he must be planning something. Never before, so he tells me, has he taken a whole month off, unless he was convalescing, of course. And he is taking me to meet his folks."

"If he proposes, are you going to accept?"

She hadn't known trip-hammers could play "The Wedding

March." Or that she could feel light-headed for no reason at all. A flutter of her hands and a vibrating "Eyyyy" was all she managed.

"People do go all gushy at a wedding." Benny pursed his lips. "Though the possibility of Colonel Darby Baxter going all gushy at anything has the same likelihood as certain regions freezing over."

Benny stiffened and cocked his head with a miniscule movement. He straightened up and his hand automatically reached down to smooth his T-shirt over his jeans, so no skin—and no scars—showed. As usual, Pepper was a beat behind him. Unlike Benny, with his combat-hardened early warning system, she had to wait until sounds actually became audible. She heard soft footfalls on dirt and a swish of leaves a few seconds before Randy Fulford came into sight on the path.

Randy had turned thirteen a few days earlier. In the past six months, he'd sprouted into a tall, skinny young man, with his brown hair cut short to resemble photographs of his father at the same age. He came down the path switching a long twig through leaves at the side of the path.

With a start, Pepper realized that Randy was always doing something to announce himself. Today it was ruffling leaves with a stick, but it might as easily have been whistling or stopping to toss rocks into the creek that ran beside the glade. Living in close proximity to three Viet Nam veterans must have heightened Randy's awareness that creeping up on adults wasn't a good idea. Pepper ached as though she had a tiny metal splinter under her fingernail. Children should be protected from even small losses of innocence.

All knees and elbows, Randy collapsed into a faded slingback canvas chair. "Daddy Ben, can I ask you something?"

"Certainly you can, as soon as you make a proper greeting."

"Good morning, Aunt Pepper."

27

"Morning, Randy."

Randy didn't look at either of them. His toe scuffed the dirt in front of his chair. "I asked Father Fred about this after confirmation class last week, but he said he didn't have any experience and I should ask you."

Oh, God. Was this it? *The talk!* Pepper had been after Benny for weeks to talk to Randy about the facts of life sooner rather than later. She didn't think he'd done it, and she had no intention of picking up his slack. "I have something to do back at the house."

"No, Aunt Pepper, you stay. I'd kind of like your opinion about this, too. I mean, since you're a woman and all."

Her face grew hot. "I really have to go."

Benny's fingers closed like an iron manacle around Pepper's wrist. "If Randy wants to talk to both of us, both of us will listen. We're ready, Randy, whenever you are."

Randy pushed a longish strand of hair off his forehead. "It's just this. If all of my grandfathers were soldiers, and my dad was a soldier, and you were a soldier, and Aunt Pepper was a solider, and Aunt Avivah was a soldier, and Colonel Darby is still a soldier, do I have to be a soldier?"

Blast Memorial Day. Benny was right; he should have gone with Randy to tidy up his father's memorial stone. Pepper said, "Of course not. No one has to be a soldier unless he wants to be one."

Benny let go of her wrist. He got up and walked over to look at the creek. His fingers picked at the bark of an old tree, as if he were picking at a scab. Pepper's shoulders tensed. Randy's question had, after all, been about the facts of life.

"What your Aunt Pepper said isn't exactly true. Sometimes your country can make you be a soldier, even if you don't want to be one."

"You mean being drafted?"

Benny turned around. Pepper recognized his carefully crafted bland expression. Being able to shut down emotions was a quality Darby and Benny shared. "Yes."

"Only there isn't a draft."

"Not today."

Suddenly thirteen was next-door to eighteen, the age at which, when the draft existed, young men had to register. Pepper had no idea what she would have said if Randy had come to her alone with his question. She only knew that her mixed emotions would have shown more on her face.

Benny said, "There's only one choice that would disappoint me, and it would have disappointed your dad, too. I assume you know what desertion is?"

"It means you've promised to do something, but when things get tough, you break that promise."

"Close enough. Being a soldier has consequences; not being a soldier has consequences. Whatever decision you make about soldiering, I expect you to live with the consequences. When the time comes that you have to make a decision, will you promise to talk to me before you decide? If you can't talk to me, to Aunt Avivah or Aunt Pepper or Colonel Darby?"

Pepper squeezed her eyes shut. Please, God, not me. Come to think of it, better her or Avivah than Darby. Although that wasn't really fair to Darby. He would give Randy's question the same consideration that Benny was doing. It's just she wasn't sure she wanted Randy to hear Darby's take on soldiering. Standing still, without even opening his mouth, Darby was a recruiting poster. She opened her eyes.

Randy still slouched in his chair, "Yes, sir, I promise."

Benny let out a deep breath. "Good. Remember that thing about not counting your chickens too early. You don't have to worry about soldiering for a long time. Now, Pepper and I are going to see about lunch. If you want to stay down here for a while, that's okay. We'll leave you a plate of food if you don't make it back by the time we eat."

"Thanks."

They walked up the hill toward Pepper's house. "You said *when* the time comes for him to make a decision."

"He's male. The time will come."

"I don't want him to be a soldier."

"I meant what I said. It will be Randy's decision, not yours or mine. Truth to tell, it's Mark I'm more concerned about. He won't be old enough for Cub Scouts for a year, but I caught him practicing a quick-draw Cub Scout salute in front of his mirror. I know it's just Cubs, but there's no telling where wearing a uniform and saluting can lead."

Pepper thought of several places. Taking out a machine gun in the Argonne Wood. Raising a flag on Mount Suribachi. Descending into tunnels beneath the Iron Triangle. Placing yourself, armed with only a flamethrower, between an A-camp and assaulting Viet Cong. She shivered. "How come you never had plastic surgery?"

"What?"

"On your burns, to reduce the scars."

Benny's hand went to his right side. "I never thought about it. Do you think I should?"

"I assume the boys have seen you without your shirt on."

"Yeah."

She could tell from one word it hadn't been an experience Benny cherished.

"And?"

"You know Mark. Things either roll off of him or give him nightmares. Fortunately, this rolled off him. He never said anything. Randy was seven when I was wounded and med-evaced to the States. His exact words were, 'That looks icky.' We don't talk about it."

They came out of the tree-shaded path into bright, hot sun. A small tarp covered a mound of construction materials stacked beside the smaller of two houses. Pepper's property had started life as a mountain homestead. Seventy years earlier the original owner built a small house. Years later the second generation built a larger house—the one Pepper, Avivah, and Benny shared—across the driveway.

Pepper had been concerned, at first, about what the neighbors might think about their living arrangements. It turned out the neighbors didn't care. That part of Madison County had seen so many communes in the past decade they didn't give a second thought to three Army buddies and a war widow living on the same property. What the neighbors found strange was that two of the veterans were women.

Pepper pulled an errant piece of electrical wire out of the ground and deposited it in the oil-drum refuse bin beside the house's open front door. Leaning through the open door, she called, "Benny and I are going to make lunch. Want some?"

Pepper's friend, co-worker, and new tenant, Frannie Maddox, worked her ample jeans-covered bottom out from under a double sink. Not so ample a bottom anymore, Pepper had to admit. Frannie had lost twenty-five pounds in the past eight months.

Frannie wiped the back of her hand against her forehead, leaving a dark streak of plumbing compound. She pointed at the old refrigerator. "I brought my lunch, but I'd do almost anything for something cold to drink."

"One pitcher of lemonade coming up."

The young woman beside Frannie worked her way to a sitting position as well. Benny's only sister, Ginny Mae, had straight, coal-black hair, green eyes, and a heart-shaped face. She'd be even prettier without a perpetual scowl. "I hope you don't expect me to stop what I'm doing and make lunch, just because I'm a girl."

Benny made a grunting, exasperated noise. "I thought I'd make lunch for all of us. You know, get in touch with my feminine side."

"Fuck off, why don't you?"

Benny turned on his heel. "I'll be in the kitchen."

Pepper found Captain Elizabeth Pepperhawk's officer's voice, the one she reserved for special occasions. "Virginia Maeve Kirkpatrick, come with me."

She stomped away, trusting that Ginny Mae was following her. She'd rather have carted the brat along by the ear, but some decency had to be observed. Ginny was, after all, nineteen, even if she was acting like a recalcitrant twelve-year-old. Pepper marched to the other side of her new garage, where the building would block the sound of their voices. As Benny said, the kitchen wasn't soundproof.

She turned to face Ginny Mae. "Your brother and Lorraine waited a long time to marry. Every one of us, you included, have a responsibility to help them through the next week."

"Yeah? What responsibility? All we've done since we arrived is sleep, eat, and sit around the bed-and-breakfast discussing the wedding, of which I'm not a part."

"I'm sorry that Lorraine didn't ask you to be in her wedding party. She didn't ask me or Avivah either."

"But Benny asked you to plan his party and the reception."

"Would you like to do that? Avivah and I have a two-inch thick file we would be delighted to hand over to you."

"It wouldn't be the same as *him* asking me."

Ginny Mae had spent her entire life as the kid sister to three older brothers. Benny was the first brother to marry. For the first time in her life, Ginny Mae had to share Benny with another woman. Was that a little green imp Pepper saw sitting on Ginny's shoulder?

"Take your choice: help Avivah and me deal with the butcher, the baker, and the wedding-cake maker, or help Frannie turn the old house into her art studio. No more garbage-mouth. And, it's going to be *please, thank-you,* and an occasional smile, or you will stay at the bed-and-breakfast until it's time for the wedding. This is my house, my land, and I get to say who is allowed on it. Whiners don't get a vote. Got that?"

Ginny Mae pulled herself into a decent civilian approximation of standing at attention. "Ma'am, yes, ma'am."

In spite of herself, Pepper laughed. "Where did you learn that?"

Ginny Mae relaxed. "You can't have a brother in Special Forces for ten years without picking up something."

"What I just did is known in the Army as pulling rank. A good officer doesn't do it. A better officer knows how to do it judiciously. Come on, this wedding will be fun if you let it be."

"I suppose so." She could certainly get a lot of sulk into three words.

"So what's it going to be: nut cups and dry-cleaning-bag flowers or plumbing?"

"Plumbing."

"Good choice. I know Frannie appreciates the help. Now for lunch, yes or no?"

"Yes. Please."

She hadn't had two consecutive words, in a civil tone, from Ginny Mae since she arrived. Be blessed with small victories, Pepper thought as she went into the house.

Half an hour later she heard a car drive in.

Benny craned his neck to see who it was. "What's Avivah doing home? Wasn't she supposed to be on duty until three?"

Pepper dried her hands on a kitchen towel. "I hope she's not sick. We do not need anyone contagious this close to the wedding."

Avivah shepherded a silent Mark into the kitchen. "Go wash your hands, and have a lie down in my room before lunch."

Benny crouched down in front of Mark. "You okay, son?"

Mark flew into Benny's arms, sobbing. Benny picked him up.

Pepper felt Mark's forehead as Benny carried him past her, but he didn't feel feverish. She could think of only one reason that Avivah had brought Mark home. There had been an accident. Grace was in the hospital, or worse. She didn't want to think about worse. She turned to Avivah.

Avivah said, "There's no easy way to say this. Grace has been kidnapped and Joseph is in police custody. New York City police picked him up on an international warrant on suspicion of involvement with the Irish Republican Army."

CHAPTER 3

No one slept Friday night.

Early Saturday morning, wind whipped sheets of rain across the Asheville airport's open observation deck. Pepper and Ginny Mae huddled as close as they could to the terminal building's rough brick walls. They might have been waiting for Ilsa and Victor's plane to arrive from Casablanca. Come to think of it, who had met Ilsa and Victor in Lisbon? No doubt, it was someone from the underground. In the pewter-colored morning, Pepper studied Ginny Mae's face.

If the underground had nineteen-year-old agents, Ginny Mae would have fitted right in. She wore a thick wool coat, buttoned to the neck. Benny's black wool watch cap rested low over her ears. Rain stood in little silver beads on the wool.

"Hamilton is so dumb! Why couldn't he take a plane at a decent hour?"

Because, as Pepper had learned in Viet Nam, in the middle of a crisis it was better to keep going than to lay down and not sleep. The inside of her eyelids felt raw. "I imagine he wanted to get Joseph out of New York City as fast as possible."

"He is such a jerk."

"Hamilton or Joseph?"

"Hamilton. I haven't seen Joseph in twelve years. He may be a jerk, too, for all I know."

All Pepper knew about Benny's brother Hamilton was that he lived in Chicago and traded commodities, whatever those were. "Your brother did manage to fly from Chicago to New York *and* get Joseph out of police custody in less than twenty-four hours."

"Okay, so he's an efficient jerk. I still don't see why I had to come with you. How hard could it be to recognize two men, one of whom will be carrying a fiddle case?"

"Maybe your dad thought it would comfort your brothers to have you meet them."

Ginny Mae shoved her hands deeper into her pockets. "Provide solace to air travelers. A woman's role, all right, to say nothing of catching pneumonia while we're waiting for them."

Her words sounded tired and scratched, like a phonograph played too long with a nickel taped to the tone arm. Ginny's hand moved back and forth in her coat pocket, where Pepper had seen her put a rosary before they left for the airport. Pepper forbore mentioning that it had been Ginny Mae's idea to wait on the observation deck, so they could see the plane the instant it arrived.

A Piedmont Airlines plane descended out of the dark clouds. Its little windows were shining with a yellow light and two landing lights connected their white beacons to the runway. Fountains of water sprayed up when the wheels touched down.

Pepper had no trouble picking out the two Kirkpatrick brothers from among a dozen passengers. They met the men inside the terminal, at the luggage carousel.

Hamilton had the build of a runner, or a man who played squash on his lunch hours. The tallest person in the Kirkpatrick family, he wore a tailored, black London Fog raincoat. Joseph was a younger version of Benny: short, with a round face and the beginning of a little bald spot at the back of his head. He wore jeans, an intricately knitted sweater, and a light gray jacket.

Ginny Mae hovered behind Pepper, as though trying to hide. Pepper could feel an aura coming from her. Or maybe that was just water vapor steaming off of Ginny's wool coat and hat. What would it feel like not to have seen your brother in twelve years?

Pepper's eyes narrowed. It had been three years since she'd seen her own sister. Regret lay under that fact. A hollow feeling that she had no idea what her sister's life was like. Relief that they led their own lives. A shade of guilt, perhaps. Family was supposed to be family, no matter what.

Hamilton retrieved a black-and-chrome suitcase from the moving luggage belt, set it down, and opened the tag holder to check the name inside. He stood up and his gaze met Pepper's. The look in his eye said, "Cross me, outbid me"—or whatever it was they did in the commodities market—"at your peril." He strode forward. "Elizabeth Pepperhawk?"

"Yes."

"Thank you for meeting us."

At the sound of her name, Joseph turned. He thrust his worn and mended violin case at Pepper, then elbowed her aside to throw his arms around Ginny Mae, whom he lifted off the floor, twirling her around twice before setting her down again. "My God, Virginia. You're lovely. Not a single woman in County Monaghan could touch that face of yours. You should come back to Ireland with me. I'd have you married inside of three months."

Joseph didn't have an Irish accent, and he didn't not have one. His voice sounded as though it had picked up a Gaelic lilt and rhythm in the same way a black skirt picked up every speck of lint it brushed against.

From what little Pepper knew about Benny's sister, being married in three months wasn't Ginny's preferred option. Pepper waited for the explosion, but Ginny Mae, her face filled with pleasure, stood with her forearms resting on either side of her brother's neck. "This husband of mine, would he own a

37

hardware store?"

"He'd own ten hardware stores if that would please you."

"One will be enough for me."

Benny often joked about his sister's singular goal in life.

Kirkpatrick and Daughter Hardware

Serving southern Missouri since 1922

"If we don't have it, why would you be needing it?"

Right now, the sign over the door didn't say *and Daughter* except in Ginny Mae's imagination.

Hamilton asked, "Is there news?"

Pepper turned from hardware to the harsh reality of the past twenty-four hours. "No, at least nothing as of a couple of hours ago, when we left home. I'm sorry. The police are doing everything possible."

"I'm sure they are."

Pepper and Hamilton, who pushed the luggage cart, walked in front; Ginny Mae and Joseph followed. Pepper caught reflections of the two of them in the airport shop windows. They held hands, looking for all the world like Hansel and Gretel, lost in the forest. Pepper could understand that. There were times when holding Benny's hand had helped her find her own way out of several dark forests.

Then Ginny Mae screamed, a piercing adolescent shriek usually reserved for rock-and-roll idols. Pushing Pepper aside, she ran across the airport lobby.

Pepper hopped on one foot, rubbing her shin, which she'd scraped against a luggage cartwheel when Ginny pushed her. Darby always said that looking at a person who screamed was a waste of time. Find out what caused them to scream because that posed a greater threat. Ginny ran toward another woman. It took Pepper a moment to realize that woman was Grace Kirkpatrick.

Near the main entrance, a stairway to the lower level was under renovation. Flimsy plastic cones with tape strung between them guarded each corner of the hole. Grace glanced over her shoulder, apparently unaware as she moved straight toward the gap in the floor.

Joseph yelled, "Ma, the hole!"

Hamilton's long legs broke into a runner's stride. He easily outdistanced Ginny Mae. With the back vent in his London Fog coat flapping behind him like a duck's tail, he made a flying tackle at his mother and grabbed her around the waist. They skidded sideways, away from the hole and into a bank of candy and soda machines. By the time Pepper and Joseph reached them, a crowd had gathered.

Grace clawed at Hamilton's face and aimed well-placed kicks so that he was forced to let go of her. She scooted herself into the narrow space between two machines, curled herself into a ball, and screamed. Pepper could see now that Grace's clothes were torn and dirty. Her gray hair frizzed, uncontrolled, around her head.

Hamilton, having made the end-zone tackle, stood up and looked at Pepper. "Benny told me you were a nurse. Do something."

Pepper spotted a bank of pay phones. Her fingers scrabbled in her pocket for coins, trying to remember if an emergency call required money.

Joseph put his hands around his mother's ankles and, with one forceful motion, slid her from between the machines. He sat on the floor, pulled her into his lap, and began crooning a soft, slow song in her ear. He looked up, his face so like Benny's that Pepper's heart melted.

"Mother of God, someone phone for an ambulance."

Sunday evening, Avivah and her lawyer sat in the psychiatric

39

unit's dingy waiting room. John Ferguson wore his customary white shirt, suit, tie and pained expression. "You need to put a criminal lawyer on retainer. I keep telling you, I'm an old country lawyer who does wills, deeds, and an occasional court appearance for good ol' boys."

The *old* lawyer was a pose. John was in his late thirties. The country lawyer bit was true. Lawyer Ferguson held the confidences of half the farmers in Madison County.

The linoleum floor made creaking sounds as Avivah paced. She tapped the edge of a long, white envelope against her fingers. "You were the only lawyer I could think of at five o'clock on a Sunday afternoon."

"Mrs. Kirkpatrick made front-page news two days in a row, and you only figured out four hours ago that she might need a lawyer?"

"What I figured out was that she might be coherent enough by tomorrow morning for the police to interview her."

John sighed. "Where's her family?"

"The doctor sent them home. He said they were hovering too much." Avivah handed him the envelope. "Her husband asked me to find a lawyer."

John slit the envelope labeled *To Whom It May Concern.* He pocketed the money. "I've read the newspaper accounts. Sit down and tell me everything that's not in the papers, then I want to interview my client."

Half an hour later, Avivah asked the nurse for paper and a marker. She posted a sign saying *Family Conference/Do Not Disturb* on the waiting room door. A nurse escorted Grace from her room.

Grace lowered herself unsteadily into one of the vinyl chairs. She wore a hospital gown and a faded green chenille bathrobe. She'd been showered with hospital soap and had her hair washed with hospital shampoo. It gave her a faint disinfectant smell and the new perm she'd gotten for the wedding lay plastered against her skull in limp gray waves.

Mr. Ferguson, sitting on a sofa, balanced a legal pad on his knee. "Mrs. Kirkpatrick, my name is John Ferguson. I'm a lawyer in Marshall, North Carolina. Miss Rosen thought it would be a good idea if you talked to me before you talk to the police."

Grace's head weaved a little, as though she were trying to bring his face into focus by moving her eyes just the right distance away from him. Her voice sounded raspy and tired. "What are your politics?"

Mr. Ferguson frowned. "I beg your pardon?"

"Democrat or Republican?"

He cleared his throat and looked at Avivah. She raised her hands in a "you're-on-your-own" gesture.

"Closet Republican."

"Why closet?"

"I'm a poor country lawyer in a small town. When you're in the political minority, you offend fewer people by keeping a low profile."

Grace uncurled her backbone, one vertebrae at a time. "You're honest. You'll do. I want to hire you."

"Your husband already gave me a hundred dollars as a retainer."

"I suspect you're not as impecunious a country lawyer as you pretend."

Avivah pursed her lips. That was the longest, most complicated sentence Avivah had heard from Grace in the past day. Could a woman still under the influence of drugs use the word *impecunious* correctly? How much of Grace's shambling state was a pretense? *Never assume that a victim isn't a perpetrator as well* was an old police axiom.

"*Poor* better not refer to your lawyering skills, or you'll be out on your ear."

Mr. Ferguson had the courtesy to blush. He took Grace through going to the airport Friday morning. Her story matched Mark's.

"What did you think when the car pulled up behind you?"

"Maybe the driver wanted our parking spot."

"When he got out of the car, did you recognize him?"

Grace's hands tightened on the chair's arms. Avivah looked around for a box of tissues, just in case. The only box in the waiting room had one tissue left in it. Who ever heard of a hospital waiting room without tissues?

Grace fumbled in her robe pocket for a well-worn blue bandana. She took a full minute to smooth the folded cloth meticulously across her right thigh. Avivah recognized a delaying tactic when she saw one. In other words—or rather, a lack of words—Grace didn't want to say she'd recognized her abductor.

Grace finally said, "Not until he spoke to me."

"What did he say?"

" 'Grace, I must talk to you.' As soon as he said my name, I knew him."

"Who is he?"

Her fingers played with one corner of the bandana. "Peter Taft."

"Where did you know him from?"

"Alaska."

Alaska? Grace had left there almost thirty years ago. What did Alaska have to do with anything? Avivah swallowed her confusion, lest it show on her face.

Mr. Ferguson asked, "What were you doing in Alaska?"

"I was born there."

"And you knew this Peter Taft there?"

Grace folded a corner of the paisley-patterned cloth back on itself, cocked her head as if evaluating the result, then unfolded it and smoothed it out again. "Yes."

"What was your relationship?"

"I'm not sure what you mean."

"Were you friends? Enemies? Next-door neighbors? Co-workers?"

She plucked at a stray piece of lint. "Enemies."

The cold, dead way Grace said that one word made the hair on Avivah's neck stand up.

"Why enemies?"

Grace's gaze slowly rose to look at Mr. Ferguson. Even through the robe, Avivah saw Grace's shoulders tighten. A gray, steel-like quality replaced the pillow softness in her voice. "Peter Taft was an unprincipled conniver, who would do anything to make money."

"Do you know this for a fact, or was it hearsay and rumor?"

"It was a fact that Peter conned Quinn's men into stealing Army supplies. I was an eyewitness when Quinn took Peter out behind the Northway Café, and beat the shit out of him. Peter later admitted he was responsible for getting Quinn sent to the Aleutian Campaign. Those are facts."

Mr. Ferguson took time to write Grace's exact words on his legal pad. Grace leaned back and closed her eyes.

Avivah studied Grace. She was round like many women in their early fifties, but not flabby. Benny said her hair had changed color completely one summer, as though, once gray hairs began showing up, she'd decided to turn gray all at once and get on to other things in her life.

Mr. Ferguson asked, "When was the fight behind the North-way Café?"

Grace slowly opened her eyes, as if coming back from a dream, or a memory. "Christmas Day, 1942."

Good bones was what Avivah called it when she watched

Pepper resurrect some bit of unused nursing knowledge, which had lain dormant since nursing school. John Ferguson had the same kind of good lawyer bones. Grace had thrown him a curve. He might not be a practicing criminal lawyer, but somewhere back in law school, Ferguson had learned enough about criminal law to get him through. He blinked. "Mrs. Kirkpatrick, before Friday, when was the last time you saw Peter Taft?"

"August 1946."

"Under what circumstances?"

"We met on a street in Fairbanks. He told me he was leaving Alaska."

"Had you any contact with him since 1946, letters or phone calls? Even seeing his name in a newspaper article, or hearing it in a conversation?"

"No."

"You're telling me that a man you had no contact with in almost twenty-eight years accosted you on Friday in the Asheville airport?"

"Yes."

"How did he find you?"

"I have no idea."

"Let's go back. Start with his car pulling up behind you. Taft said, 'Grace, I must talk to you.' You recognized him. Then what?"

"I called him a bastard and slapped him."

"Why?"

She had the blue cloth bunched in her right hand now, kneading it like clay. "Because I'd never had the courage to do it in Alaska."

What passion could hold sway for twenty-eight years?

Grace moved her other hand to the left side of her face. Tiny white welding scars crisscrossed her knuckles. "He hit me—here—and I passed out."

"He hit you hard enough that you lost consciousness?"

"Yes."

"I'd call that more than hitting. I'd call that slugging you."

Grace waved away the violence with a small hand movement. "Perhaps."

"When did you regain consciousness?"

"I don't know. Later."

Mr. Ferguson turned back several pages to the notes he'd taken from Avivah. "The doctors found needle marks on your arms?"

Grace rubbed the bandana over her left elbow as if she could wipe the marks away. "Yes, they think I was drugged."

"Where were you when you woke up?"

She lowered her head and closed her eyes. "Handcuffed to a bed in a motel room."

Avivah opened a silver box in her mind. Silver boxes were where she stored the stories that victims told her. Silver boxes let her listen to the most horrific stories without going bonkers because, once the testimony was over, she could close the box lid and keep what she heard from spilling out to contaminate the rest of her life. She supposed it was like people who made hats out of tin foil to keep space aliens from reading their thoughts, only she liked to believe her silver boxes were saner and worked better.

Mr. Ferguson asked, "Was anyone with you in the motel room?"

"Peter."

"Anyone else?"

"No."

"I know this may be unpleasant for you, but I need to know everything that Peter Taft did in that motel room."

"We talked."

Avivah had made a big silver box this time, one that could

hold rape and torture. *We talked* clattered to the floor of the empty box and lay there looking small and alone.

"Talked?"

"About Alaska. Did I remember this person or that event?"

"Peter Taft knocked you unconscious, drugged you, and handcuffed you to a motel room bed so he could talk to you about Alaska?"

"Alaska and my family. Were Quinn and I still married? Where did I live? What had happened to Hamilton and Ben?"

"How did he know your sons' names?"

"He knew them as infants."

How strange that Taft remembered the names of boys he hadn't seen in twenty-eight years. Avivah added that to her evidence box.

"What did you tell him?"

"Lies. That Quinn died years ago, and that I lived in Philadelphia and worked as a meter maid. I had to tell the truth about Ben."

"Why?"

"Ben lives here and Peter was here, too. Maybe he knew Ben; maybe he'd found me through him. But I made up stories about Hamilton, and I was careful not to mention my other two children. Peter talked about his son, too. I gather the boy is in prison. Peter kept repeating that he had to get him released, that no one would give him a pardon."

There was a knock on the door. Avivah looked at her watch. It was probably the nurse coming to say that Grace had to go to bed now. Blast hospital routine.

Mr. Ferguson rose, moved the chair aside, and opened the door. Two men stood there and Avivah knew them both: Detective Alexander and his uniformed driver. Their presence hit her like a one-two punch. One, thank goodness she hadn't waited until tomorrow to find a lawyer. Two, if the police were here so late on a Sunday evening, something had to be terribly wrong.

Detective Alexander looked straight at Avivah, but he didn't acknowledge her. He asked Mr. Ferguson, "Who are you?"

"John Ferguson, Mrs. Kirkpatrick's lawyer."

The detective flashed his badge. "I hope you're a good one. We've located a car and person fitting the description of Mrs. Kirkpatrick's abductor."

Avivah looked at Grace. The persona had slipped. Gone was the slightly befuddled, plastered-hair woman, playing with a bandana. Grace's expression was sharp, chiseled, and more than a little afraid. Avivah's cop's instinct told her that Benny's mother had lied. Whatever story Peter Taft would tell about the motel room, it wasn't going to match what Grace had just told them.

Mr. Ferguson asked, "Where did you locate him?"

"We found his car in the airport long-term parking lot. Reverend Peter Taft's body was in the trunk."

Reverend? Grace had carefully left out the small fact that her assailant was a clergyman. Avivah didn't know what was going to be more painful, telling Benny that his mother was a liar, or telling him that she was a murder suspect.

Grace pressed the bandana to her face with both hands, looking as though she had buried herself in a large blue-and-white flower. Avivah sat close enough to her to hear her whisper, "Oh, Quinn, you promised me. You promised me."

Make that telling Benny that his mother *and* father would soon both be murder suspects.

CHAPTER 4

Under the electrician's work light, Benny's family resembled a cast call for *Night of the Living Dead*. Frannie's art-studio-in-progress smelled of sawdust and dry wall. At least they had electricity and a hint of warmth from the space heater in the corner. Avivah thought it better to hold a family conference here instead of cramped into Pepper's tiny living room.

Avivah's eyelids slid over dry and burning eyes. Just a few more minutes and she could cross the yard and go to bed. Five hours of sleep would be better than none at all. Tonight she wouldn't even brush her teeth before falling into bed.

On the battered couch, Darby and Pepper sat with their sides touching and their arms and hands decorously entwined around one another. Ever since Darby arrived, Pepper had resembled a limpet mine, magnetically attached to his side.

Colonel Darby Baxter, ex-Captain Elizabeth Pepperhawk. Master and pupil, though Avivah suspected even they lost track of who was which. In the past three years, she'd watched Darby mellow and Pepper toughen up. She tried to look benignly on them, like a loving aunt, but all this wedding stuff only made the chill in her own love life more noticeable. Chill? Heck, her love life had been in deep freeze mode so long that she probably had ice crystals growing between her legs.

Quinn Kirkpatrick, Benny, and Joseph looked like triplets, down to the wrinkled clothes, red eyes, and stubby, day-old beards. Lorraine and Ginny Mae sat next to one another, looking tired and bewildered. Lorraine might be having second thoughts about marrying into the Kirkpatrick clan.

Hamilton's pad of paper was covered with notes he'd made earlier, while Mr. Ferguson outlined Grace's legal position. Calculations filled the bottom of the page. The figures had more zeros on the end than Avivah dealt with in her bank account.

Hamilton said, "The farm, as always, is in a marginally positive income position, predicated on a successful harvest, but there's excellent equity in the hardware store. Our best option is to get approval for a loan, using the store as collateral. That will give us access to a pool of background funds if legal costs spiral, which of course we're hoping won't happen. Among dad, myself, and Benny we can probably fund mom's legal costs without the loan, especially if the police are quick to realize they have the wrong person."

Avivah wouldn't bet money on that happening.

Joseph said, "I may be a traveling musician, but I'm not penniless."

Hamilton didn't even look at his brother. "Save it for your own legal defense."

Benny took Lorraine's hand. "We have money set aside toward building our house. It's yours, if you need it, Da."

Lorraine didn't pull her hand away, but she didn't look happy either. Maybe Benny should have checked with her before making so magnanimous an offer.

Ginny Mae sat silent, slouched in her chair.

Quinn covered his face with his hands, his fingers entangled in his sparse hair. His voice sounded close to tears. "I can't use the business as collateral."

Hamilton reached out to give his dad's arm a perfunctory pat. "I know how you feel about unnecessary financial entanglements, but this is exactly what you and mom worked so hard to achieve: a good financial position in case of emergency. It's not as though you're actually going into debt. All you're doing is applying for a loan authorization, to be there as a backup against future contingencies."

Quinn lowered his hands. He was only in his late fifties, but Avivah thought tonight he looked a lot older, and she suspected it wasn't just the poor lighting.

"We sold everything."

For a moment the only sound was the tail end of a two-day rain falling on the old roof.

Benny found his voice first. "You sold the farm?"

Ginny asked, "You sold the business?"

Joseph asked, "You sold our house?"

Quinn looked as though he'd been given a tiny reprieve. "Not our house or grandda's. We deeded those over to you four children."

Lorraine asked, "But how will you live?"

"We're provided for." Quinn looked around the table, focusing for a few seconds on each child's face. "We were planning to tell you, but not like this, never like this. I'm sorry we made such a mess of things."

Hamilton folded up the bottom of his paper, creased it, and tore it from the tablet precisely along the crease. "The business must have brought a good price. That means you have money in the bank, which is all to the good side in our current situation."

Quinn said, "There is no money in the bank."

Hamilton's face took on a greenish tinge. "What did you say?"

"All the money your mother and I made from the sales is tied up. I can't use any of it."

"Tied up how?"

"We agreed we wouldn't tell you about it until the details were settled. I have to honor that agreement until I can talk to your mother."

Joseph tensed up the same way Benny did, his body looking like a tightly coiled spring. "You didn't do this to pay for my plane fare, did you?"

Hamilton made a little moue with his mouth. "Don't be an ass. With what the store was worth, they could have paid for plane tickets for every person in your little village, plus all of the sheep and goats."

Ginny Mae stood up so fast that her chair hit the wooden floor. "I hate you. I wish you were all dead."

She ran out into the rain. Pepper untied herself from Darby's arms and went after her.

Darby said, "Everyone stay where you are. Pepper will handle it."

Ginny Mae ran with the speed of youth, but Pepper had the advantage of knowing the ground. Halfway across the yard Ginny Mae tripped on a root and went face-down in wet grass. Pepper slid into a sitting position beside her and gathered the sobbing woman into her arms. "It's all right, baby, it's all right."

Ginny Mae pounded her fists into Pepper's chest. "It's not all right. It will never be all right again, not ever in my entire life."

Pepper noticed that Ginny Mae hadn't objected to being called *baby*. That southern term of endearment must have made it as far north as Missouri. By the time Ginny Mae had cried herself out, the rain had soaked both women. Pepper stood and pulled Ginny to her feet. "Come on."

Ginny Mae wrenched her hand free. She stood with her feet spread a little apart, looking like a boxer. "I'm not going back in there."

"No, you're not. I'm taking you into Asheville to stay with Frannie."

"I don't need a social worker!"

"No, but you do need a place to stay—away from your family—while you catch your breath."

Ginny Mae plucked at her wet blouse. "I'll get your car all wet."

"It will dry. Just let me get my purse, and we'll be off. Unless you'd rather wait around until your dad or Benny comes looking for you."

"Let's go. Now."

By two A.M. Ginny Mae, bathed and wearing pajamas and a robe that Frannie lent her, sat on Frannie's sofa, picking through unpopped popcorn kernels at the bottom of the bowl for the tiny popped bits. Pepper's mother would have referred to Ginny Mae's tone as the *go-out-in-the garden-and-eat-worms* voice. "I was an afterthought. There's nine years and three months between Joseph and me. When the doctor told my mother she was pregnant, she told him he must have gotten his medical degree out of a Cracker Jack box."

Frannie, who had been exceedingly polite about being awakened and expected to provide dry clothes, food and a sympathetic ear, had developed an edge in her voice, too. "There's almost sixteen years between me and my partner. There comes a point where age gaps no longer matter."

Ginny Mae glanced down the hall. "Are we keeping your partner up?"

No, Pepper thought, you're just keeping us up.

"Cody is away at school. He's studying prosthetics."

Ginny Mae went back to pawing the popcorn bowl. "I'm always the odd person out in my family. I'm the only girl. I'm the only child not born in Alaska. I'm the only one saddled with a stupid name. Why couldn't my grandmothers have been named Mary or Susan or Barbara instead of Virginia and Maeve? Ginny Mae makes me sound as though I should have an Uncle Jed and a Cousin Jethro. I'm the only one still living at home. By the time Benny was nineteen, he'd joined the Army.

Joseph had moved to Ireland. Hamilton was already a commodities runner. I'm the only one without money. Joseph lives hand-to-mouth and he has more money than I do. All I have is college loans."

Frannie asked, "What's a commodities runner?"

"Like an office boy, only he dresses better and has prospects. I'm the only one who ever wanted to go into business with my dad."

Pepper's previous attempts to break up Ginny Mae's family life angst hadn't worked, but she tried, "Maybe your dad *had* to sell up. I keep hearing stories of how farming's not what it used to be."

Ginny Mae set the bowl on the coffee table. "Okay, maybe it *was* getting tougher to run a successful business. When customers are in a financial squeeze, they don't pay their bills. But mom and dad were making it work, just like my grandma and grandda before him. We have tradition. We have a name; Kirkpatrick Hardware is famous in southern Missouri. We're part of a community, and I'm developing solid business acumen that would have kept us viable in the marketplace."

Did she realize how much that last sentence sounded like Hamilton? Quite likely, Ginny Mae wasn't as much of an outsider in her family as she thought.

She wailed, "Why did they do this to me?"

Frannie stood and picked up the popcorn bowl. "Because life sucks."

Ginny Mae looked up. "What?"

"It sucks doubly if you're a woman. Get used to it. Chocolate helps." Frannie looked down at her still-ample belly. "Maybe chocolate doesn't help. Forget I said that. Lettuce and carrots help. Doesn't sound the same, does it?"

Pepper chuckled and stood to help Frannie collect dirty cups. "No, it doesn't."

"If you hate your name, change it. If that hardware store is all you want in life, go into partnership with the new owners, or find a way to make a ton of money and buy it back."

"I'm nineteen. I have college loans. I could never make that kind of money."

"Not by sitting on a couch, whining, you won't. You want to run a business, run a business. I'm doing it. I'm twice your age, and I don't have your advantage of being a business major in college."

"It wouldn't be the same. Someone else other than a Kirkpatrick would have owned the store. My parents ruined my whole life."

"Your mother was abducted by force, the Royal Ulster Constabulary wants to talk to your brother, and it's *your* life that's ruined. I suggest you forget the hardware business and devote yourself to a life of penance and good works. I'll see if I can find addresses of cloistered convents that are taking applicants, or perhaps you'd prefer missionary work? I have to be at my day job in six hours, so I'm going to bed. Sleep in, help yourself to anything that's in the kitchen. The food and bed are free, but if you make long-distance calls, leave the money for them on the table."

Ginny Mae set her mouth in a hard, thin line. Before she could say anything, Pepper said, "My house, my land."

Ginny Mae stood, arched her neck with great dignity, and collected the borrowed robe around her body. "Thank you for your hospitality. I'm sorry to be such a bother."

She sailed down the hall to the guest bedroom with the presence of a condemned queen on her way to the Tower of London.

Pepper collected the rest of the dirty dishes. "I'm sorry, too. I should have taken her to the animal shelter."

"What, and bother the poor animals? It's okay. As soon as she started whining, I put on my super social worker's cloak.

It's impervious to everything from caustic invectives to whiney children. What was that my house, my land thing?"

"I pulled rank on her. She behaves like an adult or she sits by herself at the bed-and-breakfast until time for the wedding."

"She has had a hard couple of days."

Pepper put the dishes in the sink. "And we haven't?"

"How is the rest of the family?"

"Grace has a lawyer. Hamilton is hiding behind dollar figures and cool detachment. Lorraine looks as though she wishes she'd checked the Kirkpatrick family tree more closely. Quinn, Benny and Joseph soldier on."

Frannie turned on the water and reached for the dish detergent. "Do the police have any leads on the kidnapper?"

"Brace yourself for tomorrow's headlines. The police know exactly who kidnapped Grace, a man she knew years ago in Alaska. Only he ended up dead in the trunk of his car. We have a whole new problem, not who kidnapped Grace, but who killed the Reverend Peter Taft."

An arc of detergent missed the sink and dribbled down the kitchen window. Frannie grabbed a dishcloth to mop it up. "I agree with Lorraine. Any sensible person should run as far as possible from this whole mess."

By morning the rain had stopped. Pepper parked her car in her garage and took a deep breath of the clean mountain air. That smell, all by itself, made living here a good idea.

Darby sat on her porch steps. His blond hair curled tightly to his head, the way it always did after a shower. He held open one side of his jacket and she sat on the steps beside him, snuggling into his warmth. He smelled almost as good as the clear air.

"You finished your run?"

"It just about finished me. I'm not used to this altitude."

"How far did you go?"

"Only three miles. What did you do with Ginny Mae?"

"Took her to Asheville to stay with Frannie."

"Did you get any sleep?"

"I caught a couple of hours on Frannie's couch."

"I saw Lorraine's list for you on the fridge. I'll pick up the wedding programs and matchbooks from the printer for you."

"Oh, blast the wedding! They'll have to postpone it, won't they?"

"Kirkpatrick said his nerves couldn't stand a postponement. Besides, his best man ships out two days after the wedding. Kirkpatrick said that if the police arrested his mother, he and Lorraine would marry twice, once here and once at the city jail, but they *will* get married on Saturday."

Pepper rubbed her cheek against Darby's shirt. "Benny is having nightmares about Randall and the boys. Talk to him, will you?"

"Not unless he comes to me. I'm not his chaplain."

She yawned. "I know." It had been worth a try. "Lorraine has a list for you, too."

Darby's fingers played with her hair. "I saw it. What are nut cups and why do we need so many?"

Pepper managed, "Later." She laid her head on Darby's shoulder and let the fatigue of very little sleep for three nights take her. In a moment his breathing fell into sequence with hers, and she drifted down into a dark and peaceful hole. The sound of a car on gravel startled her awake.

She felt Darby's body tense. Viet Nam had left him with a profound distrust of unexpected visitors. "Who the hell is that this early in the morning?"

Pepper looked at the secondhand car being parked next to the studio. "Frannie's assistant."

"She hasn't even opened the business. How can she afford an assistant?"

"Charity case. Sandra is trying to get into the job market. No job experience, no resumé. She's volunteering in exchange for a reference."

Sandra Waine got out of her car and bent to retrieve a briefcase. Darby stood abruptly, letting Pepper fall to the porch as though he wasn't even aware she had been leaning on him.

Sandra's and Darby's gazes locked. Even in her sleep-befuddled state, Pepper recognized the looks that passed between them. Sandra was one of Darby's ex-girlfriends, possibly even an ex-lover. Had to be! Pepper knew a whole slew of them were out there, but like other unseemly things in life she'd ignored the idea that she'd ever meet one. If Ginny Mae had one jealous imp on her shoulder, Pepper had a whole pack of them, and they were all cranky from lack of sleep.

Darby strode across the yard. He cupped Sandra's chin in his hand, and ever so slowly, with a lover's touch, he turned her face one way and then another. The imps howled like beserkers.

Darby's voice was flat. "I can't see any scars."

Sandra backed away a single step. "You won't. I paid for quality plastic surgery."

"Why?"

"Because a certain Lieutenant Baxter wouldn't give me the time of day. Grow up, he said. Well, I grew up. Oh, and it's Sandra now, not Sandy. Like the changes?"

"Can't say that I do."

Sandra stalked away. Her high heels dug up divots of grass as she stormed toward Frannie's studio, unlocked the door and slammed it once she was inside.

Darby looked after her as though he were a pole-axed calf.

Pepper tentatively approached him. When Darby Baxter was riled, the more distance between him and anyone else, the safer for all concerned, but Pepper had to know if he and Sandra had been lovers. "Who is she?"

Darby dug his car keys out of his jacket pocket. "Someone pretending to be my ex-wife." He climbed in his car. "Tell Lorraine I'm sorry. I'll get to her list later. Right now, I have to get away from here." He backed his car up so fast that the wheels cut large troughs in the grass.

"Call me," Pepper yelled after him.

He didn't answer.

Wait a minute. If Sandra Waine had never had a job, how had she paid for plastic surgery? Pepper headed for the art studio.

CHAPTER 5

Sandra Waine stood at the makeshift kitchen counter. She resembled an elegant blue heron standing on one foot, assuming a heron used a paper towel to clean grass from its high heels.

Pepper stood in the center of the doorway, blocking the opening with her body. "Who are you?"

Sandra hopped as she changed feet to clean her other shoe. "You know who I am; Sandra Waine."

"Who does Darby think you are?"

She dropped the paper towel into a waste can, rinsed her hands, and drew water into a percolator. "Sandra Waine."

"Are you his ex-wife?"

Overflowing water splattered on Sandra's suit. She turned off the tap with a forceful wringing motion. Her voice was gooey-sweet; her Texas accent more pronounced. "Goodness gracious no. The great Darby Baxter has far more refined tastes." She brushed water beads from her suit. "At least he did. I noticed his standards have slipped. Have you been dating long or are you one of his passing fancies? Women bore him easily, you know."

"But you know his wife?"

"Nancy is my cousin. Quite a bit older, I'm afraid."

Pepper thought she understood now. Sandra had been the kid cousin, infatuated with Darby, and he'd rejected her. That must have been some infatuation, and some rejection, to drive

Sandra to plastic surgery.

"Where is your cousin?"

"The last I heard, Hanoi."

"North Viet Nam?"

"That's the only Hanoi I know. Of course, I never bothered my head with geography. It's like nursing. So practical."

"What's she doing in Hanoi?"

"Talking incessantly. It's what she does best." Sandra picked up a scratch pad and carpenter's pencil from beside the sink, carefully wrote something and handed the page to Pepper. "You might try her office. They'll know if she's still away."

Nausea rose in Pepper's throat when she recognized the Washington, D.C., area code. For all the power concentrated there, *Foggy Bottom,* as Darby laughingly referred to the capital, was a village. He and Nancy might move in the same social circles, attend the same parties. So she wasn't at her best after a night on Frannie's couch, but she cleaned up as well as Sandra, as well as Nancy, as well as . . . who was she kidding?

"How much do you look like your cousin?"

"Enough to satisfy me, and more than enough to twist Darby's tail. I must say, him being here this morning came as a complete shock. Will he be staying long?"

"Long enough to satisfy me."

Pepper hurried across the yard to her house. Darby wasn't a man who ran from confrontation, but he'd run from Sandra. Maybe he wasn't even coming back. Maybe he'd phone and say ship his suitcases to Washington on Greyhound. Her toe caught on a hillock of grass. She fell, planting both palms firmly in the dirt. She didn't have to turn around to see if Sandra was watching from the window. There were some things Pepper just knew. She picked herself up, retrieved the dirty and crumpled piece of paper Sandra had given her and followed Ginny Mae's example. More than one queen had gone to the Tower of London.

Her palms stung and her dirty fingers streaked the phone as she dialed a local number.

"Pisgah Mountain Veterans' Hospital, Social Work. Ms. Maddox."

"Frannie, it's Pepper. How did you and Sandra meet?"

"Why?"

Frannie sounded ill. Too little sleep, just like the rest of them. Pepper hoped Ginny Mae had behaved herself this morning.

"Because Darby knows her. They have history."

She could hear Frannie breathing, stuffy as though she were getting a cold. "I'm sorry. I had no idea."

"Not that kind of history. Sandra is Darby's ex-wife's younger cousin. How did you meet Sandra?"

"She attended my first art therapy workshop for the MIA relatives."

Pepper's throat tightened. "She has a relative who's missing in action?"

"Her best friend did."

"Did?"

"The friend died."

"And?"

"That's Sandra's story to tell."

In other words, Sandra was one of Frannie's private clients as well as her assistant. In her private practice, Frannie specialized in counseling women who, as Frannie put it, "had to stop stewing in their own juices before they could move on."

"You might ask her how she paid for plastic surgery, and why she had it done."

"What plastic surgery?"

"Just ask her."

After she'd hung up, Pepper smoothed out the paper scrap, turned it upside down, turned it back again, read the numbers left-to-right, then right-to-left, then every alternate number, as though they might be a code hidden in ten digits. Heck, it might be a plumbing-and-heating business or a pawnshop. Washington had to be full of normal businesses. She could always pretend she'd reached a wrong number. She dialed.

"State Department, Dr. Kissinger's office."

The kitchen spun. Pepper leaned back against the wall for support. "I'd like to speak to Nancy Waine."

She wasn't going to speak to her, of course. She just wanted to hear Nancy's voice to see if she sounded like Sandra.

"Dr. Waine-Baxter is currently unavailable. I can connect you to one of our other interpreters."

The scariest thing was that this receptionist, who worked for one of the most powerful men on earth, hadn't even hesitated. She knew exactly who Dr. Waine-Baxter was. So Nancy had kept Darby's last name. How dare she! That name was reserved for Mrs. Elizabeth Baxter. Mrs. Elizabeth *Pepperhawk*-Baxter! God, her mother would have a cat at a daughter with a hyphenated last name. Maybe she'd better suggest that her mother get a supply of cat food because she had no intention of giving up her own name, not even to become a member of the Baxter clan.

Doctor. Probably PhD, though Pepper didn't rule out a medical degree. She had no idea what a person's qualifications had to be to work for the State Department. Darby never talked about his ex. She'd assumed that was because he was ashamed of her; one of those quickie marriages with a beehive-hairdo, airhead waitress he'd met in one of the tawdry clubs that inevitably sprang up near military bases. Had she ever guessed wrong!

"Hello? Are you still there?"

"Yes, sorry. I just had a personal message for Dr. Waine-Baxter." The name burned her tongue. "About a social engagement. Nothing urgent. When will she be available?"

"I couldn't say. She checks in for messages. May I say who called?" Pepper detected a change in the woman's tone, cooler, more suspicious.

Cover stories flitted through Pepper's head. She'd met Nancy at a cocktail party. Or they went to university together and she was verifying mailing addresses for a college reunion. Or she wanted Dr. Waine-Baxter to work on a charity ball committee. Darby had taught her that the best cover story was none at all.

"No, thank you. It can wait." She hung up, trying to decide if she'd been on the phone long enough for them to trace the call. Stop it. She'd caught Darby's paranoia. Even the State Department didn't trace every call they got. At least she didn't think they did. If a couple of men in dark suits showed up at her door, she'd tell the truth. She hoped Darby would ask her to marry him, and she was curious about his ex-wife. With the right southern accent, she might pull it off.

Colonel Darby Baxter would eventually have general's stars on his shoulder. Plural. No way he would stop at one. Pepper had never thought about it before, but if Darby proposed, and she said yes, men in dark suits would be a regular part of her life. She'd held a low-level security clearance in the Army. Her background was clean, but there was no way she wanted to be on someone's watch list for the rest of her life.

A patrolman passed Avivah on the police station's back stairs. She recognized him as the man who had been with Detective Alexander at the hospital last night.

As she passed him, he reached out and grabbed her arm. "I won't forget this."

"Take your hand off me."

He gave her arm a painful, come-along squeeze, the kind applied to uncooperative felons when shifts were long and patience thin.

Avivah rubbed her arm as she climbed to the floor where the detectives' offices were located. Forget what? As she knocked on Detective Alexander's door she mentally wrapped herself in protective gear. He probably wanted to know why she had been in the room with Grace and Lawyer Ferguson. "Sergeant said you wanted to see me?"

Three desks filled the large, old-fashioned office, but Detective Alexander, standing at a filing cabinet, was the only one in the office this morning.

Alexander wore the same black suit, white shirt, and black tie that he'd worn the previous night at the hospital. No, this suit coat had three buttons on the sleeve; the one last night had two. This tie had a tiny red-and-yellow fishing fly embroidered on it. She wondered if he had a closet full of fifteen-year-old suits, each so like the other that they fit him like uniforms.

"Come in and close the door."

She stood with her back almost touching the closed door and resisted the urge to assume either attention or parade rest. He wasn't her commanding officer.

Alexander removed a manila folder from the filing cabinet and shoved the drawer closed. The metallic clang reverberated in the high-ceilinged room.

"You're my driver for the next two weeks."

"What?"

He sat behind his battered desk. "Detectives have a uniformed driver assigned to them."

"I know that."

"You're mine."

"What about your usual driver?"

"He's on vacation."

The patrolman on the stairs hadn't looked as though he were on vacation. "I just passed the man who was with you at the hospital last night on the stairs."

"That's a replacement driver. My regular driver goes on vacation the first two weeks in June, every year, like clockwork."

"If you already have a replacement driver, what do you need me for?"

"I changed my mind about who I wanted as a driver. Nothing wrong with a man changing his mind, is there? Women get to do it all the time."

Now she understood what the patrolman had meant. He'd been the replacement driver, and she'd beaten him out of a nice two-week break from street duty. She stiffened her spine to keep from sagging. Body fluids in the locker, here we come. "This isn't going to make me popular."

"I wasn't under the impression that being a police officer was a popularity contest. Sit down. You're making me nervous."

Avivah sat on the edge of the gray metal chair beside his desk. Close up, Alexander's suit smelled faintly of both body odor and dry cleaning fluid. White flakes decorated both shoulders. A man who had dandruff shouldn't wear dark suits.

"Why me?"

"Why not you? How do you take your coffee?"

"What?"

"Your coffee, how do you like it?"

"A little milk, no sugar."

"I like one of each. You bring me coffee in the morning; I'll bring you coffee in the afternoon. Fair enough, equal enough for you?"

Avivah couldn't figure out if Alexander was intentionally making an ass of himself or if he was a good old boy trying to play by new rules he didn't understand. "Stop doing that. It's really irritating."

He looked confused. "Stop doing what?"

"Stop making veiled references to equality."

"Affirmative Action. It's in. Haven't you heard? I'm only trying to get with the program."

"You don't have a clue what the program is."

For an instant, his face lost its chiseled hardness. Avivah saw a middle-age good old boy, who was making a nominal attempt to follow baffling new rules. "I'm sorry. My remark was uncalled for," she said.

He compressed his lips and nodded. "Being a detective's driver means more than providing chauffeur service. You'll do scut work, make phone calls, track down reports, and take notes during interviews."

"I can't be your driver. You're investigating Peter Taft's death."

"Among other crimes."

"I've got a conflict of interest here."

His chair creaked as he sat back in it. He studied her for a minute. "You related to Taft?"

"No."

"You related to Grace Kirkpatrick?"

"No."

"You related to anyone who is related to them?"

"I shared a house with Grace's son."

"Shared? Past tense?"

Last week, Benny had moved into the bed-and-breakfast to be with his family. "Recent past tense."

"Then I don't see that we have a problem."

"I think we do. You know I was present last night when Grace's lawyer interviewed her."

"I spoke to the Chief about that."

"That doesn't bother him?"

"Not really. You graduated top of the class at the police academy, right?"

It still rankled Avivah that, after spending ten years as a military police officer, the Asheville City Police made her repeat their six-week training program. Nonetheless, Alexander wouldn't know her class rank unless he'd checked up on her. In the presence of the enemy, name, rank and serial number were all that was required. Only Avivah couldn't decide if she was in the presence of the enemy. She tried a tentative, "Yes."

He spun around in his chair and removed a dusty three-ring binder from the shelf behind his desk. He propped it up, with the spine facing her. "Administrative policies. You tell me where in here I can find a written policy about conflict of interest."

Avivah looked down at her hands. "I don't think there is one."

"There isn't."

He shoved the binder back in its spot. With his index finger he slid the manila file folder across the desk to her. "Here's the Taft file. Read it. Let me know when you get to the conflict of interest part."

He might as well have waved a bottle of whiskey under the nose of an alcoholic. Her fingers scrabbled for the file.

It was paper-thin. Two pieces of paper, to be exact: the patrolman's report of finding the car and body in the airport parking lot, and a summary of what was known so far about Peter Taft. Grace's interview was probably still in the secretarial pool, being typed.

Peter Taft had been sixty-one when he died. He had a Tennessee driver's license, which showed an address in Murfreesboro. A note clipped to the file had a phone number and said that no one had answered at that number on Sunday.

Avivah closed the folder. The brown cardboard felt rough under her fingers. Without a written conflict of interest policy, she was on her own. Thank the Almighty that she had a military background. The Army had rules up its ying-yang. They wouldn't mind if she borrowed a few, starting with *never look a gift horse in the mouth* and *more reconnaissance is better than less reconnaissance.*

Peter Taft had hurt Grace; no, hurt all of the Kirkpatricks. Someone had hurt him. A good dose of justice was due all around. Justice for whom? She'd have to work on that question.

"Coffee: one sugar, one cream. Right?"

CHAPTER 6

The ringing phone had been annoying, now it was obsessively annoying. It wasn't a usual ring, but rather a *brrp-brrp* sound, which made Avivah wonder if the Murfreesboro phone system was connected to the rest of the world. She hung up the phone once again and massaged her ear.

The first thing she'd done after she and Detective Alexander finished coffee was to hike half a block up Pack Square to the library. An atlas showed that Murfreesboro was about three hundred miles west of Asheville. Driving between the two would take six, maybe seven hours driving time, depending on how much of I-40 was finished and open to traffic.

She doodled numbers. If Peter Taft met Grace at the airport about nine A.M., Friday morning, he would have had to leave Murfreesboro by two A.M. Equally likely was that he'd spent Thursday night in Asheville. Maybe his effects held a clue about where he'd stayed.

She'd stopped by the evidence room and collected the envelope with his personal possessions. She opened the envelope and a set of keys clanked on the desk. Keys. That meant whoever stuffed Peter Taft in the trunk of his car either had their own set of keys, or more likely, had parked in the airport parking lot, opened the trunk, and put the keys back in Taft's pocket. Rummaging around a trunk containing a dead body in a public parking lot took balls. They were looking for someone who didn't panic easily.

The rest of the items in the envelope were the usual: comb, checkbook, wallet, breath mints, and a worn leather portfolio, which held a blank pad of paper, several ballpoint pens, and a selection of business cards.

She riffled through his checkbook stubs. Taft hadn't been a meticulous checkbook keeper. Most entries contained only single phrases such as *groceries, dry cleaning,* or *car payment,* plus an amount. No dates, no notes to self. If he paid rent or utilities, he didn't do it with a check. She examined the space between the checks and the preprinted deposit slips. There were no ragged edges to show that deposit slips had been used. Taft apparently didn't deposit his paycheck using these slips. He must have had an income; he was buying groceries and making car payments.

His wallet held a hundred dollars in small bills and a driver's license. No photos, no slips of paper, no receipts. No one went around with a completely empty wallet, she thought. Someone had cleaned out this wallet, but left the cash.

She turned her attention to the leather portfolio. When she ran a pencil over the top sheet of paper, no faint marks from previous notations appeared. Peter Taft was an absolute cipher and that wasn't normal.

At least the business cards were interesting. Three different cards, all with a Christian cross and colored images at the bottom of the cross: *Cross of Joy* (flowers in yellow ink), *Johnny's Kids* (teddy bear and toys, blue ink), and *Bible Study by Mail* (a book, red). All of the cards said *Reverend Peter Taft,* a post office box address in Murfreesboro and a phone number. The first three digits of each phone number were identical, but the last four digits weren't even sequential. She lined the cards up in order of phone numbers. If she could put any stock in sequencing, Peter had had the phone number for *Bible Study by Mail* and *Cross of Joy* for about the same length of time. The numbers were close in sequence. *Johnny's Kids* appeared to be a new addition because the last four digits for that one were higher than the previous two.

In script letters on each card was *2 Corinthians 9:6–7.*

Finding a Bible in the police station was harder than finding an atlas in the library. Avivah was about to trek up the hill again when Claiborn Denham, the dispatcher, unearthed a tattered Bible in a box behind the dispatch radios.

He wiped the dust off the cover with a paper towel and planted his skinny ass in the worn chair behind the console. "What do you need out of here?"

"I can look it up."

"Be better if I did."

Of course it would be better. She didn't know Claiborn's religious preference, but she'd bet coffee and a doughnut that he wasn't going to let a Jewess's hands soil even a dusty and tattered Bible. Some things never changed.

"2 Corinthians 9:6–7."

He flipped through the pages, cleared his throat, and read, as if from a lectern, "Remember this: Whoever sows sparingly will also reap sparingly; and whoever sows generously will also reap generously. Each man should give what he has decided in his heart to give, so let him give; not reluctantly or under compulsion, for God loves a cheerful giver."

"Show it to me."

He turned the Bible around, his nicotine-stained fingertip marking the passage so that she could see for herself that he'd read the right passage.

She went back to the third-floor office, where she lined up the three cards: red, yellow, and blue. What struck her was that there was no church or denomination name on any of the cards. She pressed the intercom. "Claiborn, can you find me a number for the Tennessee Department of Corrections?"

From June 1950 to February 1951, a John Peter Taft, with the same birth date on Reverend Taft's driver's license, had served nine months in a Tennessee state prison for a confidence game gone wrong. The con had involved a bogus campaign to raise building funds for a nonexistent church. He'd served out the remainder of his sentence under parole, and disappeared out of the Tennessee justice system. That would make John Peter Taft a most unusual success story, a confidence man who had gone and sinned no more. Except Avivah didn't believe that. More likely, Taft had found a way to stay under police radar for almost twenty-five years.

For the rest of the morning, Avivah attempted to call all three numbers, rotating through the three cards. No one answered at any of them. Either Peter Taft was a one-person operation, now permanently closed, or God's fiscal advisors were taking Monday off.

She and Detective Alexander were away from the station all afternoon. Peter Taft's death wasn't the only thing on his caseload. It was three when she parked their cruiser in the station parking lot. As she got out of the car, a voice called, "Avivah!"

Avivah looked around. Saul Eisenberg, a friend of hers who edited a small town newspaper, unfolded himself from his car, which was parked across the street.

Alexander asked, "Friend of yours?"

"Yes."

He looked at his watch. "You're off duty in fifteen minutes anyway. See you tomorrow."

Avivah crossed the street. As she got closer to Saul's car, she realized every inch of it, except the driver's seat, was filled with boxes and clothes. Saul himself looked like a refugee from a work party. He wore blue jeans so old they were almost white, hiking boots, and a grimy sweatshirt that said *Columbia University School of Journalism*. His face was dirty and she could swear a cobweb covered the back of his head like a yarmulke.

"What's going on?"

"I got fired."

"What?"

"Jim's uncle sashayed into the office this morning, court order in hand, and told me to be out of Jim's office and apartment by five o'clock this afternoon."

Jim had been Saul's best friend in journalism school. Son and grandson of newspaper owners in a small mountain town, he had waged a constant war against his uncle who equated journalism with advertising copy. Several months ago, when Jim had learned that he was dying, he had pleaded with Saul to take over the newspaper and save it from his uncle's delusion that he could run the paper as well as Jim did.

"All I can say is, I beat his deadline."

"Who put the uncle in charge all of a sudden?"

"A judge who agreed that the uncle had a right to contest Jim's will."

"You told me that this uncle had no journalism experience."

"Editor of his high school paper for a year."

She looked at Saul's sweatshirt. Two-and-a-half degrees in journalism should count for more than a year on a high school paper. "I'm sorry."

"Me, too. I was supposed to save the paper from Jim's uncle. I failed."

"No, you didn't. You kept Jim's paper running just the way he asked you to. I can't believe the rest of his family is just going to let this happen."

"They're filing a counter-petition tomorrow. Who knows how long that will take? Or who will win? Can I stay at your place?"

Darby was sleeping in Benny's vacated bedroom and they

had no guest room. "We're a little crowded this week, but I'm sure we can find you a corner for tonight."

"I mean *stay* as in move in to Benny's room. Stay until I can decide what I'm doing next. I'll pay rent. It's just that I might have a job in Lower Slobovia by next week. I don't want the hassle of finding an apartment and signing a lease." His large eyes blinked myopically behind his glasses. "Please, I'm hot and tired, and I don't have any other place to go."

He looked so much like a lost puppy that Avivah stretched on tiptoe and kissed his cheek. He tasted like dust and sweat. "I hope you're not in Lower Slobovia by next week. I'd miss you."

Saul ran his fingertips over his cheek.

Avivah cleared her throat as she took her key ring out of her pocket and worked off her house key. "Get a duplicate made. Tell Pepper I told you it was all right if you moved in. We can work out the rent and all later."

Avivah picked up the eraser to remove her name from the duty blackboard. She tried to remember if she knew what Saul's favorite food was; she'd stop by the grocery store. On a day like today, he deserved a special meal.

The evening dispatcher said, "Alexander wants to see you."

"Now?"

"No, ten minutes ago."

Avivah groaned. One problem with being a detective's driver was that she would work when he worked. She hoped they didn't have a new case. If they did, she probably wouldn't get home in time to see Saul awake, never mind cooking supper for him.

As she walked down the hall on the third floor, she heard an elderly woman's voice say, "Praise the Lord. Praise the Lord."

Her first thought was "and pass the ammunition." It was an old Army phrase. She slid in through the partially open door.

An old woman and a middle-age man sat in front of Nate's desk. The woman wore a hat and white gloves and balanced a vinyl purse on her lap. The man had taken off a sports coat and draped it across the back of his chair.

Alexander made a hand movement that Avivah should close the door. She did. The two people looked around.

The detective said, "The constable is here to take notes. I'm afraid I have to ask you to go over everything from the beginning. Whenever you're ready, Constable."

Avivah sat beside a credenza and took out her notebook. She entered the date, time, Detective Alexander's name and her own, then nodded to him that she was ready to begin.

"Could you please state your names and place of residence for the officer."

Now that she had a better view of their faces, Avivah saw how tired both of them looked. The woman's face was pale, her gray hair carelessly done up in a bun. She drew herself up and clutched her purse with both gloved hands. "I'm Mrs. Tallulah Nibb from Murfreesboro, Tennessee." She gave a rural address and a phone number.

The man ran his hand through his close-cropped hair. "Kevin McCormick. Same address and phone number."

The phone number was only one digit different from *Bible Study by Mail*. Maybe God's fiscal advisors were only on a road trip.

Alexander asked, "You were both acquainted with Peter Taft?"

Mrs. Nibb opened the clasp on her purse and handed Nate a tri-folded piece of green paper. It looked like a home-printed brochure. "We're his mission staff. We provide a practical, Christian ministry to elderly, sick, and shut-ins in God's beautiful Blue Ridge Mountains."

Avivah couldn't decide if that sounded like a church or a tourist bureau.

Alexander opened the brochure, glanced at it, refolded it and tucked it under his blotter. "The Blue Ridge Mountains are quite a ways from Murfreesboro. Wouldn't it be easier to headquarter your *mission* someplace closer?"

From the emphasis he placed on *mission*, he believed the same thing Avivah did. Once a con man, always a con man.

Mrs. Nibb's eyes teared, and reached in her handbag for a flowered, cotton handkerchief, with which she dabbed her eyes. "That's where my farm is. It's a lovely farm. At least it used to be."

Mr. McCormick reached over and patted her arm. "There, there, Mother Nibb. You know the animals were getting too much for you. You're better off without them."

She sniffled as she took a photograph out of her purse. "I still have a cat. Would you like to see him?" She handed the photograph to Detective Alexander, who passed it along to Avivah. It showed Mrs. Nibb sitting on the stoop of an old house, holding a huge gray cat with a squashed face.

It was the ugliest cat Avivah had ever seen. She handed the photo back. "He's obviously your pride and joy."

"His name is Tommy Three-Toes because he has three big toes on his back feet."

McCormick laid his hand on her arm again. "Mother Nibb, this gentleman probably has more questions for us."

"Oh, of course." She put the photograph and handkerchief back in her purse and snapped it shut.

"Did Peter Taft live on this farm with the two of you?"

Mrs. Nibb started to say something, but Kevin McCormick interrupted with, "Yes."

"How long had he lived there?"

The old woman looked as though she wasn't going to give up control of the interview that easily. "Peter was our boarder for almost twenty years. He was a business associate of my late husband."

Avivah wondered if the Tennessee Department of Corrections had any record of an inmate named Nibb. Con men tended to find one another.

"Mr. McCormick, how long have you boarded with Mrs. Nibb?"

"A year."

"Where were you before that?"

"Twenty years in the Air Force. Retired as a Senior Master Sergeant."

Avivah asked, "Were you in Viet Nam?" The question slipped out before she remembered she was supposed to be the strong, silent one here today.

He cocked his head and stared at her. "One tour, June sixty-five to June sixty-six."

Alexander cleared his throat. "What was Peter Taft doing in Asheville?" He looked pointedly at Kevin McCormick, as if hoping for short answers so they could all get the hell out of there and go home.

"We didn't know he was here."

Mrs. Nibb contributed, "He was supposed to be in Virginia this week."

"Does he do a lot of traveling?"

"Oh, my, yes. His congregation covers three states, praise the Lord."

Alexander looked directly at Kevin McCormick. "When Taft came to Asheville, where did he stay?"

"In our ministry, like Blanche DuBois, we must depend on the kindness of strangers."

Avivah would have never figured Kevin McCormick for a man who read Tennessee Williams. Maybe he'd seen the movie.

Mrs. Nibb now laid her hand on McCormick's arm. "Not

strangers, Kevin. Friends in Our Lord."

It was one arm pat too many. Stage directions. That's what all this arm-patting, cat photographs and cotton handkerchiefs were about. Two right cons, the both of them. She wrote *play-acting* on a piece of paper and handed it to Alexander. He glanced at the word, and slid the piece of paper under his blotter. "In other words, you have no idea where he stays."

Mrs. Nibb sat up straight. "Of course we do, young man. It's only good manners to send a thank-you note when someone does you a kindness. I have a complete list of everyone who has hosted us."

A complete mailing list was more like it.

"I'll need a copy of that list."

She said with great dignity. "The list is in Murfreesboro. You'll have to wait until we go home, and I don't know when that will be."

Detective Alexander folded his hand over his blotter. "What are the two of you doing in Asheville today?"

Mr. McCormick said, "We were attending a Bible camp, outside of Black Mountain, for the past three days."

"Did you stay at the camp all weekend?"

"Yes."

Avivah had no idea what a Bible camp looked like, but she assumed it was like the camps she'd attended as a child. Log cabins didn't match in any way the room where Grace described she'd been held captive.

"News of Reverend Taft's death was in this morning's paper, but you told me you only learned about it at two o'clock this afternoon. Why was that?"

Mr. McCormick continued, "Saturday at one o'clock, we started a forty-eight-hour prayer marathon for world peace. For two days, we only left the prayer room to go to the bathroom and the dining hall."

Nate steepled his fingers. "You've been awake two full days?"

Kevin McCormick ran his hand through his hair again. "Mostly. I nodded off now and then. I'm afraid Mother Nibb has more stamina. She's been awake since six o'clock Saturday morning."

Thirty-three hours without sleep. Tired witnesses were bad witnesses. A clever lawyer would make mincemeat of anything either of these people said today.

"I wish you'd told me that before we started. I wouldn't want anyone as—conscientious—as Mrs. Nibb to answer questions when she's tired."

From the pause she bet he'd cycled through *old, frail,* and possibly a few more adjectives before he settled on *conscientious.* Maybe, just maybe, he was a good old boy who was actually trying to change. After a day with him, Avivah was willing to give him the benefit of the doubt.

Alexander sketched a map on a piece of paper, and wrote an address. Avivah saw the word *morgue* on the drawing. He folded the paper and handed it to Mr. McCormick. "I'd appreciate it if you—just you—could meet me at that address tomorrow morning at nine o'clock."

McCormick opened the page, read it, and folded it again. His face looked pale. "I suppose one of us has to, don't we?"

Morgue wasn't anyone's favorite word.

"Yes, please."

Their visitors stood. Avivah escorted them all the way to the front door.

When she came back to the office Alexander didn't look up from the notes he was completing. As Avivah closed the door, he said, "That woman's cornbread is not baked."

"What was all that 'Praise the Lord' I heard just before I came in?"

"She wanted to make sure that Peter Taft hadn't been struck

by lightning. When I told her that there was absolutely no lightning involved in his death, she started praising."

"Weird."

"I agree. Now, let's get straight who asks questions and who takes notes."

Avivah held up her hand. "Sorry, but when someone says they were in the military, the next thing I ask is if they were in Viet Nam. Automatic reflex."

"Un-automate it. So what about his military career?"

"I'm more familiar with the Army than the Air Force, but twenty years' time and only one tour of Viet Nam makes him either very smart or very lucky."

He locked his desk. "I've never trusted in luck. I think we have a couple of very slick characters there."

"Want me to check with Tennessee to see if they have a record of a Mr. Nibb serving time?"

Nate stood. "I think that would be an excellent idea, Avivah. You don't mind me calling you Avivah, do you? When we're alone, I mean."

"Not a bit, and you won't mind me calling you Nate, will you? When we're alone, I mean."

CHAPTER 7

Pink tulle squares covered every available surface in Pepper's kitchen. Pepper moved among them, placing precisely two tablespoons of birdseed in each one. Her back ached. Tallies of decorated nut cups, plastic-bag flowers, birdseed packets, and engraved matchbooks whizzed around in her head like errant pigeons.

Quinn Kirkpatrick knocked at the kitchen screen door.

"Come in."

He took off his boots and hung his weathered cap on the peg beside the door. "What are you doing?"

"Making birdseed packets. More earth-friendly than throwing confetti."

Quinn hefted one of the packages that she'd already tied with pink and green ribbons. "Can't say I'd like to be hit with too many of these."

"You don't throw the whole packet. You open them and throw the seed."

He set the tiny bag down in a different place from where he'd picked it up.

"Don't do that! I'll lose count."

He moved it back. "Sorry." He pointed to the tall kitchen stool on which rested two brown paper bags full of flowers made from dry-cleaning bags and pipe cleaners. "All right if I move those bags and sit there?"

"Fine. Just don't touch anything else."

After setting the bags on the floor beside the stool, he put his sock feet on the fold-down steps, and his hands in his lap, as though he were trying to make himself as small as possible. "Grace and I got married after Mass one Sunday. Eight people came. The sewing circle ladies baked a cake, and my best man tied tin cans to a truck. That was it. Oh, and I think people threw rice. Was that earth-friendly?"

Pepper set the bowl of birdseed in the sink, stretched, and rubbed her eyes. "It wasn't bad. I'm sorry I snapped at you. I've been making wedding doo-dads all day. I am *not* an arts-and-crafts person."

He propped his elbow on a miniscule unencumbered slice of kitchen counter and, looking morose, put his chin in his palm. "Can I invite myself to supper?"

"Where's your family?"

"Renting cars. Visiting Grace. Taking my grandsons out for pizza."

"You didn't feel like pizza?"

"I didn't feel like family. I desperately love every one of them, but I'd forgotten what it was like to have them all in the same place."

Pepper opened her chest freezer, took out a foil-covered disposable baking pan, and turned on the oven. She took two Cokes from the refrigerator. "Left-over lasagna is the best I can do. It comes with a side order of peace and quiet."

Quinn accepted a Coke. "Miss Pepper, both sound wonderful. I haven't seen that young fella, Baxter, around today. Will he be at supper, too?"

Pepper's stomach did a flutter dance. Nut cups and engraved matchbooks had pushed aside any thoughts of Darby all afternoon. "I don't know."

"You two have a fight?"

Pepper began to tie up little bags with pre-cut lengths of

colored ribbon. "Something from Darby's past came back to bite him this morning. He needed time by himself."

Quinn watched her. After a minute, he took a handful of ribbon pieces from the table and began to tie bags, leaving each one exactly where he'd picked it up. "How much time?"

"You sound just like Benny."

"He is my son. I hope you won't take offense for me asking, Miss Pepper, but is there anything between you and Benny?"

Pepper's hand faltered over a bow. "Wouldn't do me any good to pretend to be aghast at that question, would it?"

"Not much. I've watched the two of you. You enjoy each other's company. You shared a house at Fort Bragg; you've shared this house. You sold him half of your land, so he and Lorraine could build just down the road. I love Lorraine, and I like you."

"And you want to know if Benny and I are sneaking around behind Lorraine's back."

"That'll do for a start."

Were she and Benny that transparent? Or had Quinn picked up on their friendship just because he was Quinn? Benny said his dad didn't miss much.

"We kissed once, and both realized it was a mistake. Benny is my good buddy, probably the best buddy I've ever had. I'm not sure I can explain why, but we hit it off from the moment we met."

"I've got a buddy like that from the Army. Thirty-five years and we're still in touch. Can't say I ever had the urge to kiss him though. Does Lorraine know about that kiss?"

"We agreed not to tell her. I've kept my end of that bargain and I assume Benny kept his."

"Some things are best kept private."

"That's what Benny and I thought."

Pepper picked up completed packets, five in each hand, and

put them in a plastic bag, recounting to herself as she went. "As long as we're not taking offense, I'm furious with you, you know."

"If it's about breaking Ginny Mae's heart by selling the store, you'll have to take a number. It's all I've heard all day. This wasn't the way everything was supposed to turn out."

"Why did you sell up?"

He stopped tying packages. "Where were you in July 1947?"

"Mostly in my crib. I was four months old."

"That's when I brought Grace and the boys home to Missouri from Alaska. The Monday after we arrived, she and I were at the store, with my father, at six A.M. Except for holidays, family vacations and sickness, Grace and I have opened that store every morning, six days a week, for twenty-seven years. We want to take time off, be able to travel, buy a boat and go fishing, work part time for someone else instead of being the boss."

"Where is what Ginny Mae wants in all this? That store was going to be her life."

"She's nineteen. She's not ready to take on a store by herself."

"She'll be twenty in a few days."

"Miss Pepper, you just have to trust me. Grace and I believe that what we've done is the best thing for Ginny Mae."

"I don't agree."

"That's your privilege."

"Why won't you tell anyone what you've done with the money from the sale?"

Quinn pulled a length of ribbon through his hands over and over. "We've got a line on a place to live, a part-time job, even a secondhand boat, but the people we're dealing with asked us not to say anything until the details could be worked out. Believe me, we were going to tell all of our children once the deal was settled."

Pepper bet they were moving to Florida, probably buying a

trailer in a retirement community. From the way Benny had described Missouri winters, she couldn't blame his parents for wanting to leave ice and snow behind.

Quinn hit the table with his open palm. "Blast Peter Taft!"

Pepper sat down beside him. "Tell me about him."

Quinn's hands shook as he laid the ribbon he'd held in a squiggly line on the kitchen table, anchoring each end with birdseed bags. This time Pepper didn't object; some things were more important than accurate counts. Quinn's finger traced the ribbon's curve. "Big Delta, Alaska, at one end to Whitehorse, Yukon, at the other end. Not the whole Alcan Highway, you understand, just my part of it. Five-hundred-and-four miles of the most mother-fucking wilderness I ever hope to see. It was gumbo mud up to your ass, insect swarms, twenty-hour workdays, and days so cold that exposed flesh would freeze in under a minute. We had to keep fires burning under our trucks all night or our engines would be frozen solid by morning. Sometimes had to keep fires under the gas tanks as well."

"Wasn't that dangerous?"

"What do you think?"

"Sorry, I forget we were talking about the Army."

"I was a Quartermaster sergeant. Food, fuel, shelter, truck parts, medical supplies, anything the men building that road needed, getting it to them was my responsibility." He put a few grains of errant bird seed about two-thirds of the way along the ribbon. "Northway, where Grace and Hamilton lived."

"How big a town?"

Quinn laughed. "A runway, café, civilian truck maintenance yard and a couple of dozen tents."

"Grace and Hamilton lived in a tent, in Alaska, in winter?"

"They had a room in back of the café, but I lived in a tent. The Army used what it had. At least we were fed, even if we had to hunt most of it ourselves. No one shot at us, and Grace and I could see each other. We had it better than most couples did during the war. Then Peter Taft showed up."

"Was he in the Army, too?"

"He and his father owned a trucking company, and we used every truck, military or civilian, that could limp along the road. Peter was a con man and a dope pusher."

Pepper knew her mouth had dropped open. She closed it. "Dope?"

"You young people think Haight-Ashbury invented drugs. Most guys preferred liquor, but alcohol was in short supply and prohibited. Grace always carried beer in her truck. A quart of beer bought a full tank of gas, or meals and a night's lodging. The problem with liquor was not only did you have to hide it from the Military Police, but you had to keep it from freezing, too. Carrying cocaine or heroin in a foot powder tin was a lot easier."

"And more profitable?"

"A select, desperate market. Not that either one of us held with getting rip-roaring drunk, but a quart of beer wasn't going to make anyone so drunk that they couldn't take care of themselves. Heroin was different."

Quinn moved the bird seed bags back where they belonged, picked up the ribbon and pulled it so taut between his hands that the ribbon stretched irrevocably. "I know for a fact that Taft was responsible for at least one death. Conned one of my men into stealing truck parts, traded him heroin for them. The guy shot up, and got so addled he froze to death."

"Was Taft charged?"

"Of course not, but I knew what had happened. We found the body on Christmas Eve. The next day, I hauled Taft's ass out behind the Northway Café and beat the shit out of him. That was the only punishment he got. In retaliation, he saw to it I got shipped off to the Aleutian Campaign."

"We're a long way from Alaska."

"If you're asking did I hold a grudge for thirty-one-and-a-half years, the answer is no. Until this weekend, I hadn't thought about Taft in decades. I almost passed out when Mr. Ferguson said his name."

"Any idea how he found Grace?"

"None. Benny and Lorraine swear they'd never heard of him."

"Did anyone ask the boys?"

Quinn's eyes opened wide.

"Randy and Mark knew when and where Grace was going to pick up Joseph. Maybe they told someone."

"I don't think anyone thought to ask them."

A car clacked its way over the cattle guard. Benny had installed a large circular mirror just outside the kitchen window, so that the entire parking area was visible. Pepper checked the mirror. Even in the distorted view, she recognized Darby's car. The pigeons stopped fluttering in her stomach. As a bonus, Sandra had left hours ago.

Pepper threw a quick, "Excuse me," at Quinn. The screen door slapped behind her as she ran to where Darby was parking his car beside Frannie's car. She put her arms around him and they melted into one another's contours.

He buried his face in her hair. "I'm sorry, pretty lady. I let the side down. I promise to do all my errands tomorrow like a good boy."

"I did your list and mine."

"I owe you one. How about if I take you out to dinner? Someplace fancy where they have great food, dancing and maybe a view of the mountains. Only we don't talk about Sandra or Nancy—agreed?"

All day, she'd been dying to find out if Darby knew Nancy worked for Henry Kissinger, but suddenly, that question didn't seem so important. "Agreed. Oh, bother."

"What?"

"I promised to feed Quinn Kirkpatrick. He's taking a day off from his family. I already put lasagna in the oven."

"A man of his age should be able to take lasagna out of an oven. If he doesn't know how to do that, I'll be his principal instructor. When I get finished with him, he will be able to fix his own supper, without reference, and without error."

Without reference and without error, one of the first things Pepper had ever heard Darby say. It had become their catch phrase. She laughed and all the fear she'd been holding in check all day melted away.

"Frannie is here. Maybe she'd like to have supper with Quinn. He could use some non-family company."

Darby kissed her on her forehead. "I need *your* company. I'll go talk to Frannie while you change. You're always beautiful, but go make yourself gorgeous. When we walk into that restaurant, I want everyone in the place to wonder how a plain Joe like me ended up with a goddess."

God, was he in a strange mood. If there was one thing Darby Baxter wasn't, it was a plain Joe, and he knew it. Pepper caught him preening in front of a mirror often enough. "Sorry, all the goddesses have a meeting tonight on Mount Olympus. You'll just have to settle for an ex-Army nurse."

Another car rattled over the cattle gate. What in the world was Saul Eisenberg doing here with his car loaded to the gunnels and towing a small U-haul box-on-wheels behind him? Avivah hadn't mentioned that he was going on vacation.

Saul inched the U-haul into place beside Darby's car. He got out. "Sorry I took so long. I decided the best thing would be to buy a bed. It took me longer than I thought to find one to fit me. Then I had to rent the trailer to put it in."

Pepper asked, "What bed? What are you doing here?"

His long face grew even longer. "Avivah didn't tell you? I lost my job and my apartment this morning. Avivah said I could move into Benny's room, after Darby leaves of course. I was planning to camp in the living room until then."

Pepper heard a rustling of crinoline petticoats. An imaginary hand clamped itself firmly over her mouth. Her southern hospitality gene was awake, the one that said family—Saul was close enough to family—was always welcome to sleep on the couch. The couch, not bring their own bed with them.

Darby was already untying the rope that secured boxes in Saul's roof rack. He asked, "Shall I start with these?"

It wasn't just crinoline Pepper heard swishing. There was a vest, coat and trousers as well. Darby had the same southern hospitality genes she did. With their combined military and southern backgrounds, their married life could be a constant stream of unexpected company and neither one of them would ever turn away a single person. Their only hope for privacy would be to hire a frosty English butler who'd vet every visitor as rigorously as they did at Buckingham Palace. Pepper opened one of the car's back doors and took out a cardboard box. So much for a romantic supper.

Quinn came from the house and Frannie from her studio. Everyone stood in the yard, swatting at mosquitoes, while Saul told his story. Just as the ant party, with everyone carrying something, moved toward the house, Avivah arrived.

Frannie, carrying a small suitcase, bent down to look in the car's windows. She asked, "Did Ginny Mae change her mind?"

Avivah got out and tucked her car keys in her uniform waistband. "What do you mean?"

"Ginny Mae wasn't there when I came home this afternoon. She'd left a note on my kitchen table, saying she was going to find her own way home. I assumed she'd catch a ride with you."

"I haven't heard a word from her. I figured she was staying another night with you."

Everyone stood fixed in a tableau, which Pepper christened "Like Mother, Like Daughter." A chill traveled through her backbone. Peter Taft wasn't in the running to abduct Ginny Mae, but his killer might be.

CHAPTER 8

The tableau shattered.

Quinn said, "I'll phone the hospital. Maybe she went to see Grace."

Avivah said, "I'll phone my Sergeant in Juvenile."

Saul said, "I'll phone the Asheville paper. I know the evening editor."

Frannie asked, "Saul, where do you want this box?"

Darby climbed in his car. He reached across the passenger seat and opened the door for Pepper. "Get in."

Other people made phone calls; Darby went in person. She laid a box on the roof of Saul's car and got into Darby's car. As they turned onto Highway 251, Pepper wondered if Batman felt the same warm glow when he pulled out of the Bat Cave.

"Frannie's would be the best place to start looking."

"We're not looking for Ginny Mae."

"We have a duty."

"Fuck duty."

The Bat Cave image shredded. "A nineteen-year-old girl is missing."

He pulled to the side of the road and jerked the parking brake so hard that Pepper jolted forward.

Darby said, "Nineteen-year-old girls are adults. They have their own lives and, by my count, Ginny Mae has a police officer, a social worker, a journalist and her father looking for her. She can slide by without us. You and I are going to supper."

They ended up at the only Mexican restaurant in Asheville. Darby spooned refried beans on a tortilla and rolled it with the same ease farm boys rolled corn cigarettes. "I don't know anyone who gets out of Fort Sam without loving Mexican food."

Honestly, the boy acted as if he hadn't eaten all day. Maybe he hadn't.

Pepper tossed her napkin on the table. "I'd better phone home."

Darby waggled his empty beer bottle at their waitress. "You'd better stay right where you are."

He made it sound like an order.

Pepper aligned two empty beer bottles in front of his plate. A drop of beer ran down the side of the second bottle onto her finger. She scrubbed at it with her napkin, afraid absorbing even that miniscule amount would break the promise she'd made to Darby and Benny, that she'd never take another drink.

"High-fat food and three beers in one evening. What next, planning to take up smoking?"

Darby laid down his tortilla. He placed his forearms protectively on the table between the plate and his chest. "Could you and I please pretend we're on vacation? It doesn't even have to be a real vacation like civilians take. It can be Rest-and-Recreation. If it makes you feel better, pretend there's a war out there somewhere." He waved one hand in a vague direction where a war might be. "People like me are being shot and people like you are trying to save them. Only, we've caught the freedom bird and, for the next little while, it's copacetic for us to enjoy ourselves. Even the Army approves of soldiers taking R-and-R."

Pepper hadn't taken a vacation without booze in the past three years. "But Ginny Mae—"

"Pepper, please, please, can I have your undivided attention for a few hours? Is that too much to ask? Then we can both go back to saving the world."

An overwhelming urge rolled over her to empty her water glass into one of Darby's beer bottles, swish the liquid around, and down it in one long swallow. Surely the few drops remaining in the bottle would be enough to give her the taste, without her actually having taken a drink. Bad idea. Very bad idea.

To keep her hand away from her glass, Pepper reached across the woven tablecloth and rested her fingers on Darby's hand. The blond hair on his forearm looked golden against his skin. "You have eyes a woman could get lost in."

Darby relaxed. He picked up her hand and kissed her fingertips. "And you, pretty lady, are a woman a man would conquer kingdoms to possess."

The waitress, a non-Hispanic-looking woman in a peasant blouse and ruffled skirt, rolled her eyes, put Darby's fresh beer on the table, and took away the empties without saying a word.

Pepper and Darby broke down, laughing. Darby ordered more guacamole.

An hour later, they came out of the restaurant into a cold, almost full-moon night. It might be June, but when the sun went down in the mountains, temperature plummeted. They sat in the parking lot, waiting for the car to warm up. Darby kept both hands on the steering wheel and looked straight ahead. "Shall we get a motel room? Separate beds, like old times."

When she'd been stationed at Fort Bragg and he at Fort Benning, one weekend a month they'd meet halfway between the two bases, squeezing all the time together they could into a weekend pass. They'd shared half a dozen motel rooms, but never the same bed. It had been more of a sleepover than a tryst, long nights in the dark, her in one bed and him in the other, talking. People who knew her believed that story. People who knew Darby . . . didn't.

She pointed to a phone booth. "Pull over there. I have a better idea. Got any change?"

She shut the glass booth door behind her and fed coins into the phone.

Benny answered, "Kirkpatrick."

"It's Pepper. Any word?"

"She's not in the hospital, the morgue, or jail. She's too old for Juvenile to take an official interest, and the police won't take a missing-person report on an adult until forty-eight hours have passed. The guy Avivah works with in Juvenile made some un-official calls. We know she hasn't bought a plane or bus ticket. She didn't take a cab from Frannie's house, which means she left by city bus or on foot."

Or, the one possibility neither of them wanted to say out loud—with someone.

"Is Frannie still there?"

"Yeah. You want to talk to her?"

"Please."

Pepper stamped from foot to foot to stay warm until Frannie came to the phone.

"What's up?"

"I need a favor. Can you sleep in my room tonight and let Darby and me stay at your house?"

Frannie hooted.

"It's not like that. Darby and I need a place to talk."

Frannie hooted again. "In case you have a power failure while you're talking, you'll find candles in a kitchen drawer. There's a basket in the bathroom closet with toothbrushes, lotion, and other things. Have a good talk."

"Stop chortling."

A few minutes later Darby parked in Frannie's driveway. Wildflowers and stone paths covered the front yard; white flowers and pale leaves shimmered in the moonlight. Darby said, "A moon garden."

"How did you know that? I never figured you for a garden guy."

"I spent a couple of hours one night crouched in a moon garden in Na Trang."

"Business or pleasure?"

"Business. We stood out like target silhouettes. Scary as hell."

"There's been too much business in your life. Let me show my favorite part."

She reached down and tweaked a few leaves beside the stone path. "This would work better if I had on a long, trailing skirt, but maybe if I just brush against the plants like this." She rubbed her leg against some plants. Mint, vanilla, and an undercutting of sharp thyme filled the air.

Darby took a deep breath. "That's gorgeous."

"It's a strewing garden. You crush the leaves as you walk and they release fragrance."

"You think I could grow a strewing garden in my apartment? Then I could smell an intruder."

Only Darby would use gardening as a defensive perimeter. Pepper put her arm around his tight, lean waist. "Your landlord might object to dirt in the carpet."

"He might."

Wisps of scent and moonlight trailed them to the front porch. Pepper put her key in the lock and opened the door. "Ginny Mae, it's Pepper. Are you here?"

Darby put his hand on the door frame to block her entering the house. "If you brought me over here to help you look for clues about Ginny Mae, I'm leaving."

"Suppose she came back? Do you want to walk in on her sleeping in the buff?"

"How do you know Ginny Mae sleeps in the buff?"

"I don't, but she might. I brought you over here because it's nicer than a motel."

"How come you have a key?"

"Last winter, I slept here a few times after my shift, when roads were icy."

They stepped into the dark, silent house. Pepper rotated a dimmer switch. Warm, peach-colored light rose in three translucent globes, strategically placed around the living room.

Darby walked over to the far wall and studied black-and-white photographs of the front garden. "These are nice. Peaceful."

Pepper swished her fingers through a bowl of dried pennyroyal and lemon balm. "Frannie took them. She calls them light-and-shadow studies."

"Is she going to open a photographic studio at your place?"

"She's going to do art therapy. She's tired of therapy groups where the only physical activity women do is pass around Kleenex boxes. She wants women to have fun while they are recovering. Pound clay, weave, write poetry, paint. Get naked under a full moon, if that's what it takes."

"You approve of nudity in your backyard?" He sounded hopeful.

"It's not like they're going to run naked under my kitchen windows. She's going to use that clearing down by the stream for the more . . . um, private sessions."

"Did she quit her job at the Veterans' Hospital?"

"That is, as they say in the art world, her day job. She also started a private counseling practice, women clients only." She stopped herself before she added, "Sandra is one of her clients." If Ginny Mae was off-limits, Sandra Waine was way, way off limits. "Want to give me your clothes?"

A blush rose and fell in Darby's face, like a small tide coming in and going out. "What?"

"Mine are full of glue, glitter, and birdseed. I don't have

clean ones for tomorrow. I might as well wash yours at the same time."

"What will we wear?"

"Frannie keeps a robe in the bathroom closet for unexpected visitors. Bother, she lent it to Ginny Mae last night. Let me see what else I can find."

Darby followed her down the small hall. She flicked on the light in the guest room. The bed was made, the wastebasket emptied. Pajamas and the robe, looking newly washed, lay folded on the spread. Unless Pepper wanted to play out an unlikely scenario of a killer holding Ginny Mae at gunpoint and making her do laundry and tidy the room, Benny's sister had left this house in her own time and according to her own wishes. A voice in Pepper's head entreated, "Wherever you are, please be safe." It would have been a prayer, if Pepper still prayed.

She handed the robe to Darby. "Frannie said there was a basket in the bathroom closet with toothbrushes and such. Make yourself at home."

"I think I'll shower. There's only one robe. What are you going to wear?"

Pepper slid open the closet door, and took out a faded blue robe. "Sorry to disappoint you, but I keep a few things here."

On the way back from the basement laundry room, Pepper stopped in the kitchen. She ran her fingertips down the smooth, white table candles Frannie kept in her odds-and-ends drawer.

She was twenty-seven years old. For years, Darby Randolph Baxter had been the only boy who held her heart. Benny's words came back to her. *Put that boy out of his misery.*

She supposed *boy* was out these days. People got upset at the strangest words. But there was a sweetness to that term, like the fizz of a cherry coke, or the taste of ripe watermelon, or women of her mother's generation fanning themselves and saying, "He's such a *fine* boy." Darby would understand what they meant, and not be the least insulted. Embarrassed, maybe, but not insulted.

The table candles weren't right: too white, too long, too formal, too something. She rooted around in the drawer and came up with a dozen tiny tea lights and a box of kitchen matches.

The candles made Frannie's bedroom glow. Pepper opened all four windows, and closed the inside wooden shutters over the screens. She liked the arrangement, fresh air and privacy combined. She might do something like it at the homestead.

Darby came in, drying his hair with a towel. His blond, curly hair always screwed down into tight curls when it was wet. He stopped in the doorway, and caught the tip of his tongue between his teeth.

Pepper's heart dropped to the soles of her bare feet. She'd thought. She'd assumed. Oh, God, the one thing in her life she hadn't wanted to mess up, and it looked as though she had.

It was the robe. He'd probably imagined her wearing something slinky and black when this moment came. Or maybe peach-colored. He was from Georgia, after all.

Courage. One day they would both laugh about this.

Darby slung his towel over his shoulder, and walked slowly by the dresser, trailing his fingers along the top. He picked up a silver-framed photo of Cody Doan. "How's Doan doing?"

"Prosthetics school is hard for him. Frannie's worried that he won't pass."

"Is he still playing his disabled veteran card?"

"Half of his classmates are disabled veterans. One is a double amputee. You might say Cody has discovered that ploy doesn't have a leg to stand on."

Darby slid his towel from his shoulder, and snapped it at her. She threw a pillow at him. They tussled playfully until Darby backed her, squealing, into a corner.

He pulled her to him and kissed the nape of her neck. A

honeysuckle-laden breeze drifted through the windows. Crickets chirped. Darby took her hand and led her to bed. "You ever get to the central highlands in Nam?"

"No."

"When the French were in charge, the well-to-do had summer homes in the highlands. That's what this room reminds me of, even down to the wooden shutters on the windows."

Her heart pounded. Thank God she and Darby had been in Viet Nam at different times, in different places. She knew she wouldn't have been able to resist the smell of war on him. She would have fallen for him too hard, too fast for it to be good for either one of them. "I always feel funny being in someone else's house. I can smell Frannie and Cody here."

"How do you know what Cody smells like?"

"I know what a lot of my patients smelled like."

"The nurses did that to me. Put their noses right up against my wound and took a deep breath. It was unnerving."

"You can't beat a trained nose."

Darby's finger brushed against her bare skin. "Aren't you afraid of catching something?"

"Haven't caught anything yet."

He kissed the nape of her neck again. Butterfly kisses drifted toward her left shoulder.

Pepper rolled to her back. Sweat covered her body. "Am . . . I . . . supposed to be . . . this out of breath?"

Darby traced a fingertip from the point of her collarbone down to her stomach, where he circled her belly button. "If you're lucky."

"So that was it, was it?"

He licked her earlobe. "One version of it. Vacation is just starting. We can try out a lot of other versions."

"I guess I'm going to have to buy Frannie some new sheets."

"I guess so."

Pepper pulled the top sheet over them. Most of the candles had burned out, leaving only two spots of light in the dim room. Something she couldn't name, something transparent, which had stood between her and Darby, had burned out as well. An incredible, secure peace flowed over her. She asked, "Where did you meet Nancy?"

"At a garden party in Atlanta."

White summer dresses against tanned skin. Clunky jewelry. Bourbon and Coke in tall glasses. The smell of barbecue. Not that a railway mechanic's daughter was invited to that kind of party, but Pepper knew they existed. She'd caught glimpses of them, as a child, riding her bike around Biloxi.

"Nancy had trapped a group of men in a corner and was intimidating them about FDR's foreign policy. The first thing I said to her was, 'You just misquoted Cordell Hull.' Hull was Roosevelt's Secretary of State."

"I knew that." Pepper picked at the sheet. "No, I didn't."

Darby turned on his back and put his hands behind his head. "Let me see if I can do this without putting my foot in my mouth. You're smart. I'm smart. Nancy is brilliant. Most men ran when they saw her coming. She scared the hell out of me, too. Before I'd write her a letter, I'd go to the library and study up on whatever we were discussing. She demanded more intellectual honesty than any of my instructors."

"Did you ever study up before you wrote me a letter?"

"For you, pretty lady, I had to study up on what was in my heart, not what was in the West Point library."

His honesty opened up a pit in her stomach. "Why did you two marry?"

"We saw potential in each other. Drive. A whiff of the success we would have conquering the world together—well, conquering Washington, D.C., for a start."

"You, in politics?"

He winced. "We were young."

"What happened?"

"Viet Nam. Nancy thought going there was like showing up for homeroom. You got your name checked off to show you'd been there, and then you cut out early. Only I didn't cut out early. I stayed so long after school that she got tired of waiting."

Pepper muttered, "Then what is she doing in Hanoi?"

"What is who doing in Hanoi?"

"Nancy."

Darby raised himself on one elbow. "Why do you think she's in Hanoi?"

"Sandra told me she was."

"I wouldn't put too much stock in what Sandra says."

"Kissinger's secretary said Nancy was away. She gave me the impression she wouldn't be back for a while."

He stared at her. "Henry Kissinger?"

"Sandra gave me this Washington, D.C., phone number. I didn't know it was Henry Kissinger's office, or I'd never have called. Anyway, the woman who answered the phone knew exactly who Dr. Waine-Baxter was, and that she was away, and that she couldn't say when she would be back."

"Hmh, she kept my name."

She couldn't tell from Darby's tone if he was pleased or dismayed. What he sounded was possessive. Pepper got up and blew out the two remaining tea lights. The room settled into darkness. She felt her way back to the bed.

Darby asked, "Do you still have the phone number?"

"I threw it away. Why?"

"Nothing. It's not important. Come here."

Pepper did. Darby molded his body against her back. She could feel the scar in his chest pulsating.

"One of the nicest parts of sleeping together is falling asleep together. I love you, pretty lady. Whatever else happens, always remember that I love you."

CHAPTER 9

Detective Alexander—his Tuesday's black suit distinguished from Monday's black suit by having two front buttons instead of one—peered through the round window into the morgue's waiting area.

Kevin McCormick sat on one of the scuffed plastic chairs. He wore slacks, a sports coat and an opened-necked shirt, and he held a soft, black leather case on his lap. Avivah remembered Army chaplains carrying their Bibles in similar cases. She wondered if he planned to say a few words over the body. Nate pushed the door open.

A few minutes later the three of them stood in front of the viewing window. Detective Alexander punched the intercom button. "We're ready."

Kevin McCormick looked anything but ready. His skin tone brought out the color of the thin green thread woven through his jacket. Doing his good Christian duty, no doubt.

Curtains rattled along the slide. A morgue attendant stood beside the stretcher, where a man's body lay covered with a white sheet. The sheet was pulled back to neck level, revealing a pale, thin face.

What surprised Avivah most was how, even in death, Peter Taft looked like a good-old mountain boy. If she'd been pressed for an opinion, she'd have said he came from Tennessee or Kentucky instead of Alaska. He had a hawk-like nose, and deep lines etched the corners of his mouth. His gray hair was sparse and dry, but the dryness might have been because he was dead.

Kevin McCormick took a deep breath. "Those are the physical remains of the man I knew as Reverend Peter Taft. His spirit has departed for a better place."

That qualified for her weird body identification collection. McCormick's pretentious religiosity sounded as cheap as his suit looked. She hoped they got him out of there before he began to testify or pray.

Detective Alexander punched the intercom again. "That's good. Thank you."

The curtains slid shut. When he turned from the window, Kevin McCormick's face was pale and he had sweated handprints onto the leather Bible cover. She looked around for a chair to push under his knees before he collapsed. McCormick closed his eyes. "Could we get a cup of tea?"

A few minutes later the three of them were wedged into a back booth in a combination bakery and coffee shop.

McCormick said to the waitress, "Tea, please. I'll put the tea bag in myself. And whole-grain toast, two slices, dry, no butter, no margarine."

Avivah and Detective Alexander ordered coffee.

As soon as the waitress left, McCormick placed his leather case on the table and unzipped it. Avivah noted that the zipper pull was in the shape of a cross. Instead of a Bible, the inside was filled with gray foam, the kind photographers used to protect their cameras and lenses. The cut foam held glass vials, jars, a shot glass, a set of measuring spoons, and syringes. Kevin McCormick removed one of the syringes, and pulled open its paper wrap. "Sorry. I normally take my medications by mouth, but seeing Peter's body was more of a shock than I thought it would be."

Detective Alexander asked, "Are you a diabetic?"

With deft fingers, McCormick selected a small vial, inserted air and withdrew a tiny amount of clear liquid. He repeated the motion with a second vial. Then he twirled the syringe gently between his palms. "I'd welcome something as simple as diabetes."

He pushed up his left coat sleeve and inserted the tiny needle just under his skin. Injecting the liquid raised a weal, no bigger than a mosquito bite, on the soft side of his forearm. He recapped the needle and removed a paper packet and small jar from the case before he zipped it closed. Avivah was glad that the booth had a high back. Otherwise, other patrons might assume that two police officers had just watched a drug addict shoot up.

The waitress returned. Ignoring the tea bag beside the metal hot water pitcher, McCormick emptied the contents of the paper packet into the pitcher. A vegetative odor, reminiscent of cut hay, rose from the pot. He smiled apologetically. "It creates less confusion to order tea instead of a pitcher of hot water."

He poured a cup of vile-looking liquid, held the cup between both hands and inhaled the aroma for two long, slow breaths. Then he drank deeply. Some of the color returned to his face. Setting his cup back on its saucer, he said, "Lung cancer. Terminal, according to some of my doctors."

Alexander asked, "What's with the drug paraphernalia?"

McCormick opened the small jar and spread something on his toast that looked like honey, but was full of bright yellow specks. "Naturopathic medicines and nutritional supplements. This is unrefined honey with bee pollen. I don't usually use needles in public, but my naturopath says it's essential to immediately counteract any strong negative emotions, which could feed the tumor."

Avivah was certain McCormick had brought no case with him yesterday afternoon when he and Mrs. Nibb came to see Nate. Why not? An interview with police detectives almost certainly could be counted on to produce negative emotions.

From his coat pocket, Detective Alexander took Peter Taft's three business cards and laid them on the table. Each card made a little crisp sound, as though he dealt a poker hand. "We found these in Mr. Taft's notebook. Do you know anything about the businesses?"

"Not businesses, services provided in Christ's name."

He sounded like a parrot, repeating what Mrs. Nibb had said yesterday, but without her conviction. Avivah wondered how Peter Taft would have sounded: sincere, probably. He'd been on the con—and she was sure these cards had something to do with a confidence scheme—for decades.

Alexander managed to look apologetic, as though he'd made a social *faux pas*. "My mistake. Do you know anything about these *services?*"

McCormick picked up the *Bible Study by Mail* card. "Peter recruited people from Christian churches to record cassettes of Bible study lessons, which he mailed to people who couldn't read or who preferred to listen rather than read. Twenty-nine-ninety-five, plus postage and handling, for twelve inspirational monthly cassettes, plus special Christmas and Easter messages as a free bonus. An ideal gift for shut-ins or elderly relatives."

Bulk cassettes were cheap. Avivah bet the readers volunteered their time. Taft's profit on each ideal gift could have been as high as ninety percent. Mail fraud involved the U.S. Postal Service; investigating it came under the jurisdiction of the Federal Bureau of Investigation. Peter Taft must have been both crafty and lucky to stay inside the law on that one.

Detective Alexander pushed forward the card with the blue teddy bear and toys at the foot of the cross.

"*Johnny's Kids*. Mrs. Nibb's only grandchild died in a freak lightning-strike accident. Peter set this up as a memorial fund in Johnny's memory. It provides nonviolent toys and art supplies for children in war-torn countries."

"Is that why Mrs. Nibb was so concerned about Mr. Taft being struck by lightning?"

"Tallulah had a rough time when Johnny died. She's still terrified about anyone else she knows being struck by lightning."

That left the *Cross of Joy* card on the table. The yellow flowers at the base of the cross were the same bright yellow as the flecks in Kevin's untouched toast and honey.

McCormick tapped the card. "These are the people who will be hurt the most by Peter's untimely death."

Alexander gathered up the cards, and put them in his pocket. "Who are they?"

"Old mountain people, abandoned by their children, who went off to work in northern factories, or sank into alcoholism, or simply left to find a better life outside the mountains. There're dozens of old people up and down the Appalachian chain who lost track of their children as long ago as the Great Depression. Peter created a special ministry for them. Their cross will be lifted when they're reunited with their children in Paradise."

The cheapness disappeared from his voice. Either he seriously believed in the *Cross of Joy* work, or his medications had kicked in. Avivah bet on the latter.

Nate asked, "Why?"

McCormick tilted his head. "Why what?"

"Why was Taft especially interested in these people? Why did he create a ministry just for them?"

"Because he abandoned his own son. Peter had never had any contact with the boy after he left Alaska."

Avivah felt as though a hand had pushed her back against the booth. If Peter had never had any contact with his son, how did he know the boy had ended up in prison? Had Grace Kirkpatrick's statement just fallen apart?

A skeletal old man, dressed in clean overalls and a faded plaid work shirt, sat on the bench outside the police station's front door. His back bent in an osteoporotic curve. One arthritic hand rested atop a wooden cane; with the other he clutched a worn manila envelope. When Detective Alexander nodded a greeting to him, he pushed himself to a standing position.

"Excuse me, are you the young fella investigating this Peter Taft business? They said inside I couldn't miss you 'causen you'd have a lady cop with you."

Nate turned. "Yes. I'm Detective Alexander."

The man peered at Nate, as though he couldn't see well, then held out a gnarled hand. "Pleased to meet you. I'm Deputy Sheriff F. J. Cantrell from Yancy County."

Not likely. Not any time recently. Avivah asked, "Been retired long, deputy?"

"1957."

She had been fifteen when Deputy Cantrell retired.

"I got inside knowledge about your victim you might find beneficial."

Nate asked, "Which victim is that, sir?"

"I told you! Peter Taft!"

He said each word carefully, as though Nate thought might be deaf or simple. The kooks had started to come out of the woodwork. The juicier the case, the kookier the kooks.

Detective Alexander put his hand under the man's elbow. "Why don't we go up to my office?"

It took an eternity for the old man to shuffle across the marble floor into the elevator. Twenty minutes passed before they had him settled, with a cup of coffee in front of him.

Detective Alexander placed a clean pad of yellow paper in the middle of his blotter. Avivah noted he didn't ask the old man to identify himself, as he would have if he considered this a real interview. She wondered if Deputy Cantrell noticed he was being humored. She took up her position, standing with her arms folded in a corner of the room. She doubted Nate wanted her to take notes either.

Detective Alexander leaned forward. "You were acquainted with Mr. Taft?"

"Going on two months."

"How did you meet him?"

"He came to my house on Hog Branch Road, out north of Burnsville."

Out north of Burnsville was strictly rural, a landscape filled with the highest peaks and deepest valleys in North Carolina. Avivah doubted she would even find Hog Branch Road on a map. It sounded as though it was one of those places people talked about being so far back in the coves that you had to pipe in sunshine.

"Why did Mr. Taft come to see you?"

"Offered up what he called a Christian connection. Wanted to drop by and read the Bible with me when he was in the neighborhood. Said he believed in muscular Christianity; that Jesus was a carpenter and He intended for people to put their hands where their faith was. Asked if he might set my porch to rights. The steps were in bad shape, I admit."

It sounded a lot like what Peter's business card called his *Cross of Joy* ministry.

"Wouldn't your family be doing that kind of thing for you?"

"Ain't no family left. My wife died and my last boy ran off in thirty-two, planning to hop a train north. Ain't heard from him since."

It sounded exactly like the *Cross of Joy* ministry. A bitter taste filled Avivah's mouth. How dare Taft use religion to prey upon vulnerable old people, like F. J.?

"Asked for money, did he, for repairing your porch?"

"Five dollars. I knew that wouldn't even cover lumber, but he wouldn't take no more. Said church people subsidized his work, and I'd be denying them the grace of their offering by not accepting help."

Smart move. Mountain people hated to accept charity. Cantrell might have become suspicious or offended if Taft offered to do the work for free. By taking five dollars, Taft set himself up as someone who respected that take-no-charity value.

Cantrell moved as though he were trying to straighten his crooked back to relieve a muscle strain. Only he kept going until his back was straight and firm as a young tree. Avivah swore his hands grew less gnarled as she watched, like seeing, in reverse, that old black-and-white movie where the man turned into a werewolf. He sat back at ease in his chair. "Course I played along. That was what he expected me to do."

Detective Alexander opened his desk drawer and shoved the pristine yellow pad into it. He closed the heavy wooden drawer with a thunk. "Who the hell are you?"

The old man grinned and reached for his wallet in a back pocket. He opened it to show a gold badge. *Retired* was engraved on the badge's face. "Exactly who I said I was. F. J. Cantrell. Retired deputy, Yancy County. I may be eighty-two, but I'm neither feeble nor feeble-minded. The men in my family are blessed with long, healthy lives, and, Detective Alexander, if you intend to take my statement, I suggest you do it in the proper form."

Alexander's face turned red. "What's this all about?"

"Real estate fraud. My great-grandson, down to Appalachian State University, got to studying what happened to old folks' homesteads when the family ran out of blood kin to inherit. He looked up a lot of wills and bills of sale. Two names kept cropping up suspiciously often on the wills: Reverend Walter Nibb and Reverend Peter Taft. I got involved because my great-grandson wanted to know what I remembered about Aunt Ethel-Birdie's land leaving the family."

Avivah had a mental image of a piece of mountain real estate fluttering its handkerchief as it waved good-bye to the Cantrell family.

"I thought you said your great-grandson was studying people who had run out of relatives to inherit the land? Sounds like your Aunt Ethel had kin left alive to inherit."

"Aunt Ethel-Birdie. Both names together. She was very particular about that. Aunt-by-marriage. Her blood kin died out or left the mountains long before she died, and once her husband was gone, she didn't have much truck with the Cantrells. She willed her land to a Reverend Walter Nibb, a man none of our family knew anything about. My folks figured it was church business. Aunt Ethel-Birdie was an odd sort, and the land wasn't worth much then, so they put no-never-mind to it when it happened."

Avivah asked, "You said then. What about now?"

"Some developer went and put a tourist trap on it: restaurant, gift shop, and petting zoo. This Reverend Nibb made himself a nice bit of money when he sold the land, only none of that money went to any church on record that I could find."

Nate took the yellow pad out of his desk again and uncapped his pen. "How do you know that?"

"My great-grandson and me, we been researching together almost two years now. The boy's going to get some high-fangled degree out of the book he's writing, *Forty Years Gone: Lingering Effects of Northern Migration During the Great Depression, Extinction of Blood Lines, and Extra-Family Transfer of the Hereditary Land Base.* Can't say I cotton much to the title, but he says that's what his teachers want."

F. J. Cantrell didn't look like a man who'd spent a lot of time in a university library. Avivah asked, "How did you help your great-grandson with his research?"

"Talked to people. I've always been good at talking to people. He'd give me names of people who willed their land to one of the reverends. I'd go visiting neighbors and friends to find out what they remembered about what happened to this or that piece of land."

F. J.'s back curled slowly once again into the osteoporotic curve. His voice sounded tremulous. "Always did like making up stories and playing out parts. Might have gone for an actor, if 'en I weren't Baptist. We don't hold with play-acting, you know." He winked at Avivah and straightened himself out. He scratched the back of his neck. "Finally decided I wanted to meet one of the reverends, only I'd waited too long. Nibb passed on last year, but I figured I could still take a look at this Taft fellow."

If Taft and Nibb had been partners, that might explain Kevin McCormick. Nibb died; Taft needed a new partner.

Nate asked, "What did you do?"

"Set up a sting of my own. You see that movie? Good movie. Having been a deputy—even if it was donkey's years ago—I understood the difference between collecting evidence and entrapment. Plus, my family had a cabin I could use for a stage prop."

"How did you contact Peter Taft?"

"A good Christian lady I'd known for years wrote to him. Said she'd heard about his good works and wanted to talk to him the next time he came through these parts about an old man in Yancy County in dire straits." He picked up the manila envelope. "These are my notes. You're welcome to make copies."

Alexander passed the envelope to Avivah. She took it down the hall to the photocopier.

If Mr. Cantrell was telling the truth, and she thought he was, how did Peter Taft's real estate scam relate to Grace Kirkpatrick? For the life of her, Avivah couldn't see any connection.

A piece of pink stationery fell out of the envelope and floated to the floor. Avivah picked it up.

April 4, 1974

Dear F. J.,

Peter Taft answered my letter. He expressed concerns about my "old friend," and is eager to hear how you might be in need of strong Christian charity. I made sure I slipped a paragraph into my letter about your lonely little cabin and nice piece of land. I'm meeting him next Wednesday, in Asheville. Prepare yourself for a visit from him.

Regards, Frannie

CHAPTER 10

The soft sheet slid over Pepper's cool shoulders. At least Darby hadn't gotten up at 0500 for his morning workout and run. She'd have to be content with that much, even if she didn't like the distracted way he was dressing this morning. She said, "I'll need a ride home. When will you be back?"

He fastened his watch around his wrist. "Soon."

"You want breakfast?"

He picked up his keys from the dresser and came back to the bed to kiss her forehead. "I'll eat while I'm out."

In other words, they weren't even going to enjoy the proverbial scrambled eggs on the morning after. So much for Hollywood movies reflecting real life.

She lay in bed after he left, but the bed felt cold and empty. Pepper turned over and nuzzled her face into the pillows. Yes, she could smell him, and so would Frannie. Pepper threw back the covers. Laundry, breakfast, and airing out the bedroom. She slipped on her T-shirt and threw open the wooden shutters to a green-and-gold morning. If the world looked beautiful, why did she feel abandoned?

By nine-thirty, she decided her and Darby's definitions of *soon* were different. She phoned the bed-and-breakfast where the Kirkpatricks were staying.

Benny's voice sounded tired. "Still no word."

"Where is everybody?"

"Da and Lorraine have gone to get Mom. The hospital is

114

discharging her today. Hamilton, Joseph and I are hanging around the phone and getting on each others' nerves."

"Do you have any recent pictures of Ginny Mae, ones that show her face?"

"A few."

"Bring them to Frannie's house as soon as you can, and bring your brothers. I have an idea about how to look for Ginny Mae."

"Where's Baxter?"

"On a secret mission."

"Are you all right?"

Pepper poked around in her head. She'd live. "Yeah. You know, fantasies don't always play out the way you thought they would."

An hour later, Pepper sat under the cool shade of Frannie's front porch. Meeting the Kirkpatrick brothers on the porch was a courtesy to Frannie. She'd asked if she and Darby could sleep over, but that didn't give her the right to invite the whole Kirkpatrick clan inside.

Meeting them on the porch didn't have one single thing to do with what she and Darby had done last night. Not one thing to do with freshly laundered sheets, and having every window in the house open. As soon as he stepped into Frannie's house, Benny would know; she just knew he would. He wouldn't say anything, but she'd be able to read it in his eyes. Nope, staying on the porch had nothing to do with any of that.

Benny and Hamilton emerged from opposite sides of Hamilton's rental car. Benny slammed his door first. "Selling the store isn't a decision you or I would make, but it doesn't mean Mom and Da are crazy."

Hamilton slammed his door with equal force. "All I'm saying is that I know an excellent doctor in Chicago. He consults for competency hearings. It might be a good idea to get both of them a complete medical assessment. When was the last time Da consulted a doctor?"

"I have no idea, and neither do you."

Joseph had slipped out of the back seat and come to sit next to Pepper, with his fiddle case resting on his lap. Pepper inclined her head toward his two brothers and raised her eyebrows, trying to ask Joseph if they were always like this. He returned the gesture with a polite, noncommittal stare. Either he couldn't figure out what she was trying to say, or he didn't care to make a comment. Pepper shrunk a little inside. Maybe Joseph didn't like her.

Hamilton and Benny sat on porch chairs.

Benny asked, "So what's your idea?"

"I don't think Ginny Mae left here under duress. She took time to do laundry, straighten her room and wash her breakfast dishes. The police won't even take the missing persons report on her until tomorrow afternoon, but we can get a jump on them by canvassing the neighborhood today. Someone might have seen her leave."

Hamilton's fingernail worried a fleck of paint on the chair's arm. "It's the middle of the day. Everyone will be at work."

Maybe where he came from. "Some people won't be, people who do shift work, or are retired, or are on vacation."

Benny got a city map and pencil from Hamilton's car. He drew a dot where Frannie's house was located and penciled in an irregular shape around it, following major streets. "Let's start with four blocks in each direction. We'll divide up into pairs and each take half of the area."

Hamilton frowned. "We'll look like people from those religious groups who hand out tracts. People won't want to open their door to us."

Pepper wondered if Hamilton had whined this much all his life.

Benny added two more lines. "All right, we'll divide up into quarters instead and go individually.

Joseph said, "I'll go with Pepper."

He was just being contrary. From the look Benny shot his brother, Benny thought so, too. He tried to erase one of the lines. The eraser was hard and all it did was smear the pencil line. Benny tapped the map with the pencil point. "Hamilton here, I'll do this part; Pepper and Joseph the long stretch. We'll meet back here."

Benny distributed the photographs he'd brought. Hamilton and Benny left, going in opposite directions. Joseph sat. A small summer breeze ruffled his hair.

"We'd better go, hadn't we? I mean, we have the largest area to cover."

"The problem with people in this country is that they're in too much of a hurry."

He opened his fiddle case. The inside was even more worn than the outside, the red velvet lining faded to pink and carefully mended. The fiddle looked equally well cared for.

Joseph put the instrument under his chin and played a few exploratory notes, then tuned it. He drew the bow over the strings in long, slow strokes. Gradually, the strokes shortened, picking up a rhythm. He played with his eyes closed and his head thrown back. He looked transported.

The desire to hurry flowed from Pepper's body. She closed her eyes and leaned back against the post, reveling in how the music and the scents from the strewing garden complimented one another. By the time the last note floated away on the breeze Pepper knew things were going to be all right. Wherever Ginny Mae was, she was all right, too. She opened her eyes. "That's lovely. Did you write it?"

"Hardly. I'm no composer—yet. That's *Maeve's Lament*. My sister's name is really Virginia Maeve."

"I know. After her grandmothers."

"I thought . . . that is, I hoped wherever she is now, the music might reach her. Tell her we are thinking about her."

Pepper reached over and squeezed his hand. "That's a very kind thing to do."

Joseph blushed. "Can I leave my fiddle here? I didn't want to leave it at the bed-and-breakfast. Not that I don't trust our hosts, but some beautiful things have a way of their own. They naturally draw people to admire them. Would you mind if I looked at the room where Ginny stayed before we go?"

"Why?"

"I want to see if I can pick up any aura, maybe handle some of the things she handled here."

Pepper wondered how much twelve years in Ireland had twisted Joseph's Catholicism. Next thing, he'd be asking if she believed in elves and fairies. Truth to tell, after Joseph's beatific music, a fairy or two peeking out from Frannie's garden wouldn't shock her.

"Everything has been washed and tidied. Would there still be an aura, do you think?"

He closed the fiddle case clasps. "I suppose not. It was just a thought."

Ginny Mae might think she was the outsider in the Kirk-patrick family, but Pepper suspected the true outsider was Joseph.

"You've been away from your family a long time."

"Maybe too long." He stood. "Where shall I put this?"

Pepper took the house key from her pocket. "In the living room will be fine."

A few minutes later, as Pepper turned from the sidewalk to stop at the first house next to Frannie's, Joseph took her arm and turned her away from the house. "Always walk your perimeter first, then work your way in."

They walked to the four-block limit Benny had defined. Had Joseph learned that bit of military lore about perimeters from Benny? Not likely. Pepper was hazy on dates, but she thought that Joseph had moved to Ireland the same month Benny joined the Army. And she couldn't imagine Joseph in even a Boy Scout uniform. Where had he learned about walking a perimeter?

From the day they met, she and Benny had been totally honest with one another. She couldn't imagine confiding in Hamilton, but, in spite of not quite trusting Joseph, she was curious as to which brother he favored. "How come the Ulster something-or-other wants to talk to you?"

He didn't answer, and just when Pepper had pegged him as more like Hamilton, he said, "Royal Ulster Constabulary. They have me confused with another Joseph Kirkpatrick who lives in County Monaghan."

"Do you know him?"

"If you found out there was another Elizabeth Pepperhawk in the next town over, wouldn't you be curious to meet her, maybe see if you were related?"

"Of course I would. Were you?"

"Was I what?"

"Were you related to the other Joseph?"

"Second cousins, three or four generations back. I wish now I hadn't met him. He spends too much time over the border for my liking. Do you know what I mean by *over the border?*"

"Northern Ireland. Catholics fighting Protestants. It doesn't make sense."

"Catholics fighting Protestants is shorthand. It's history fighting history, culture fighting culture, old injustices fighting old injustices. Plenty of shame to be shared around on both sides."

"I thought you lived in Ireland itself, not Northern Ireland?"

"It's called the Republic of Ireland. My cottage is a mile from the border with County Tyrone, which is part of the North.

The Irish government pretends the violence doesn't spill over, but they're not in the Carrickroe pub of a Saturday night."

They stopped where two larger streets came together. Joseph looked around. His body language was so like Benny's that Pepper's heart gave a little jump. She wondered what the perimeter of the Carrickroe pub looked like.

Joseph asked, "Have you worked out a fiddle?"

"We left your fiddle at Fannie's house."

"Being on the fiddle means to have a scheme, a plan, as in how we're going to do this."

"I thought we'd walk up to a door and ring the bell."

"You've no sense of presentation. Here's what we're going to do . . ."

No one was home at the first three houses they tried. At the fourth house, a woman in her fifties answered the door. Pepper stood a few feet from the door, holding up Ginny Mae's photograph. Joseph, who kept back on the walkway, said, "Please, Missus. The girl in the photograph, she's my sister, only a girl. She disappeared from this neighborhood yesterday. All we're asking is, if you've seen her, to please phone Sergeant Lambert at the Asheville City Police Juvenile Division. We're that worried about her."

Pepper couldn't tell if it was Joseph's Irish lilt, or that he implied Ginny Mae was underage and that the police were already involved, but the woman held out her hand. "Let me get a better look."

Pepper handed the photograph to her.

The woman studied it and handed it back. "No, sorry, I haven't seen her."

Joseph touched two fingers to his forehead. "Thank you, Missus. Sorry to bother you."

Even a good presentation couldn't produce information where none existed. By the time they'd circled back to Frannie's street, Pepper had to admit her idea had gone bust. She wondered if Hamilton or Benny had faired any better.

The woman who lived four houses down from Frannie was a tiny woman who could have been any age past eighty. She raised her spectacles and peered at Ginny Mae's face. "What was she wearing?"

Pepper described the clothes Ginny Mae had worn Sunday night.

"She got on a bus to go downtown."

Pepper forced herself to hold still when what she really wanted to do was kiss the woman. She and Joseph could have saved themselves a lot of time if they'd canvassed on this street first. No, Joseph was right. Having a protocol meant they knew now, for a certainty, that they hadn't missed anything. "When?"

"Yesterday morning just before eleven o'clock."

"Was she alone?"

"She was."

Joseph asked, "Which bus?"

The woman pointed to a bus stop in front of her house. "The only one that stops here."

Her mind full of who should contact the bus company, Pepper turned away. "Thank you so much."

The woman called after them, "Don't you want to know where she got off?"

Pepper spun around. "How do you know where she got off?"

"I rode the bus with her."

Joseph was bouncing on the balls of his feet, "Where did she go?"

"Down to St. Lawrence Cathedral. She got off right in front of the church."

Pepper almost slapped her forehead. Her parents had drilled it into her since she was a child. If you're in trouble in a strange city, find a Catholic church. The priest will help you.

Father Vincent, one of the priests at St. Lawrence's, was non-committal. He required identification from all four of them, then sat back in his black leather chair and listened while the Kirkpatrick brothers talked. From her vantage point in a corner of the room, Pepper watched how Joseph deferred to his brothers, playing the proper role of youngest brother. He almost disappeared.

Joseph had complained that the other Joseph Kirkpatrick, his namesake, spent too much time, as he called it, *over the border*. By the way he moved, by the way he planned, by the way he stood on that street corner surveying the landscape, Pepper knew that Joseph had spent time in a war zone. Even if she had no idea what County Tyrone and the Northern Ireland troubles were like, one soldier could always recognize another.

She and Benny kept an article of faith between them: always be honest with one another. Some time soon, she was going to have to tell Benny that his little brother might be the person the Royal Ulster Constabulary was looking for after all. Doing that would give her no pleasure.

Father Vincent finally consulted a red, leather-bound address book, and dialed a number. Pepper could tell it was long-distance from the long sequence he dialed.

"Father, it's Father Vincent again. We spoke yesterday about Miss Kirkpatrick. I have her three brothers in my office right now. Apparently, we've all been taken in . . . Certainly, which one?"

He held the phone out to Benny. "He wants to speak to you."

Benny took the receiver. "Kirkpatrick."

His whole body language changed as he listened, became more deferential. "Thank you, Father. Yes, the wedding is Saturday. Prayers and blessings would be most welcome. So would any information you have about Ginny Mae . . . I see. When? . . . No, whatever you do, don't tell her we called. She's safe, that's the important thing, and she's almost twenty. She's got a right to make her own choices. Thank you so much."

He hung up and folded his arms over his chest. "She's on a Greyhound bus, on her way back to Missouri. The priest from our parish church will pick her up at the Springfield bus station this evening. He'll drive her home."

So that's what Ginny Mae had meant in her note to Frannie about finding her own way home. Her note to Frannie hadn't referred to coming back to her family, but to home-home, back to Missouri. Pepper wondered if Ginny intended to follow Frannie's advice about offering to work for the store's new owners, or if she just wanted time away from her family. She was glad Ginny was safe, but leaving like that proved Quinn Kirkpatrick was right. Ginny Mae wasn't mature enough to run a business.

Hamilton protested, "But that policeman, Sergeant Lambert, checked the bus station. They said she hadn't bought a ticket."

Father Vincent stood. "I'm afraid one of our nuns bought it for her. Your sister told me she was trying to escape from an abusive boyfriend, and that he might be watching the bus station. We gave her some clothes out of our poor box, so that her boyfriend wouldn't recognize her when she got on the bus."

Hamilton reached in his pocket. "How much do we owe you?"

The priest waved Hamilton's money aside. "She reimbursed me for her ticket with traveler's checks. However, the next time you're in contact with her, you might suggest she go to confession. She lied to a priest."

CHAPTER 11

Avivah didn't have to look at her watch. She felt the pace change around her: fifteen quiet minutes as the hospital's day shift ended and the afternoon shift began. Pisgah Mountain Veterans' Administration Hospital hadn't changed since she'd left. Her hand brushed against her gun, and she jerked her fingers away. Maybe the hospital hadn't changed, but she had.

Nate asked, "You developing a nervous tic?"

"I don't feel right, carrying a gun here. This is a hospital, not Dodge City. The hospital administrator's words. He was adamant about security not carrying weapons."

Nate pushed open a swinging door into the Social Work Department. "You're not hospital security any more. You've graduated to being a real peace officer instead of a rent-a-cop."

"No cracks about security, okay? They might not be hardball street cops, but they do important work, and I won't stand for you making fun of them."

"Loyalty. I like that. Still, no one seemed to be sending out for fatted calves to celebrate your return."

She'd smoothed the way for Nate, showing him how to cut through red tape from the administrator down, so they could interview Frannie at work. Everyone from the hospital adminis-trator to her old boss in security had been, at least, cordial. "They were surprisingly polite, considering what we're asking. Frannie's note, which mentioned a meeting with Peter Taft, had nothing to do with the Veteran's Administration Hospital. What do you hope to gain by talking to her here?"

"The element of surprise."

He knocked on Frannie's office door, which jerked open. Nate showed her his badge.

"My supervisor said you wanted to see me."

Frannie's voice sounded tight. Maybe the element of surprise was a good thing, after all.

Avivah stepped into Frannie's line of sight.

Frannie's hand circled the bottom of her throat. "It's not Ginny Mae, is it?"

"She's safe. Her brothers located her."

Frannie's hand fluttered on her chest as she patted her heart. "Thank goodness." She stepped into the corridor, moved the round, red magnet on her message board to *Out,* and locked her door behind her. "I booked a conference room. We'll have fewer interruptions there."

They'd painted the conference room pale green since Avivah left, but rehung the same olive green curtains and sun-bleached prints—now faded to an overall unpleasant blue—so nothing matched. The room was small and contained only a square table with four chairs.

Avivah took up her post, standing with her back against the door. Detective Alexander waited until Frannie was seated before he sat directly opposite her. "Miss Maddox, do you have any idea why I'm here?"

Frannie looked down at her hands in her lap. "Peter Taft's death."

The way she said those three words held the same potential as drops of boiling water falling on plate glass. If Frannie gave many more answers like that Avivah was certain something would shatter.

Detective Alexander took the photocopied note out of his notepad and slid it across to Frannie. "Are you the 'Frannie' who wrote this?"

Frannie picked up the paper and studied it longer than it could possibly take her to read the few lines. "Yes."

"Did you keep the meeting with Peter Taft?"

Frannie's blazer tightened across her shoulders. "Yes."

"When?"

"Early April. I'd have to check my day timer."

"So you've been aware of Taft's death, you met with him several weeks ago, but you haven't contacted the police. Why was that?"

Frannie raised her head and looked at Alexander. "Our meeting couldn't possibly have anything to do with his death. Dozens of people must have met with him over the years. How many of them have come forward?"

Go, Frannie. Oh, wait—she was supposed to be on Nate's side.

"Where did the two of you meet?"

"At the Lord's True Salvation Motel in Swannanoa."

The Salvation Motel. Some days it didn't pay to get out of bed. Alexander turned and nodded to Avivah, their prearranged signal that she was to follow up on whatever information had just been revealed. Good drivers pinched clues before they could escape, leaving their detective free to work uninterrupted. She slipped out to find a phone.

Marsenia Pullins owned the Lord's True Salvation Motel. She was "well known to police." And sheriff, fire, mental health hot line, ambulance, taxi dispatchers and probably a few long-distance trucking companies. Every night dispatchers across Buncombe County eyed the clock. Between nine-fifty-five and ten-oh-five, Marsenia favored one of them with a phone call. Sometimes she reported a prowler; sometimes having seen Jesus in her back garden; but most often she confessed she'd been the person behind everything from developing the atomic bomb to

Patty Hearst's kidnapping. Listening to Marsenia was a civic duty the dispatchers shared.

Finding Peter Taft's body had been front-page news Monday. They would have to track down who Marsenia favored with a phone call Monday night. If Taft *had* been staying at her motel, she might have reported it, and no one noticed.

It was now Tuesday afternoon. In any other motel, rooms would have been cleaned several times since Friday evening. At the Salvation Motel, who knew? They might get lucky; they might not, but it came down to whomever told Marsenia Pullins they had to search her motel should qualify for combat pay.

Swannonoa was outside Asheville city limits, so Avivah phoned the Buncombe County Sheriff's office. "Detective Alexander of the Asheville City Police requests your assistance in checking to see if a Peter Taft was registered at the Salvation Motel last Friday. If he was, please secure the room he occupied."

The deputy's eloquent silence lasted a good thirty seconds. "This better not be a joke, Constable, because if it is, I'll find where you live, and make your life miserable."

"You have my sympathy, and it's no joke."

She found her way back to the conference room door, and slipped inside. Alexander slid a chair out for her at the table.

"Constable, no notes for now. I have not advised Ms. Maddox of her rights. We are just chatting." He turned to Frannie, "Continue, Ms. Maddox."

Miss to *Ms.* in ten minutes. She'd love to know what Frannie had said to Nate to bring that about.

Frannie pressed her palms together tightly. "The day after I turned twenty-one, I ran away from home and married Porter Jackson. We'd been married three weeks the first time he assaulted me. It took me two years to find enough courage to leave him, and file for a divorce. The Reverends Peter Taft and

Walter Nibb appeared as character witnesses for Porter."

Avivah doubted that either man had had the slightest theological training. Would Kevin McCormick carry on the ecclesiastical tradition by pretending to be a minister? As they said in the mountains, that dog wouldn't hunt. McCormick couldn't spout a single religious sentiment without sounding cheesy.

"You knew both Taft and Nibb?"

"I'd never laid eyes on either one before the divorce hearing. My husband was a traveler. He sold house siding and gutters. I suppose he met them through his work."

Frannie was around forty. The divorce hearing had to have taken place in the fifties. Avivah tried to imagine a world of white-shirts, ducktail haircuts, and fast-talking traveling salesmen. There was that photograph of Mrs. Nibb and her ugly cat. The farmhouse in the background had worn siding on it. Possibly Frannie's husband had sold that same siding.

Frannie twisted her hands in her lap. "They were slick, both of them. They testified what a righteous man Porter was, and what a cold, cruel wife I was, not fulfilling Bible injunctions. The judge had a strong religious bent. In his denial judgment, he wrote that my 'withholding of conjugal duties was, in large part, responsible for the friction between me and my husband.' "

"You must have been angry."

"I was scared spit-less. As soon as we left the judge's chambers, Porter grabbed one arm and Taft the other. They told me that they were going to take me to Tennessee, until 'I knew my place.' "

One of the olive green curtains wavered in a small puff of air from the air conditioner. Avivah's heart pounded in the silence. She'd known that Frannie had been married, and that it had ended badly. She'd asked Pepper about it once, but all Pepper said was, "She never talks about it." No wonder.

"Porter didn't know I'd started carrying a gun. After we'd crossed the state line into Tennessee, I managed to get free, and wreck Taft's car, a brand new, black 1956 Buick Century Riviera. When we stopped at a rest stop, I shot out the front window and put the rest of the bullets into the tires, radiator, and engine block."

"Were you arrested?"

"Peter Taft took out a warrant. I went on the run—from my husband, not the warrant—changed my name constantly, and worked for cash only, no questions and no records."

Detective Alexander pursed his lips. "Becoming a social worker, working for the Veterans' Administration involves questions and records. What happened to the warrant?"

"Porter caught up with me in Yancy County. That time, he beat me in front of witnesses. The Yancy County Sheriff discovered the Tennessee warrant and arrested me, not Porter."

"Is that how you met F. J. Cantrell?"

"He was the deputy who responded when Porter assaulted me. I pleaded no contest to destruction of property, carrying a firearm without a permit, and public endangerment. There wasn't a trial, just a sentencing hearing. The judge was going to let me off with supervised parole, but F. J. persuaded him to give me ninety days. F. J. saved my life. Jail was the one place Porter couldn't get to me. Porter died while I was in jail."

"How?"

"Blood poisoning from dirty needles. He was a heroin addict. He'd become addicted in Japan during the Korean War."

Avivah asked, "Does the VA know about your conviction?"

"I was granted a pardon of forgiveness by the State of Tennessee ten years ago. I was arrested, sentenced, and pardoned under my married name. Mrs. Franchesca Jackson's criminal record can be found in Tennessee, if anyone cared to look for it, and thought to connect it to Ms. F. Maddox, social worker in

North Carolina. As long as I have no other criminal charges laid against me, I'm not required to disclose my history."

In other words, the VA didn't know. If they found out, Frannie would, almost certainly, be out of a job.

"How long was it between when Peter Taft testified at your divorce proceedings, and when you met him at the Salvation Motel?"

"Eighteen years."

"Did he recognize you?"

"No. The Mrs. Jackson he knew was a skinny chain-smoker, with bleached hair right out of a beauty parlor. We danced around each other nicely. He called me Sister Maddox; I called him Brother Taft. What I really wanted to do was scratch his eyes out."

Detective Alexander held up his hand. "Ms. Maddox, before we go any further, I am going to advise you of your rights. Do you have an attorney?"

Frannie looked down at her hands again. Her voice grew small. "I haven't got anyone."

Pepper and Saul sat at the kitchen table in Pepper's kitchen. A metal file box and papers covered the table.

She and Avivah were still going to have to work out who could invite people to live with them, but it pleased Pepper the way that Saul fit into her kitchen, rather like auditioning a lamp or new throw rug to see if it worked with the decor. Of course, maybe it was just that she already knew Saul's natural affinity for kitchens. "Saul, meet food," had the same result as introducing The Assyrian and his cohorts to the fold.

Saul turned to the last page of the three-page house-sharing agreement. "You're sure you're a nurse and not a lawyer?"

Pepper handed him a pen. "Benny's idea. He said the surest way for friends to turn into enemies was to share quarters without having a written agreement. He and I signed one when we shared a house at Fort Bragg, and again when he moved in here."

Saul signed each page. "I've suspected for a long time that ex–Special Forces Sergeant Kirkpatrick was more than your average G.I. Joe."

"Wait until you meet all his buddies this weekend."

"I can't wait."

Pepper put the rental agreement in a folder and picked up a butter knife, which she used to slice open envelopes from the pile of mail sitting at her left elbow.

"Wait a minute, that one has Avivah's name on it."

"I know." She took the letter out of the envelope. "Avivah never told you about her fan club, did she?"

"Fan club?"

"It's our little joke. It's better than calling it hate mail, though the truly hateful ones have tapered off." She ran her gaze down the letter. "Okay, this will give you an idea. It's from a Fine Arts graduate student at one of those fancy Eastern colleges. She starts with this is who I am, so-on-and-so-forth. Here's the relevant part." She cleared her throat.

My graduate thesis is a stream-of-consciousness novel, condemning the patriarchal industrial-military dictator-ship. My point of view character will be a woman Army officer, but I can't decide if the book should be in the *bildungsroman* or *roman à clef* tradition. Any advice you could provide would be most appreciated, as would an interview at your earliest convenience.

"She gets letters like that all the time?"

"She even gets marriage proposals. Being the only female military police officer to serve in Viet Nam, and notorious to boot, is a magnet. At least this letter is just pretentious. Some she got after your articles were published about what happened in Long Bien were downright sickening. Scary people took exception to her being a woman, an officer, and a veteran. That's why I open all of her mail that isn't from family or friends."

"I'm sorry. She never told me."

"Don't be sorry. You did her a big favor. A fine, a downgraded efficiency report, and losing the valor citation on her Bronze Star was almost a slap on the wrist, when you consider she could have ended up in military prison. She didn't even lose the Bronze Star itself. Your articles made all that possible."

Saul ducking his head shyly resembled a long-necked bird's mating dance. "I was just doing my job. I suppose you ignore the letters?"

"Heck, no. That's the fastest way to make a quest out of it. Find Avivah Rosen. The nasty ones we turn over to her lawyer. Avivah says I've turned answering harmless ones like this into an art form." She pulled a yellow pad to her and bent over it for a few minutes, writing, crossing out, and writing again. "I'll start with the usual stuff: thank you for writing, interesting question, so on."

Unfortunately, I do not feel sufficiently versed in literary traditions to suggest a course of action, but I believe you will find that writings of the Prussian General Carl von Clausewitz will be of inestimable assistance in helping you reach a decision. My personal opinion is that his English translators never represented the General's arguments in this area with the clarity and insightfulness present in the original German. You may wish to read him in both German and English to see if you come to the same conclusion.

As for an interview, I would love to give you one, but I have joined the Peace Corps and am leaving tomorrow morning for a two-year stint overseas. Perhaps I can contact you when I return.

Saul grinned. "Pretentious people cross your path at their own risk, don't they?"

Pepper paper-clipped the letter and her response together. "I guess they do."

"Clausewitz wrote a lot?"

"Enough to keep this woman busy for a long time."

"What did he say?"

"Beats me. All I know is a few quotes Darby throws around. Probably the usual about seeing a light at the end of the tunnel, and never give a second lieutenant a compass, a map, and a need to call in an air strike, though since Clausewitz wrote in German, in the 1800s, he probably said never give an *leutnant* a compass, a map, and a need to lead a cavalry charge."

A car pulled into the graveled parking lot and Pepper heard the garage door open. She looked at the clock. "At least Avivah is home on time today."

A few minutes later Avivah came through the back door, already unbuckling her gun belt. She nodded at both of them and, without speaking, went to her bedroom. Saul's gaze followed her.

Pepper got up and went to the refrigerator. She took a can of frozen lemonade concentrate from the freezer, and put it to defrost in a bowl of warm water. "Avivah and I usually sit down for a few minutes when we get home from work, have something to drink, and talk. You care to join us?"

Saul still looked at the doorway. "I'm not sure I should be here at all."

"Why not?"

"What you just told me about Avivah's letters. I caused that."

"Forget that nonsense. You going to tell me you would have

pulled back on your story if you thought Avivah might get nasty letters later?"

"Pulling back wouldn't have been honest journalism."

Pepper put her hands on Saul's shoulders and turned him so he faced her. "Avivah doesn't blame you for the letters. Stop feeling guilty."

Avivah came back, still in uniform, but without her gun belt or name tag. She'd replaced her uniform boots with fuzzy bedroom slippers. Pepper handed Avivah the letter and her reply. Avivah barely glanced at the two pages before she tossed them on the table. She hadn't even smiled.

Pepper looked at their household calendar, which was taped to the refrigerator. Avivah was assigned to Community Services this week. She'd probably had one of those hell-on-wheels days dealing with the public. Pepper picked up the lemonade and shook it. It was still frozen. She put the can back in the bowl, and began to clear the papers from the table.

Another car pulled in. Frannie parked her car next to Sandra's. After she got out of her car, Frannie reached back and took something from the front seat. When Pepper saw it was a large bag of potato chips, and that Frannie was eating nonstop as she hurried toward her studio, Pepper's stomach did an elevator free fall. She threw papers in a heap back on the table. "I have to stop her."

Avivah asked, "Stop who?"

"Frannie. She has potato chips."

Pepper started for the door, but Avivah reached out and grabbed her hand. Pepper jerked to a stop under Avivah's strong grip.

Avivah said, "Leave her alone. This is none of your business."

"I promised Cody that I'd look out for her while he was gone. He was afraid she'd break her diet."

Avivah let go of Pepper's arm. "That does not make you the

potato chip police. Frannie is an adult, who will have to take the consequences of whatever choices she made."

Sandra Waine slammed the studio door behind her as she came barreling out of the building. Instead of heading for her car, she stalked across the backyard. The back door flew open.

"You slut. You told that cow to fire me, just because Darby and I have history. I need this job."

Maybe the potato chips had been courage food.

Sandra picked up the can of lemonade and threw it at Pepper, who ducked. The can's edge caught Pepper on the side of the head. She lost her balance, careening into Saul's lap. She retched and rolled off of Saul, lest she throw up on him.

On her hands and knees on the floor, Pepper closed her eyes and took a deep breath. She came up in one fluid movement, imagining she was in the gym with a ten-pound weight in her hand. Breath, stance, arm back, swing underhand from the shoulder. Her fist caught Sandra in the middle of the stomach with so much force that Pepper imagined she could feel the woman's backbone through her skinny little body. Sandra went down in a heap, making animal noises. Avivah was on Sandra in an instant, holding Sandra's arm behind her, with her knee in the middle of her back.

Pepper rose over Sandra, panting, her hands balled into fists. Never before in her life had she answered violence with violence. She felt as though she could take on the world. Forget lemonade and cookies; she was taking everyone out for a steak dinner. "Fucking hell, son-of-a-bitch. It worked."

Avivah pulled Sandra to her feet and marched her to the back door. "Don't show your face around here again."

Pepper yelled, "Wait!"

Avivah and Sandra turned toward her.

"Can I press charges, assault-and-battery or something?"

"Technically you can, but you probably don't want all the hassles."

Pepper rubbed the side of her head. Her fingers came away without any blood. She picked up the phone. "That's where you're wrong. Hold that bitch until I get a Sheriff's deputy out here."

Avivah opened her hands and let Sandra go. "I can't. We're outside the city limits. I have no authority here."

Sandra ran for her car. Pepper continued dialing. "The Sheriff will just have to track her down. Frannie must know where she lives."

Pepper noticed the look on Saul's face. She'd seen the same stunned expression on an expectant father who'd just been told he and his wife were going to have triplets. She turned to the wall to hide her smile. Poor Saul. Living with two Army-conditioned women was going to be a new experience for him.

CHAPTER 12

"Wait until the Sheriff is up for reelection. Don't forget I vote," Pepper yelled. She slammed down the phone, which was a big mistake. Her headache resembled monkeys improvising jazz in a foundry. She took an ice bag out of the freezer, wrapped it in a towel, and applied it to the side of her head.

Avivah, who had changed into shorts and a T-shirt, came back to the kitchen. "The Sheriff was less than enthusiastic about arresting Sandra?"

"They suggested I come by the office tomorrow to file a complaint. Sandra could be long gone by then."

Avivah had brought her camera. She leaned down to get a shot of melting lemonade oozing from the split can. "Good riddance to her. Hold your hair out of the way so I can photograph your bruise."

Pepper gently slid her hair against her scalp. "How does it look?"

"You're going to have a nasty bruise, but your hair should cover most of it. Shouldn't you see a doctor?"

Pepper reapplied her ice bag. "So he can tell me I have a concussion? Big deal. If I go unconscious in the next forty-eight hours, then take me to a doctor."

She fortified herself with three aspirins and a large Coke. When half of the monkeys had departed for better banana fields, Pepper walked across the yard and knocked on the studio door.

Frannie lay curled in a ball on the dilapidated couch. A wash

137

of tears covered her cheeks and her eyes were red and puffy. The empty potato chip bag sat at her feet, with crumbs trailing along the floor. Pepper couldn't decide if her queasy stomach was from her knock on the head or having failed to keep Frannie on her diet. Cody was going to be upset. Pepper sat on the edge of the couch and rubbed Frannie's back. "Shh. Shh. It's going to be all right."

"It's not going to be all right. I don't have an alibi."

"You don't need an alibi. Sandra was trouble, you're the boss, and you can fire anyone you want."

"Not about Sandra. I don't have an alibi for the time Peter Taft died."

Pepper brushed hair off of Frannie's face. "Why would you need one?"

Frannie wiped her hands over her eyes and pulled herself to a sitting position. "I knew Taft a long time ago. Avivah and a police detective want to question me about his murder."

Pepper wished there was a mirror in the studio so she could check her pupils. Maybe she'd been hit harder than she thought because Frannie made no sense. "Avivah is working Community Services this week."

"I don't think so. She came to the hospital with a detective. He advised me of my rights, and I told him I wanted a lawyer before they interviewed me again."

Pepper rubbed her forehead. Frannie couldn't be right. Even if Avivah had been reassigned to work with a detective, wouldn't investigating Peter Taft's death be a conflict of interest?

Frannie hefted herself off the couch and wandered around the room, picking up things at random and putting them in a cardboard box. "This art therapy idea was a mistake. I thought a few minor renovations and slap some paint on the walls, and I'd be ready to go. With my job, and my private practice, it's too much. I can't do it."

And a volunteer assistant like Sandra, whom Frannie said was great with paperwork, but wouldn't pick up a paintbrush for fear of ruining her manicure.

"I won't leave the place like this, I promise. I'll finish what I can. Can we work a deal? I'll trade you building materials for rent."

Yeah, right. Leaving Pepper with an art studio for which she had absolutely no use. At least if this were still a house, she could rent it. "You're quitting?"

"Done. Over. Walking away from a bad idea."

"But you haven't even opened."

"And I won't. I'm going to cancel the workshops I've booked for the summer, and return the money."

"Hold on. Just calm down. All of us are out of kilter right now, what with the wedding, and what happened to the Kirkpatricks, and—other things." Like discovering Darby's first wife was brilliant, educated, and drop-dead gorgeous. "Cody will be here for the wedding. Once you two spend a few days together, life will look brighter."

Frannie smoothed her hand repeatedly over the curved end of a can of turpentine. "Cody won't be here for the wedding."

"Of course he will be. He's just forgotten to send back his reply card, saying he would attend. I put him on the guest list anyway."

"He's never coming back, not for the wedding, not ever."

Pepper growled. She stopped herself just sort of slamming her palms into both sides of her head. "It's not that stupid age difference again, is it? So what if you're older than he is?"

"It's not our ages. He's not coming back because I told him not to. Did you know Cody when he was addicted to narcotics?"

"I met him after he'd gone through rehab. Please, please

don't tell me he's using again. I don't think I could stand to hear that."

"As far as I know, he's clean."

Pepper sank back against the lumpy cushions. "Thank God."

"The problem is me, not him. I never told you about my first marriage. Porter was a vet and a heroin addict. Cody is a vet with a history of prescription drug abuse. I can't believe I've been so stupid to repeat the same pattern. It's one of those things I always warn my clients against."

A few hairs stood up on Pepper's neck. If she'd known details of Frannie's first marriage, she might have been more reluctant to root for Frannie and Cody as a couple. "What pattern, falling in love with a vet with a drug problem?"

"Thinking I could love the war and the drugs out of them. Make everything all right for them if I was just gentle and patient enough. I'm not a twenty-year-old working at dead-end jobs anymore. I'm a social worker, in a damn VA hospital. I know every vet-related con there is. Between the hours of eight and four, I can weed out liars, drunks and druggies better than most, but my brain seems to go off-duty at four P.M. There must be something wrong with the way my brain is wired."

"You tell Cody any of this?"

"All of it, before he left for school."

"And he said?"

"That I was overreacting. That he didn't expect me to solve his problems. He was the one who said I wasn't twenty and naïve anymore."

Pepper got up, took the turpentine can out of Frannie's hand and pushed her gently toward the door. "Go home. Phone Cody. Tell him everything, including this nonsense about needing an alibi."

"I can't."

"Why not?"

"When he went away to school, we agreed we wouldn't phone or write to each other, not while he was at school, not ever again."

"He's been gone two months. You haven't talked to him in two months?"

"No."

"Letter? Telegram? Carrier pigeon?"

Each time Frannie shook her head.

"Don't make me phone him on your behalf."

"You wouldn't."

"Damn straight I would, and I'll start by telling him you still have his photograph in a silver frame in your bedroom."

"What were you doing in my bedroom? Oh, right. Monday night."

Pepper handed Frannie her car keys. "You have twenty-four hours to phone Cody, before I do the deed for you."

Frannie took her keys. "In twenty-four hours, I could be under arrest."

The bed-and-breakfast the Kirkpatricks had rented for a week had started life as a big farmhouse. As she locked her car, Pepper admired the sparkling white paint job and the riot of colors in the flowerbeds. Delightful odors of early summer flowers, frying chicken, and wet, newly turned earth washed over her. Maybe, just maybe, everyone could relax for one evening.

She walked the flagstone path around to the side. Two tables covered with white cloths were set in a V shape. Balloons and pots of flowers decorated the tables. Citronella tiki torches ringed the yard like a medieval palisade. She hoped they would keep away mosquitoes.

Tonight's party, arranged by Randy and Mark, was Kirkpatrick family and guests only. Benny had confided to Pepper that the boys had kept everything, including the menu, as top secret as plans for the Normandy invasion.

Apparently, she was the first to arrive.

The two boys waited beside a table set aside for drinks. They wore dress pants and knit shirts, their haircuts fresh and standing straight up probably thanks to liberal doses of Brylcreem. Grace stood behind them. She'd had her hair done, too. Except for the dark circles under her eyes she didn't look anything like a woman who had been abducted, drugged and confined to a mental ward. Pepper decided that, if she ever grew up, she wanted to be the kind of woman who had enough courage to push on in the face of events that would have had most people quivering.

Randy shook her hand. "Good evening, Aunt Pepper, thank you for coming."

Mark extended his arm stiffly, a gesture often seen at Christmas pageants, accompanied by the line, "Lo, behold a star in the east." Instead he said, "Would you like a drink before dinner? We have lemonade and tomato juice."

Hopefully, not mixed. She was relieved to see separate glass pitchers. It seemed to be her day for lemonade, but considering how the Kirkpatricks raved about the bed-and-breakfast's food, at least this was likely to be made from scratch, instead of from a can. She poured herself a glass.

Grace leaned down and whispered something to Randy, who said, "Dinner will be served in half an hour. Perhaps you would enjoy a walk in the garden before dinner."

Just beyond the back steps was a large kitchen garden. At least, it would be a large garden once the isolated baby vegetables grew up and joined forces. Small water puddles stood on wet, dark loam. A middle-age woman in a loose smock, straw hat, and green rubber boots wound a hose around a large wheeled carrier. "You must be one of the boys' guests. I'm Mrs. Somerset. Sorry about the mess, dearie. I'd planned to finish watering long before any guests arrived, but one thing ran into another today."

Her accent was English.

"No need to apologize. I admire your kitchen garden. I'm thinking of starting one."

"Not much to admire right now. We had vandalism a few days ago. Stupid teenagers. My jobbing gardener put what he could to rights. I did so want everything to be perfect for those boys."

Pepper looked over to where Randy and Mark were greeting Benny's brothers. "I think it is perfect for them."

"So sad about their real dad. I lost my oldest brother when I was younger than Randy. Merchant Marine, he was. His ship was torpedoed in the North Atlantic, so I know how hard it is. I'm so relieved that horrible war is over."

She wasn't sure if Mrs. Somerset meant World War II or Viet Nam. Whichever war, Pepper could agree that she, too, was glad it was over.

By six-thirty everyone had arrived. Randy or Mark escorted each guest to his or her seat. Pepper looked at her hand-drawn place card and tried to figure out what the two blue things were that held up the banner with her name. If she squinted just right, they might be bluebirds of happiness.

Benny and Lorraine sat on either side of the sharp point of the V. Benny's parents sat beside him and the two boys sat beside Lorraine. Joseph, Avivah, Saul, Pepper, Darby and Hamilton were arranged down the sides of the V.

Pepper counted noses. If she were the slightest bit superstitious, she would be glad that Ginny Mae had taken off for Missouri. If Ginny were here, they would have been thirteen at the table.

Benny took Lorraine's hand as he bent his head to say a blessing before dinner. Lorraine's blond hair was oily. She'd pulled it back into a ponytail the way women did when they didn't have time to wash their hair and hoped to look present-able anyway, which they never did. Grace might have dark circles under her eyes, but the patches under Lorraine's eyes resembled the purple-green color of tornado clouds.

For an instant, Pepper feared Lorraine might have some terminal illness and was keeping it a secret until after the wedding. But no, she wouldn't have kept a secret like that from Benny. And, if Benny knew, he would tell Pepper.

So many people—herself included—had promised to help Lorraine, but because of the Peter Taft business, none of them had. I'll do better, Pepper promised herself. After tonight they would be plenty of help. Benny's best man and groomsmen, Lorraine's attendants and her parents were all due to arrive tomorrow.

When Benny finished grace, Mark tapped his brother on the shoulder. His pudgy fingers curled like a clamshell around his brother's ear. He whispered something.

Randy whispered back, "After we eat, doofus."

"I want to do it now!"

Randy considered. "Okay." He looked at his mom. "May we be excused for a minute, please?"

Lorraine looked wary. "They're about to serve the food."

"It won't take long," Randy said, already working his way out of his chair.

The two boys went into the house and came out a moment later carrying two fishing rods and reels, with big bows on them and white envelopes dangling from the sinkers at the ends of the lines.

Randy gave the one he carried to his mother. "We tried to wrap them, but it didn't exactly work."

Mark handed his to Benny. "Merry Wedding and Many Happy Returns."

Since it was hard to accept large fishing rods sitting at a crowded table, both Benny and Lorraine stood. They read their cards, and thanked the boys. Lorraine stepped away from the table and made a few practice casts. She was, Pepper knew, a more devoted fisherman than Benny, who often used fishing trips as an excuse to sleep with his hat pulled over his eyes.

Mark said, "Grandda Kirkpatrick got them for us wholesale, because he's in the business."

Randall punched Mark on the arm. "You're not supposed to tell them that part."

Benny pressed his lips together. He took his truck keys out of his pocket. "Why don't you guys go put them in my truck, so they'll be safe. I'd hate it if anyone stepped on them accidentally."

The boys left and Benny turned to his parents. "Thanks, guys. I hope you didn't subsidize them too much."

Quinn grinned. "It's smart business to know when to give your best customers a good deal."

The boys returned and supper was served. Fried chicken, potato salad, biscuits, and homemade pickles, with rhubarb crisp and ice cream for dessert. Pepper suspected a guiding adult hand in choosing the broccoli-and-tomato salad.

During the meal, Darby, Benny, and the boys talked fishing. Joseph told his parents, Avivah, and Saul stories about Ireland. Pepper was left alone with Hamilton at their end of the table.

Among the things Pepper had learned from the nuns in convent school were social graces, and southern social graces to boot. She smiled at Hamilton, "You're on the Chicago Stock Exchange, I believe?"

"The Chicago *Mercantile* Exchange. We're a commodities market, dealing in farm futures."

"Is that like what's going to happen to farms when the current owners die or retire?"

When Hamilton sighed, he sounded like Benny. He placed a bread plate in front of him. "This is a tofu factory that needs ten thousand pounds of soybeans on August first." He took a pot of flowers and placed it a little distance away from the plate. "This is a farmer who has soybeans in the ground. My job is to make sure those ten thousand pounds of beans end up at the factory gate on August first. Obviously, I can't wait until the farmer harvests his crop to buy them. So I buy them while they are still growing, sometimes before they've even been planted."

"What happens if, between the time you buy them and August first, there's a hailstorm or a flood, and there aren't any soybeans to harvest?"

He held up both index fingers. "That's what makes trading in future commodities interesting."

Benny came to Pepper after supper. "Thank you for being kind to Hamilton. I was afraid everyone would ignore him this evening."

"It was no hardship. He's just like you."

"He is?"

"Both of you are natural teachers. You both make the most obscure topics fascinating. With you, it's principles of battlefield communication. With him, it's soybeans."

"Hamilton, fascinating? I may have to rethink my brother."

"Lorraine doesn't look good. Is she all right?"

"She's exhausted. This big wedding was a mistake."

Pepper didn't think that was all. During supper, while she listened to Hamilton talk about soybeans, she'd watched Lorraine push food around her plate without eating.

She found Lorraine sitting in the vine-covered arbor beyond the kitchen garden. Apparently the vandalism hadn't reached this far. The twisted vines must have taken years to grow so solidly packed. Pepper sat on the bench beside Lorraine, who

did something she'd never done before. She reache
Pepper's hand. Lorraine wasn't a touchy-feely person. Ter
illness was definitely back on the agenda.

Pepper tried humor. "You look, as they say in my f
'plum tuckered out.' "

"I haven't been this tired since just after Mark was bor

As far as Pepper knew, Benny and Lorraine honor
Catholic prohibition against sex before marriage, but N
night had shown her how easy it was to let your guard d

"Should Randy and Mark expect a brother or sister?"

Lorraine pulled her hand away, and turned red. "No!
mean no, not ever; Ben and I want more children, but
I'm not pregnant. I have to talk to somebody, but you
promise me that you will never, ever tell anyone, especia
about this."

Who better to tell that you were dying than a nurse?
voice wavered, "All right, I promise."

Lorraine reached into her dress pocket and t
something, which she pressed into Pepper's hand. Pepp
down at a set of dog tags. *Fulford, Randall.* Lorra
husband. So there had been thirteen people at dinne
only one of them was a ghost. She closed her finger
tags. "I can't make Randall's memory disappear. I wisl

"Look at them."

Enough light filtered through the arbor leaves for
read the engraving. There were two tags, one on a lor
be worn around the neck, and the other on a mu
chain. In theory, if a man was killed, the soldier next
supposed to jerk off the tag on the smaller chain
with him, to be turned in later to Graves Regist
remembered being told in basic training that the
tag—the one on the long chain—was to be jammed
casualty's front teeth, up into the hard pallet, on the

if the skull survived, the tag would, too.

At the time, that had sounded not only yucky, but also impossible. She was grateful she'd never had the need to find out how much brute strength it took to drive a rounded-edge piece of metal into the hard palate.

She read the first tag. It contained Randall's name, serial number, blood type, and religion. Then she read the smaller tag. Name, serial number, blood type—wait a minute. She compared the two tags. "The religion isn't the same."

"One of those stupid Army mistakes. They put Roman Catholic on one tag and Episcopalian on the other. Randall was supposed to get new ones, but he never did. Peter Taft gave me those dog tags."

Peter Taft? Pepper clutched the tags. Rolled metal edges pressed into her skin. She put her hand up to her head, feeling the bump there, wondering if a concussion could produce auditory hallucinations. With first Frannie confessing a connection to Taft and now Lorraine, this was a very bad day to be hit on the head.

Lorraine asked, "Do you remember that Valentine's Day workshop that Frannie and I put together for the family and friends of men missing in action?"

"Yes."

Lorraine twisted her hands. "I met Taft there. His son is a Navy pilot, shot down over North Viet Nam. The Navy lists him as missing, presumed dead. I gave Peter my card and told him to phone me if he needed to talk."

Over the past few months, Lorraine had gradually divested herself of the duties of being regional chair of a MIA support group, but people still phoned her.

"I gather he did?"

"About two weeks ago. He was in Swannanoa, and asked me to meet him the next day."

"Why?"

"He said his conscience bothered him, and he had something to show me. We met in some strange motel. Peter showed me proof that his son is alive and held captive."

"What proof?"

"A home movie, smuggled out of North Viet Nam, showing his son in captivity. I almost passed out watching it. I kept seeing Randall in it."

Pepper clutched the tags tighter. "Do you mean you actually *saw* Randall? That he was in the film with Taft's son?"

"No, I kept imagining him as the man in the film. You have no idea how horrible those images were. I never felt so helpless in my life. Then Taft gave me the dog tags."

"Where did he get them?"

"From the person who made the film. That person told him there were at least eight men, including Randall, confirmed alive."

This was Patty Hearst's kidnapping, flying saucers, and the JFK assassination cover-up rolled into one. Pepper knew, in her heart, that no American prisoners remained alive in Southeast Asia. Not because the U.S. government said there weren't. Not because the MIA wives, driving around the White House with their *All POWs are NOT home* bumper stickers, hoped there were, but because two years ago, during the Paris peace talks, every returned U.S. serviceman would have been a drop of gold for Hanoi, one more tiny edge to get a better settlement. Still, a voice whispered, "Maybe," at the edge of her conviction.

"I gave Peter Taft the three thousand dollars Benny and I saved to build our house."

"Whatever for?"

"Establishing proof with the U.S. government that those men are still alive. If the government couldn't be shamed into sending another delegation to North Viet Nam, I wanted to arouse so much public anger that a national newspaper or TV network would send one."

Pepper opened her palm. "Are you absolutely certain that these belong to Randall?"

"I thought I was."

"But?"

"You know how things age, they get a mark here or a wear line there. If there were three black umbrellas in a row, could you pick out yours by how it had worn?"

"Probably."

"It's like that. They look right, but not exactly right."

"I gather you haven't told Benny about this."

"I can't. I put him through hell over Randall before I came to my senses. My life with Randall is over. He's legally dead. If he showed up this minute, I'd go through whatever legal procedures I had to so Ben and I could marry, but if Randall is alive, I don't want him to spend the rest of his life in the filth and degradation I saw in that film."

"What are you going to do when Benny finds out the house money is missing?"

"Tell him I made a bad investment, or make up some story about a destitute woman in the MIA group."

"Lie to Benny if you want, but I won't. I'm sorry, that came out more holier-than-thou than I intended."

"Especially since he was honest with me about the two of you kissing?"

A burden she hadn't realized she was carrying lifted from Pepper's shoulders. "When did he tell you?"

"Last year."

"I'm glad. I was always scared that I'd blow it and say something accidentally."

"I'm grateful the two of you got it out of your system with one kiss."

"So was I."

"All right, I'll tell Ben the truth, but not until after the wedding, and I desperately need a favor."

"What do you want me to do?"

"Not you, Darby. I know he has connections. I want to know if Peter Taft really *had* a son and if he's really missing in action. If Taft was honest about that, then yes, I believe these are Randall's dog tags, and he may still be alive."

"Doesn't your MIA support group have lists of all men missing in action?"

"I turned my binder over to the woman who succeeded me as regional chair. She's, well, nosy, and I'd rather not ask her. Besides, this is something I want to hear from a friend. Will you ask Darby to find out for me?"

"Yes."

Even if Darby answered Lorraine's question, that left a lot of questions unanswered, including who killed Peter Taft. What if Benny already knew about Lorraine and Peter? As much as Pepper loved and respected Benny, she wouldn't go so far as to say he'd never kill again. The man had been a Green Beret for a decade, for God's sake. She'd have to go to the police, of course, but maybe it would be better to wait until after Darby had the answer to Lorraine's question.

CHAPTER 13

Wednesday morning, Pepper's breakfast grew cold as she stared at a few lines written on a note pad. Darby had ferreted out the information faster than Pepper thought possible.

Name: John Taft/D.O.B.: 31 October 1935/Home of record: Tok, Alaska
Next of kin: aunt and uncle in Alaska
Thirty years old, unmarried, no children
Navy Lieutenant, shot down over North Viet Nam 22 March 1966
Status: missing, presumed dead. Next of kin have not filed to have him declared legally dead.

Still, the name might be a coincidence. Pepper had heard of criminals adopting names on tombstones or from newspapers. Maybe Quinn would remember if Peter had ever mentioned a son.

She phoned the bed-and-breakfast. Grace came to the phone. "Quinn isn't here. Can I help you?"

Pepper had oodles of things to do. She couldn't sit by the phone waiting for Quinn to call.

"Do you feel up to answering a question about Peter Taft?"

Grace's voice was hesitant. "I'll try."

"Did he have a son?"

Pepper heard a large clock ticking somewhere on Grace's end

of the line. Finally Grace asked, "Why?"

"Because we have information about a person who might be his son."

"Who are *we?*"

What was that slogan from World War II? Loose lips sink ships. In this case, loose lips might sink a wedding. She couldn't risk mentioning Lorraine. "Darby and I accidentally tripped over a connection. You know, one of those weird coincidences."

"Yes, Peter had a son. I met him once; Peter had him tagging along in his truck."

"How old was he when you met him?"

"Seven or eight. I can't remember. It was a long time ago."

"Do you remember his name?"

"No, sorry. What's this all about?"

It was about a boy who, if he were seven or eight in the early forties, would be the right age to be shot down in 1966. "Like I said, a coincidence. It probably doesn't mean anything."

"Is he really in prison?"

"Who?"

"Peter's son. Peter told me no one would help him get his son out of prison."

"Did he actually say *prison,* or did he say something else?"

"Like what?"

Like a prisoner of war camp. "Like jail or in custody?"

"No, I'm sure he said prison. I must go. Lorraine and I are leaving to pick up her family at the airport."

Grace's voice quavered on the last word. Why hadn't she asked someone else to take airport duty? Maybe it was like getting back on a horse that threw you, or maybe it was seeing how thin a line you could walk between courage and stupidity, a quality Pepper always assumed came down to Benny through his male genes. In the case of Benny's family, maybe the double-X chromosome played a bigger part than she'd imagined.

Pepper looked at the kitchen clock. Nine A.M. Wednesday morning to one P.M. Saturday afternoon. She had seventy-six hours until the wedding. She'd once done a massive single shift almost that long when the 101st Airborne had gotten creamed and had to evacuate casualties as far south as Qui Nhon. Funny, she'd felt much younger then.

All right, pace herself. Sensible food. Enough sleep. Focus on the tasks at hand. She could do seventy-six hours, then she and Darby could collapse together.

A flicker of movement on the hill behind her house caught her attention. Four men, walking single file, came from the path that connected her land to Benny's. Pepper grinned when she recognized the first man in line and ran out of the house to meet him. She called, "Morning, Tank."

The bear of a man hurried over, picked her up, swung her around, and set her down again. "Morning, Captain."

She'd met Benny's best man the previous November when they unveiled Randall Fulford's memorial stone.

"I hear you're shipping out next week."

"Yes, ma'am. Two years with NATO Command in Greece. Quarters in a villa overlooking Athens, Greek women, ouzo and dancing every night under a starry sky. Woo! This ole boy done died and gone to heaven." He broke into an impromptu Zorba the Greek dance. The other men, coming up behind him, chanted and clapped.

She'd seen Tank's rows of medals and unit citations on his dress uniform. He deserved a little heaven.

Tank said, "These here are Jeff, Warren and The Saint. They're Benny's groomsmen. This is Captain Pepperhawk, U.S. Army Nurse Corps."

She shook hands with the three men. "Just plain Pepper, ex-

Captain, ex-Army, now one hundred percent civilian."

Jeff was ordinary looking, the kind of man who could lose himself in a crowd. Warren was one of those whipcord tight small men, and The Saint had a polished, shaved head, with a bird tattooed over his left ear. She hoped it wasn't a vulture. Sometimes Special Forces could be a touch too crude for her liking.

Tank shaded his eyes with his hand. "Benny sent us over to help you with wedding stuff. He said we're yours until tomorrow afternoon. Do with us what you will."

Everything left on her to-do list was fussy, like making final arrangements for the champagne luncheon Lorraine was giving for her attendants. The mental image of The Saint discussing asparagus salad and raspberry mousse wasn't reassuring. Still, Benny had sent them over to keep them temporarily out of his own hair. She had to find a make-work project for them. She looked across the yard at Frannie's studio. "You guys ever do any Civil Action Programs?"

Tank said, "Shoot, we've done the works. MED-CAP. SAR-CAP. Just tell us what you need."

"Construction work."

The four of them pulled themselves into a football huddle, with their hands around each other's shoulders. After a lot of whispering, Tank raised his head. "Among us we've built an orphanage, half a dozen medical dispensaries, two schools, and a Montagnard long-house."

"Good enough. Follow me."

She led them across the yard and unlocked the building. "It's supposed to be an art studio. There's a pile of materials outside, covered by a tarp. I don't know what's there or where they go, but you guys can probably figure it out. There might even be a blueprint. If not, use your imagination, but try not to make it look too much like a Montagnard long-house. The lady you're doing this for is named Frannie Maddox. She might show up this evening."

Pepper crossed her fingers behind her back. Please let Frannie show up, not give up.

"She might be embarrassed you're doing this, even offer to pay you. Don't let her. Benny likes her; if he weren't so tied up in the wedding, he'd be over here doing this himself, so you're doing this as a favor to Benny. Got it?"

"Got it."

It wasn't exactly a lie. Benny had never said one way or the other if he liked Frannie, but he knew her, and he hadn't said anything bad about her, so maybe he liked her.

Tank said, "Just in case we run out of supplies, give me directions to the nearest hardware store, pizza parlor, and liquor store."

She told him how to find a hardware store and a pizza parlor. She could guess all too well the ratio of the number of liquor store runs versus hardware store runs they were likely to make. "As for the liquor, tell you what. I've got snacks and sodas in the house. Help yourself. I know you guys will be at Benny's bachelor party tomorrow evening. How about you hold off on the serious drinking until then?"

The Saint stepped forward. "I'll keep them in line."

Pepper grinned up at him. "Who are you, their chaplain?"

"Yes."

She looked more closely at his tattoo. It was a dove with an olive branch in its mouth. "Fine then. I have to go out, but I'll leave the kitchen door open. Make yourselves at home. There's a guy named Saul asleep in the living room. Try not to wake him."

Tank put his finger to his lips. "We'll be as quiet as kittens."

Right. Of course they would. Saul would just have to fend for himself.

Pepper tread quietly past a sleeping Saul, and opened the door to Darby's room. It was empty, the bed neatly made. She'd hardly seen Darby since he'd left her at Frannie's house yesterday morning. He'd arrived at the bed-and-breakfast just before supper, left while Pepper was talking to Lorraine. By the time Pepper arrived home, he'd hung a *Do not disturb* sign on his door. She'd left a note pinned to the door with the request to track down any Viet Nam POWs with the last name of Taft. This morning he'd been gone when she got up, the only evidence he'd been there at all was the note pad with John Taft's information on it.

She picked up a pillow and held it to her chest. It smelled like Darby's hair. No way was he a morning-after, I-promise-I'll-call guy. She'd been such a fool to tell him about his ex-wife Nancy and Hanoi. No, she hadn't. He had a way of finding out the damnedest things. It was a question of when, not if, he would find out where Nancy was, and also find out that Pepper had known where she was. The Marines might favor the motto *Semper Fi*, always faithful, but she and Darby believed more in *Semper honestus*, and there was no honor in holding back the truth.

Darby was probably trying to get in touch with Nancy, or getting information about her. He'd need a phone and privacy, and the latter would be in short supply in Pepper's kitchen. She discarded the simple expedient of him checking into a motel and using the room phone. Too many records, too much of a chance that a switchboard operator would listen in.

Darby wasn't exactly paranoid about security. Who was she kidding? Darby was grade-A, first-class, bordering-on-needing-therapy paranoid about security. Where were there military personnel in Asheville? High school ROTC. A local militia unit. Army Recruiting. Bingo. Shoot, he might even do a little business for them in exchange for using their phone.

"Sit down, son. Have you considered the benefits that Army life offers? Are you interested in adventure? Would you like to travel?"

Yes, Army Recruiting would be delighted to have him. She went to the kitchen and looked up their phone number. Nothing ventured, nothing gained. A sergeant answered the phone.

"I'd like to speak to Colonel Baxter, please."

"Wait one, ma'am." He apparently put his hand over the receiver, but not tight enough. His voice sounded muffled, but still understandable, "Colonel, line three. A woman with a southern accent. This might be the call you've been expecting."

So Darby knew she would track him down. Pepper smiled, quite pleased with herself.

"Nancy?"

Darby's voice was as close to frantic as she'd ever heard. At the same time there was some other emotion, riding below the surface. Could it be love? Pepper gritted her teeth. "Um, no. It's Pepper."

The silence that followed was complete and deadly. Pepper broke it with, "I talked to Grace. She met Peter's son during World War II. The boy was about seven or eight at the time. She couldn't remember his name. He fits the age group to be the pilot who was shot down. That's all I wanted to tell you. I'm hanging up now."

"Pepper, wait. I'm sorry. I just . . . I'm sorry, that's all."

She drew a ragged breath. "I have to be at the Azalea Café at eleven-thirty. Meet me there, if you want to."

Her hand trembled as she hung up. She hadn't told Darby where the Azalea Café was. Heck, he'd taught her compass-and-map reading. Chances were he could look up an address in the phone book. So why did she feel as though she'd just abandoned him in the middle of the Sahara?

★ ★ ★ ★ ★

The arrangements at the Azalea Café were a disaster. Pepper sorted out the menu, corrected the number attending, inspected the private dining room, and convinced the person in charge of special functions that she really, truly could find time to make up six gift baskets by the next day at noon. As she went down the flagstone steps to the café's lobby, she basked in the glow of actually having done something useful for Lorraine.

At the foot of the stairs, she spotted Darby pacing back and forth in front of the lobby pay phone. Before she could say anything, the phone rang. Darby dove for it, Pepper reached the receiver a second before he did.

"Colonel Baxter's office."

At worst, someone would think they had a wrong number.

"This is the duty officer at the Pentagon. May I speak to Colonel Baxter?"

Darby had managed not only to get the cafe's address, but pay phone number as well. Pepper held out the receiver. "It's the Pentagon. I think World War III might have broken out."

Darby frowned and took the receiver. "Colonel Baxter here. Yes. Yes. Go ahead with the message." A pause. "You're sure? Repeat it to me again, word-for-word the way it came over the wire." Another pause. "Yes, there's a reply. Ready for copy? The message is fifteen Delta, zero-five Romeo, four-zero Bravo."

Whatever it was, it couldn't be World War III. For that Darby would have used a tighter code than D.R.B.—his initials—and hisbirthdate.

"Yes, that's the entire message. Thank you." He hung up the phone and rested his forehead on the receiver.

Pepper slid her hand cautiously through the crook in his elbow. She relaxed a little when he didn't pull away. "Let's take a walk. There's a nice park on the other side of Pack Square."

His hand felt like a vice-grip around her fingers. After they'd walked—no, make that double-time marched—about a block, Darby said, "You're probably confused."

"You've been trying to reach Nancy. You either found her or she found you. There's a problem, which is going to require some military falderal—perhaps another land war in Asia—to take care of. What I really want to know is if that weird phone conversation with the Pentagon came with a decoder ring? Because if it does, I have to start saving my box tops to get me one."

Darby stopped abruptly and put his hands on her shoulders. He turned her to face him. "I know you think I'm a good officer, but there was a time when I was a newly minted, young and stupid second lieutenant."

"All shiny and green?"

"The shiniest, the greenest. I'd just graduated from West Point and had my commission. Nancy had graduated *cum laude* from Baylor and was interning with the State Department. We were going to save the world, but we had enough sense to know that there were real bad guys out there. We came up with a code, things we could say in a letter or a tape that would send a secret message to the other person. This morning, I finally reached someone who said he could get a message to Nancy. I sent her a coded phrase. That phone call was her reply."

"What was her reply?"

"It translates to 'I'm in real trouble.' "

"So your initials and birthdate mean what?"

"Sit tight and don't give up hope. I'll get you out of this. Translate that into as soon as I can find a plane heading in the right direction, I have to go to Hanoi."

The sun moved from behind a building and their square of concrete was suddenly brightly illuminated by hot, midday sun. Pepper felt heat rising in her body. "Like hell you do. It's already been too close a thing between us. You could have bled to death on the floor of that helicopter and we'd never have met. Or you could have vanished into whatever hole you fell into the last time you disappeared for months. I refuse to end up like Lorraine, never knowing. The adventure is over. No more secret codes, no more mysterious friends sending you on clandestine errands. No more! You hear me, mister?"

A policeman came out of one of the shops. "Is there a problem, miss?"

"Yes, there's a problem. Too much testosterone, that's the problem."

Over the policeman's shoulder Pepper saw two middle-age ladies smile as they passed. One of them raised her fist in a sisterhood salute.

The policeman looked at the small crowd gathering on the sidewalk. "You're scaring the tourists, miss. Why don't you and the gentleman go somewhere cool? Have a nice glass of iced tea and talk this over."

"I don't want iced tea and I don't want to talk this over." She faced Darby square on. "Either you phone your family and tell them you are bringing me to meet them next week or you get on that airplane. You have one choice—and only one—from column A. I'm getting on with my business. You can come with me or not, as you choose."

Pepper turned on her heel and marched across the crosswalk toward the police station. She didn't turn around to see if Darby followed.

CHAPTER 14

Air Force record heaven—the place that stored retired military personnel files—said the story Kevin McCormick had told them about his military service was legit. Avivah brought the information to Nate's office and plopped herself down in an empty chair. Today's suit was an exact duplicate of the one he'd worn on Monday, except it was navy blue instead of black. Maybe this riot of color change celebrated Wednesday as the week's hump day.

"Kevin Frances McCormick. Enlisted in the Air Force in January 1952. A twenty-year man. His MOS—his job description—was flight mechanic, and later crew chief. No record of dependents, so he probably never married. Retired with the rank of Master Sergeant in March 1972. He was either successful or lucky because he did only one Viet Nam tour, back in the mid-sixties. Most lifers would have done two or three. Service ribbons, outstanding unit citations. No medals for bravery. No disciplinary actions. Honorable discharge, full pension, no disability rating."

Nate pinched the bridge of his nose. "That last one is important, isn't it?"

"It means he had a clean bill of health when he left the military. His lung cancer would have had to show up between 1972 and now."

"If he has lung cancer. Does he look sick to you?"

"No. That natural medicine stuff might be working."

"I think not. All that mixing and injecting and bee's pollen was for show." He handed her some papers. "Taft's autopsy report arrived a few minutes ago."

Avivah waded through the medical jargon. Cause of death: heart attack. Other findings: enough amphetamines and street drugs in Peter Taft's body to knock out a horse. The pathologist was equivocal about whether the drugs caused the heart attack or not. "Hell's bells."

"Exactly. If Taft self-injected, it's not a murder investigation, and we have to close his file. If someone injected him, it could be murder, but a good attorney would argue that there's no conclusive way to know that the drugs caused the heart attack. We can't even investigate Mrs. Kirkpatrick's kidnapping because we have sufficient evidence from her testimony, and her grandson's, to believe that Taft was her kidnapper."

"He had to have an accomplice. He didn't put himself in his car's trunk and drive his own body to the airport."

"There's not one thing in Mrs. Kirkpatrick's statement or her grandson's to indicate Taft didn't act alone as her abductor. For all we know, he could have had a dozen associates waiting in the room next door, but that's not relevant to our investigation, unless we can produce hard evidence that they injected him with the drugs."

"In other words, we tidy up the paperwork and go on to something else. What about the discrepancy between Taft allegedly telling Grace that his son was in prison and military records showing that his son is missing, presumed dead?"

"Family information, not a crime. How well do you know this Elizabeth Pepperhawk?"

"You mean besides sharing a house?"

"Besides that. Would you give her a character reference?"

What would she say? Bends reality to her own whims. Fiercely loyal. Carrying a load of southern, Catholic, and Viet Nam baggage. In love with a man who will eventually break her heart. Hasn't had a drink in eight months. Lying through her teeth about *accidentally* discovering information about Peter Taft's prisoner-of-war son, probably to protect Benny, or Lorraine, or both. Avivah said none of the above.

"Police officers are rarely asked to give a character reference for nurses."

Nate cocked his head to one side as though he was a bird studying a particularly interesting object to see if it was edible. "She seemed angry. Has she got an ax to grind here?"

"Pepper is always ticked off about something. Her boyfriend is visiting. There's tension."

"You known her long?"

"A few years. We were old Army buddies before we became housemates."

Nate leaned back. "You have no idea how strange *old Army buddies* sounds coming from a woman."

"You did a tour, right?"

"Old history. Thirty years ago."

"There were thousands of women in the military during World War II."

"They were clerks, telephone operators, and cooks."

"They were also mechanics, pilots, parachute riggers, code breakers, and spies."

"Why do you turn every one of our conversations into a gender issue?"

Avivah tossed the autopsy report on his desk. "Why do *you?* I didn't ask for this assignment, you know."

Ollie Lambert's big body filled the doorway. He came into the office and closed the door. "Amazing, isn't it, how the marble floors in these old buildings carry sound?"

Avivah hooked a chair with her foot and pulled it toward her. "Sit down, Ollie. Nate was just about to get us some coffee."

Nate glared at her. Avivah tapped her wristwatch. "It's afternoon. You've got coffee duty."

Ollie waited until Nate finished slamming the door before he asked, "Going well, is it?"

"I still haven't figured out why you set me up to be Nate's driver."

"Because it will do you both good to spend time together."

"That's no answer."

"It's the only answer I've got."

An idea wiggled its way into Avivah's brain. Nate had a problem and Ollie expected her to solve it. Forget that. Nate Alexander was not her problem. "What happened with your daughter last weekend?"

"That's why I wandered down here. I heard you and Nate discussing the Air Force. My daughter was hysterical because her husband had enlisted in the Air Force. Never asked what *she* wanted—just up and boom, he's gone to basic training. After he graduates, both of them go off to the Azores for two years. I had to look up the Azores. It's a bunch of tiny islands, stuck in the middle of the North Atlantic."

"I assume he had a good reason for enlisting."

"He thought so, at the time. A couple of weeks ago they left Davie with his grandmother. When they picked him up, she said Davie had gotten into some markers. The kid is only a few months old. Holding a rattle is a big deal and he's playing with markers? When they got Davie home, they checked him out. The marks were only on his right arm and they weren't random. Someone drew lines on that kid."

"Whatever for?"

"That's what my son-in-law wanted to know. He hot-footed it back to his parents' place and demanded an explanation. Turns out grandma took Davie to an orthopedic surgeon. He drew the marks to show her where he would amputate Davie's hand. She had brochures about how life-like an artificial hand would look.

"My son-in-law slammed out of the house, yelling he'd arrange it so his mother couldn't see Davie for a long time. On the way home, he enlisted, on the condition that the Air Force send him some place far, far away."

"I think you can still get to the Azores from South Carolina."

"Not her. She's terrified of flying, and gets seasick in a rowboat." Ollie bent forward and put his hands between his knees. "The problem is they're not only taking Davie away from her—can't say I disapprove of that—but they're taking him from me and Madge, too. Two years. By the time they come back, I'll have missed his first word, his first step, a couple of birthdays—you get the idea."

"I'm sorry."

"You don't know any military magic, do you? Something I could use to get my son-in-law out of the Air Force?"

"Afraid not. There is such a thing as an unaccompanied tour. He could go to the Azores alone."

"I don't want my daughter to have to choose between her husband and her parents. Besides, this whole stupid plan was to get Davie away. God, I'm so glad Viet Nam is over. I think it would kill me if I knew he was going to a war zone."

Avivah started to say that Viet Nam wasn't over for everyone. She pressed her lips together. No sense adding to Ollie's burden.

Nate brought back three Styrofoam cups in a cardboard tray. "Drink up. The lab just finished in Swannanoa. Avivah and I have a date with Marsenia Pullins and the Lord's True Salvation Motel."

Ghosts of faded, fifties-style letters on the white clapboard building hinted that the Lord's True Salvation Motel had started life as the *Swannanoa Motor Camp.* Six small white cabins dotted the property; wooded areas separated each building. Those trees could muffle a lot of sounds, and the remote location was great for privacy. Since a Buncombe County Sheriff's car was parked in front of the last cabin, Avivah assumed that was the place Peter Taft had stayed.

A hanging swing creaked back and forth on the office's porch. The large woman in it could have been any age. She wore a blue-and-white seersucker muumuu, white cotton socks and sandals. A large straw hat shaded her face.

Nate acknowledged her with a wave as they drove by the office, but she didn't respond.

"Is that Marsenia Pullins?"

"In the flesh."

Between the office and first cabin, Avivah caught a glimpse of Marsenia's backyard. She slowed the car. A faded, life-size statue of Jesus offered a tin bucket, planted with marigolds, to a plastic deer. The torso of a Greek statue sat on an aluminum lawn chair, surrounded by garden gnomes. Zeus does storytime at the library. Through breaks in the trees, Avivah glimpsed perhaps a dozen more groupings.

"I wouldn't stare at her collection if I were you. She's suspicious at the best of times."

They parked beside the Sheriff's car. The deputy who had been leaning against the car introduced himself. "The lab boys finished half an hour ago. I thought I'd stick around until you got here."

He unlocked the cabin door. Avivah stepped inside and took off her dark glasses. As her eyes adjusted to the cool, dark interior, she discovered that she'd walked into a time warp.

A double bed, with a carved wooden headboard, filled most of the room. Like the faded letters on the office, the chenille bedspread could have come straight out of 1954. Cheap bedside stands with lamps on them stood guard on either side of the bed. Avivah bet no electrician would vouch for the safety of their braided plug-in cords. Opposite the bed was a three-drawer dresser with a round, bevel-edged mirror over it. Two wooden chairs, a mended web-strap luggage holder and a green metal wastebasket, which looked like government surplus, completed the room. There wasn't a phone.

In the bathroom, a white vinyl shower curtain stretched itself across the stand-up stall. One edge was wavy, as if someone had cut a full-size curtain in half in order to use one curtain for two bathrooms. Above the pedestal sink, an old-fashioned tin medicine chest stood empty and open. As a child Avivah had wondered where used razor blades, dropped into the back slot, went.

In spite of the starkness and age, the rooms were clean, except for fingerprint dust. A tear in one lampshade had been carefully mended. The dresser had a hand-embroidered scarf on it. For all of her other failings, Marsenia Pullins cared about this place.

Nate squatted down beside the bed. A series of scratches, some deeper than others, had been gouged around one cutout in the headboard. "The lab boys have any idea what made these marks?"

The deputy's leather belt creaked as he hooked his thumbs behind it. "Something hard and round. They didn't find anything that could account for them in the room."

Avivah ran her fingertip through one of the grooves. That silver box in her head opened again. She tossed into it an image of Grace handcuffed to this bed, and then slammed the box lid shut. It never paid to identify too closely with a victim.

Nate asked, "Any useful prints?"

The deputy shrugged. "What you'd expect from a motel room."

In other words, Avivah knew, probably not.

"When was the last time the room was cleaned?"

"Last Thursday morning."

"Today is Wednesday. No one cleaned for a week?"

"Marsenia gave her hired girl the long weekend off. The women who minded the office didn't do any cleaning. She— Marsenia, not the girl—heard about Peter's death on Monday morning. She locked the cabin. She said that on television the cops are always upset if evidence is disturbed."

Avivah asked, "Did you ask her why she didn't tell anyone Taft was staying here?"

"She phoned the *feel-good* lady Monday night and told her."

"Who's the feel-good lady?"

Nate picked up the wastebasket. "Probably the mental health hotline. Check their call log for Monday night to see if Marsenia favored them with a call. If she did, set up an appointment to talk to the counselor who worked that night."

Avivah already had her notebook out and wrote the tasks down.

"Did the lab boys take the liner?"

"Wasn't any liner. This isn't exactly the Grove Park Inn."

Avivah peered into the can. Like the room, the can looked old, but pristine.

Nate said, "People chuck nasty things into waste baskets. Eventually they rust. No rust; hence, a liner. Go check in another cabin to see if the can there has a liner."

The deputy left. Nate opened and closed dresser drawers.

Avivah asked, "I think handcuffs made those marks on the bed."

"So do I."

"Where are they?"

"Probably the same place as the food containers."

"What food containers?"

"In her statement, Mrs. Kirkpatrick said Taft left at one point, and returned with takeout food. If no one cleaned for a week, and there were no wastebasket liners when the deputy arrived, where are the containers? More important, where's the food odor?"

Avivah took a deep breath. There was no rancid oil, no old food smell. "Someone not only cleaned up, but aired the place as well. Do you think it was Marsenia?"

"That's my first guess."

The deputy came back, red-faced. "You're right. The wastebaskets in the other cabins have plastic bags in them. You want me to have a look around outside, go through the garbage cans and all?" He looked resigned. A policeman's lot was not a happy one.

"Let me talk to Miz Pullins first. Did you interview her?"

"Tried to. Between the 'Praise the Lords' and the Bible-cracking, I didn't get very much. Not that I'm against Bible-cracking. My granny sets store by it. It just makes it hard to conduct an interview."

"I imagine it does."

The deputy took a small notebook from his uniform pocket. "She's known Taft all her life; he was a friend of her parents. Been coming here five or six times a year as long as she can remember. A woman named Nibb always made reservations for him."

So Tallulah Nibb had been lying. She'd known exactly where Peter Taft was staying.

Avivah wrote, "Arrange for a follow-up interview with Nibb. No McCormick."

Nate said, "Set something up with Mrs. Nibb. Without Kevin McCormick this time."

Avivah grinned at him.

The deputy turned a page. "Except this time, he showed up without a reservation. Marsenia thought it strange, because he'd stayed here from May sixteenth to nineteenth, then he was back on the twenty-fifth."

Nate consulted a small black pocket calendar. "Arrived on a Thursday, left on Sunday, was back again the following Saturday?"

"Yep."

"He give Miz Pullins an explanation?"

"I was trying to make my way through the Bible quotes to that question when the lab arrived."

Nate and Avivah walked to the motel office. Would Marsenia, who was obviously obsessed with religion, somehow magically recognize her as a Jew? Would it matter? She resisted a vision of being sent to sit in the car so her presence wouldn't impede the interview. Religion shouldn't matter like that, but she knew it did.

Marsenia Pullins had a round face. The fat hid her age, but from the wisps of gray hair straggling from underneath her straw hat, Avivah put her age at closer to fifty than thirty. Nate stopped a couple of feet from the porch's bottom step. He took out his wallet and opened it to show her his badge. "I'm Detective Alexander from Asheville City Police. The constable is my driver."

Marsenia rocked back and forth a few times. Her left hand rested on a Bible in her lap, and she fanned herself languidly with the woven fan in her right hand. "Have you accepted Jesus as your personal savior?"

Nate put his badge away. "I was baptized in Spivy Creek the summer I turned fourteen."

Marsenia eyed Avivah. "Has she been saved?"

"The constable has her own path to God."

And that was that.

Nate asked, "Can I ask you some questions?"

"Ain't got no place to go until supper time."

They walked up the steps. Nate sat down in a metal chair. Avivah squeezed past him and sat on a rickety bench along the far side of the porch.

"Miz Pullins, may I borrow your Bible?"

She pressed her hand down on the book. "What for?"

"I believe it's helpful to take counsel before I talk to some-one."

After a few seconds' hesitation, Marsenia handed him the book. Its soft cover bent under its own weight.

Avivah had read about Bible-cracking. She expected Nate to put the book on his knee and allow it to fall open wherever it would. Instead, he turned to the back of the book, ran his finger down the small, dense text, and then turned the flimsy pages.

" 'You shall know the truth, and the truth shall make you free.' *John 8:31.* That's a good start to a talk, don't you think?" He closed the Bible and put it behind his back.

Marsenia Pullins's eyes had the same desperate look Avivah associated with junkies trolling for a fix. Her fingers made little scrabbling motions on her knees. Avivah wondered what Nate would do if Marsenia demanded her Bible back.

"Miz Pullins, I'm going to ask you some questions, but you don't have to say a thing to me you don't want to say. The constable there is going to write down what you and I say to help me remember it. Some people like to have a minister or a lawyer with them when they talk to the police."

"I don't got no lawyer."

"Most people don't, so it's part of my job to find a free lawyer for them, if they want."

"Why would you find me a free lawyer?"

"Cause a judge says it's fitting and proper to do that."

"Which judge?"

"The one down to the courthouse in Asheville."

"That's all right, then."

"Do you want a lawyer before we talk?"

"No."

"Just so we understand one another, you stop me any time you are thinking on needing a lawyer."

Avivah wrote, "*Miranda* given." She resisted the urge to add, "I think." She wondered why Nate had chosen to do the *Miranda;* usually it was done only if someone was a suspect. Given Marsenia's mental health history, maybe he thought it safer to be sure.

"You knew Peter Taft since you were a little girl. He stayed here, on and off, maybe five or six times a year, always making a reservation. Except this last time, it was different. Is all of that right?"

"Right enough."

"He give you a reason for turning around and coming back here after he'd just left?"

"No, but when I puzzled on that I decided one of his old people had been taken powerful sick, and Peter had to help with the farming."

"What makes you think that?"

"He left every morning, dressed for suckering tobacco, and came back, all wrung out, after supper."

"Can you describe his clothes?

"Long-sleeve shirt, overalls, work boots and a straw hat. The old fellow he was helping must have up and died."

"Why?"

"Last Friday morning Peter left long before I was to feed him breakfast. He had on his ministering clothes. Figured he was off to hold a funeral."

"You feed all your guests breakfast?"

"Only the ones I like."

"What time is breakfast?"

"Eight o'clock."

"So this was last Friday morning, Memorial Day that was,

Peter Taft left here, all dressed up, before eight o'clock in the morning?"

"Yes."

He'd been on his way to the airport to meet Grace, Avivah thought.

"When did you see him again?"

"Never saw him again. My cousin came for me after breakfast. We spent all day prettying up family graves, then I stayed out to her place 'til Sunday night."

"If you were gone for two days, who took care of the motel?"

"Got a hired girl who comes in to the office. Business is real quiet this time of year. Folks don't start their summer traveling for a couple of weeks yet."

"When did you hear that Peter Taft was dead?"

"Monday, on the radio news."

"Monday was hot, wasn't it?"

She fanned herself. "Passing hot."

"Too hot to let old food sit around, especially if it had chicken or hamburger leavings in it."

She eyed him suspiciously. "Might have been?"

"You keep up this place real nice with the statues and flowers. Being the manager, it would be only right if you took a peek in Peter's cabin before you locked it up. Maybe saw some old food there, flies buzzing around, and noticed the place smelled bad. I can see how a God-fearing woman like you would want to tidy up, open the windows for a breath of fresh air."

The woman's fingers picked at a loose palm frond in her fan. She bent it back and forth until it broke. "Didn't take no food. Weren't none to take. Weren't no smell, neither."

Marsenia pushed her feet hard on the porch. The swing creaked in a big arc.

Nate let her rock back and forth for several minutes before he asked, "What *did* you take out of Peter's room?"

She planted both feet hard on the porch and the swing came to a stop that shook the porch. Moving surprisingly fast for a big woman, Marsenia pushed herself out of the swing and stomped down the porch stairs and around the side of the building. Her arms swung at her side, making her look like a hiker starting a cross-country walk.

Nate and Avivah followed. Marsenia strode through her backyard to the statue of Jesus. She ran her hand over the statue's hair, like a parent might stroke a child. "I'm sorry, Lord Jesus. I'm sorry. Peter made him sad, you know. The devil tempts ministers most sorely."

"Marsenia, what did you take out of Peter's room?"

"Tools of the devil. Instruments of depravity for the binding of harlots. 'You are to live with me many days; you must not be a prostitute or be intimate with any man.' *Hosea 3.3.*"

"What did you do with what you took from the room?"

She pointed to an oil drum, the kind used for burning trash. Burning was illegal, but people still did it. "Purified them in the fire."

Marsenia picked up a rusted water can and dipped it in scum-covered water filling a claw-foot bathtub. "The woman cried," she said. "Not that happy-sad crying neither, like when that little girl clicked her magic shoes and went home. This was sad crying, like when the boy shot his old yellow dog. It was one of those sinful films that tempt men. Imagine showing that to a woman."

Grace hadn't mentioned being shown a movie.

Nate tried to take the watering can out of Marsenia's hand. She swung back in an arc and hit him full in the chest with it. Algae-covered water washed down the front of his suit. The green tinge shimmered in sunlight. Marsenia appeared not to notice. She wandered toward a grouping that looked strangely like DaVinci's Last Supper painting. Only instead of Christ and his apostles around the table, there was a large stuffed raccoon in the middle. Plaster squirrels surrounded him. They appeared to be having a last supper of green-glass telephone pole insulators.

"Tarted up, with that blond hair so fancy on her head. Big blue flowers on her dress. Oh, yes, tall and pretty, but I knew what she was. Whited sepulcher, that's what I call it."

Avivah's world tilted. Friday, exactly a week ago, before Grace was kidnapped, Avivah had dropped by Lorraine's trailer. Lorraine was getting into her car. Her hair was done up in French braids and she wore a summer dress with big blue hydrangeas.

Marsenia had reached the other side of the yard. She closed her eyes, raised her arms to heaven, and sang a hymn.

The patrolman came up behind Nate and Avivah. He whispered to Nate, "Want me to phone the guys with the straight jackets?"

Nate tried to brush water and slime from his suit with his pocket handkerchief. "Ask the public health nurse to visit. Miz Pullins may not be taking her medicine. The good news is you don't have to search the garbage. Someone else took the liner, and they wouldn't have gone to all that trouble just to toss it away around here. The bad news is there's likely to be a pair of handcuffs and a key at the bottom of that trash-burning barrel."

The deputy rolled up his sleeves. "This is a new uniform. Ain't that always the way."

Avivah and Nate walked to their car. Avivah said, "Mrs. Kirkpatrick's statement didn't say anything about being shown a movie."

"I don't think it was Mrs. Kirkpatrick who saw the movie." He started to wipe his forehead with his handkerchief, looked at the green streaks on it, and blotted his skin with the back of his wrist. "First thing when we get back to the office, I'm going to check with the lab. See if they hauled away any drug paraphernalia or suspicious substances. If not, we go on the assumption that Peter Taft did not self-inject, and that whatever drugs or syringes there were in that room were carted off by the same person who took away the fast-food containers. That makes it a murder investigation. We also start looking for a tall, blond woman wearing a blue-flowered dress."

All it would take was three words—*I know her*—but the words stuck in Avivah's throat. *Let's see what the lab had to say first.* She was certain now that Lorraine was the person Pepper was protecting. She had to talk to Pepper before she went around blurting out Lorraine's name.

Nate took off his suit coat and hooked it over his shoulder. He was sweating and panting.

"Are you all right?"

"Of course I'm not all right. This is my best suit."

"I mean more than that. Are you *all right* all right?"

"Why wouldn't I be?"

"Ollie said it would be good for both of us to spend time together. I don't know what he meant."

"Ollie should mind his own business." He opened the car door. "Late May is too early to sucker tobacco. We have to figure out where Taft went every morning dressed as Farmer Brown."

For the first time Avivah realized how tired Nate sounded.

177

CHAPTER 15

Avivah threaded her way through a maze of cars and trucks parked along the road, on the lane, and even in front of her house. Sounds of sawing, hammering, and cursing ripened the afternoon air while Merle Haggard belted out "Montego Bay" from a huge boom box. A couple of dozen men—most of them stripped to the waist—swarmed over Frannie's studio. Frannie stood, with her hands on her hips, in front of the studio. She yelled to a man on the roof, "Warren, where did you put the paint thinner?"

A small, tight man, wearing only swim trunks and sandals, scurried down a ladder.

Saul sat on the front porch with a bottle of wine in an ice bucket beside him. He raised his glass in greeting.

"What is going on here?"

He handed her a glass of wine. "I don't know."

"Who are all these men?"

"I don't want to know."

He appeared pleasantly tipsy and after the afternoon she'd had, tipsy didn't sound bad. Avivah sat beside him. "Saul Eisenberg, premiere journalist, doesn't want to know something? That's a first."

"This morning while I was brushing my teeth, I bent down to spit in the basin. When I stood up, this huge, bald guy with a tattoo over his ear was standing beside me. It was like he'd walked through the wall. He wanted to know if I had an extension cord. I gave him every extension cord I could find. Then I went to Boone for the day. When I left there were four men here, and when I came back, there were more."

Two more men walked down the lane. One of them put both little fingers in his mouth and gave a sharp whistle. Everyone paused. One of the men who was painting yelled, "Sweet William," threw down his paint roller and jogged over to embrace the guy in a sweaty hug. There were introductions all around and someone shoved cans of cold soda into the newcomers' hands.

Saul said, "That happens about every forty-five minutes. Some of them seem to know everyone, but not everyone seems to know all of them."

"Can you repeat that?"

Saul stared into his wine glass. "I don't think so. Most of them have nicknames, or code names, I'm not sure which. They're partial to country-and-western music, and they are drinking pop rather than beer, which I find fascinating. Since Frannie is with them, I assume this is the universe unfolding as it should, even if I have no idea what's going on. My contribution has been memorizing the phone number for the volunteer ambulance and fire brigade just in case one of them falls off the roof, or they set the place on fire."

Avivah chuckled. Saul said he wasn't interested in a story, but his hindbrain was still taking notes. "What did you do in Boone?"

"Said my good-byes. Had the electricity, gas, water and phone disconnected from Jim's place."

"I thought you told me Jim's uncle moved in to his place."

A little vulpine grin showed Saul's teeth. "He did, but the accounts were in my name. Best to close out my accounts and let him open up new ones. It will probably take a week or two to complete his paperwork."

"The power of the press?"

Saul offered more wine. "The power of friends in essential services."

Avivah ran her finger over her glass's edge, stopping short of producing a squealing sound. "Can I ask you an ethical question?"

He set down his wine glass. "A question that might not be ethical to ask or one that requires an ethical assessment to answer?"

"Maybe a little of both."

He reached over and took her hand. His long, thin fingers felt cool and comforting.

"What's up?"

"As a journalist, you have to protect your sources, right?"

"Yes."

"Take a hypothetical situation. Suppose you were reporting on a murder. A man you interviewed told you he knew nothing about the victim. But later—"

Saul squeezed her hand. "Wait a minute. You already know I don't do off-the-record interviews. I also don't do hypothetical situations. It's too easy to get important details wrong. Tell me the real scoop."

"The scoop, that's what I'm afraid of. Am I talking to Saul Eisenberg, first-class journalist?"

He thought for a moment. "How about Saul Eisenberg, editor? Or Saul Eisenberg, teaching assistant at Columbia School of Journalism? Or Saul Eisenberg, friend? Would any of those help?"

"Teaching assistant might."

He let go of her hand. "Oh."

"What?"

"I hoped you'd choose friend."

Avivah rubbed her hands together. "Friendship is the problem."

"Our friendship?"

"Not ours."

"That's a relief. Just say what's on your mind, straight out and get it over with. I'm listening as a friend, not as a journalist."

"I have reason to believe that Lorraine met Peter Taft several days before his death, and that something very weird, something possibly related to the murder, went down between them. I know for a fact that Lorraine hasn't come forward to the police with that information. What are the ethics of me using insider information and telling the detective in charge of the case that she might be the witness he's looking for?"

Sweat slid down Pepper's neck. Blast Avivah. She hadn't even had the decency to come up with a plausible excuse, just said she and Saul were in the middle of a long talk, and weren't coming to the party. Some days you couldn't rely on anyone.

Pepper counted the people on the open-air patio behind the steakhouse. Benny, Lorraine, Mark, Randy, Quinn, Grace, Joseph, Hamilton, Lorraine's parents, her two sisters, her brother, two in-law spouses, five nieces and nephews, three bridesmaids, Benny's best man and three groomsmen, Darby and herself. Twenty-eight people. Mark and two of his cousins, on sugar overload from the death-by-chocolate dessert bar, shrieked as they ran past the back of her chair.

Pepper tossed her napkin over the unappetizing bone, gristle, and soggy baked potato skin remaining on her plate. She wiggled her way out of her chair and went to the ladies' room. Safely locked in a bathroom stall, she allowed the craving to roll over her. Just one tall, cool beer—that was all she wanted—just one. She'd been perfect for nine months, and this was a celebration, not only of the wedding, but of Benny's thirty-second birthday tomorrow. Just one beer to celebrate. The sweat-beaded glass would feel so good in her hand.

And the beer would burn like acid. Even if it didn't, Darby and Benny would walk out of her life forever. They promised her that would be the consequence if she ever had another drink; they were two men who always kept promises.

She had to get out of here. She and Darby had driven into Asheville together. If he was ready to leave, fine. If not, also fine. He could catch a ride with someone else. She went back to the dining room for her purse.

Lorraine's father was standing, thanking everyone for coming. "Benny's brother is a musician. He's come all the way from Ireland for the wedding."

He made Ireland sound as though it were on another planet. "And he's brought presents for the kids. So, Joseph, why don't you come up here?"

Joseph picked up a cloth sack from beside his chair, and made his way to the stand beside Lorraine's father. "Music can bring all sorts of people together, and I want to encourage all of my new nieces and nephews to learn music. So if all the kids would come up here, I have a gift for you. Come on, all the kids."

Randy, Mark, and their cousins made their way to Joseph, the smallest one carried by one of Lorraine's sisters.

"There's a present in here for each of you. So dig your hand in, and pull out the one that feels right for you."

He opened the sack and a round, black object, about the size of a baseball, fell out of the bag onto the concrete.

Randy yelled, "Grenade!"

He shoved Mark out of the way, scooped up the object, and threw it overhand in the best Hollywood war movie tradition. It landed with a clunk against the huge old-drum barbecue at the end of the patio. Every soldier and ex-soldier on the patio dived to protect the closest child. Pepper landed on top of a curly-headed three-year-old, who took umbrage and bit Pepper's forearm. Ignoring the pain, Pepper put her hands over her ears and the back of her head. She wished she still had a flak jacket and helmet.

One-one-thousand, two-one-thousand. Nothing! Oh, God, it was a dud, or the timing mechanism was off. Move and die or stay put and die. Not much choice. Whiffs of yellow smoke burned her eyes. She gagged on the smell of rotten eggs and burned rubber.

She raised her head cautiously. Benny climbed off Randy, but pinned the boy's shoulders to the ground with his hands. "Stay here!"

Benny walked over and toed the object. "Stink bomb," he announced. He picked it up, put it in a trash can and slammed down the lid. Her eyes watering, Pepper got up and allowed the child's mother to scoop up her wailing daughter. She looked down at her arm. No blood, but a perfect oval of teeth marks sank deep into her skin. She'd bruise by tomorrow. Hit with a lemonade can yesterday, bitten today. At this rate, she'd be black-and-blue all over by Saturday.

Lorraine's father had a ball of Joseph's shirt in his hands. "What the hell are you up to, boy?"

Joseph's face was white. "I don't understand. It was only tin whistles. Tin whistles." He upended the sack. Seven tin whistles, with various colors of mouthpieces, tumbled onto the table.

"Sweet Jesus!"

Nestled among the whistles were three shiny, bare razor blades.

Around the room, some people were vomiting, others had hysterics. She hadn't had any alcohol, but the putrid rotten egg smell was making her nauseated, too. Pepper's emergency room reflexes went into overdrive. She tried to be everywhere at once, calming and soothing. The restaurant owner called the police. It was almost ten o'clock before frightened parents and children were allowed to go home.

Somewhere in the chaos, Pepper lost track of Darby. When almost all the guests had gone, and Darby hadn't reappeared, she went outside to look for him. She circled the building twice. Her car was still in the parking lot, but no Darby. As post-crisis adrenalin beat a retreat out of Pepper's body she realized she had to sit down before she fell down.

Beside the restaurant's front door was a deep alcove with stone benches. Pepper found refuge in the dark alcove. Tears welled up in her eyes and she let them come. It had been that kind of day.

The door opened. Pepper scrabbled back into the darkest corner, wiping her face with her hands. Crying was okay, letting someone see her cry wasn't. She had to be strong for everyone else. That's what nurses did.

Her brain chanted, "I am not here. You do not see me. I can pass as the wind among you and you will not see me." She couldn't remember if she'd learned that mantra from Darby Baxter or Kwai Chang Caine.

Benny and Hamilton had Joseph's arms slung around their shoulders. Joseph fought his way out of Hamilton's grasp, and connected a well-placed kick to Benny's shin, falling to his hands and knees as he delivered it. Benny interlaced his fingers and raised his interlocked hands to deliver a blow to the back of Joseph's neck. Joseph rolled, hooked his hand around Benny's ankle and brought him down with a sharp tug. They wrestled, but before Benny could get the upper hand, Joseph spit on him, yelled *"Marfóir"* and broke Benny's grasp. He rose and stumbled off down the sidewalk.

Benny was on his hands and knees. He said to Hamilton,

"Let him go."

Hamilton helped his brother to his feet. "You okay?"

Benny ignored Joseph's spittle on his shirt, and ran both hands through his short hair. "Where the fuck did Joseph learn street fighting?"

"Ireland, I imagine. He's a traveling musician. Some Irish pubs aren't genteel."

The two men sat on a bench a few feet from Pepper's alcove. She cringed. She couldn't show herself now, and her whole body had gone from cold to numb.

Benny leaned over, panting. Hamilton ran his hand briefly over his brother's spine, then took two bottles of beer from his coat pocket and handed one to Benny. "I had an Irish period."

Benny straightened. "The folks mentioned it."

"Studied Irish history. Went to the clubs. Even learned a little Gaelic. *Dia's Muire duit. Cá mhéad atá ar an im inniu?*"

"What does that mean?"

"Good day. How much is butter today?"

"Useful."

"Depends on how often you buy butter from a Gaelic-speaking shopkeeper."

"So what did Joseph call me?"

Hamilton ran his fingers along the edge of the concrete bench. "It wasn't part of the vocabulary in my Gaelic primer."

"Maybe not, but you know. I can see it in your face."

"Killer."

Benny's shoulders sagged. "I figured it was something like that."

"We've never talked—about Viet Nam I mean. Hell, Benny, we've hardly talked about anything since I moved to Chicago."

"No, we haven't, and now that you've brought that up, why aren't you married? Are you gay?"

Hamilton threw back his head and laughed. He sounded so

much like Benny did when he laughed, that Pepper felt she was watching twins who had been separated at birth and just found one another again.

"I'm not gay, just focused."

"On soybeans?"

"Soybeans. Wheat. Pork. Nothing is going to stop me from making something of myself. It's hard to compete with a Green-Beret brother who went to Viet Nam twice, was wounded, and brought home a chest full of medals."

"You're not going to give me a line about Mom and Da loving me more than you, are you? You know that isn't true."

"It's just that *my son, the war hero* makes for better stories than *my son, the soybean merchant.* I'm aiming for *my son, the millionaire.*"

"If it makes you feel any better, most of what you call my chest full of medals are service ribbons."

"What's the difference?"

"Service ribbons you get for showing up, medals you get for being aggressively stupid."

"How many times were you aggressively stupid?"

"Twice, that the Army caught me at."

"Maybe a few more times that they didn't catch you?"

"Maybe."

"Let me see your scars."

Benny stood, and unbuttoned his shirt. His belt buckle clinked as he unfastened it.

After a moment, Hamilton spoke. His voice sounded husky, "I've always been curious."

There were sounds of Benny redressing. "It's no big deal." He sighed. "Okay, I'm lying, sometimes it is a big deal. I always thought it would be with you, but it wasn't, and I'm glad."

"I'm glad, too. You want to go back inside?"

"No. Lorraine will think we took Joseph home. Let's split.

I've had all I can take for one night."

Hamilton's brow furrowed. "Should we go look for him?"

"Not unless you want to. He's not falling-in-the-river drunk. It's summer; he's in no danger of laying down and freezing to death. Let little brother take care of himself for once."

"Suits me."

The restaurant door opened again. Randy came out, looked around and started to go back inside, but Benny waved for him to come over, opened up a place for him to sit and patted to the empty spot on the bench. Randy sat down.

Hamilton ruffled his hair, "You're quite a hero."

Randy pushed his hair back in place. "Oh, yeah, some hero. It was a stink bomb. Those are real dangerous." He stared straight ahead. "Besides—"

Benny drank a swig of beer. "Besides, you saw it roll out of the bag. Something snapped. The next thing you knew you were lying on the floor, the place smelled like rotten eggs, and you thought maybe you'd crapped because you were so scared."

In her hidey-hole, Pepper understood, for the first time, why Lorraine hated any military influence on her boys. Randy had reacted entirely too fast for any normal boy his age. Whether or not Lorraine liked it, Randy and Mark were both Army brats. Their lives would always be different from those of civilian children.

Randy shrugged. "Something like that."

"It happens like that."

"Did it happen when you were burned?"

"Yes."

"Do you think it ever happened to my dad?"

"I know it did." Benny held out the beer bottle. "You want some of this?"

Randy took it. "Thanks." He took a swig in the same way Benny had. His whole body tightened. He swallowed and wiped the back of his hand across his mouth. "That is so gross."

Benny chuckled and took the bottle back. "You keep thinking like that for a few more years."

Keep thinking like that forever, Pepper wished. She'd had the same reaction as Randy to her first taste of bourbon. She couldn't remember when, or why, liquor had started tasting so sweet.

CHAPTER 16

Thursday morning, Azalea Café staff were hosing down the outdoor patio when Pepper arrived. As she climbed the outside iron staircase to the private dining room, a waitress put her finger over the hose's nozzle and sprayed terra-cotta tubs full of herbs. Odors of sage and basil filled the air; sunlight turned the water fan into a rainbow. Pepper hurried upstairs before the rainbow dissolved into something ghastly. She'd had all of ghastly she could take in one week.

At least café staff had gotten off their asses. Grape vines, woven with ribbons and flowers, in what Pepper assumed were dusty rose and celadon, draped from the chandelier to each corner. Why not call Lorraine's wedding colors pink and green and get on with it? On a buffet table, fresh greenery formed little nests waiting for food bowls. Six elaborate cellophane-wrapped baskets, filled with North Carolina goodies, rested on a separate table. The baskets were Lorraine's gift to her attendants, Grace, and her own mother. A large, round table sparkled with seven place settings of crystal goblets, pink-and-green china, and gold flatware.

On the other side of the room a second door led into a hall. Frannie came through that door, carrying an open cardboard box.

Pepper asked, "Why aren't you at work?"

Frannie set her box down on the floor. "I took a leave day. I promised Lorraine a centerpiece and I didn't finish it until early this morning."

"I figured you'd have a florist deliver an arrangement in dusty rose and celadon. I never heard of celadon before Lorraine picked it as one of her colors. Had you?"

Frannie took a round mirror from the box, and placed it in the center of the table. Rocks and artificial moss had been glued to the edges of the mirror. "Celadon is a Chinese pottery glaze, usually, though not always, pale green."

"Oh."

Frannie rubbed her hands together. She bent down and reached deep into the box. Pepper expected her to pull out a precious cut-glass bowl or one of those modern flower arrangements with spiky things. What came out of the box was a small wooden building. When Frannie set the building on one side of the mirror, it appeared to be a tiny fairy house, sitting at a lake's edge.

Pepper bent down until her eyes were level with the table. "Oh, my."

"You like it?"

"I love it."

The wooden building had obviously started life as a nativity manger. A doll bride, no more than three inches tall, with long blond hair like Lorraine, sat in a woven twig chair, attended by four other dolls dressed in acorn caps, moss clothing, and shimmering wings. One of the attendants combed the bride's hair, one gave her a pedicure, the third had a miniature wedding dress draped over her arm, and the fourth carried so many envelopes and brightly wrapped packages that she couldn't hold them all. A trail of tiny envelopes cascaded out behind her.

"It's not perfect. The comb isn't to scale, and the dolls wouldn't bend the way I wanted them to."

"It's charming."

Frannie took a tent card from the box and put it beside the centerpiece.

FRAN-TASTIC ART, FOR WOMEN MOVING ON

"I thought you usually gagged over *charming*."

Pepper sat down, careful not to disturb anything on the table. "This is different. It makes me feel happy and warm inside. I had no idea you did this sort of thing."

Frannie sat down, too. "You thought that my studio would have been filled with angry women tossing purple and black paint on large canvases, or feminist-angst poetry readings fueled by herbal tea and Goddess lore."

"Something like that."

Frannie moved two pieces of gold flatware, precisely aligning them. "Some of that, too. You have to get the anger out before you can let the fun in."

"Will be filled."

"What?"

"Your studio will be filled with women, not would have been filled. You can't give up, not when you can do great stuff like this. Did you phone Cody?"

"Yes."

"And?"

"And nothing. We talked. Nothing changed between us. And nothing has changed with the studio. The idea is gone, over, finished. Maybe a couple of years from now, if I can get a little ahead, I might try again."

Footsteps clinked up the iron staircase. Grace Kirkpatrick appeared at the door. She'd had her hair done again. Soft curls framed her face. Grace wore a lilac pantsuit, gorgeous amethyst jewelry, and a purple orchid corsage. Behind her Sandra Waine, dressed in big sunglasses, a floppy white straw hat, white sundress, and clunky red plastic jewelry, carried half a dozen corsage boxes.

Pepper rose and balled her hands into fists. "What the hell are you doing here?"

Sandra busied herself distributing corsages to six of the seven place settings. "I'm Mrs. Kirkpatrick's chauffeur and special personal assistant, another service provided by her bed-and-breakfast hostess." She wrinkled her nose at Frannie. "I see you finished your craft project. Amusing, but too cutsey-wootsey for my tastes."

Frannie started to come out of her chair. Pepper put her hand on Frannie's shoulder and pushed her back down. "That's because you *have* no taste."

"Oh my, the claws *are* out today. When did Darby get home last night, or don't you know? He's not happy with you. We had a long talk, over coffee at my apartment."

Pepper wasn't about to tell Sandra that she had no idea when, or if, Darby came home. None of the steakhouse staff remembered seeing him leave. If he could find the Azalea Café, he could have found Sandra's apartment, but Pepper couldn't figure out why he would bother. Pepper wished she had long, sharp nails instead of her sensible, stubby nurse's nails. It would have been so gratifying to rake blood-red nails over that surgery-perfect cheek. "We won't need you anymore. I'll make sure Grace gets home."

"That's up to Mother Kirkpatrick, isn't it? I'm her assistant, not yours."

"She is not your mother!"

Grace stepped between the two women. She took a ten-dollar bill from her purse. "Sandra, dear, I'm grateful for your help this morning. Lorraine and her mother will see I get home."

Sandra plucked the money from Grace's hand. She gave one of those bend-from-the-waist hugs so only her arms connected with Grace's body. "You have a wonderful party. Don't let any spoil-sport ruin it for you."

At the door she turned and gave a little finger wave. As the sound of her footsteps receded Grace sidled up to one of the windows, and peered cautiously out of it. "Thank you. Any more of Miss Sugar-Sweet, and I'd want a blood test for diabetes. She is efficient; I'll give her that. She railroaded me through my hair appointment and the florist, but she's not my first choice for a companion." She turned from the window. "Lorraine's dress fitting will probably take another hour. Why don't the three of us go downstairs and have coffee?"

Frannie put her empty box in a corner, out of sight behind a table skirt. "I'll have to take a rain check. I've got an appointment in twenty minutes." *Lawyer,* she mouthed at Pepper.

So delivering the centerpiece wasn't the only reason Frannie wasn't at work today. Pepper gave her a hug. "Let me know how it goes."

Grace watched Frannie depart. "She said *appointment* with the same enthusiasm I have for my yearly gynecological exam. Frannie's not ill, I hope?"

"Not ill, just under a lot of stress."

Grace turned from the window. "Aren't we all? I gather both of us had problems last night keeping track of people we love."

"Did Joseph make it home?"

"He was at breakfast, but he wasn't interested in anything but coffee and Anacin. That horrible thing with the tin whistles set him off."

"Sandra is who set Darby off. She's his ex-wife's cousin, and she told him his ex is in trouble. Now he feels compelled to help—some kind of stupid mutual assistance pact they made when they first married."

"Nothing wrong with loyalty."

"There is with pigheadedness."

"I don't know your young man that well, but he doesn't impress me as pigheaded."

"Not him, me."

Grace smiled. "I think that might be jealousy. Darby appears to a fine young man. I'd hang on to him, if I were you. Want to stay around until the others get here, and keep an old broad company?"

"Love to. I even promise not to call you Mother Kirkpatrick."

"See that you don't."

They sat down at the table. Grace noticed the centerpiece. "Oh, my word!"

"That was my reaction, too."

Grace ran her finger gently over each doll, lifting tiny details with the ball of her finger to examine them more closely. Pepper remained still. Silence seemed to suit Grace.

Through the open door Pepper heard people on the patio below them. Ice tinkled in glasses; chairs scraped on flagstones. A woman's voice called, "Over here. We thought you'd forgotten." Smells of coffee and fresh baking wafted up the stairs.

Pepper asked, "How do you do this?"

Grace smoothed the folds of the tiny wedding dress. "Do what?"

"Last weekend you went through an experience that would have most people curled in a ball, gibbering. You're sailing through this week as though nothing happened."

"Looks can be deceiving. My mother's motto was, 'survive now, collapse later.' I guess it comes from growing up in bush camps. A grizzly or a blizzard won't wait while you have a nervous breakdown. When my first husband died, and years later, when we received word that Benny had been wounded, both times I did what was expected of me, but I have no memories of either of those times. The same thing is happening this week. When I lay down at night, I can't describe to Quinn one thing that I've done or seen that day. When we get through this, I will have missed my son's wedding." Tears welled up at the bottom of her eyes. "I hope people take a lot of pictures, so I can look at them later and figure out if I had a good time."

Pepper took her hand. It was warm and dry and she felt calluses built during a lifetime of welding and handling hardware. "I wish you had told me about the pictures. I'd have photographed every minute of every day for you."

Grace picked up a napkin with her other hand and dabbed at her eyes. Purple eyeliner stained the pink fabric. "This is cousin Myrtle, standing in front of the wedding cake, only you can't see the cake because Myrtle is standing in front of it. I hate those self-indulgent slide shows people put together after vacations."

Pepper let go of Grace's hand and gave it one pat. "The two other times, did your memory come back gradually? One day you remembered a small thing, then the next day a little more, and so on?"

"You mean like Novocain wearing off after you've been to the dentist?"

"Something like that."

"Not at all like that." She touched her left side, just under where her corsage was pinned. "I have a scar here. My kids think I fell on a broken bottle; Quinn knows I didn't. A few weeks after my husband died, after the funeral and settling his estate, and all the necessary things had been done, I tried to stab myself in the heart."

Pepper's stomach gave a little lurch.

"All very Romeo and Juliet. Fortunately, both my aim and my knowledge of anatomy were piss-poor."

Pepper didn't have the time or energy to mount a suicide watch on top of everything else. If she had to shove Grace back into a mental ward for Grace's own protection, she'd do it.

"What about when Benny was wounded, did you have any thoughts of hurting yourself then?"

"I tried to hurt the Army instead. There was a group of us, all mothers whose sons had been horribly burned, most a lot worse than Benny. We'd meet every morning in a coffee shop to plan what battles we thought we could win that day. The burn unit staff used to flatten themselves against the wall when they saw us coming. They might even still have the plaque at Brooke Army Medical Centre."

"What plaque?"

"The one the other patients put up outside his burn ward the day Benny was discharged."

To "Colonel" Grace Kirkpatrick, Officer-in-Charge of the never-take-no-for-an-answer squad. Up the Mothers!

Pepper laughed at the typical Army-patient humor. "Benny never told me that story."

"I don't imagine he will. I embarrassed him. A tough Green Beret shouldn't depend on his mother to fight his battles. He forgot I'd been a mother a lot longer than he'd been a green-beanie. What he didn't know was that by saving him, I was saving myself."

"How will I know if you need help this time?"

"Thank you, dear, but I don't expect you to save me from myself. Quinn and I will manage. Fortunately, we planned a treat for ourselves after the wedding, something I've looked forward to for a long time. I'm hoping that will carry the day."

A knock on the inside door startled Pepper. "That's probably the serving staff, coming to set up the food. Do you need more time for yourself? Shall I send them away?"

"What, and get the reputation as one of those mothers-of-the-groom who treats people as though they were Victorian servants? Besides, I think we need a clean napkin here."

A second knock, harder this time, followed by the door opening. Pepper had been wrong. No way had Detective Alexander and Avivah come to set up food. She looked down at the detective's shoes. Yesterday, when she'd told them about Peter Taft's son, she hadn't been able to see them because he'd been behind his desk. His dark suit and perfectly square, white pocket handkerchief reminded Pepper of fifties TV cops. She'd bet herself that his shoes were spit-shined. She'd been right.

Avivah closed the door and stood in front of it. All of the muscles in Pepper's neck tightened. It wasn't Avivah being in uniform. The first time they'd met, Avivah had been in a military police officer's uniform. What was irritating her was the inequality. Alexander was in charge; Avivah had to guard the door. Pepper wanted to tell him that Avivah was just as good a police officer as he was.

Grace stood, clutching the crumpled napkin in her hand. "Has there been a development?"

"We're looking for Mrs. Fulford. Mr. Kirkpatrick said we would find her here."

"Why do you need to see Lorraine?"

"I need to take a statement from her." Detective Alexander took several photographs out of his inside suit pocket. "Does this room look familiar to you?"

Grace took the photographs. Pepper craned her neck to see what they were, but Grace held them close to herself. "Where is this place?"

"Just outside of Asheville."

Grace's hand trembled as she handed the pictures back to Alexander. "This may be the place Peter took me."

"Can you identify it positively?"

Since she'd returned the photographs, Grace had gripped a chair back with both hands. Her voice was flat. "Would I be willing to stand up in court and say so positively? No, not until

I've seen that room in person. You still haven't told me why you need a statement from Lorraine."

"We have reason to believe that Mrs. Fulford met with Peter Taft, in this same motel room, a week before he abducted you."

Pepper held back a groan. Truth will out. It had taken Avivah less than twenty-four hours to figure out that if a missing-in-action Navy pilot was somehow involved in this, Lorraine, with her extensive MIA family connections, was involved, too.

"That's impossible."

"We'd like Mrs. Fulford to confirm that impossibility for herself."

Grace stood tall. "Colonel" Kirkpatrick in a lilac pants suit and amethyst jewelry. It all hinged on which battles she thought she could win. Grace obviously found one she *intended* to win. "Detective Alexander, do you have daughters?"

His face lost color. Must be the heat, the tightly knotted tie and that dark suit.

"One."

"Then you'll understand how important today is for Lorraine. Amid all this wedding confusion, all the things she is doing so other people will have a good time, this is her day. Please show a little respect and not spoil it. Her mother and I will be with her the rest of today. She won't leave town. I give you my word that I will bring her to your office tomorrow morning. Will ten o'clock be all right, or should we come earlier?"

Alexander turned around and looked at Avivah, who nodded at him. So maybe the relationship between them wasn't that one-sided after all. Alexander went up a notch in Pepper's estimation.

"Ten o'clock, tomorrow, my office."

"Perhaps tomorrow, after you speak with Lorraine, you might take me to that motel."

"I'll see what I can do."

Once the door closed behind them, Grace grabbed Pepper by both arms. Pepper felt the strength in those welder's hands. "Find Quinn. I'd go myself, but I gave my word. I have to stay here and wait for Lorraine."

Her voice sounded as though they were suddenly in *survive now* mode. Pepper's emergency room background kicked in. Colors were suddenly brighter; she could hear the air moving in and out of her lungs. "The guys are probably back from getting their tuxedos fitted. I can phone Quinn from downstairs."

"No, find him in person and be sure you're alone when you talk to him."

"Then what?"

"Ask him what he was doing at that motel. When I looked at those photographs, I remembered Quinn bending over me. He was in the motel room that night. I'm sure of it. He's the person who drove me to the airport in Peter's car."

CHAPTER 17

As the police cruiser pulled into the parking lot of Mrs. Nibb's motel, Nate asked, "You sure McCormick isn't here?"

Avivah cruised the full lot for a parking place. "The morgue tech promised to keep him busy filling out forms and making phone calls. Apparently, if you want it to be, getting permission to transport a murder victim's body across a state line can become complicated."

She spotted a car leaving, and swung into the parking spot. The patrol car's nose ended up inches away from a black iron railing. Beyond it, a woman in a print dress and straw hat was doing something to the flower boxes that hung on the railing. A waitress—who looked young enough to be a high school student—faced the woman. "For the third time, ma'am, it's the bus boys' job to take care of the flowers. We pay them to do it."

"Boys ain't no good at deadheading. Got no sense 'bout a flower's going to seed."

Avivah's brain did a double take. The gardener was Mrs. Nibb. The old woman snipped more flowers and tossed them into a basket, which sat beside her on the sidewalk.

The waitress resembled a puffer fish in full defense. "If you don't stop this minute, I'm calling the police."

Nate opened his door. "Enter, stage right, badge drawn."

He exited the car, pulled his badge, and showed it to the waitress, who clung to his arm and screeched, "Do something with her!"

Avivah was right behind him. She circled around to Mrs. Nibb's other side and put her hand around the woman's elbow, but without any pressure—for now. "Mrs. Nibb, I'm glad to see you. We came to take you to lunch."

Nate gave Avivah a confused look, which she ignored.

The clipper blades wavered, taking out a couple of buds instead of a flower past its prime. "Take *me* to lunch?"

Poor old thing. Probably no one ever took her out.

"Mr. McCormick's been delayed downtown, so we thought we'd keep you company." She hoped she was channeling correctly for Pepper, who would have known just the right amount of southern honey to drip into her voice.

Mrs. Nibb's hand picked at her dress bodice. "Am I dressed enough for a restaurant?"

"You look fine."

Nate asked the waitress, "Could you find us a quiet booth, inside, out-of-the-way?"

The waitress picked up three menus. "Anything you want. Right this way."

Mrs. Nibb tried to excuse herself to tidy up, but Avivah went to the ladies' room with her. She wasn't taking any chance on the old woman wandering away. Once they were safely ensconced in a rear booth, behind artificial palm fronds, their waitress hovered over them with a poised pencil.

Mrs. Nibb put on her glasses. She studied her menu from top to bottom, cover to cover.

The waitress shifted from foot to foot.

"I don't often eat in fancy restaurants. There're so many choices that I can't make up my mind. Kevin or dear Peter always has to order for me."

Nate picked up a laminated card, which listed daily specials. "How about a chicken salad sandwich, French fries, and iced tea?"

"That would do nicely."

Nate took the menus from Mrs. Nibb and Avivah and handed them to the waitress. "For three."

Avivah glanced at her watch. She'd let Nate get away with ordering for her this time because it was exactly noon. Not her time or his. And because she was as anxious as Nate to get this interview over. Truth to tell, she'd probably have ordered the special anyway.

Mrs. Nibb pulled on the waitress's apron, like a child wanting an adult's attention. The waitress looked down at her.

Mrs. Nibb's voice sounded small and frail. "Could I have a slice of lemon in my tea, if it's no bother?"

"Anything you want."

Anything to keep her shears away from the flower boxes outside.

After the waitress left, Mrs. Nibb leaned over the table. "A fresh slice of lemon looks so pretty in a tall glass, don't you think?"

The Mrs. Nibb with them today was different from the woman in Nate's office on Monday. Something was wrong here, but Avivah didn't know what.

The waitress brought their tea, along with an entire bowl of lemon slices. Mrs. Nibb beamed, and what was wrong slipped into place. There hadn't been one mention of Jesus or the Bible. Today Mrs. Nibb was small, meek and lost in the big city. Or was she?

Avivah ventured, "Why were you cutting the flowers?"

She sipped her tea. "Kevin has gone to . . . well . . . make those delicate arrangements that we shouldn't discuss at the table. I had to do something to keep myself busy, so I wouldn't think about that."

And she just happened to be traveling with a straw hat, a gardening basket and a pair of shears? Some of Avivah's aunts were ferocious gardeners. Even the most determined among them didn't tend their flower beds under a noon sun, but a woman who wanted to be noticed might want hot sun. The hotter, the better. Work up a sweat, put a delicate, veined hand to her forehead, appear faint and the restaurant would be quick to offer a free meal, and who knew what else. Was that why Mrs. Nibb's trimming shears faltered when Avivah offered to buy her lunch? The old woman thought they had discovered her con.

Was the lunch theater they'd witnessed a knee-jerk reaction to being in the same house with two con men for decades? Or had Peter Taft's death put his organization, and Mrs. Nibb, in a precarious financial position? Maybe she really could no longer afford restaurant meals.

Their food arrived. Detective Alexander took several healthy bites of his sandwich, chewed, and swallowed before he asked Mrs. Nibb, "Have you ever heard of the Lord's True Salvation Motel?"

She looked up from squirting ketchup over her fries. "Of course I have. Walter and I were friends with the people who built it. A good Christian couple, who have been taken up into the bosom of the Lord."

Here come the religious references. So, the chameleon could change colors.

"Did Mr. Taft ever stay at that motel?"

"Every time he came to Asheville."

"You said on Monday that you had no idea where he was staying."

"That's because he wasn't *supposed* to be in Asheville. He should have left on the nineteenth, for a trip through Virginia, then back home to Tennessee."

"You also told us you couldn't be certain of dates without looking at your book, which was back in Tennessee."

"I've thought a lot about Peter the last three days. I

remembered a lot of things."

She was good. Her voice held just the right tint of grief.

"When did you find out that Taft hadn't gone on to Virginia?"

"Tuesday morning, May twenty-first. One of our faithful supporters phoned to tell us that Peter never showed up for a prayer group in Galax on Monday night."

"What did you do then?"

"I phoned dear Marsenia. I thought Peter might have been taken sick and stayed over."

"Was Peter sick often?"

"He took spells."

"When he was using drugs?"

Mrs. Nibb folded her hands primly. "I will not speak ill of the dead. We are all weak in the flesh."

So she knew that Peter used drugs.

"After Miz Pullens told you that Peter had left the motel, what did you do?"

Mrs. Nibb's bony hand patted hard against her chest. A real reaction this time. Avivah signaled their waitress to bring another glass of iced tea.

"I had to lie down for a while. I was so afraid that he'd been struck by lightning, like my grandson. Peter said that our children are in the care of the Lord, but I get so afraid sometimes."

Mrs. Nibb accepted the glass of tea and took her time adding sugar and lemon slices.

Avivah asked, "Did Peter have children?"

Mrs. Nibb took a delicate bite from her sandwich. "He had a son."

"Do you know how to reach him? Has anyone informed him of his father's death?"

"I imagine he knew before the rest of us did. He and Peter are in the same place. Diphtheria took him."

Avivah paused with a French fry halfway to her mouth. Yet another version of Peter and his son. "When?"

"Years ago."

If that were true, who was missing-in-action Navy Lieutenant John Taft of Tok, Alaska?

Detective Alexander's foot nudged Avivah's leg under the table. He apparently wanted the conversation back. "On May twenty-first, after you lay down to recover your strength, did you do anything else to try to locate Reverend Taft?"

"Kevin did. He made a lot of phone calls, but no one had seen him."

Of course they hadn't. He was safely at the motel, dressing like a farmer every morning. Did Taft carry overalls and a straw hat with him, the way Mrs. Nibb carried gardening tools? As soon as they got back to the station, Avivah wanted to take a closer look at the items found in Peter's car. For all she knew, he could have had enough props and costumes to supply a small repertory company.

"Did you file a missing person's report?"

"Goodness gracious, no."

"Why not?"

"We never imagined anything had *happened* to Peter. Kevin said the Lord had simply taken him on a different journey, like Saul on the road to Damascus."

You might say that. Or, McCormick didn't want the police asking too many questions about what Peter and the rest of them were up to.

"Will Mr. McCormick carry on Reverend Taft's work?"

"Not if I have anything to say about it."

For the second time, Avivah felt they had gotten through the facades to the real Mrs. Nibb. She'd been bordering on true hysteria when she talked about her grandson, but the way she held herself now, the fire in her eyes was pure, unvarnished fury.

"Is that because Mr. McCormick isn't a minister?"

"It's because he's a thief and a liar. He stole my grandson's money."

So many Mrs. Nibbs—sweet old lady, Bible-spouting Christian, confidence trickster, furious grandmother—kaleidoscoped in front of Avivah that she was getting a headache. Would the real Mrs. Nibb please stand up? Whatever else the woman was capable of, her grandson had meant everything to her.

"Do you have any proof of that?"

"In my room."

"Would you show it to us?"

Mrs. Nibb looked down at her remaining half sandwich. "Could I take this with me, for later?"

Detective Alexander signaled for their waitress, who packaged the food in a take-away container. Avivah paid the bill and collected a receipt for expenses. It was afternoon, after all. They went to Mrs. Nibb's room.

She opened an old-fashioned striped suitcase, releasing an odor of mothballs. The faded pink satin lining snapped into place around the case. Mrs. Nibb undid several snaps and slid her hand between the lining and the case. She pulled out three letters, but handed only one to Detective Alexander.

He took it without hesitation. Who knew how many people had handled it? No sense wasting time trying to preserve fingerprints. Avivah looked over his shoulder.

The letter was typed on standard paper, dated in February, addressed from *Johnny's Kids* to a community center in Omagh, County Tyrone, Northern Ireland. Mrs. Nibb apologized for the delay in sending the money promised for sports equipment. The bank had finally sorted out converting U.S. dollars to Northern Ireland currency. A money order was enclosed to pay for basketballs, baseballs, gloves and bats. The letter was unsigned, but there was white space for a signature between *Yours, Sincerely* and *Tallulah Nibb (Mrs.)*. The word *Copy* in blue ink was stamped on one corner of the letter. Nibb and Taft might be con men, but they were business-like con men.

Avivah asked, "Your grandson was named Johnny?"

"Yes. We got the idea for the name, *Johnny's Kids*, from that entertainer, the one who has that TV marathon every year to raise money for kids in wheelchairs."

Smart marketing. That entertainer's name also began with "J." Avivah wondered how many people might confuse the two charities.

Mrs. Nibb handed the detective a square of thin, blue airmail paper, the kind that was both letter and envelope in one. "I got this in March."

The handwriting had a European look. It was a tactfully worded enquiry from the same community center asking if Mrs. Nibb had changed her mind because they had never received her promised money.

Mrs. Nibb held the last letter to her chest. "This third letter arrived the next day. It was for Kevin, but I was so upset when I saw the Northern Ireland stamp that I opened it. You know how things go astray and end up on the wrong person's desk."

Detective Alexander had to almost pry it from her fingers. It was another airmail letter, white this time, with no return address. Inside, a single scrawled line read, "The gift is appreciated. Jos. K."

Avivah's lunch turned to lead in her stomach. She wished she had a sample of Joseph Kirkpatrick's handwriting for comparison.

"We had to go to the bank to get a special money order. They don't understand dollars in Ireland, you know. I remembered signing the letter to go with it and wasn't to anyone named Joseph!"

"Who was the money order made out to?"

"The Omagh Youth Project. The lady at the bank said that was the way to do it."

"How much was it for?"

"A hundred of those things with the funny-looking *L*."

"Pounds?"

"Perhaps. I don't know how much that is in real money, but Kevin said that was the right amount to send."

Avivah didn't know the conversion rate either, but a hundred of anything sounded like a lot of money.

"I think Kevin took the money order out of my letter and sent it to this Joseph person instead. I want to charge him with stealing my grandson's money. Can I do that?"

Detective Alexander collected up the three letters. "Yes, you can bring charges, but if fraud was committed, it was done in the state of Tennessee. I'd advise you to wait until you get home to bring charges. I'll need to take these letters long enough to make copies of them. You'll get them back, I promise."

As they walked down the motel corridor, Nate looked at his watch. "It's almost one. Call the station and tell them to send someone to the morgue office to pick up Kevin McCormick and escort him to my office. I want him waiting there when we get back."

Kevin McCormick was as red-faced as the waitress had been. In her case, it was youthful frustration. Avivah was concerned that McCormick might pop a blood vessel and die of a stroke on Nate's office floor. He clutched his zippered folder, a handkerchief, and a small brown bottle.

"You had no right to question Mother Nibb without me being present."

"This is a suspicious death investigation. I can question whomever I want, whenever I want."

Kevin McCormick unzipped his case. He took out two pieces of paper. All Avivah could see was that the first one, which he handed to Detective Alexander, had a gold seal at the bottom. "In this case you can't."

While Detective Alexander read the paper, McCormick opened the brown bottle, lifted his tongue and let three clear drops fall underneath his tongue.

Nate ignored what might be illicit drug use right in the police station. "This says Peter Taft, not you, is Mrs. Nibb's legal guardian."

McCormick handed him the second piece of paper. "This is a notarized statement, dated March of this year, stating that Peter has a petition before the court in Murfreesboro applying for both of us to be named joint guardians and, if anything happened to him, he wanted me to see that Mrs. Nibb was cared for."

Oops. Any good judge would suppress evidence learned from Mrs. Nibb. Heck, it wouldn't even take a *good* judge.

"Why didn't you tell me about this earlier?"

"I would have, if I'd known you had any intention of questioning her without me being present. Who was she today? The Bible-quoting Christian? The grieving grandmother? The meek old lady lost in the big, confusing world?"

Yes, she'd been a little of all of that.

"Are you telling me she has a multiple-personality disorder?"

"I'm telling you she has bats in her belfry. I have no idea what five-dollar word the doctors call it. Look, Walter and Tallulah Nibb had one child, and from him, one grandchild. The son and his lady—I don't think they were married—took off when the grandson, Johnny, was two years old. No one has heard from them since. Tallulah and Walter raised Johnny. Walter died;

three months later Johnny died, and Mother Nibb went off her rocker. Johnny was all the old lady had, even if he wasn't, well, right in the head."

"Retarded?"

"A little. He never developed adult interests; he liked hanging around with younger kids."

"Boys or girls?"

Avivah saw exactly where this was going.

"You have a dirty mind."

"I'm a cop. I'm paid to have a dirty mind."

"It wasn't like that. Johnny liked puzzles, board games, marbles, model airplanes, things most boys outgrow by the time they're seventeen. It was as though he was permanently stuck in being ten or eleven. Johnny helped a coach with a Minor League softball team, more of a bat boy, really, but the coach called him his assistant to please Johnny. A year ago this month, he was standing in the middle of the outfield one afternoon, showing a boy how to catch pop flies, and boom, lightning comes out of a clear, blue sky and whacks him dead. The kid next to him was frazzled, but unhurt."

Even without Mrs. Nibb's religious obsession, that sounded like the wrath of God to Avivah. It would be enough to drive even a sane person over the edge.

"Peter was away when Johnny died. The postman found Mother Nibb. She'd put choir robes on the cows and pigs. She'd made wings and crowns out of construction paper and glitter and tried to glue them to the chickens. She'd stolen an expensive set of dishes from a neighbor, set a table outside, and filled the plates with things like broken glass and raw animal parts from animals she'd butchered with a kitchen knife. What little sense they could get out of her was that she was building a place for Johnny in the presence of his enemies. Psalm 23:5, in case you're interested."

"Did she get psychiatric help?"

"Several weeks in Central State Hospital. The Society for Prevention of Cruelty to Animals agreed not to press charges as long as she didn't have access to animals again. That's when Peter became her guardian."

It was silly, but Avivah had to know. "What happened to the cat?"

McCormick looked puzzled. "Tommy Three-Toes? He disappeared, I imagine, when she slaughtered the animals. I think animals sense danger, don't you? He came back a couple of months later. He's pretty much gone feral, but he sleeps in the barn when it's cold."

Detective Alexander held out his hand. "Let me see that bottle, if you don't mind."

So he hadn't been ignoring the drug use, just biding his time. The more Avivah watched Nate, the more she realized he was really good at that. Maybe she should try to be more like him.

"Rescue remedy. Essence of flowers. Perfectly legitimate, I assure you."

The detective smelled it and handed it to Avivah. There was a commercially printed label that said *Rescue Remedy*. She unscrewed the dropper and took a deep breath. It smelled like flowers. She took another deep breath. Truth to tell, she did feel calmer. Maybe it worked. She recapped the bottle and handed it back to McCormick.

Detective Alexander asked, "Tell me about *Johnny's Kids*."

"Peter set that up to give Mother Nibb something positive to focus on. The money went to places like children's hospitals, social clubs, and detention centers, anywhere there were children under stress. It paid for toys, games, sports equipment, things Johnny liked to play with."

"Was it successful?"

"Not really. There were donations right after Johnny died, but they tapered off. An unknown seventeen-year-old who died bizarrely isn't a big charity attraction. When Peter came back from the riding circuit, he'd kick in money, say he collected it from groups he visited. Mostly, it was Peter's own money."

Which McCormick ripped off and sent to a man named Jos. K. in Northern Ireland. Avivah couldn't wait to see how he'd try to explain that away.

Detective Alexander sat back in his chair and gave McCormick an appraising look. "Does Peter Taft have a son?"

"Did have. Navy pilot, shot down over North Viet Nam. Died in a POW camp."

Ka-ching. McCormick had just changed the rules again. No son. A son. A son who died from diphtheria. A son who Peter thought was alive and held captive. A son whose bones had come home. Too many sons and too many stories.

"You're sure the boy is dead?"

"I carried his bones home myself." McCormick looked from one of them to the other. "Sorry. That sounded weird. My last Air Force assignment was to return to the U.S. remains of servicemen turned over by the North Viet Nam government. My crew brought home what was left of Lieutenant John Taft. That's how Peter and I met."

Avivah felt her face grow hot with excitement. She had this bastard stone, dead cold in a lie. If the Navy flier's remains had been brought home, that information would have been in the records Darby had located. The Navy listed Lieutenant Taft as "missing, presumed dead," not "deceased; remains recovered." Moreover, his remains would have gone to his aunt and uncle in Alaska, who were listed as next-of-kin, not to a father Lieutenant Taft hadn't seen since he was a child.

As a career military man, McCormick had to know that. What he didn't know, Avivah realized, was that she had a military background too, and that she had caught him out.

Score one for their side.

She managed to contain her excitement until a patrolman escorted McCormick out of the office, and then Avivah banged her fist on Nate's desk. "God-damn, frigging son-of-a-bitch. I'm going to nail McCormick's sorry ass to the barn door."

Nate looked stunned. "Obviously, you know something I don't."

She explained about the discrepancies between what McCormick had said and official military records. She finished with, "When Lorraine comes in tomorrow, go easy with her, okay?"

Nate retrieved his suit coat from the coat rack. "Why?"

"Because the only connection I can imagine between Taft and Lorraine hinges on prisoners of war. You can't imagine what she's been through the past few years. If anyone deserves consideration, she does."

"Even if she's our killer?"

"Lorraine Fulford didn't kill Peter Taft. I'd stake my life on it. Oh, and don't order for me in a restaurant again. Okay?"

Nate massaged his forehead with his fingertips. "Sorry. I was just trying to hurry things along. That woman could have sat there all day without ordering." He checked his desk drawers to make sure they were locked. "You think that rescue remedy works?"

"Who knows? Even if it doesn't, how much could flowers hurt you?"

"That's what I thought. Where would you buy that stuff?"

"Maybe in a health food store. You thinking of getting some?"

"I'm thinking smelling flowers would be better than some of the ways cops use to relax. I might try a bottle."

He'd already said he was okay. Avivah didn't dare ask the question again, but if a seasoned cop was thinking about sniffing something that smelled like perfume, Avivah very much doubted that Detective Nate Alexander was okay at all.

CHAPTER 18

Within sight of Quinn's bed-and-breakfast Pepper pulled to the side of the road and sat with her car's blinkers flashing. The lights beat out a rhythm. *Kill-er, kill-er, kill-er.*

Pepper tried to override with *fath-er, fath-er, fath-er.* She knew in her bones that Quinn wasn't ordinarily violent. Knew it in the respect Benny had for his father. If Quinn killed Peter, it must have been an accident. "He fell and hit his head. I panicked." Except that Quinn himself admitted giving Peter a sound beating, decades ago when both men were younger and hotter, and there was a war on. Old grievances were the worst grievances.

If Quinn had known where Grace was, why hadn't he phoned the police? "Come alone, no police, or you'll never see your wife alive again." Okay, so where was the part about "bring X amount of dollars in unmarked bills"? Even if Peter had contacted Quinn with a ransom demand, how could Quinn lay his hands on big money on a Friday night, Memorial Day weekend, when all the banks were closed? Kidnappers didn't take checks.

Pepper jabbed off the blinker button and pulled back onto the road. She liked Benny's family better at a distance. Close up, they came with too many questions.

Mrs. Somerset stood on her porch, watering hanging baskets filled with multicolored flowers as she talked to a young woman dressed in pink shorts and a white blouse. The woman's back was to Pepper, but something about the way she carried herself looked familiar. Probably a bed-and-breakfast employee. Mrs. Somerset had that British idea about servants being neither seen nor heard—simply pop up at the right moment, offering the right thing. Pepper couldn't remember having had a conversation more extensive than "Please" and "Thank you" with any of them in all the times she'd visited the b-and-b.

Mrs. Somerset's voice drifted down the drive. "I know I've no say in the matter, dearie, but I think you're making a mistake."

The sound of Pepper's tires crunching on gravel as she pulled into a parking space obliterated the younger woman's reply. The screen door slammed and, when she got out of the car, Mrs. Somerset was alone on the porch.

Mrs. Somerset shaded her eyes with her hand. "Miss Pepperhawk. Nice to see you."

Pepper mounted the stairs. "It's nice to see you, too, but I'm afraid I have a complaint."

The woman screwed the hose nozzle shut. Water trickled down her arm. "Oh, dear. What?"

"That woman you sent with Grace Kirkpatrick this morning talked incessantly. It was quite irritating actually. I wondered if you'd had complaints from other guests?"

She frowned and laid the hose on the porch. "This will never do. This isn't my month for staff. My regular gardener broke his leg, my jobbing gardener left me after five days, and my housekeeper just told me that her husband has been transferred."

Ah, the woman in the pink shorts must be the housekeeper.

"Now this. To tell the truth, I only hired Miss Waine early yesterday morning."

"Were you advertising for someone?"

Mrs. Somerset pushed damp hair back from her forehead.

"No, she just showed up at breakfast time, with a proposal for offering personal service assistance to our guests. Said she'd give me ten free hours so I could see what she provided. I'm always on the lookout for something extra we can offer. I thought, why not? She seemed a personable thing, bright and bubbly."

"Maybe a little too bubbly."

Sandra was up to something, but Pepper couldn't figure out what. After she straightened out this mess with Quinn, she and Sandra were going to have it out, even if Pepper had to swallow her pride and ask Darby where Sandra lived.

"Miss Waine won't bother any of the Kirkpatricks again."

"Thank you. I came to see Mr. Kirkpatrick. Is he here?"

"Which Mr. Kirkpatrick?"

"Senior. Quinn."

"He's in his room. Up the stairs, last door on the left."

Pepper hesitated at the landing, running her fingers over the narrow-board wainscoting, feeling every ridge. Wasn't there some famous French trial where someone stood up and yelled, *"J'Accuse"*? She couldn't just burst into the room, point her finger at Quinn, and shout that she accused him of murdering Peter Taft.

A loose splinter jabbed her in the finger. Darby's voice said in her head, "When the going gets tough, the tough advance." Benny's voice said, "Or retreat. That's always an option." Oh, great, now she had two professional soldiers arguing tactics in her head.

Behind her a bedroom door closed. She looked around, but the corridor was empty. She shivered, certain someone had been watching her from one of the rooms. As she hurried to Quinn's room, she wasn't sure if she were advancing or retreating, but standing in a hall wasn't going to accomplish anything. Pepper knocked on the closed door.

"Come in."

Quinn sat in an overstuffed brocade armchair, staring out of a large window. The white lace curtains were pulled back, giving him a view of the backyard and vegetable garden. Light from the window picked out gray threads in the ruff of hair around his bald head. He wore a faded plaid shirt and jeans. Both were ragged around the edges. The cloth and the man had the limpness of age.

The wooden chair creaked as she sat down facing Quinn and said, without preamble, "Grace remembered."

He turned toward the garden, and closed his eyes briefly. Pepper couldn't tell if his expression was acceptance or surrender. He asked, "How?"

Down the hall, a door opened. Faint creaking sounds came toward them.

The Kirkpatricks had reserved the entire b-and-b for this week. The only person likely to be in the hall was one of the boys, or maybe that maid in the pink shorts, come to bring fresh towels. How many times had Benny drilled perimeter security into Pepper? She'd left the room door unlocked, and the transom above it, open. Anyone could walk in or stand in the hall and hear everything she and Quinn said.

There was a faint tapping on the door, as if someone didn't want to wake Quinn if he were napping. Quinn put his finger to his lips. Both of them sat absolutely still. Silence, another faint tap, and footsteps retreated down the hall. A stair creaked.

Thank heavens for Mrs. Somerset insisting on mouse-quiet staff.

Pepper got up and locked the door. She took the big, old-fashioned key from the lock and put it on the dresser, then used the long handle turn-rod beside the door to close the transom. The room felt sealed, the right atmosphere for secrets.

"The police found the motel room where Grace was held.

217

They showed her photographs. She remembered seeing you in the room."

Quinn hunched over and linked the fingers of both hands. "Who knows that she remembered?"

The smart thing would be to say that the police knew, just in case Pepper didn't know Quinn as well as she thought she did. Honesty won out over smartness. "Grace and I know. She can't get away from Lorraine's luncheon, so she sent me to find you. Benny and I never pulled any punches with one another. I suspect he learned that from you, so I'm not going to beat around the bush. Did you kill Peter Taft?"

"No."

"Did you drive Grace to the airport in Peter's car?"

"Yes."

"Did you know Peter's body was in the trunk?"

"I put it there."

"You are in a shit-load of trouble."

He smiled weakly. "Maybe that lawyer Avivah found will give us a family rate."

"You want me to call Mr. Ferguson?"

"No, not yet. I have to decide what I'm going to do first."

He got up, took a suitcase from the closet, laid it on the bed, and worked open the small combination lock.

"Friday night, after the conference at your place, Benny and I got back here about two A.M. I found this on the bed."

He handed Pepper a clear plastic bag. Inside were a cheap box, paper, and an inexpensive glass candy dish, the kind of knickknack bought as a generic, last-minute gift. The white-and-silver paper could be found in any drug store.

He handed her a second plastic bag, this one containing a card, which lay flat and open inside the bag.

Your wife is with Peter Taft, cabin 6, the Lord's True Salvation

Motel. Underneath was a sketchy map.

"Any idea where it came from?"

"None. Mrs. Somerset told me that two young men, in a pickup truck, delivered it about seven o'clock Friday night. She'd never seen them before."

"Why didn't you phone the police as soon as you opened the box?"

Quinn took the candy dish and card from her, relocked them in the suitcase, and put the case back in the closet.

"Peter Taft. It was quite a shock not only to have that man reappear in my life after thirty years, but to be told that he and my wife were together in a motel. We had only Mark's word that Grace had been kidnapped. As much as I love Mark, six-year-old boys sometimes get things wrong. I thought Grace might have gone willingly with Taft."

"Leaving Mark alone?"

"Maybe she'd planned to leave Mark with Joseph, and she and Taft hadn't allowed for Joseph's plane being late. I was jealous, hurt and not thinking clearly."

Pepper could testify to how powerfully jealousy could muddle thinking. "Did Taft and Grace have a relationship thirty years ago?"

"I don't know, but Grace posed for semi-nude photographs that Peter sold to men building the Alaska Highway."

Just when Pepper thought she knew the Kirkpatricks, the ground fell out from underneath her. Imagine sturdy welder Grace Kirkpatrick posing for pornography. She had a fine figure, but it wasn't dirty postcard material, especially with her scar.

"This was before she fell on the broken bottle?"

"She told you about that?"

"She told me the truth about it."

"You should take that as a compliment."

"I do."

"I assume you know what a pin-up girl was?"

"I've seen pictures in books about the war."

"The ones that made it into those books were the classy ones: good-looking girls posed in high heels, short shorts, and skimpy halters. Tame by today's standards, but not then, and there were other, more provocative poses."

"Downright dirty?"

"Even to a soldier's way of thinking."

Pepper was intimately acquainted with that version of soldiers' ways of thinking. It was a part of her Army memories she usually refused to visit. "Grace was how old when she posed for the pictures?"

"Eighteen, so yes, it was before she had her scar."

Pepper started to say that she'd done crazy things at eighteen, which she now regretted, except that she hadn't. At eighteen, she was still in her goody-two-shoes period, before the Army and Darby Baxter joyfully corrupted her. The best she could do was, "Some eighteen-year-olds make bad decisions."

"That's the way I figured it. By the time I met Grace she'd been married, widowed, and had Hamilton—and her scar. She didn't need a youthful indiscretion coming back to haunt her. Christmas Day, after I beat the shit out of Taft, I made him give me the negatives to those pictures."

"Did you plan on beating the shit out of him Saturday morning?"

"I don't know what I planned. I felt as though the whole life Grace and I built had come unraveled. I was mad enough to kill, but when I got to the motel, I found Grace passed out on the bed and Peter, half-naked, dead on the floor."

"Why didn't you call for help?"

"I know death when I see it. No ambulance would have helped Taft. There were handcuffs hanging on the bedpost, taunting me, saying I'd never really known my wife at all. I couldn't bear the thought of my kids finding out their mother was a woman like that."

"Did you think Grace killed him?"

"I didn't think anyone killed him. There was no blood, no sign of a struggle or a weapon. He wouldn't have been the first man his age to have a heart attack in the bedroom."

"So why not put Grace in your car and leave?"

Quinn came back to his chair. He sat down and rubbed his hand across his forehead. "Rage. All those times Grace went away to farm conventions. The year she was Christmas shopping in St. Louis and didn't come home for three days. Car trouble, she said. The more I thought about it, the more times I found that she and Taft could have carried on behind my back. I wanted to punish both of them, maybe punish myself for being so stupid all these years."

Just like she had wanted to punish Darby for carrying on at fancy Washington parties with his ex. Only he hadn't been carrying on, but Pepper herself had come close enough to wanting revenge to understand exactly how Quinn had felt.

"I hid my rental car, put Taft's body in the trunk of his car and Grace in the front seat. A couple of miles from the motel I came to my senses. I'd stolen a car, had a body in the trunk and an unconscious woman beside me. The honest thing would have been to drive to a police station or a hospital. Honesty failed me."

Other than "I love you," Pepper had never heard so much emotion summed up in three words.

"How did you get back to your car from the airport?"

"Took a taxi."

Great. He'd left a trail that might as well be neon. There was no way a cab driver would forget a fare from the airport to Swannanoa. "The longer you wait, the more it's going to cost you to get that honesty back."

"I know. When Grace couldn't remember anything—or said she couldn't—I felt as though I'd been given a gift. I was going to turn myself in after Benny and Lorraine were safely on their honeymoon. They've waited so long to marry. I didn't want them to go to the altar with me in jail."

"The police want to question Lorraine. Grace negotiated a deal: she keeps an eye on Lorraine today and tonight, and they allow Grace to bring her to the police station tomorrow morning."

"What does Lorraine have to do with Peter?"

"Her relationship with him is difficult to explain. Knowing the truth about what you did might influence how they question Lorraine."

Quinn stood. "Will you drive me to the police station?"

"I'm going to take you to see Mr. Ferguson. He'll shit a brick if you talk to the police before you talk to him."

"Good enough."

"Bring that stuff in the plastic bags. He'll want to see that." Pepper hesitated. "Grace told me about the two times her memory blanked out. I can tell you, as a nurse, that her mental health is at high risk right now. When you're arrested—no sense fooling ourselves that you won't be—your children are going to have to protect her. They have to know the truth about where her scar came from."

"Not Benny, not today of all days. His bachelor party is tonight. He hasn't seen some of these guys in years. He may never see some of them again. I won't ruin that reunion for him. I suppose it will have to be Hamilton. He's my calm and logical child."

"Is he here?"

"I think so."

"Get yourself ready. I'll go find Hamilton."

Pepper unlocked the door, opened it, and stood eyeball to

eyeball with Ginny Mae Kirkpatrick, dressed in pink shorts and a white blouse. Pepper tried to remember how to breathe.

Ginny Mae pointed to the oversized keyhole. "Big keys require big key holes."

In other words, she'd heard everything.

Ginny Mae stepped into the room and closed the door behind her. Quinn slowly straightened up from trying to winkle his suitcase out of the closet again. His face had gone dead white. "What are you doing here?"

"Helping my brother get married."

"How did you get here?"

"Flew."

Color crept into Quinn's face. "I thought you didn't want anything to do with us."

Ginny sat on a corner of the bed. "A bus ride from here to Missouri is dead boring. I could only look at so much scenery. I had a lot of time to think. You and mom sold the store out from under us, and that wasn't right."

Quinn looked at the floor. "Maybe it wasn't."

"Every one of us kids worked in that store. Weekends. Summer vacation. Pre-Christmas rush. We deserve something from the sale. I worked out a formula for the percentage each of us should get. I'm taking my share, and buying into a hardware business somewhere, maybe in Missouri, maybe not, and there's not a thing you can do to stop me."

"Honey, I wouldn't try to stop you."

Ginny Mae stood and put her arms around her father's neck, burying her face in his shoulder. "I'm so sorry, Da, so sorry about all of this. I love you. Tell me about Mom. Tell me what I can do to help."

Shortly after lunch, Frannie appeared at the door of Nate's office. "I've spoken to a lawyer. He directed me to give you a statement."

Avivah looked into the empty hall before she closed the door. "Is he planning on being here?"

"He had to close a house deal this afternoon, but he knows everything in my statement."

Avivah wished Frannie had not picked a lawyer who thought a real estate deal was more important than a murder investigation, but beggars couldn't be choosers. She sat down and prepared to take notes. Nate reached into his suit pocket and took out a couple of stomach tablets. "Let's start with the day that F. J. Cantrell asked you to write to Peter Taft. You've already told us that Peter Taft brought charges against you, which eventually resulted in you going to jail. Why would F. J. Cantrell ask you to contact Taft, of all people, and why would you agree to do it?"

"Hubris."

Nate looked confused. "I beg your pardon?"

"That old mountain expression: don't get above your raising. F. J. and I have kept in touch for a long time. In his own way, F. J. always was as bad a confidence man as Peter, though fortunately, always on the right side of the law. He convinced me how much fun it would be to pull Taft's nose, you know, conning the con man. It was pure false pride, just seeing how much we could get away with."

"When did you first write to Taft?"

From her purse, Frannie produced a thick day timer, crammed with bits of paper and held together with a rubber band. She flipped through a few pages. "March sixth of this year."

Nate led Frannie through her letter exchange with Peter Taft and their meeting in early April. As she came to the end of describing their meeting, Frannie laid her right hand on her day timer, as though it were a Bible and she was preparing to take an oath. "I lied when I said Peter Taft didn't recognize me when we met. I think he did."

Avivah had never really gotten to know Frannie. She was just Pepper's overweight friend. If Frannie were guilty, then Grace and Lorraine couldn't be. Would it be any easier for Benny to have a woman he knew and liked instead of his family as the guilty party?

Nate sat upright. "Why do you think that?"

"He phoned me, at home, last Thursday. I hadn't given him my phone number, but he found me anyway."

"What did he want?"

"I don't know. As soon as he said who he was, I disguised my voice and pretended I didn't speak English. He asked for Ms. Maddox. I said Miz Maddox was in the hospital having a baby, and then I hung up. My phone number hasn't been listed for twenty years, a holdover from being on the run from Porter."

Nate asked, "Did F. J. know your home phone number?"

"Yes, but he didn't give it to Peter. I asked him if he'd done that."

Avivah wouldn't have put it past Reverend Taft to distract the old man and go snooping in F. J.'s cabin. "Could he have seen it accidentally when he visited F. J.? A lot of people keep a list of phone numbers beside their telephone."

"F. J.'s cabin doesn't have a phone, and the only things he brought out there were what he wanted Taft to see, like old, worn clothes. Props. Stage dressing."

Avivah picked up a phone book. The name Maddox was listed eight times. It wouldn't have taken Taft long to go through the whole list. "Do you have family in town? Could he have phoned one of them and asked for your number?"

"My uncle was my only local relative, and he died last year. I inherited his house."

"Was he listed?"

"He was before he went into the nursing home."

Good odds that Marsenia Pullins had an outdated phone book lying around the motel office. They would have to check the motel's phone records and phone the other Maddox listings to see if anyone remembered a man calling a week ago, asking for a Frannie Maddox.

Nate asked, "How did that phone call change things for you?"

A single tear rolled down Frannie's cheek. She found a tissue in her purse and wiped it away. "If he had my phone number, he had my address. Taft always had a rough streak in him. Before I worked for the Veterans' Administration, I worked in child protection services. You learn a lot about meanness in that job. I was scared."

"What did you do?"

"I phoned that motel in Swannanoa. The woman who answered said he was registered there. That meant he was in town. It's been twenty years since I was on the run, and Thursday night I almost chucked everything and ran again. As soon as it was daylight Friday morning, I went to Pepper's place."

"Why?"

"Benny Kirkpatrick was a Green Beret. I felt safer knowing he was nearby."

"Did you tell Mr. Kirkpatrick about Peter Taft?"

"I told him that I'd received a threatening phone call from a man."

"Did you mention Taft's name?"

"No."

"The Swannanoa Motel?"

"No."

"What was Mr. Kirkpatrick's reaction?"

"He said that as long as I was on Pepper's property, or his

own, he'd see to it that no one bothered me. He suggested that I sleep at the studio for a few days, or, if I insisted on going home, he would escort me. And he told me to talk to Avivah, that is, Constable Rosen, because it sounded like a police matter."

A year ago Benny would have suggested turning the homestead into a military compound and protecting Frannie himself. Maybe civilian life was finally rubbing off on him.

"When did you learn about Grace Kirkpatrick's kidnapping?"

"About noon on Friday, when Constable Rosen arrived at the homestead with Mark."

"Did you have any idea that Peter Taft was the person who had kidnapped Mrs. Kirkpatrick?"

"Absolutely none."

"You knew of no connection between the Kirkpatricks, or Lorraine Fulford, and Peter Taft?"

"None whatsoever."

"How long did you stay at Miss Pepperhawk's place on Friday?"

"I slipped away about four o'clock. I didn't ask Benny for an escort. He had too much on his mind with his mother being missing."

"What did you do?"

"Went home, locked the house, turned off all the lights, and hid."

"For how long?"

"All weekend."

"Was your car in the driveway?"

"No, in the garage behind my house. I covered the windows so it wasn't possible to see if the car was there."

So none of the neighbors could support Frannie's alibi.

"You were obviously in a highly emotional state. Did you have a weapon?"

227

"I have a felony conviction involving the use of a firearm. One of the conditions of my pardon was that I am not permitted to be in possession of a firearm."

From the practiced way she said each word, Avivah knew that Frannie had rehearsed that line. In other words, she was in violation of her pardon. *Weapon* might have meant a baseball bat or a nail file, yet Frannie had immediately focused on a gun.

"In your work at the VA do you have contact with drug abuse?"

"I can't—"

"I'm not asking you to violate an individual patient's confidentiality. All I'm asking is if, in your professional opinion, some patients at the Veterans' Administration Hospital might use or deal drugs."

"Yes, they might."

Nate had established that Frannie could get access to street drugs. Syringes wouldn't have been a problem. Pepper often came home with uniform pockets full of syringes, alcohol wipes, or tourniquet tubing. The detritus of working in a hospital, available to anyone, even social workers.

"When did you hear that Peter Taft had died?"

"About midnight Sunday. When Pepper brought Ginny Mae Kirkpatrick to my house."

"What was your reaction?"

"I managed to hold together until I went to bed. Then I screamed and cried into my pillow for a long time. For the first time in three days, I felt as though I had my life back."

CHAPTER 19

Cars and pickup trucks, parked carefully on the verge, lined both sides of the road. It looked like your average Madison County wedding or funeral, except for the Ft. Bragg parking tags and Green Beret decals many of the cars sported. The lane and parking area at the homestead was even worse. They'd left Pepper a straight shot, right into the garage, but with no space on either side for mistakes.

A faint odor of paint, sawn wood, and barbecue drifted through the air. Frannie's studio was dark and locked. Pepper had no idea how far her ersatz crew had gotten, but the pile of construction materials had disappeared. She hoped The Saint had kept the crew sober long enough for them to escape with limbs intact. As Pepper walked to her back door, a plume of green smoke from a smoke grenade rose above the clearing where she and Benny had strung lights.

Party time!

The aroma of hot barbecue descended like a curtain as soon as Pepper walked into her kitchen. Half a dozen round foil containers covered the sink drain board. Pepper's saliva glands went into overdrive.

Avivah, dressed in jeans and a sweatshirt that bore crossed gold flintlock pistols and the words *U.S. Army Military Police*, was on the phone. "Yes, it's going to be noisy, and it's going to go on all night, but we've got it under control. Up to sustained automatic weapons fire, how about letting us police it ourselves?"

She listened and rolled her eyes, "Come on, dispatcher, I'm kidding about the automatic weapons. I know they are Green Berets—and Viet Nam veterans. This isn't the first all-night, good-old-boys bachelor party held in these hills. We've taken away everyone's car keys. We've got a bartender mixing drinks, and enough barbecue to feed even this Army. We've warned the neighbors that there is a bachelor party going on. We've got a first aid kit and a nurse. I'll be here. I've got a Green Beret colonel, who works at the Pentagon, standing by in case orders need to be given in a loud and commanding voice. Send a car by if you have to. We'll feed the deputies, too."

She hung up the phone hard. "Civilians!"

Pepper opened a foil container and pulled out a drumstick. She sucked off the sauce as if she were eating a Popsicle. Chunks of meat came off in her mouth. She interspersed chewing with, "We got a problem?"

"The Sheriff's bent out of shape because we have a bunch of veterans up here getting ready to cut loose. They are afraid the place will be littered with bodies by tomorrow morning."

"It will be, but hopefully most of them will still be breathing."

Avivah said in a sing-song voice, "For public safety, Madison County Sheriff's deputies will make regular patrols all night."

Pepper tossed the denuded bone in the garbage. "Let's lock the gates."

"What?"

"This is private property. As owners, Benny and I have a right to lock our gates if we want to."

"The deputies will just come the back way, over the mountain."

Pepper rinsed her hands and dug in their kitchen junk drawer.

"Maybe not. They'd have to park at the top of the hill and come in on foot. If you were already nervous about dealing with a bunch of liquored-up, war-crazed veterans, would you want to approach them by sneaking around through the woods after dark? Here they are." She took two locks from the drawer.

They walked toward their gate. Pepper asked, "Is that sweatshirt your uniform of the day?"

Avivah looked down at her chest. "I figured, even plastered out of their minds, they'd recognize Military Police insignia. Conditioning, like Pavlov's dogs. That green smoke was a signal that supper was being served."

"We invited?"

"Benny sent up the food in the kitchen."

"I guess that means no."

"Guess so."

"Is Darby down there?"

"For supper. He figured it would cramp their style for a full colonel to hang around too long."

"Where's Saul?"

"Down there, too."

"For supper?"

"For the duration, if he wants to be."

"Does Saul have any experience as a war correspondent?"

"No."

"Oh, my, my, my. I think our little journalist is about to have his cherry broken."

They looked at one another and laughed. Avivah stooped and picked up some trash from beside the lane. "You wish you were down there?"

"Hell, yes. You?"

"Absolutely, and without the sweatshirt."

"I'm in the mood for some no-shit-there-I-was stories, and a few beers."

"Pepper!"

She waved her hand. "A thought, not an intention."

While Avivah deposited the trash in the barrel beside the gate, Pepper swung the gate closed. "It really is the end of an era. Like Quinn said, a lot of those guys will never see one another again. Heck, half of them are civilians already. I don't know whether to be sad or not."

"They lived long enough to become civilians, thanks to people like you."

Avivah was right. Maybe she hadn't helped these particular guys, but she had others, who were out there somewhere. Embarrassing, actually. If she thought too much about it, she'd start believing those recruiting ads for the Army Nurse Corps. Better to move on. She put the lock through the hasp and rammed the bar home. It closed with a click.

Pepper hung the key-festooned shoestring around her neck. "One point for our side."

They trudged along the road, up the slight incline toward Benny's gate. Avivah said, "We know all the paths. We could sneak down and spy on them."

"My mama didn't raise no fool."

The North Carolina Tourist Bureau would love to bottle an evening like this, Pepper thought. The air was cooler now and a faint breeze blew in fresh air from the mountains. The sun, still three hours from setting, had mellowed from a hot yellow ball into a ripe peach. Shadows lengthened over the landscape. Crickets chirped in the grass.

The problem with murder was that it spoiled even sunsets and crickets. All the way to Benny's gate, Pepper debated whether to tell Avivah about Quinn. It was no secret; at least it wouldn't be as soon as Lawyer Ferguson escorted Quinn to the police station tomorrow. After all, Avivah hadn't told Pepper about her being assigned as Detective Alexander's driver. She'd walked into the police station cold and gotten a big surprise. Ah, hell, she wasn't into payback. So Avivah hadn't told her she'd been promoted to detective's driver. Big deal.

They stepped inside Benny's land and closed the gate. Pepper stood on the bottom rail so that she could lean over and put the lock in place. "Quinn Kirkpatrick moved Peter Taft's body from the motel to the airport."

Avivah did a double take. "Do you know that for a fact or is it speculation?"

"He says he did it. He described the motel room to me."

"How did he know where Taft was?"

"Someone delivered a fake wedding present to him Friday night. It included a card with a map. Was there really a pair of handcuffs dangling from the head of the bed?"

Avivah's body sank like a rag doll with stuffing removed. "Where is Quinn?"

"Taking counsel with Lawyer Ferguson. And Ginny Mae is back. She flew in from Missouri yesterday afternoon. Mrs. Somerset at the b-and-b has been hiding her out."

Avivah turned toward the path that connected the two homesteads. "You remember when we first met Benny? How he told us all those stories about his wonderful family."

Pepper followed her down the path. "Made you want to go to Missouri and ask to be taken in as a foundling. I have this theory. I think the Kirkpatricks are like sulfuric and nitric acids. In separate containers, they're only a little dangerous. Put them together and things happen."

Avivah didn't care how Pepper knew the chemicals used to make nitroglycerine. After hanging around soldiers for years, both of them were wellsprings of dangerous, esoteric military knowledge.

She and Pepper managed to make it through supper by ignoring the music and noises coming from the far end of Pepper's property. Pepper went to her room, and Avivah, who had kitchen patrol this week, washed dishes and packaged leftovers for the freezer.

Through the kitchen window, she watched a man, wearing either a loin cloth or a pair of jockey shorts and combat boots, sprint across the far yard from left to right, his arms pumping as he ran. Close behind him, two more men, similarly attired, with streaks of paint decorating their faces, ran after him. One of the men—who looked an awful lot like Saul—appeared to have a rubber tomahawk tucked in his waistband.

The curtain rings rattled on the brass rod as Avivah firmly closed the kitchen curtains. Playing cowboys and Indians wasn't against the law, though all three men were perilously close to violating nudity bylaws. They were on private property, no one was screaming for help, and you couldn't do much damage with a rubber toy. At least, she hoped you couldn't.

The phone rang.

"Constable Avivah Rosen, please."

The woman had an Irish accent and the line had the faint, hollow sound of an overseas call.

"Speaking."

"I have a reverse charges call for you from Martin Fitzgerald. Will you accept charges?"

"Yes, operator."

There was a series of clicks, then a man's voice said, "Constable Rosen? Martin Fitzgerald here. The Omagh Youth Project. My wife said you phoned earlier, and left your number."

Avivah looked at the clock. She had no idea what time it was in Northern Ireland, but it didn't matter because Mr. Fitzgerald had sorted it out before he called. She sat down in the relative privacy of the small space between the end of the counter and the stove. One day she had to get an extension phone installed in her bedroom.

"I'm with the Asheville, North Carolina City Police. Detective Nate Alexander is following up on donations made by a charity called *Johnny's Kids.*"

"So they weren't legitimate after all. Too bad."

He sounded like a man who had been disappointed often.

"As far as we know, it is a legitimate charity. We—that is, Detective Alexander—is investigating the suspicious death of a man connected to that charity."

"I'm not sure how I can help you."

"*Johnny's Kids* promised you money for sports equipment, is that right?"

"That's correct."

"Did you contact them or did they contact you?"

"A woman named Tallulah Nibb wrote me a letter. I remember her name because it was odd, like the American film star, Tallulah Bankhead."

"How did she hear about you?"

"She said a woman in an American church group gave her my name and address. Almost everyone I know has a relative or friend who's gone to America. I thought it was a connection like that."

Might have been; might not have been.

"Do you know a Kevin McCormick?"

"No, though McCormick is a common name here. I know a Diamuid McCormick, and a George McCormick, and three Ian McCormicks, but no Kevin. Though it's possible that one of the men I know has a relative named Kevin."

"Do you know a Joseph Kirkpatrick?"

"I know several."

"A young man, American, a fiddler."

"Ah, Joey. He comes over from County Monaghan every month to play music for the kids."

Drat. If Joseph routinely came to the center, could he have

intercepted Mrs. Nibb's check?

"Could you tell me how your mail is delivered?"

"What an odd question. The postman gives it to our secretary."

"What does she do with it?"

"Puts it in a basket on her desk until she can get to it."

"It might stay in the basket for a while?"

"Like many volunteer groups, we've got too few people and too much work. So yes, sometimes it sits in her basket a day or two before she can get to it."

She would have to find out when Mrs. Nibb mailed the check, calculate when it might have arrived in Omagh, and match that to the days Joseph Kirkpatrick came to play music. It would have been a second's work to slip an envelope from the mail basket to his pocket, that is, if Joseph Kirkpatrick knew which envelope to watch for.

Avivah's muscles cramped. She worked herself out of the small space, stood, and stretched her back.

"Mr. Fitzgerald, I don't know much about Northern Ireland politics, so I'm not sure how to phrase this question, but to your knowledge, is Joseph Kirkpatrick involved in politics?"

"What sort of politics?" He sounded wary.

"Groups with an illegal agenda."

If a porcupine baring its quills had a sound, that was the sound of Mr. Fitzgerald's voice. "Illegal by whose definition?"

"Sir, it is not my intention to discuss politics with you, but I need information. Let me rephrase the question. Has the American fiddler, Joseph Kirkpatrick, the man you call Joey, given you reason to believe that he favors a particular point of view in relation to the situation in Northern Ireland?"

Avivah watched the second hand on the clock eat up this month's phone budget.

"Yes."

For the second time that evening, Avivah's stomach plummeted. First Quinn, now Joseph. Sulfuric acid and nitric acid indeed.

"Can you tell me what that point of view is?"

"There are some things worth a man's life to discuss too freely."

In Mr. Fitzgerald's clipped Irish accent, that sentence was one of the most sinister things Avivah had ever heard. "We may require further details related to your correspondence with Mrs. Nibb. Detective Alexander will be in touch with you."

"If you must."

She hung up and dialed information for New York City. By the time she had answers, she'd blown several months' worth of phone bills. The police department better reimburse her, or Pepper would hit the ceiling. She dialed one final number, thankfully local this time.

"Alexander."

She tried to imagine Nate talking on a pink princess phone, but it was no go. He'd have a heavy, black Bakelite phone, one that matched his dark suits and spit-shined shoes.

"It's Avivah. Mr. Fitzgerald called me back from Northern Ireland. He knows Joseph Kirkpatrick, but he's never heard of Kevin McCormick. Joseph could have had an opportunity to intercept Mrs. Nibb's check after it arrived in Omagh. For what it's worth, Joseph has political leanings. Mr. Fitzgerald wouldn't be more specific about what they were. The problem is, when Peter Taft was killed, Joseph was in a holding cell in New York City. The police escorted him off the plane and into detention. He stayed there until his brother negotiated his release. There's no way he could have killed Peter Taft."

"Unless he had a partner who did the killing, and that whole New York thing was a ruse to establish Joseph's alibi."

Somewhere in the twilight, beyond the closed curtains, howls went up that sounded like Indians attacking a wagon train.

She hoped Benny reveled in playing tonight. Soaked in play. Played until he collapsed. Tomorrow was not going to be a play day.

CHAPTER 20

Pepper came in the kitchen door as dawn curved a blue-and-gold outline over the mountain ridges. She wore jeans and a thick sweater. The green canvas bag, marked with a red cross, which they used for a first aid kit, hung from her shoulder.

She laid the bag on the kitchen table. "It's over," she said with such finality that she sounded as though one of her patients had died.

What was the phrase obituaries used? *Peacefully at home, after a long struggle, bravely fought.*

Pepper poured herself a cup of coffee and plopped into one of the kitchen chairs. "All present and accounted for. The bartender—who is remarkably cheerful after having slept on a cot behind the bar—is serving tomato juice, coffee, and breakfast to those able to take nourishment. You'd better prepare yourself. Saul has a pierced ear."

Avivah turned from making an omelet. "Whatever for?"

"Quite nicely done, actually. One of the medics did it. A little gold stud. It was either an induction ritual or the collective unconsciousness of fifty alcohol-soaked brains. Damn." She got up and grabbed her car keys from the peg by the door. "I've got to get away from here for a while." She ran from the house to her car, started it, and managed to back through the rows of parked cars without demolishing any of them.

Fifteen minutes later Benny and three other men walked out of the woods to the parking area. They did the male hug thing.

Avivah wondered why men felt a need to pound each other on the back so hard, as if dislodging a piece of food. One of the men tossed his gear in a car and inched out of his parking spot. With a wave and a toot of his horn he was gone, leaving a gap like a missing tooth in the row of tightly packed cars. Two of the men headed up the hill. Benny headed for the kitchen.

He was red-eyed, with a two-day growth of beard, his hair sticking out at odd angles, and grass plastered to his bald pate. "Where's Pepper?"

"Gone."

He sat down at the table and picked up Pepper's cup. "Yours," he asked.

"Pepper's. I don't think she'll be back for it."

He drank.

"What did you guys do to her down there?"

"Gassed her with testosterone—and memories. Too many unwashed soldiers. I'm not sure *I* can stand us right now. The clearing resembles a casualty clearing station, or the railway scene in *Gone With the Wind*." He drank more coffee. "So this is it, is it? The kids are right. Never trust anyone over thirty. You turn thirty-one and old age creeps in."

"You're thirty-two now."

"Oh, yeah, I forgot. It was some birthday party. I can truthfully say a good time was had by all."

Avivah put her breakfast dishes in the sink. "Does Saul really have a pierced ear?"

"It's okay. He can take the stud out today and it will heal over so you can't even see it."

Avivah wasn't convinced. She had visions of blood poisoning and Saul's ear falling off. "Whatever possessed you people to pierce his ear?"

"It's like one of those vivid dreams you can't remember after you wake up. It made sense at the time."

The sun crested the mountain, turning the day from dawn into just another Friday. Avivah unplugged the coffee pot. "I need to talk to Joseph. Did he spend the night with the rest of you?"

Watching Benny's face resembled watching a house where someone was turning on the lights one-by-one. "He was invited for supper, but he never showed up. At least Hamilton came for a while. He even tried to fit in. Soybeans weren't mentioned once. I owe him for that. Why do you need to talk to Joseph?"

"Because this thing with your mom may have a Northern Ireland connection."

Benny blinked at her, shook his head, and blinked again. "Are you saying Joseph is involved?"

"I'm saying I don't know. That's why I have to talk to him."

Benny used both hands to push himself up from the table. "I'll say my good-byes, get cleaned up, and look for Joseph. This is what really happens when you're thirty-two, isn't it? You wake up one morning and realize you *are* an adult, and the world isn't such a fun place anymore."

Wait until Quinn turned himself in. Benny was going to find out what *not a fun place* truly meant. Oh, bother! Grace had promised to bring Lorraine to the police station at ten. She and Nate were going to spend the entire day pulverizing Benny's father, fiancée, and brother.

Benny asked, "When I find Joseph, shall I bring him to the police station?"

She wished she could tell him to take Lorraine and run. Far and fast. Just get out now. "Call me. We've got a full day already."

He left. Avivah went to the door and called after him. "Benny."

He turned. "What?"

"You're one of my best friends in the whole world. I love you."

His shoulders hunched. "Joseph is in that much trouble, is he?"

She watched him walk away.

The phone rang.

"Hello."

"It's Nate. I'm glad I caught you before you left for work."

"Another ten minutes and I'd have been gone."

"Tallulah Nibb just dropped dead in the coffee shop at her motel. Meet me there."

Some people had no luck. The young waitress, Beth, who had served lunch the day before was working days today. Mrs. Nibb had died in her arms, or rather under her hands.

Avivah sat across from Beth in the same booth where they'd had lunch yesterday. A glass of water and several crumpled tissues littered the table. At least the booth's high walls muted the activity that was going on behind them, on the other side of the coffee shop.

Beth twisted a tissue. "I did CPR just like I'd learned in phys ed. I got an A. I did everything right. I know I did."

Avivah used the voice she'd practiced especially for her weeks in Community Services, her cop-as-friend voice. "I'm sure you did."

"CPR is to be used in cases of sudden and unexpected death," Beth recited. "She keeled over into her scrambled eggs. That was sudden and unexpected, wasn't it?"

"I'd say so. Mrs. Nibb was an old woman. She'd been under a lot of stress. This wasn't your fault. Whatever chance she might have had, you gave it to her."

"That's exactly what my CPR instructor told us in class."

Avivah figured it must be part of the canned lesson. "Mine, too. What you can do to help her now is help us sort out what happened. You arrived at what time?"

"Five o'clock. We open for breakfast at five-thirty."

"What time did Mrs. Nibb come in?"

"A little after five-thirty."

"Was that her usual time?"

"I don't know. I usually work the lunch shift. I only came in this morning because I traded shifts."

"Were you her waitress?"

"Yes. I brought her coffee, water, and a menu. She took her pills with the water, then she must have looked at the menu for ten minutes. I mean, our breakfast menu is only one page. How could it take someone so long to decide?"

"So it would have been about five-forty-five when she ordered?"

"About that. Maybe a few minutes later. Scrambled eggs, ham, white toast, and orange juice."

"When did you bring her food?"

"I wasn't watching the clock. We were busy by then. I brought her food when it was ready. Scrambled eggs don't take that long and her order was the second or third that I put in."

So figure the food was delivered about six A.M.

"She did all that ritual stuff. Salt. Pepper. Cream and sugar in her coffee. Cut up her ham into little pieces. Spread orange marmalade on her toast. We studied rituals in social sciences last year. That's why I was watching her. Rituals are fascinating, don't you think?"

Avivah thought about Saul's ear. She was full-up with ritual today.

"And she said grace. At least I guess that's what she did. She clasped her hands together like this and bowed her head." Beth unclasped her hands and put her fingers on either side of her mouth. "That was good, wasn't it? I mean, she was praying just before she died. That was a good thing."

"What did she do after she said grace?"

"She picked up her fork and started eating. A couple of minutes later, bang, face down in her eggs."

Nate came to the booth and worked his way in beside Avivah. Friday's suit had, perhaps, a nuance of change: wider lapels, different trouser cut. By now they all looked so much alike that Avivah didn't care. He said, "Doc's first guess is a stroke."

Beth looked brighter. "I'm glad CPR didn't work. I wouldn't want her to be paralyzed or anything."

Avivah turned back in her notes. "Beth, you mentioned that Mrs. Nibb took medicine. Was it in a medicine bottle?"

"It was in one of those little round boxes. The kind you can buy at a drug store, with the painted china top. Hers had birds on it."

Nate worked his way out of the booth again. "I'll have the uniforms search the area."

After he'd left, Avivah said, "You're going to have to come down to the police department later today and make a formal statement. Are you eighteen?"

"Seventeen."

"Then you'll have to bring a parent or guardian with you. Can you do that?"

"Sure. My mom will come. The supervisor told us all to go home anyway. They can't open the shop again until you guys get finished."

"Do you need a ride home?"

"I was going to take the bus, but a ride would be great."

Avivah picked the youngest, cutest constable to take Beth home. She still had a vague memory of being seventeen. A few minutes later, she bent down to speak to Beth through the patrol car window. "Don't call your friends, don't talk to anybody until you've given us a statement. Can you do that?"

"Could I go now and give a statement?"

Avivah guessed Beth would explode if she didn't call her

friends soon. She remembered that, too, about being seventeen. "Yes, the officer can drive you to the station, instead of home. You can phone your mom to meet you there."

Beth held out her hand. "Thank you so much for your kindness."

Avivah shook her hand. She recognized a young Pepper-in-training. Southern womanhood would continue for another generation.

She went back inside. A man stood at the check-in desk, with his back to the lobby door. "Looks like you've had a bit of excitement."

The man at the desk was Hamilton Kirkpatrick. Avivah dropped into one of the lobby chairs, grateful that the artificial foliage hid her from the desk. She used her index fingers to pry the plastic fronds open a fraction.

The desk clerk, a woman dressed in a blue blazer and red-and-blue neck scarf, said soothingly, "One of our elderly guests had a medical emergency. It's being taken care of." She handed Hamilton a leather case, the kind men carried on a trip for their toilet articles. "Here's your case. We hope you will stay with us again soon."

Hamilton handed her money. "Please give this to the chambermaid who brought it to you."

"That's not necessary, sir." Even as she said it, the woman sealed the money in an envelope and wrote something on the front.

"I know it's not, but I want to do it."

The envelope disappeared under the counter and Hamilton disappeared through the exit on the far side of the lobby.

When had Hamilton left his toilet case behind? Pepper had picked up him and Joseph at the plane Saturday morning. He'd ridden from the airport to the hospital in the ambulance with his mother, and from there, gone directly to the bed-and-breakfast. She couldn't imagine Hamilton being in Asheville at another time and not phoning or seeing his brother. But she was sure that Benny and Hamilton hadn't seen each other in a long time before this week.

Avivah picked up a promotional card from the table beside her chair. It had the hotel's phone number on it. She found a pay phone down the hall and dialed the number. The desk clerk answered.

"I'm trying to reach Hamilton Kirkpatrick. He said he was stopping by this morning to pick up his toilet case. Has he been there yet?"

"I'm sorry, he was just here moments ago. I can try to catch him in the parking lot, if you want."

"Don't bother. Maybe you can help me. I'm Mr. Kirkpatrick's secretary. We're having a problem with accounts payable. They refuse to reimburse Mr. Kirkpatrick's travel expenses because the dates on the invoice he submitted don't match the dates on the receipt you gave him. Could you verify the dates he checked in and out?"

"I'm not supposed to give out that information."

Today, of all days, Avivah didn't have time to apply for a warrant.

"I know you're not, but I'm trying to clear my desk so I can leave on vacation. My husband is home right now packing the car. The kids will drive him crazy if I don't get home soon." She considered adding a colicky baby, but there was no sense overplaying her hand.

"Are you going any place special?"

"Disney World."

"We have a lovely motel in Orlando. If you haven't already booked your reservations, we'd love to have you stay with us."

Avivah turned the card over. On the back was a list of other motels in the chain. "As a matter of fact, we *are* staying at your hotel. The one that's only a mile-and-a-half from the front gate. Mr. Kirkpatrick was so complimentary about your service, we picked it as our first choice."

"Thank you for staying with us. Just a moment, I'll see if I can find those dates."

A little flattery would get you somewhere.

She was back in less than a minute. "I have a copy of his reservation right here. Thursday, May thirty, Murfreesboro, Tennessee, one night. Friday, May thirty-first, Asheville, North Carolina, one night. Ah, I see the confusion. He missed his night in Murfreesboro and was here instead on Thursday. Then, with that awful thing that happened to his mother, he checked out shortly after twelve noon on Friday. Is his mother all right? I didn't want to ask."

With a dry mouth, Avivah managed, "Yes, his mother is recovering."

"I'm glad. Would you like me to mail an amended stay sheet to Mr. Kirkpatrick's business address? I see we have it on file."

"Thank you. That would help."

Avivah hung up. Her coin clinked deep inside the phone. Hamilton Kirkpatrick had been in Asheville the night Peter Taft was killed. He had planned to be in Murfreesboro the day before. She hoped they grew lots of soybeans around Murfreesboro. If they didn't—maybe even if they did—Hamilton Kirkpatrick was suddenly in a shit-load of trouble.

CHAPTER 21

Pepper tried to ignore the colorful recruiting posters. Photographs of young men—and the rare woman—dressed in crisp duty uniforms stressed mental challenges, seeing more of the world than your home town, and a positive, meaningful, productive way to spend the next two years. In her day, posters featured men rappelling from helicopters and sweat-stained officers yelling "Follow me!" It just wasn't the same, though a couple of years' enlistment for mental challenges no doubt produced fewer body bags. Be grateful for small mercies.

Two recruiting sergeants in uniform looked from their desks. The slightly older man stood. "Can I help you, ma'am?"

"I'd like to see Colonel Baxter, if he's available."

"Yes, ma'am, who shall I say is calling?"

"Elizabeth Pepperhawk."

The man walked down a short hall and knocked on a door. He opened the door. "Elizabeth Pepperhawk to see you, sir." The man beckoned to her. "Right this way, ma'am."

It was a miniscule office. Pepper wondered if it had started life as a closet. Darby didn't stand as she closed the door. He was working at a bare desk that contained only a telephone and a yellow legal pad. The poster in this room proclaimed *Today's Army has a lot more to offer.*

"If you've come to reenlist, we're full up on our quota of nurses." He threw his pen on the desk and turned the yellow pad face down. "Who am I kidding? We'd take you back in a heartbeat."

Pepper sat on the edge of a gray metal folding chair, and tucked her purse under the chair. Her knees touched Darby's desk. "If you'd said that to me an hour ago, I'd have raised my right hand and sworn to 'support and defend the Constitution of the United States against all enemies, foreign and domestic . . .' "

Darby's eyes narrowed. "What happened an hour ago?"

"I took a swing through the clearing this morning before dawn. Just to see if everyone was breathing, you understand." Her voice wavered. "You know the way men smell when they've worn a set of fatigues too long? They . . . I . . ."

"You had a flashback, didn't you?"

Pepper rubbed the heels of her hands across her eyelids. "I didn't know they came in a kaleidoscopic version."

He leaned forward. "You want coffee or something?"

"I want a double-shot of bourbon, neat, and a coke chaser, with lots of ice."

Darby picked up the phone and punched one of the buttons. "Sergeant, would you mind going next door to the cafe? Get me an RC cola and a moon pie, please. Thank you."

Southern first aid.

When the food arrived, Darby set it on the desk in front of her. "Eat."

She did as he commanded. It would be nice to take refuge in a time when life's problems could be solved by a huge hit of sugar, carbonated water, chocolate, graham crackers, and marshmallow cream.

Pepper wiped her hands on a paper napkin and threw both it and the moon pie wrapper in the garbage can. "I didn't come to reenlist. I came to listen. It's past time that you and I stopped dancing around one another and started listening to one another. Tell me about Nancy and the trouble she's in."

"Why this sudden interest?"

"You know what happens when a car is stuck in a ditch and the drive spins your tires?"

"Eventually, you burn out your clutch."

"My clutch is burned out. I'm tired, and I don't want us to go on like this. You deserve the courtesy of a hearing."

Darby's clear, blue eyes played a game of visual chicken with her. He blinked first. "I believe that Nancy is under house arrest in Hanoi."

He believed. So this wasn't a generally accepted theory. Pepper got more comfortable in her chair. "Why isn't the State Department doing something about it?"

"I don't think they know she's there. Their official line is that Dr. Waine-Baxter is on extended leave."

"If the office of one of the most powerful men in the world doesn't know where one of their own employees is, how did Sandra?"

"Nancy sent her a letter from Hong Kong. She wrote that she was going to Hanoi. Sandra thought her cousin was on one of her usual State Department junkets."

"Why is Nancy under house arrest?"

"I can only guess. Nancy speaks Vietnamese, French, enough Chinese to get by, and a smattering of indigenous dialects. She was at the wrong meeting, saw the wrong documents, somehow got access to information she shouldn't have. Very soon, the man in the Oval Office is going to have to be told that one of his CIA interpreters, with top-level security clearance, is missing. Once the U.S. government officially makes enquiries, she is going to disappear without a trace."

"Don't you mean State Department?"

"What?"

"You said CIA. A CIA interpreter."

"That just shows you how upset I am."

Pepper studied him, looking for any twitch of body language that said that Darby wasn't telling the truth. There weren't any. Maybe it had been a slip of the tongue.

"This can't be happening. Regular, ordinary people don't end up under house arrest in Hanoi."

"You and I—and Nancy—gave up being regular, ordinary people a long time ago."

"Not me. I'm your average nurse and homeowner."

Darby prompted, "To those who fight for it . . ."

". . . life has a flavor the protected never know," Pepper finished without hesitation.

She'd never seen the sentiment on a recruiting poster, but it was a code a lot of good soldiers, including Darby and Benny, lived by.

Darby leaned forward, with his elbows on the desk, interlocked his hands, and pointed his index fingers at her. "Do *you* believe what you just said?"

"I've hung around you and Benny long enough that it's probably engraved on my heart, whether or not I believe it. Oh, hell, yes, I admit to being brainwashed. I believe it."

"Completely and without reservation?"

"Yes."

"Nancy doesn't. Whatever reason motivated her to get into this mess, it will turn out to be some piss-ant reason that benefits Nancy first. *The world revolves around me* is one of the less charming characteristics women in the Waine family share."

"Why bother rescuing her?"

"For the same reasons you don't walk away from a patient who's a smoker, or a wife-beater, or creamed a car full of teenagers because he was drunk out of his mind."

"I don't like all my patients."

"And I don't like all of the people I deal with, but getting people out of tight spots is what I do. I'm good at it. If Nancy wasn't my ex-wife, if I told you that an American woman, a diplomat, was secretly under house arrest in Hanoi, that she might be killed, and that I'd been assigned to get her out if I could, what would you say?"

"I'd say go. Do your job. But, no one has asked you to do this, and neither of us can ignore that she *is* your ex-wife. As long as we're using the nurse–patient analogy, I would take myself off a case like a shot if the patient were a relative or close friend."

"In other words, because she's my ex-wife, I shouldn't go."

"Of course you shouldn't, but that's not going to stop you. So go, but take me with you."

The words sprung from Pepper's mouth without her permission. The Army had a phrase about volunteering: Never let your iron head overrule your eggshell ass. She hoped the room wasn't so small that Darby could hear her eggshell ass cracking. Under no circumstances did she want to go to Hanoi.

"What about your job?"

"You have to be back at the Pentagon in three weeks, so I assume all of this has to go down by then. I'll work something out, use all of my vacation time, maybe a leave of absence. If Nancy can take one, I can, too."

Apparently the iron head was still in charge.

Darby rubbed his chin. "Us traveling together opens up possibilities I hadn't considered before. Let me think about it."

Pepper grabbed her purse from under the chair. She had to leave. Poster propaganda had seeped into her brain, activating some dormant alien military virus, like in those science fiction movies. "In the meantime, you can take me to breakfast. The snack was nice, but I'm starving for real food."

Darby picked up his yellow pad and stuffed it in a vinyl folder, which he zipped shut. "You're sure about not reenlisting? Your old rank back, no loss of seniority. I can guarantee you a place in staff school within six months."

Completing staff school was a requirement to be promoted from captain to major. Only lifers went to staff school. But he had to be joking, surely?

"And while you're waiting for that opening, you could see some of the world. Hawaii. Panama. Japan. Germany. You could have your choice of assignment. Think of it as a holiday with paid accommodations."

She tried not to read too much into the fact that he hadn't suggested Washington, D.C. Walter Reed Army Hospital was just down the road from the Pentagon. They could be neighbors. Darby sounded more like a recruiter all the time. The military virus in his brain had been activated, too. She had to get him out of here, permanently.

They went down the short hall. On the sign-in board, Darby moved a magnetic dot beside his name from "In" to "Out." He'd been using the office four days, and they had already put his name on the sign-out board. Getting him out of here might even be worth a trip to Hanoi. Pepper wondered if her passport was still valid.

Avivah glanced out of Nate's office window. In the public parking lot down the block from the police station, Benny, Lorraine, and Ginny Mae climbed out of Benny's pickup. The rest of his family emerged from a car, and Lawyer Ferguson from a second car.

Avivah rubbed her hand across the wire-reinforced window, clearing an oval big enough to see them better. Quinn and Grace held hands, Lorraine was on Grace's right, Benny on Quinn's left. Joseph, Ginny Mae, and Hamilton—also holding hands— formed the second row. It reminded her of a children's game. Red rover, red rover. From the way everyone stood tall, marching in step, no one would be able to break through those lines. John Ferguson brought up the rear, clutching his leather note-case to his chest as though it was a Bible carried by an Old West preacher.

"Nate, we got company."

He came to the window. "Company, hell. I feel like Wyatt Earp watching the Clantons and McLaureys arrive in Tomb-stone. Tell Claiborn to put them in the big conference room."

"You're not going to interview them all at once, are you?"

"I need a place to store them while we make it through their individual statements."

Avivah flipped the intercom switch. "Claiborn?"

"Yes, ma'am." The dispatcher hadn't called her *Rover* once this week.

"There is a large group of people coming to see Detective Alexander. Please have someone show them to the big confer-ence room."

Nate cocked his hip and sat on the corner of his desk. "You know about horses and zebras?"

"No."

"When a patient comes to a doctor with a set of symptoms, the doctor looks for the horse—the most common illness—first. After he exhausts the simple possibilities, he looks for zebras—the weird diagnoses. What's our horse?"

"Peter Tate injected himself and died of a heart attack. Quinn Kirkpatrick came along later, tidied up, put Peter's body in the trunk, and drove Grace, and the body, to the airport. Suicide or accidental death, with Quinn being an accessory after the fact."

"Mrs. Nibb's death?"

"Natural causes."

"The zebra?"

"Both deaths premeditated and unrelated. Two killers: one who injected Taft and one who did something to Mrs. Nibb's pills to cause a stroke. Quinn is still guilty of two felony counts: concealment of death and larceny of goods over one thousand dollars."

"How about if Quinn had help, maybe took one of his kids or Lorraine with him to the motel?"

"How about if he took all of them, like that murder mystery where everyone on the train was part of the conspiracy?"

They looked at one another and laughed. Nate said, "I like a partner who can visualize a whole herd of zebras."

Avivah's fingernail made a metallic click as she tapped her badge. "Uniformed constable. Your driver, not your partner."

"How'd you like to be my permanent driver? Detective-in-training. I've watched you this week. You're good and you could get better. We could start this morning by dividing up the interviews."

"What about your regular driver?"

"Maybe it's time he went back on the street."

For the past five days, Avivah had felt protected, almost cosseted. No standing role call with the rest of the constables, watching them smirk at her with their *we're-going-to-get-you* looks. No jibes or bloody raw bones from Claiborn Dexter. "You mean promote me ahead of male constables because I'm a woman?"

"It's called Affirmative Action. It's all the rage. Everyone is doing it."

Not her. She didn't need Affirmative Action. She had brains and talent and being a Viet Nam veteran on her side.

In one clarifying moment, this week made sense. "You, the chief, and Ollie cooked this up. The chief could get a lot of publicity out of a first female detective-in-training, without really making me responsible for anything I might screw up. But, you good-old boys guessed wrong. I'm not playing. I will not use my gender as a weapon. I won't work with you, and I won't work with Ollie again. If that relegates me to permanent Community Services, so be it. If I have to go back into that stupid dog suit, I'll do it."

"Don't penalize Ollie."

He hadn't said she was wrong.

There was a knock on the door.

Nate growled, "Come in."

John Ferguson entered. "I'm John Ferguson. We met when you interviewed Grace . . . Avivah, what are you doing here?"

Nate stepped between them. Hell, first Affirmative Action, now he was acting as though she needed physical protection. There was no way she was coming back as Detective Alexander's driver next week. She'd turn in her badge first.

Nate said, "She's my driver."

Watching her lawyer's face was like listening to safe tumblers click into place. She knew all of the Kirkpatricks. Click. She'd shared a house with Benny. Click. John Ferguson would see all of this as a big-time conflict of interest. Click. Except that she could give a rat's ass. She'd done her job well and there hadn't been any conflict of interest as far as she was concerned. An imaginary hand reached out and twirled the safe dial back into its locked position.

"Has she been present at any time during your investigation of the matters surrounding Peter Taft?" As he spoke, his eastern North Carolina drawl became more pronounced.

"She's been everywhere I've been."

And she was damned proud of that, even if Nate and Ollie had cooked it up.

"This conflict of interest is intolerable. I will not have my clients subjected to this kind of subterfuge. I will be petitioning for another detective to be assigned to the Taft investigation, and I will advise my clients to make no statements until that detective has been assigned." He turned to Avivah. "Miss Rosen, in addition, I am sorry to inform you that I am no longer your lawyer of record."

Avivah was sorry about that. For all of his old boy pretense, she knew that John Ferguson was a good lawyer. As for the other, now she could relax. It was Friday morning. There was no way another detective could be assigned to the case before Monday. Next week might be hell-on-wheels, but Benny and Lorraine could get married without worrying about Quinn being in custody.

Nate depressed the button in the intercom. "Claiborn, it's Detective Alexander. Send a couple of constables to the big conference room. I want Quinn Kirkpatrick taken into custody for questioning immediately."

Avivah glanced between Nate and Lawyer Ferguson. She had, at most, only a couple of minutes to prepare the Kirkpatricks for what was about to happen. Conflict of interest be damned, she was still their friend. She ran down the wide stairs, her duty boots slipping on the marble floor. As she reached the conference room, two officers came from the opposite end of the building.

She pushed open the door. Everyone seated around the table turned. "Quinn is about to be taken into custody. The rest of you stay calm. Meet me at Mrs. Somerset's house, without your lawyer," was all she had time for before one of the officers pushed her aside.

"Quinn Kirkpatrick?"

He stood. Grace reached over and took his hand. "I'm Quinn."

"Keep your hands visible, sir, and move away from the table. Lean forward, put your hands on the wall, feet apart."

Quinn complied. One of the policemen patted him down, while the other one stood about three feet away, with his hand resting on his gun butt.

257

"You have the right to remain silent . . ."

Avivah fled. She found the duty sergeant leaning on the reception counter, talking to Claiborn.

"I'm booking off sick."

He frowned. "You didn't say anything about being sick when you signed in this morning."

"It came on me suddenly. The details are delicate. Shall I describe them for you?"

The sergeant's face turned bright red. "Get the hell out of here."

"I doubt I'll feel well enough to work Monday either. You'd better find Detective Alexander another driver for next week."

As she pushed open the station's front doors, Claiborn said, "I told you this would happen when we hired her."

Wouldn't use her gender, ha! She'd show Nate Alexander some affirmative action.

CHAPTER 22

Through the open lace curtains in Grace's room, Avivah watched a black man ride a lawnmower around the lawn in ever-decreasing circles. Sunshine and odors of gasoline and cut grass filled the room. Avivah doubted anyone in the room had enough energy left to appreciate summer. She didn't.

Ginny Mae sprawled on the bed with her back propped against the headboard. Hamilton brought two chairs from the hall for himself and Joseph. Joseph turned his around so the back of the chair formed a barrier between himself and the rest of the room.

Lorraine seated herself in the chair by the window, with Benny crouched at her feet. Avivah had seen him crouch Vietnamese style dozens of times, but today it looked awkward. What Pepper had said earlier this morning came back to her. "It's over." Some bond between Benny and Viet Nam had irrevocably broken at the party last night.

Grace sat on the edge of her bed, fingering the chenille trim. "Is there any possibility that Quinn can still be at the wedding?"

Avivah paced the small, open space in the middle of the room. "A small one. If Quinn is charged only with concealment of death, there's a good chance Mr. Ferguson can get him released on bail immediately."

Ginny Mae appeared overly interested in loose cuticles on her nails. She didn't look up when she asked, "What about accessory after the fact?"

Avivah wondered how much cop TV Ginny Mae watched. "There may or may not have been a *fact* to be an accessory to. Peter Taft died of a heart attack. Shortly before he died, he either injected himself or someone injected him with drugs. There's no proof that those drugs contributed to his death. Mr. Ferguson will argue that the two events were unrelated, and that the only crime was moving the body. What complicates Quinn's situation is that three of you in this room have not come forward with evidence."

In the movies, the camera would jump from face to face accompanied by diabolic background music. Here, everyone just looked tired. The lawnmower sound died in a sputter, leaving only a disagreeable blue jay that squawked his displeasure from some distant tree. Avivah sided with the bird. "Your coming forward may make a difference in the charges Quinn faces. Please, if you have some connection to Peter Taft that you have held back, go to Detective Alexander immediately. The time for secrets is past."

Lorraine's hand slipped into the pocket of her sundress. She reached for Benny's hand and put something into it, closing his fingers over the object. A loop of metal chain hung like a tongue from his closed fist.

"I'm sorry, Ben. I gave Peter Taft our house money."

Benny opened his fist. Avivah saw what he held was a set of dog tags.

"Where did these come from?"

"Peter Taft." Lorraine cried without a sound. Tears sheeted down her cheeks, turning her makeup into pink-and-black rivulets. "He showed me a movie of his son, who is alive in a North Vietnamese POW camp. He says there are eight men still alive in the North, and Randall is one of them."

Marsenia Pullins had seen Taft show a movie. Frannie had said Taft had a rough streak in him. How hard would it be to fake a film supposedly of someone in a POW camp? But why would a father, even one who hadn't seen his son in years, do that? A movie like that wasn't roughness, it was perversity.

Benny closed his eyes and ran his thumb around the edges of both tags. "These aren't Randall's."

Lorraine sucked in a wet breath. "How can you be sure? They have the right mistake."

Benny handed the tags to Avivah. She saw what Lorraine meant about a mistake. Randall was listed as having two religions. The Army processed dog tags by the thousands. Mistakes crept in.

Benny shifted painfully in his crouch, gave up and sat down hard on the floor. He pulled first one knee, then the other to him, and rubbed his calf muscles. "A couple of weeks before Randall went missing, a guy pulled a knife on him in a MIKE Force bar in Kontum. Randall's only injury was a little cut across his chest, but the knife nicked one of his dog tags. These don't have a nick."

Avivah added her own name to the list of people with a secret. The man who had attacked Randall was Benny. In a drunken rage he had taken a knife to his best friend and he hadn't found the courage to apologize before Randall went missing. Benny had vowed he would never tell Lorraine about the fight.

Hamilton said, "Maybe he got the tags replaced."

"Not possible in Kontum, and dog tags don't heal. Even if the spot had worn smooth over the years, there would still be a mark."

Lorraine wiped at her eyes, transferring the makeup glop to her hands. "You're not saying that to make me feel better?"

Heedless of the muck, Benny took her hand. "You have my word that these can't possibly be Randall's tags."

Avivah asked, "How did Peter Taft contact you?"

261

"We met at that MIA family workshop, in February. Taft came up to me after my speech. He introduced himself as the father of an MIA pilot. We exchanged addresses and phone numbers. He phoned me in May to say he would be in town and that he had something he wanted me to see."

"Where did the two of you meet?"

"Some strange motel in Swannanoa. He had a home movie projector and this movie—about five or six minutes long—that showed . . ." She drew another ragged breath. "That showed things I wish I'd never seen. Taft said that the person who had smuggled out the film also smuggled out eight sets of dog tags belonging to men who were still alive. He never asked me for money. I had to force him to take it."

Of course she had. That's the way good cons worked. "Did you give him a check?"

"Cash. Three thousand dollars."

Benny winced. "It's okay, babe. We can always save more money."

If their timeline for the last couple of weeks of Taft's life was correct, he hadn't gone back to Murfreesboro. They had found no money, movie projector or film in the motel room, in Taft's car, or in his belongings. What happened to them? "Lorraine, this speech you gave. Did you mention Randall's dog tags in it? Use them to illustrate a point or as an anecdote?"

"No."

"You're sure?"

"Positive. I can show you the speech. Only—"

"Only what?"

"I did write about them in a journal I kept for a while. I was trying to remember everything I could about Randall. For the boys, for later, if they ever asked me about their father."

"Did you write about the mistake on the tags?"

"Yes."

"Has anyone but you ever seen that journal?"

"I showed it to Frannie. She didn't read it, just thumbed through it, and said she was glad I'd kept it."

Frannie again. "Was this before or after you met Taft?"

"A month after. That weekend we moved from Pepper's place into our trailer. Frannie helped us move. I found the diary as I was packing boxes, and showed it to her."

Benny stood awkwardly. "I'm taking Lorraine home. Flat out, Avivah, am I one of the people you think hasn't been honest with the police? If I am, I've no damned idea what you believe I'm holding back, but if it will help Da, I'll turn myself in this minute."

"No, Benny, not you."

Everyone stood, hugged, and moved chairs aside to make space for Lorraine and Benny to leave. Hamilton looked at his watch. Joseph shifted uneasily from side to side. Grace dug in her purse for money. "Hamilton, take your brother and sister and find lunch for us. I think I saw a general store down the road toward Asheville. Even if you can only get cheese, crackers, and fruit, that will tide us over. I'd like a Coke, if you can find one."

The other three Kirkpatrick children left. Grace snapped her purse shut. The sound echoed in the room. "Quinn told me about the photographs," Grace said.

"I'm sorry, what photographs?"

"I guess Pepper didn't tell you. The ones that would be motive enough for Quinn to kill Peter Taft." She sat down in the straight-backed chair Hamilton had occupied. "I'm sorry, I'm not telling this well."

Avivah turned around the chair Joseph had used and sat in it. "At this point, none of us are well. Start at the beginning. Hell, start anywhere that makes any sense at all, and I'll try to follow you."

"Where did you grow up?"

Okay, that made no sense, but Avivah had promised to follow. "Schenectady, New York."

"Is that a small town or a city?"

"A city."

"Until I was fifteen, I lived in Alaskan bush camps. Life was catch-as-you-can. All my schooling was by correspondence courses. My family lived more by seasons and the weather than by rules. When I turned fifteen, my parents sent me to board in Anchorage so I could go to high school. All of a sudden, there were rules: what I could wear, what time I had to be in, where I could go in town, and who I could see. By the time I was seventeen, I was a hell-cat. The surest way to make Grace Hamilton do something was to tell her that she shouldn't do it."

"Hamilton was your maiden name?"

"Yes. My best friend had as little sense as I did. We were healthy seventeen-year-olds, whose greatest pleasure was to get away with everything we could."

Avivah grinned. "Even in Schenectady, I could relate to that."

"Guys had pin-up girls in their work sheds. We dared each other to pose like that; one July we borrowed a camera, and bought a few bottles of wine—Dutch courage. We went into the bush where no one could see us and tried to imitate the poses we'd seen."

"The more wine you drank, the more outrageous the poses got?"

"I'm afraid so."

"Who developed the film?"

"We did, in the high school dark room. Do you have any idea what Alaskan mosquitoes are like? We should have looked like lumpy pieces of dough, but we didn't. Keep in mind, for all my sass, I was raised a good Catholic girl. When I saw those photos, I was sure we would burn in hell for what we'd done. We agreed to destroy everything, but I guess my friend didn't do that."

"How did Quinn see the photos?"

"Peter Taft showed them to him; he—Peter, not Quinn—sold them to soldiers building the Alaska Highway. I was mortified when Quinn told me. All these years, I allowed Quinn to believe that he introduced me to Peter, but I'd known Peter for years." She bent double and covered her face with her hands. "I'm so ashamed."

Avivah smoothed her hand over Grace's back. "We all do things at seventeen that mortify us later."

Grace straightened her back vertebra by vertebra. Lines covered her face and small jowls sagged. For the first time Avivah thought she looked old.

"The photographs weren't all. Peter Taft raped me."

The physical exam at the hospital hadn't shown any signs of rape, but it was possible that she had showered between the rape and when she was taken to the hospital on Saturday. "Last Friday?"

"April 17, 1940. In a shed beside the runway at Northway. All these years, until last night, I wondered what I'd done wrong to make him do that. It was those damned pictures. It was all my fault."

If Avivah had known this was coming, she'd have opened one of those silver evidence boxes in her head. But she hadn't and Grace's pain spilled over her. It couldn't be shut out now. "Stop that. You didn't cause your own rape. Rape is a crime of violence and power, not sex."

"Hamilton was conceived as a result of that rape. He's Peter Taft's son."

Avivah had to force out, "Does Quinn know that?"

"No one knows but me."

"Hamilton doesn't know?"

"Of course not."

"Did Peter know?"

"No."

"Your first husband, did he know?"

"He knew I was pregnant, but not about the rape or who the father was. He was an older man, my dad's chief mechanic. I'd known him all my life. He married me to give Hamilton a name. That's how they spoke of it back then. We were only married nineteen days before he died in an accident, but that was long enough to protect my reputation. Everyone assumed Hamilton had been conceived on our honeymoon."

Rings on Grace's fingers bit into Avivah's flesh as she clutched Avivah's hand. "You said three people in this room hadn't come forward. Lorraine and I have confessed our secrets. Please tell me which one of my children is the third person. I have to know if it's Hamilton who hasn't come forward."

Hamilton and Joseph. Avivah had miscounted. She hadn't known Grace held a secret, too.

"I can't tell you."

"You said no when Benny asked. If it hadn't been Hamilton, you would have said no straight out about him, too. Whatever Hamilton knows, he has to come forward. Of all my children, he always kept secrets best. If I have to shock him into telling the truth, I'll do it, but I don't have enough courage to do it alone. Get Quinn out on bail. If we're together, I'll find a way to tell both of them. You're right, the time for secrets has passed."

Son for father. Free Quinn, arrest Hamilton. No matter how this played out, someone would not be at the wedding tomorrow.

Half an hour later, in the bed-and-breakfast's chintz parlor, Avivah dialed with one hand and placed her other hand protectively over the end of her night stick, lest it accidentally damage one of the china dogs or shepherdesses that covered every horizontal surface.

Through the beveled glass doors, she saw the three Kirk-patrick children return. Hamilton and Joseph carried brown paper grocery bags; Ginny Mae, a six-pack of Cokes. If Avivah were in Grace's place, she'd have wanted more than cheese and crackers—a good stiff drink, for a start. A calligraphic card on a sideboard read, *Devon Cream Tea from 4 to 5; sherry and biscuits at 5:30.* She wondered if Mrs. Somerset might consider starting the sherry party early.

"Detective Division, Alexander."

"It's Avivah."

He said, "Just a minute," then a muffled, "Would you mind waiting outside? I have to take this call."

There was another pause, during which Avivah heard a door close.

Nate demanded, "Where are you?"

"At the bed-and-breakfast with the Kirkpatricks."

"Why the hell did you book off sick without telling me? I don't need a smirking duty sergeant saying, 'I told you so.' Has it occurred to you that Ollie and I are sticking our necks out for you? For God's sakes, you're thirty-two years old."

Avivah knocked a note pad off the miniscule telephone table, bent to pick it up, and stopped her nightstick just before it decapitated a shepherdess. "What the hell does my age—like my gender—have to do with anything?"

"By the time I was your age, I was a sergeant and a shift supervisor."

"Big deal."

"You've been out of the Army almost a year, and you haven't even made it back to beat cop yet."

Avivah stood, stretching the phone cord tight. She unhooked her gun belt, wrapped the belt into a circle, and put it on the floor at her feet. Being armed was a disadvantage in this room.

"I was a shift supervisor, too, and a lot of other things in the Army."

"What have you done as a civilian?"

Avivah waited for a sharp retort to flow over her tongue, but nothing came. What had she done as a civilian? Worked as a hospital security guard? Dressed as a dog? Shuttled back and forth between two dead-end assignments?

"You're smart, tough, and a good cop, but if you don't kick-start your career soon, it's going to be game over for you as a police officer."

"Why are you and Ollie so interested in my career?"

"Good cops give other good cops a hand up."

"The old boys' network?"

"Maybe some of us have decided to join the twentieth century and be more inclusive. If our situation was reversed, would you help me only if I was a white, Jewess cop?"

Avivah thought about Specialist Ramerez, a Hispanic cop she'd worked with at Ft. Bragg. She'd promised him they would keep in touch. She didn't even have an address for him. "No." She toed at her holster. "Cut Quinn loose. Either don't charge him or make sure he's out on bail this afternoon."

"Why?"

"Grace needs Quinn. Come on, Nate, how much of a flight risk is he between now and Monday?"

"That's for a judge to decide. All right, I'll cut him loose, and I'll put you down for half a day's leave for the wedding. Get your tail in here first thing Monday morning."

Avivah felt herself blush at just thinking what the duty sergeant might have written on the roster's *Reason for absence* column. Could she, Ollie, and Nate actually be on the same side?

The black man who had been mowing sat on a folding chair in the shade. He mopped his face and neck with a bandana.

One of the staff brought him lunch. He picked up a sweating Mason jar, tilted his head back and drank.

Clothes made the man, and his sweat-stained clothes gave Avivah an idea. She went to find Mrs. Somerset, whom she located in a tiny office off the kitchen.

"The man mowing your yard. Is he your regular gardener?"

"Why?"

"I'm trying to find a man who works as a day laborer or a gardener. White man, late fifties, gray hair, always wears overalls, a work shirt and a straw hat. Talks like a preacher." She did her best to make up a man she'd never seen alive.

"Why are you interested in him?"

"He may have been involved in a confidence scheme that targeted old people."

"I can't imagine Paul involved in anything criminal."

Avivah's heart beat faster as she closed the door and sat down. Peter. Paul. At least Peter Taft had stuck to the apostles. "Tell me about Paul."

"He was a God-send. My regular gardener broke his leg, and then teenagers vandalized my garden a few days before the Kirkpatricks were due to arrive. I was desperate by the time Paul showed up."

"Had you advertised for a gardener?"

"I'd put up a notice at the general store and in the church bulletin."

"Was there anything suspicious about how your gardener broke his leg?"

"He tripped over a root and fell in a ditch. A man his age shouldn't be flying kites with his grandchildren."

"How long was it between his accident and when Paul showed up?"

"About three weeks."

Long enough for Taft to nose around and discover the vacant

position. It was awfully convenient that Mrs. Somerset's garden had been vandalized shortly before Paul applied for a job. She wouldn't put it past Taft to create his own job opportunity. How had he known that the Kirkpatricks would be at this bed-and-breakfast in the first place? "What was Paul's last name?"

"He was cagey about that. Travelers often are."

"Travelers?"

"That's what we call them in England. Men on the move, who don't mind working, but don't stay long in one place."

"Do you remember the date he showed up?"

"The last Sunday in May, right at dinner time. It's been a long time since I've seen that old trick. Knock on the back door at mealtime, especially on a Sunday, and even if there's no work, the lady will feed you before she sends you on your way. Worked every time with my mother."

"Did Paul give you his address?"

"I didn't ask. Chances were he was sleeping rough, and I didn't want to embarrass him. He was clean, polite, sober, and willing to work on a Sunday. I hired him on the spot. He was a hard worker, for as long as he was here. Came early, stayed late, and kept out of the guests' way. I liked that."

"You said, 'for as long as he was here.' How long did he work for you?"

"Five days."

If Peter/Paul was hired on the last Sunday in May, the five days he worked would have covered the time between the Kirkpatricks' arrival in Asheville and Grace's kidnapping. "Did he ever speak to the Kirkpatricks?"

"I told him right off, seen and not heard. Never a word to the guests, just a tip of his hat."

Grace or Quinn would have been hard pressed to recognized a gardener—dressed in overalls and a straw hat—as their old acquaintance, Peter Taft. "Do you remember the date he didn't show up for work?"

"Friday, May thirty-first. Haven't heard from him since. I'm not surprised he took off, but it does worry me a little. He had wages coming. One thing about travelers: they always collect their wages before they move along." Mrs. Somerset pointed to a small, brown box. "I put his money aside, and a few wearable clothes. I expect he'll be back one day to collect."

Avivah wouldn't bet on it. "Friday evening, a wedding present was delivered for Quinn Kirkpatrick. Were you here when it arrived?"

"Yes."

"Do you remember what time it was delivered?"

"About seven o'clock, maybe a few minutes afterward. Two young men in a pickup truck brought the box to the door."

"Did they know who Quinn was?"

"I don't think so. One of them read his name off the envelope."

"Did you recognize either man?"

"No."

"Were they a delivery service? Was there a company name on their truck?"

"Just a plain pickup truck."

"Can you remember anything about them or the truck?"

"It had a parking tag for the Veterans' Hospital."

"Pisgah Mountain Hospital?"

"Yes."

Frannie Maddox worked at Pisgah Mountain. Come to think of it, so did Pepper.

When Avivah arrived home, the first thing she noticed was that only one car, Saul's, remained. The only clue that there had been fifty people here twenty-four hours ago was crushed grass and tire ruts. It reminded Avivah of a school parking lot in

August, with a gone-to-seed look.

Saul, dressed in shorts and a T-shirt, sat at the kitchen table, thumbing idly through the Asheville paper. Avivah took his chin in her hand and turned his head, so she could see the gold ball. Other than his left ear lobe looking pink and slightly swollen, his pierced ear did look good.

"You going to keep the stud in?"

"I think so."

"Why?"

"Souvenir."

"Of what?"

He rotated the ball slowly. "Being accepted as part of the group. I've felt alone and abandoned the past couple of days."

She sat down opposite him. "I haven't exactly been a fountain of support the past few days. How are you?"

He shrugged. With his tall, bony frame he resembled a bird doing a weird mating dance. "Surviving."

"Have you thought about what you're going to do? Not that we mind having you here. You're welcome to stay as long as you want."

He patted her hand. "Thanks. I have a few feelers out, talked to a couple of fellow journalists. Something will turn up."

"Do good reporters help other reporters with a leg up?"

"Unfortunately, no. Good reporters often look at someone's misfortune as their opportunity. But good friends might help each other out, even if that friend is another reporter. Why?"

"A conversation I had with Nate today."

Pepper came into the kitchen, thumbing through a passport. "Thank goodness, it's good for another year."

Avivah got up and got glasses and milk. "You planning a trip?"

Pepper put the passport in her dress pocket. "Darby and I might be."

Saul moved his paper, so Avivah could put the milk and glasses on the table. She said, "I thought he was taking you to meet his family. Georgia hasn't seceded from the union again, has it?"

Saul turned to the paper's front page. "It didn't make the headlines."

Pepper sat casually at the table and busied herself filling the glasses. She got up to find napkins and the cookie tin. Avivah knew that behavior. When Pepper didn't want to talk about something, one way she avoided it was to go into hostess mode.

"Pepper?"

Pepper popped open the cookie tin. The smell of homemade chocolate chip cookies filled the kitchen. Avivah realized she'd missed lunch. She took three cookies.

"Change of plans. We thought we might try a more exotic destination."

"You're not eloping, are you?"

"Whatever gave you that idea?"

"All this wedding atmosphere. Just so you realize, I'm going to be very, very ticked off at both of you if you elope. I'd pay a substantial admission price to watch Colonel Darby Baxter promise to love, honor and obey someone other than his commanding officer."

"I don't think he loves his commanding officer."

"You are avoiding giving me a straight answer."

"We aren't planning to elope, okay?"

"So where are you going? Hawaii? Tahiti? Europe?"

Two white paneled vans, with *Party Rentals* emblazoned on their sides, pulled up into the parking area, followed by a station wagon. Four young men clambered out of the vans, and the same number of middle-age women milled around the station wagon.

Pepper screeched and put her hands to the sides of her head.

"The marquees! The refrigerator!" She flung the refrigerator door open and grabbed containers, two at a time. Avivah dug two plastic milk crates from behind the freezer.

Saul and his paper backed into a corner. "What's going on?"

As fast as Pepper took containers from the fridge, Avivah loaded them into crates. She said, "The rental company is here to set up wedding marquees. Those women are the Luck and Trust Volunteer Fire Department Auxiliary. They're catering the rehearsal dinner tonight. We promised them an empty refrigerator, but with everything else, we forgot."

Pepper picked up a crate. "As of right now, this kitchen is officially off-limits until Sunday morning. The Volunteer Auxiliary will be here tonight, and the caterers all day tomorrow. Frannie has that old refrigerator in her studio. We can stuff food in there. It won't hurt us to eat cold leftovers for one day."

Avivah hoisted the second crate. Wedding frenzy was upon them. Murder would have to wait.

CHAPTER 23

As Pepper unlocked the door to Frannie's studio, the loose lid on her casserole dish slid open. A tuna-and-onion perfume wafted around her face. Pepper flipped the light switch and stepped inside. Saul and Avivah crowded behind her. Saul hit her in the back with a corner of the plastic crate he carried.

Pepper whispered, "Oh, my," as she moved aside to make room for the other two.

Wood shavings and construction dust crackled under their feet. The room smelled like paint, drywall dust, and wood shavings, but a good cleanup would take care of that. Recessed light fixtures, spaced around the ceiling, had replaced the single hanging bulb. Pools of light gave a soft glow to peach-colored walls and off-white woodwork. Only the sagging brown couch and battered card table looked as though they had held until relieved and would welcome replacements.

Pepper's heart melted into a warm puddle for The Saint and his crew. She would have to find a way to thank them.

The door to Frannie's office opened with that tacky sound associated with just-painted door frames. Sandra Waine, wearing a tight-fitting summer dress, high-heeled sandals, and an upswept hairdo, came from the office to the studio, shutting the door behind her.

Pepper almost dropped her covered dish. "What the hell are you doing here?"

"Frannie rehired me." Sandra looked around the room. "I

guess Special Forces are good for something after all, besides being sex toys."

Pepper hugged the casserole. The cold boring into her chest distracted her from going for Sandra's eyes. "Your car isn't parked outside. How did you get here?"

"I caught a ride."

"With who?"

"*With whom*, dear. Object of a preposition takes the objective case. And please, take that objectionable concoction outside. I can't have Ms. Maddox's new studio smelling like a fish plant."

Avivah set her crate down perilously close to Sandra's open-toed sandals. "We've come to use the refrigerator."

Sandra's heels made little clicking noises on the new floor as she crossed the room to stand in front of the refrigerator. "I think not. This is now Ms. Maddox's place of business. As landlord, Miss Pepperhawk is required to give twenty-four hours written notice of her intention to enter the premises, and that written notice must state her reason for entering."

"That's my refrigerator!"

"Any appliances in a rental property are assumed to be included in the rental, unless the lease specifically states otherwise."

Pepper turned to Avivah. "Is that true?"

"You've probably read the landlord/tenant laws more recently than I have."

Except that Pepper hadn't read them. Frannie wasn't a tenant; Frannie was Frannie. She and Pepper had signed an agreement, similar to the ones Avivah and Saul had signed to share the house. It had never dawned on Pepper that there were laws governing a transaction between friends.

Avivah said to Sandra, "I do know that as the property owner, Miss Pepperhawk can apply for a restraining order to prevent you from setting foot on her property. While Ms. Maddox may be the tenant of this building, right of access depends on the goodwill of the owner."

Pepper wondered if that were true, or if Avivah was slinging legal bullshit. In any case, she planned to read up on restraining orders as soon as the library opened on Monday.

"So unless you plan to helicopter to work and rappel onto the roof each morning, you might want to rethink the refrigerator."

Sandra pried Pepper's hands from the dish so violently that a bit of creamed tuna splashed on the floor. Leaving Pepper to clean up the mess, Sandra bustled, putting Pepper's dish in the refrigerator and taking Saul's crate from his hands. Saul recoiled from the killer smile Sandra bestowed on him.

This woman wasn't the same air-head prattler who had been Grace's escort yesterday. Sandra filled the fridge with the precision of a field officer moving figures across a sand table. So she could be a great organizer when she wanted to be. Why had she chosen, as the Bible said, to hide her light under a basket?

Pepper asked, "Why did Frannie hire you in the first place? Don't give me that song-and-dance about never having worked and having no references. I know that's a lie."

Sandra closed the refrigerator door, hard. "Why Frannie hired me is none of your business."

Avivah stepped between the two women. "Miss Waine, I doubt you've seen Pepper truly angry. I have. It might be in your best interest to answer that question."

"Are you going to take me to the police station and shine bright lights in my eyes if I don't tell you?"

Pepper bared her teeth. "Restraining order. Helicopter. Darby is a whiz at rappelling. Would you like him to teach you?"

Sandra rinsed her hands at the sink and dried them on a paper towel. "Oh, all right, if you're going to be childish. I was fired from my last job, and blackballed. Satisfied?"

Pepper started to ask, "Fired by who?" but decided "By whom" was grammatically correct after all. She'd be damned if she would give Sandra the satisfaction of being right, so she asked instead, "What were you, an English teacher?"

"Please! I was an executive administrative assistant, and, no, I didn't make coffee."

Maybe not make it, but serve it? Pepper imagined Sandra, in her form-fitting sheath dress, handing delicate china cups of espresso to men in expensive suits. The image fit as well as the dress did.

Sandra flopped on the faded brown couch. She resembled one of those brittle, rich women in thirties films. All that was missing was the cigarette holder. "You think CEOs run companies? Think again. It's people like me who arrange meetings, manage appointments, book business trips, and order Christmas baskets that keep big companies in business."

Saul upended a crate and sat on it. "Why were you fired?"

"Friendship." She crossed her legs at the knee, showing off a little more skin in Saul's direction.

Avivah frowned and sat on the couch beside Sandra, blocking Saul's view. Pepper pulled out a chair from the card table and sat down.

"My best friend's brother died a year after he came back from Viet Nam. A lot of his buddies were sick and dying, too. Felicity found out about some powder the Army gave them. Sprinkle it on hootches, light a match, and whoof, even in the rain. Only problem was that if you were close enough to light the match, you were close enough to breathe it in. She asked me to get her a job at ChemCover. I did."

"Why?"

"Our company developed the powder. She wanted to prove they knew how dangerous it was."

Light glinted off of Saul's new earring as he leaned forward.

Avivah recognized all the signs that he was going into reporter mode.

Saul asked, "Did she?"

"She got caught, then committed suicide in my apartment, the ungrateful little wretch."

Avivah asked, "Leaving you holding the bag?"

"Leaving me fired and ineligible for unemployment insurance. I didn't dare ask ChemCover for a reference, and they saw to it that I was blackballed by every top company in the country."

Avivah pursed her mouth in a little moue. "There are millions of companies in this country. Not a single one would give you a job?"

"I'm not interested in petty infighting in a go-nowhere company. I belong in a big boardroom."

Pepper remembered Darby's take on the Waine women. Sandra had skipped over a friend committing suicide to focus on unemployment insurance. "How will working for Frannie help you? She's not exactly tied into Fortune 500 companies."

Sandra rolled her eyes as though put upon by dim-witted children. "Frannie's not just my employer, she's my therapist, okay? I kind of lost it when Felicity died."

Pepper remembered phoning Frannie to tell her that Sandra wasn't on the up-and-up. "You told Frannie that your friend's brother was missing in action."

Sandra dipped her head. Her hair swung forward seductively. "There aren't support groups for women whose best friend's brother died of chemical poisoning. I had to take what I could get." She raised her face slowly. "I needed help, I really did."

The tears pooling at the corners of Sandra's eyes looked real. Maybe, for once, she was telling the truth. Then again, maybe not. Darby didn't trust any of the Waine women, and that was good enough for Pepper.

There was a knock on the door. The door opened, and Hamilton Kirkpatrick came in.

Pepper hadn't heard a car drive up, but Hamilton could have parked at Lorraine's trailer and walked over.

Sandra purred, "Hi, Hamilton."

Sandra's ride. Pepper suddenly felt protective toward Hamilton.

"Sandra." He seemed distracted. "Avivah, can I talk to you? Somewhere private?"

They left Sandra and Pepper screaming at one another over whether Pepper had to submit a written request in order to display the wedding gifts in the studio the next day. Ladies from the Luck and Trust Volunteer Fire Brigade Auxiliary filled the house. The yard was overrun with men setting up a second marquee and carrying boxes of plates and crystal into the one already set up. Avivah changed out of her uniform into shorts and a T-shirt. She found Hamilton sitting in a lawn chair, watching the wedding preparations. Hamilton wore casual clothes, chinos and a blue-and-white summer shirt, but his drawn face looked anything but casual.

Avivah bit her bottom lip. Had Grace dropped her bombshell on him? Not yet, she decided. He looked anxious, but not distraught.

"Let's walk down to the creek. It should be private down there."

They went to the clearing where Benny had held his party. A blue plastic tarp covered the rented bar, which would stay in place until after tomorrow's reception. Only the carefully raked ground, and a few scraps of food dropped under bushes, showed that there had been a party here the night before. They sat in chairs on either side of the spool table.

Hamilton looked around. "They clean up well after themselves."

"They do."

"I had a good time last night. I didn't think I would, but I did."

"Benny said you didn't mention soybeans once."

"He noticed? Wow!"

"Did you and Benny have a falling out somewhere along the line?"

"Yes—and no. Benny was sixteen when I left home for university. Since then, we've hardly seen each other, until this week, that is."

"This week hasn't exactly been a perfect time for reunions."

Hamilton closed his eyes. He ran his hands over his face, then rubbed his hands together and opened his eyes. "Am I one of the people you think hasn't been honest with the police?"

"Yes."

"About where I was the night Peter Taft died?"

"Possibly."

"I couldn't say anything in Mom's room because I didn't dare speak in front of Joseph."

"Why not?"

"I didn't want him, or the rest of the family, to know how much danger I'd put him in."

The hair on the back of Avivah's neck tingled. Cop sense. "Is Joseph in danger right now? Should I arrange protection for him?"

"I call being detained on an international warrant being in danger, don't you?"

"You straightened that out. The police confused him with the other Joseph Kirkpatrick."

"Did they?"

"Are you telling me that Joseph is involved in something illegal in Ireland?"

Hamilton played with a wood splinter on the chair arm. "A couple of years ago, I was heavily into the Irish club scene. It's big in Chicago. The club owners know how to cater to immigrant grandsons in three-piece suits, wrapping themselves in myths from the Auld Sod. Music. Dancing. *Craic.* An occasional speaker."

"Drugs?"

He waggled his hand back and forth. "I stuck to Guinness. Being Catholic, the clubs I favored had more of a green than orange tint to them. Do you understand what that means?"

It meant people like Martin Fitzgerald and, now, both Joseph Kirkpatricks. "A united Irish Republic. The Irish Republican Army. Brits out. That song, *A Nation Once Again.*"

Hamilton looked surprised.

Avivah said, "I attended New York University in the early sixties, and spent my share of Sunday afternoons listening to folk singers in Washington Square."

"It also means collection tins on club tables, with *Widows' and Orphans' Fund* on the wrap-around paper labels. Friday night, good music, good conversation, you're feeling sentimental, you stuff a few bills in a tin before you leave."

"One-dollar bills?"

"In my crowd, twenties. Hundreds if a fella could afford it."

"You could afford it?"

"Occasionally."

"How long did it take you to figure out the money wasn't going to widows and orphans?"

"Some of it did, make no mistake about that. Some of it also ended up, as the phrase goes, 'supporting the cause.' In my club, ten percent ended up in Kevin McCormick's pockets. A finder's fee, as it were."

Kevin McCormick again. Why wasn't she surprised? What a

sweet con. Place a few tins, rake in the bucks. Avivah wondered how Kevin had stumbled into it. "Was his being involved rumor, gossip, or innuendo?"

"Fact."

"How do you know?"

"I hired a private investigator."

"When?"

"Eight months ago."

"Why?"

"Because one day my secretary buzzed me to say that Joseph Kirkpatrick was waiting at reception. I came bounding out of my office, expecting to see my little brother, only to find a middle-age stranger who tried to shake me down for a substantial contribution to the cause. When I picked up the phone to call the police, he said simply, 'I know your brother.' He knew enough details about our Joseph to scare the wits out of me. He even had photographs."

"You hired a private investigator to do what?"

"Find out all that could be discovered about this other Kirkpatrick fella. I'm not stupid. Joseph is a musician, which makes him a public figure. Anyone ever take photographs of those musicians in Washington Square?"

"All the time."

"I thought—I hoped—that my man would tell me the closest the two Josephs came to one another was being at the same concert."

"And?"

Hamilton pulled the splinter out of the chair, leaving a hole. "Both Josephs, my brother and the man who came to my office, see each other on a regular basis, mostly in Omagh, but they meet on both sides of the border. They regularly disappear at the same time, usually for a day or two. I think my little brother is up to his neck in the Irish Troubles, and no, I don't think you can protect him." He got up and walked over to the creek bank, facing away from Avivah, looking at the gently flowing water. "I couldn't protect my own mother, but I've come close enough, this week, to asking Benny and his friends to protect my family. I'm not a violent man, Miss Rosen, but if it takes professional killers to protect my family, I'm desperate enough to give them a try."

"You think your mother's kidnapping was somehow connected to all of this?"

"The IRA is no stranger to kidnapping, and Peter Taft was connected to Kevin McCormick, who is directly connected to the cause."

She didn't miss that Hamilton's voice had taken on an Irish tint. Not like Joseph, where it sounded natural, but more like whitewash laid too heavily on a door, without the older layers of paint being removed. Hamilton had either deluded himself or was trying to delude her, and they hadn't even gotten to how Peter Taft might be mixed up in all of this.

If they hurried, they could catch Nate before he left work. Finding Mr. Ferguson on a Friday afternoon might be another matter. Avivah wasn't about to interview Hamilton further without his lawyer present, and tomorrow was out. She couldn't miss Benny's wedding, even for murder.

"I need you to come to Asheville with me, right away. Will you do that?"

Hamilton looked at his watch. "Mom asked me to come back as quickly as I could. She said she had something important to talk to me about."

What Grace had to tell Hamilton beat any link Kevin McCormick had with the IRA hands down. At least, as far as what was important to Hamilton. But it was also likely to upset him so much that he'd be useless in giving a statement for who knew how long. They had to get Hamilton's statement now!

"We have to sort this out this afternoon. There's already been a kidnapping, and a practical joke that almost hurt a lot of children. If what you say is true, and there is IRA involvement, do you want to risk a shoot-out in the middle of the wedding, as well?"

She couldn't imagine any such thing happening, but with Hamilton playing the Irish martyr, that possibility might just scare the bejesus out of him enough to make him come with her. Bejesus? Almighty, the Irish were rubbing off on her.

If there was trouble at the wedding, the odds that some of Benny's Special Forces friends would be armed were higher than Avivah cared to think about, and much higher than she dared risk. If she and Nate were going to mount any kind of defense for the wedding day, Avivah had to get Hamilton to Nate in a hurry.

CHAPTER 24

Hamilton located Mr. Ferguson with one phone call, but Avivah couldn't find Nate. He'd left work early, and there was no answer at his home. She phoned Ollie, thinking the two friends might get together on Friday evenings.

"I know where he probably is, but you can't reach him by phone."

The cautious way he said it called up an uncomfortable image of a Friday-afternoon tryst. Come on, this was Nate Alexander. More likely he'd be embarrassed if his coworkers knew he stopped in a bar for a drink.

"I've found a witness who is going to confuse the hell out of the Peter Taft case."

"Can it wait until Monday?"

Not when the safety of over a hundred people was at stake. "No."

Ollie was quiet for a moment. "Riverside Cemetery. Drive all the way around to where the road starts to curve back toward the entrance. If he's there, you can't miss him. He'll be sitting on a bench. You never heard it from me."

Avivah looked down at her shorts and T-shirt, and headed to her room to change into slacks and a blouse, more befitting for visiting a cemetery.

Riverside was deserted except for three funeral home employees dismantling a green awning over a fresh grave mounded with flowers. She wondered if Nate had attended a funeral, but the men worked near the entrance, not where Ollie had told her to go.

She wound her way along the narrow blacktop until the road made a small V at the very back of the cemetery. Nate's car was parked in one arm of the V, and she saw him sitting alone on a bench, under a tree. A few feet in front of him was a gray marble triple headstone. The center grave had a small bush planted on either side of the stone.

Avivah parked behind Nate's car and walked along the crushed shell path to where he sat. He looked up, but didn't move.

She sat down, aware of the cool concrete against the back of her thighs. She was close enough now to read the inscription on the center stone.

Natash Suzanne Alexander
June 29, 1944—May 26, 1973

Instead of an inscription, a bas-relief bouquet of flowers filled the bottom of the stone.

His daughter, she guessed. From the three plots in a row— the two side ones were blank—his only child. She had died barely a year ago. No wonder Nate looked the way he did sometimes. Grief didn't fade quickly.

He stared straight ahead, but not at the stone, higher, into the trees that surrounded the plot. "This had better be important."

"Hamilton Kirkpatrick believes his mother's kidnapping might be retaliation by the Irish Republican Army, through a connection with Kevin McCormick."

Nate cupped both his palms around the edge of the bench, pushed down to stretch his shoulders, and bent his neck forward. "This isn't a murder investigation, it's a farce."

"He's afraid there might be another attempt at the wedding or reception."

"Why the hell did he wait until now to tell us this?"

"I don't know. He just did."

Nate stood. "I'd better send someone around to pick up Mc-Cormick."

"I did that. He checked out of his motel. I put out a be-on-the-lookout, wanted for questioning on him."

"Where is Mr. Kirkpatrick?"

Avivah stood also. "I hope, by now, at the police station, with his lawyer."

"You had supper yet?"

"No."

"Come on, I'll buy you a burger."

"What about Hamilton and Mr. Ferguson?"

"They can find their own supper."

Avivah glanced over her shoulder at the grave.

"Did she die unexpectedly?"

"Not unexpectedly enough."

The police station had a hollow, abandoned sound. Even the noises of the evening shift coming and going two floors down muted into whispers. The building that faced the detectives' office was already in shadow. As Nate, Avivah, Hamilton, and Mr. Ferguson entered, Avivah turned on the overhead light and Nate's green glass–shaded desk lamp. After cautioning Hamilton, Nate interlaced his fingers and rested his hand on the ink-stained blotter. "Now, Mr. Kirkpatrick, what is all this about the Irish Republican Army?"

By the time Hamilton described his Irish club involvement, and the meeting with Joseph Kirkpatrick, twilight had set in. Nate asked, "Did you ever meet Kevin McCormick in person?"

"Once."

"When was that?"

"March twentieth, last year."

"How can you remember that date so accurately?"

Hamilton shifted position on the hard wooden chair. "It was three days after St. Patrick's Day. I was still recovering from the awful burden of being Irish."

Walter Nibb had died of a heart attack in March of last year. Had Peter Taft and Kevin McCormick already linked up by the time Hamilton met McCormick? Had Peter been involved in the Irish gig at all, or had it been strictly Kevin's show?

"How did you meet him?"

"In my favorite Irish pub. I was having a drink at the bar. He introduced himself."

"What did you talk about?"

"The club scene. Music. What groups we liked."

"Politics?"

"No."

"Family in Ireland?"

"No."

"When was your next contact with Mr. McCormick?"

"His name featured in my detective's report as someone Joseph Kirkpatrick visited periodically in the U.S."

"Not your brother, Joseph Kirkpatrick?"

"No, another man with the same name."

"When did you receive this report?"

"March of this year."

"Can you produce it?"

"Not immediately. It's in my safe at work."

"What did the report say about Kevin McCormick, other than that this Kirkpatrick visited him?"

"That he has relatives in the North, including a couple of cousins *behind the wire*."

"Meaning?"

"Prisoners—political prisoners they would call themselves—in Her Majesty's Prison Maze, also known as Long Kesh Gaol." Hamilton turned to Avivah. "There are songs about Long Kesh, too. Militant songs that draw a uncompromising line between *us* and *them.*"

Nate tilted his head. "Do you think Kevin McCormick is a hard-liner when it comes to the Irish situation?"

Mr. Ferguson, who had also been taking notes, gestured with his pen. "You're asking for an opinion. Let's stick to the facts here, shall we?"

"Did the report say anything else about Mr. McCormick?"

"His address and phone number."

"Did you phone him?"

"No."

"Did you correspond with him in any way?"

"No."

"Did you try to see him?"

"Yes."

"When?"

"Last week."

"Why?"

"Why did I try to see him or why last week?"

"Both."

Hamilton and Mr. Ferguson conferred in whispers. The lawyer reached into his briefcase and handed Nate an envelope, addressed to Hamilton Kirkpatrick, at what appeared to be an office address. The envelope was postmarked from Omagh, Co. Tyrone in mid-May. There was no return address.

Nate laid typing paper on his desk, and used a pair of tweezers to take a card from the envelope. It was obviously of Catholic origin, high on iconography, with a stylized color drawing of Jesus rising from a tomb on one side. Nate turned the card over with the tweezers.

In perpetual remembrance of
Benjamin Kirkpatrick and Lorraine Fulford
Who will share in the daily Masses,
prayers,
sacrifices, and good works of the Sisters of
St. Brigit
This remembrance is made by
a friend of the family

"I'm not Catholic, so you'll have to explain this to me."

"It's a Mass card. Someone donated money to the Sisters of St. Brigit to pray for Benny and Lorraine."

"If two Catholics are getting married, wouldn't that be a good thing to pray for the success of their marriage?"

"It's those words *perpetual remembrance*. This is a memorial Mass card. It commemorates people who have died."

Subtle, and scary. Supper turned heavy in Avivah's stomach.

Nate appeared unmoved. "When did you receive this?"

"Last week."

"Did you contact the police?"

"Which police, and tell them what? That a shadowy figure in Northern Ireland, possibly in league with a man in Tennessee, might or might not be threatening two people in North Carolina, over a failed shakedown that took place in Chicago?"

"What did you do?"

"Booked a flight to Murfreesboro. If it took a donation to keep my family safe, I was going to make one."

Except that blackmailers rarely stopped at one demand.

"When did you arrive in Murfreesboro?"

"About eleven o'clock, Thursday morning. I picked up a rental car and drove to McCormick's address. An old lady answered the door. She said McCormick wasn't home."

"Did you believe her?"

"She was distracted, packing a suitcase. She said that she and

McCormick were leaving for Asheville the next day, and that whatever I wanted would have to wait until they got back. She practically threw me out. I panicked; I thought something was already in the works, and I decided I had to get to Asheville as soon as possible, so I drove straight here from Murfreesboro."

"When did you arrive in Asheville?"

"A little before six, Thursday evening."

"Did you contact your family immediately?"

Hamilton squirmed. "No."

"Why not?"

"I was a wreck. I checked into a motel, took a shower, and collapsed on the bed to try to sort things out in my head. I fell asleep. It was two in the morning when I woke up."

Hamilton sounded as though he were confessing to a capital crime, or a mortal sin. Maybe commodities traders weren't supposed to sleep when exhausted.

Avivah asked, "On Friday, how did your family reach you to tell you that your mother was missing, and that Joseph was being held in New York?"

"I phoned my secretary after breakfast Friday morning, and told her where I was. When Benny phoned my office, my secretary called me. I phoned Benny back."

Avivah had been in the kitchen while Benny made that call. Hamilton had phoned back within ten minutes. They'd both assumed Hamilton was in Chicago. Obviously, they'd assumed wrong.

Nate asked, "When your brother phoned, why didn't you go straight to the bed-and-breakfast?"

"I had a duty to go to New York as quickly as possible."

Family duty. The Kirkpatricks seemed cursed with an overabundance in that area, as well as some severe communication deficits. The whole family needed keepers.

Hamilton continued, "I flew to New York, got Joseph sorted

out with the police, and flew back to Asheville with him the next morning."

All of which they could verify with rental car receipts and plane tickets, only they weren't going to be able to do that before the wedding. Avivah speculated on the possibility of Hamilton sticking around Asheville Friday night long enough to do in Peter, then making a hurried flight to New York in the middle of the night. Probably not, plus how would he know where to find Taft?

"Did you tell your brother what you just told us, about the shakedown and the memorial card?"

"We weren't alone for a single moment from the time he left custody in New York City until the moment my mother reappeared at the Asheville airport. There wasn't a chance to talk to him in private. You will arrange protection, won't you? For the wedding, I mean."

"It's outside of our jurisdiction. I will inform the Madison County Sheriff of the situation, but what he does with the information is up to him."

Hamilton stood. "Then can you recommend a private security firm? I'll hire whatever protection is needed."

"I wouldn't recommend that."

Hamilton slammed his hand on the desk. "Then what the hell would you recommend?"

"That we all get a grip and a good night's sleep. Constable Rosen will be at the wedding tomorrow, and so will I. That's the best I can promise."

"Can we go now?"

"Yes. I'm sure Mr. Ferguson will explain to you why it wouldn't be a good idea for you to leave town until this is cleared up."

Avivah escorted the two men to the front desk, had them sign out in the visitor's book and bought two Cokes from the vending machine. When she got back to the office, Nate had his suit coat off and his tie loosened. Avivah set a Coke on the desk in front of him. "You believe Hamilton's story about last Friday?"

"You mean Chicago to Tennessee to Asheville to New York City and back to Asheville in the space of forty-eight hours? If you were going to make up a story, would it be that complicated?"

Avivah sat in the chair Hamilton had vacated and stretched her legs. "It was Byzantine, wasn't it?"

"Best guess, is Hamilton a fruitcake?"

"Repressed, anal-retentive, far too interested in money, far too likely to stew in his own juices, probably would profit from either a good bender or a good fuck or both, yes. A fruitcake, I don't think so."

"These Mass card things, are they on a rack, like birthday cards? Could someone have picked up the wrong one by mistake?"

"*Me* you're asking, already? So what have we got, horses or zebras?"

"We have a whole damn zoo, and I feel as though I've spent too much time in the monkey cage." Nate set the can down on his blotter. "What do we know for certain? Peter Taft, Kevin McCormick and Tallulah Nibb were running cons. The land scam for certain."

Avivah thought of the dog tags. "A newer one, targeting families of men missing in action in Viet Nam."

"One involving contribution tins in Chicago pubs, and possibly one involving Mrs. Nibb's grandson, though I believe that was on the up-and-up."

"Why?"

"She was fanatical about her grandson. I suspect she kept track of every penny that was paid out of *Johnny's Kids.*"

"Only Kevin McCormick diverted those funds to IRA activities in Northern Ireland."

"A supposition. As Mr. Ferguson said, let's stick to the facts, shall we?"

Avivah thought back to a week earlier. "Fact, Peter Taft abducted Grace Kirkpatrick from the airport. He took her to the Lord's True Salvation Motel and held her captive there. By early Saturday morning he was dead. Quinn Kirkpatrick got a package with a note telling him where to find his wife. He went to the motel, found Grace, put Taft's body in a car trunk and left it at the airport."

"Mrs. Nibb sent Quinn the package and the note."

"I thought we were sticking to the facts. How do you know that?"

"The handwriting on the card is old-fashioned, spidery, you know, like on a Christmas card from Aunt Myrtle. Mrs. Nibb is the only elderly lady involved. We'll have to get a handwriting expert to confirm it."

"But she was supposed to be shut up at Bible camp Friday night."

"It's Bible camp, not Bible prison. I checked with the organizers. Friday night was a fellowship potluck supper and tent revival. McCormick and Nibb could have checked in Friday afternoon, left during the tent revival—who would have missed them?—and been back by lights out."

"You think they were both involved?"

"I think that's a damn sight better theory than Hamilton's Irish Republican Army fantasies. The majority of murders are committed by someone the victim knows."

"Why both of them?"

"We know Mrs. Nibb was involved because of the gift and the card. McCormick drove Mrs. Nibb from Tennessee in her car. They had one car, and whoever left the Bible camp had to have transportation. It's in the middle of nowhere. No rental agencies, no one borrowed a car from any of the staff. So either Mrs. Nibb alone or the two of them together, and I can't see that old lady doing this by herself."

"Who do you favor for the actual injection?"

"McCormick. He practically taunted us with how good he was with a needle the morning he identified Taft's body."

"I thought that looked like performance art."

"Mrs. Nibb somehow got separated from McCormick, bought a cheap present, and found two men in a pickup to deliver it to Quinn."

They had no luck, so far, in finding the men or their truck. Come Monday, Avivah would have to wade through all the applications for VA Hospital parking tags.

"How did she know who Quinn was or where to find him?"

Nate went to his filing cabinet and unlocked it. He glanced through the case folder. "If your theory about Taft being Mrs. Somerset's jobbing gardener is correct, he'd been watching Quinn and Grace at the bed-and-breakfast. Maybe he told Mrs. Nibb before he died."

"We're still missing the piece about how he knew the Kirkpatricks were going to be at the bed-and-breakfast at all."

"Agreed. Second possibility, Grace carried a purse when she was abducted. Mrs. Nibb had an opportunity to go through that purse at the motel. Tomorrow, I want you to make a list of every piece of paper that was in it. Look for something like a receipt or business card from the bed-and-breakfast."

"Tomorrow is the wedding."

"All right, do it Sunday."

"Assuming that Mrs. Nibb knew about Quinn, why did she contact him?"

"Remorse. Guilt. For all of her problems, she might have had a real religious conviction. Murder is a sin. She was already furious with McCormick over the missing money. Having him up on a murder charge, while she went into her helpless old lady act, would have been a tasty form of revenge."

"Maybe guilt caused her to stroke a few days later."

"I'm less inclined now to believe that Mrs. Nibb died of natural causes. I want the pathologist to take a hard look at those medicines she was taking."

"What about the not-so-funny practical joke?"

"You've read the responding officer's report. Pretty convenient, wasn't it, how the smoke grenade rolled out of the bag at exactly the right moment? Created a hullabaloo and kept the children from actually getting hurt. Who had the most access to that bag of tin whistles?"

"Joseph Kirkpatrick."

"The memorial Mass card and the smoke grenade show a great deal of similarity: noise and confusion, without anyone being hurt."

"Joseph sending that card to Hamilton would be sick."

Nate held up his hand and ticked his index finger. "Grace Kirkpatrick posed for pornographic photos. Quinn moved Tate's body. Hamilton is ready to pay for hired guns to protect his family. That youngster, Ellie May—"

"Ginny Mae."

"Ran away, conned a priest, took a bus to Missouri, then turned around and flew back. Does that make sense to you? I don't think a single person in that family is capable of making a sound decision."

"Benny makes lots of sound decisions," Avivah said in a small voice, while her head tallied the number of mentally deranged, put-himself-in-danger decisions she knew for certain that Benny had made in the Army.

"Maybe he joined up to get away from his crazy family."

Avivah had once gotten a large sliver of glass in her finger. Anticipating it being removed caused her far more pain than the actual removal. She felt the same way now. Grace's secret was bound to come out, and the anticipation of that pushed words from her mouth. "Hamilton Kirkpatrick is Peter Taft's son."

Nate looked as though he'd forgotten how to breathe. His face turned pink, then red, then purple. He managed a strangled, "How?"

"Rape."

"No, how do you know that?"

"Grace told me."

"Does Hamilton know?"

"Not yet. Grace says she never told Quinn or Peter either."

"That doesn't mean one or both of them didn't figure it out. That opens a whole new can of worms." He reached for the phone. "Madison County Sheriff is not going to be happy about this."

"Since when was this business about making people happy?" Avivah tossed the empty cans in the trash. "It's not what we know, but what's missing that bothers me most."

Nate's finger paused over the phone dial. "What's that?"

"Lorraine and Marsenia both say that Taft showed a movie on May eighteenth. Lorraine gave him money that same day. He never went back to Murfreesboro between the eighteenth and when he died. Where are the movie projector, the film and the money Lorraine gave him?"

CHAPTER 25

Avivah arrived home after sunset. Frannie's studio and the homestead were dark, except for a light that showed around the curtain edges in her living room. Saul must still be up. Pepper's car was in the garage; Saul's car and Darby's rental car were parked outside. No women loading leftovers into station wagons, no caterers, no wedding party relaxing in the tents. Everyone must have had the good sense to make an early evening of it.

Might as well make a perimeter check. Her hand went to her side, but there wasn't a holster. She'd forgotten she was wearing civvies. She felt under the front seat and came up with her head-bashing flashlight.

Both Frannie's front and back doors were locked. Avivah walked through the dew-covered grass to where two marquees stood white and ghostly under a waning moon. She walked a perimeter check around each tent. All secure on the outside.

Inside the wedding tent, neat rows of chairs created an aisle down which Lorraine's attendants, Lorraine, and her father would walk. Poufy white bows decorated the end chair on each row, except for the first rows where the families would sit. Those bows were gold. Empty white, wrought-iron holders stood guard in a semicircle at the front of the tent, waiting for florists to fill them with flowers.

She walked through a tent flap into the reception tent. Bare, round tables filled the tent. Other, long tables lined the tent's far side. Plastic bins full of linens, dishes, cutlery, champagne glasses and chafing dish parts covered the table. A portable glass-front refrigerator, powered by a thick orange extension cord that disappeared under the tent side, hummed quietly behind one table. Inside, champagne bottles chilled. Avivah noted that the refrigerator had a padlock.

A lock isn't locked unless you've tested it yourself was one of the maxims of military police school. She walked over and tested the padlock. It was locked.

There was no bar. Anyone who wanted a drink stronger than punch, iced tea, or champagne would have to find their way down to the clearing by the river. If anyone intended to get plastered, Benny and Lorraine wanted them to do it away from children and more sensible guests. Avivah approved.

She broke open one of the Coke cartons and helped herself to a can. It was cool enough tonight that the can had a chill on it. It fizzed a little as she opened it.

Something small scurried behind the empty serving line. All their suspects moved around this case like that, scurrying just beyond where she could see.

The list of not-so-funny practical jokes Joseph Kirkpatrick could play was endless. She tried to imagine what her more inventive nieces and nephews would do. Remove screws from chairs so that they collapsed when guests sat down. Sneezing powder sprinkled in the floral arrangements. Phone in a false fire alarm so that the fire brigade arrived just as the vows were being exchanged.

Damn it, Nate had to be wrong about Joseph. Razor blades were serious. Someone wanted to up the odds, and they didn't care if people, even children, got hurt. Whatever might happen tomorrow wouldn't be a practical joke. It might be a hornet's nest hidden under a table so an unwary guest would kick it and cause the hornets to swarm. Or perhaps ipecac, a medicine that caused serious vomiting, would be poured into the punch bowl. She didn't want to contemplate the opportunities for food poisoning among the food and drink that would be served tomorrow.

Someone had gone quietly, cunningly crazy. Enough of the shine had worn off Benny's family that she could suspect any one of them, even Ginny Mae. She made a mental note to find out if Ginny Mae had really been in Missouri the three days that she had been gone. And she added Frannie Maddox's name to the list.

It wasn't Benny or Lorraine. She'd been too close to them for too long to think they would sabotage their own wedding.

Benny and Lorraine's wedding. "Open a new gate for us, as the old gate is closed." Long time coming and *mazel tov* to both of them.

The hard table edge bit into Avivah's backside as she leaned against it. After what she'd seen this past week, eloping had a lot to recommend it. Except that, while her family wasn't Orthodox, they'd never met a party they didn't like. She had a large family and all the way from the *ketubah* to the final toast, a parent, grandparent, aunt, uncle, best friend or rabbi would be scandalized if a particular wedding custom were omitted. Elopement would send them right off the scale. Her penance would be twenty years of variation on, "Elopement, already. I'll go to my grave not seeing what a vision you would have been in your wedding dress."

No, if she ever married, she'd end up having to do every single ritual, except maybe never being alone with her bridegroom for the first seven days after marriage. In her family, parents of both the bride and groom joined the newlyweds at their hotel for breakfast on the morning after the wedding. Then the couple flew off for a Caribbean honeymoon, though lately, Avivah heard rumors that Hawaii had become the preferred destination.

If she ever married . . . Avivah's chin sunk to her chest. Maybe at thirty-two, *when* did become *if.*

Nate was right. She hadn't paid attention while the time for being a street cop ran out. Pounding a beat was the right career move at twenty-two, but not at thirty-two, not if she eventually wanted to be—what? Chief of police? Not her style. Sheriff? She didn't fancy running an election campaign. Public defender? She had the GI bill and it would be a shame to waste it; she could go to law school. No. She was a cop, not a lawyer, and she had to jump-start her career.

If not Affirmative Action, what? Assuming a police depart-ment existed that hired women, but didn't have an Affirmative Action program, any promotion she got would look the same to an outsider. Promoted on gender, not on merit. Unless she was so fucking meritorious that even the dimmest civilian couldn't doubt she had earned every single promotion. Fat chance. She was good, but she was no heroine, no paragon. Her skin itched when she thought she might just be forced to take Nate up on his offer. That would be next week's problem.

First, they had to get through tomorrow. Unless she wanted to mount guard all night—she didn't—there was nothing else she could do tonight. Tomorrow, she would be here. Nate would be here. A whole bunch of ex-soldiers would be here. Lots of people trained in observation. Tonight: sleep; tomorrow: a battle plan.

She tossed the empty can in a trash barrel, tied all the tent flaps securely and went in through the kitchen door, laying her flashlight on the kitchen counter.

Saul called softly from the living room. "All secure?"

She called back, "All secure."

She went to the living room, where Saul was ensconced in his extra-long bed. He wore green-striped pajamas, which Avivah guessed would make his long legs and torso look even longer. He'd been reading the *New Yorker,* and he had one bony finger about midway into the magazine to mark his place. "I saw you making rounds."

He moved over a little and Avivah sat on the bed beside him. "How did the rehearsal go?"

"The usual comic opera. You know the old saying, 'bad dress rehearsal, good opening night.' " He blushed. "So to speak. The rehearsal supper was outstanding. You can't beat country women cooking country food. They made you up a platter, and I do mean platter. It's in an ice chest in the kitchen. Want me to get it for you?"

Avivah tried to pinch her waist, but even sitting, there wasn't much to pinch. "No, thanks. I ate a burger earlier. I'm going to have to go on a diet after this week."

"Benny didn't eat a single bite."

"He can't eat before a mission. Never has. Tomorrow, after the wedding, he'll be ravenous. I'd advise you to guard your plate. Benny's post-mission hunger knows no bounds."

"You're home late."

He was practically salivating. He knew that she and Hamilton had talked, then she'd changed clothes and left the house in a hurry.

Avivah picked up a small sofa pillow from the floor and bopped him on the forehead. "Curb that nose for news, okay?"

Saul stuck his lower lip out too far to be a real pout. "Be that way. I'll share with you, even if you won't share with me. I haven't been exactly indolent this afternoon. Sandra was telling the truth. A woman named Felicity Garnett committed suicide September 13, 1972, in a Houston apartment rented by one Sandra Waine. And ChemCover's personnel department wouldn't give me a reference on Sandra, other than to confirm she had worked for them from 1965 to 1972 'in a variety of secretarial capacities,' and that they wouldn't hire her again. Even the way the personnel officer said they wouldn't hire her again made me feel sticky. They don't like her there."

"How did you find all of this out?"

Saul cupped his fingers around her chin and turned her face until they gazed into each other's eyes. Avivah's heart did a little spasm. "Read my lips. I am a reporter. I make phone calls." His lips formed another word, but he hesitated and ran his tongue over his lips, and took a deep breath. "I have a new job."

Avivah took his hand in both of hers and kissed the tip of his middle finger. "That's terrific. What, when, where?"

Saul rested his hand on her thigh, and her heart did more than spasm. "Add who and why and we'll turn you into a journalist yet. I should have said a job *offer*."

He flipped the magazine open to the masthead page, and extended his finger to point to the editorial staff list. "Articles editor for the *New Yorker*."

Avivah felt as though she'd been hit in the stomach with a large, friendly marshmallow. "Oh, Saul. That's top of the line. Are you sure they want *you*?"

"From you, I expected congratulations."

"You know that's not what I meant. The *New Yorker*, it's like this fantasy place. I never thought about real people working there."

"What? You thought little magazine elves published this?"

She grinned. "Only if the elves had a New York accent. Classy. All Vassar or Yale and Manhattan."

"From Brooklyn, maybe, and I'm a potted plant?"

It was a good Brooklyn accent, considering Saul came from Terre Haute, Indiana.

"Come to New York with me." He said it quick and breathless, as though he had to get those six words out all at once. "Move in with me."

Images tumbled through her head. The arch at Washington Square. A tiny Italian restaurant she hadn't eaten at in over a decade. Her artist-aunt's *ketubah* portfolio, full of exquisitely illuminated wedding contracts. Nate asking, "What have you done as a civilian?" Her hand signing her name to Pepper's house-sharing agreement. She forced air through her mouth. It came out, "Uh." She tried again, managing a "Uoof."

Saul threw the covers back and got out of bed. She'd been right. This man should not wear vertical-striped pajamas. He looked ten feet tall. "Let me show you something."

She meekly accompanied him to Benny's old bedroom. Saul put his hand on the knob.

Avivah found enough voice to whisper, "Don't do that. You'll wake Darby."

"I don't think so."

He pushed open the door. The room was unoccupied, the bed neatly made. Saul nodded his head toward Pepper's bedroom. "Tomorrow morning, discretion might be the better part of valor."

"Are you sure? I mean, are you sure that's where he is, or are you just imagining that's where he might be?"

"I watched them walk arm-in-arm into the bedroom and close the door."

Avivah raised her right fist in a Black Power salute. Her entire body tingled. "Praise the Lord and pass the ammunition. It's about bloody time."

Saul nuzzled her neck. "If they can, why can't we? I've been in love with you since the day I met you. Come with me. The two of us could take New York by storm."

Avivah felt hot and cold at the same time. "I don't know. I just don't know."

CHAPTER 26

Shortly after dawn Saturday morning, Avivah rolled out of bed to the sound of invading caterers. She considered a quick kitchen raid to liberate their coffee maker and a box of Pop-Tarts. As it turned out, an insert-and-extract mission wasn't needed. The caterers popped open an umbrella-covered patio table in the backyard, adorned it with linen and china, and served croissants, strawberries, scrambled eggs and coffee to her, Saul, Pepper and Darby.

Their waiter, a young man in black slacks and a white shirt, sported a buzz cut and an earring like Saul's. He leaned slightly forward, one hand behind his back, to serve coffee from a silver pot. "Welcome to One Perfect Day in June."

Pepper looked at the sky. "It *is* a perfect day."

Avivah pressed her lips together to keep from smiling. Pepper's enthusiasm might have more to do with last night's sleeping arrangements than with unblemished blue sky and dew-dappled grass, she thought.

The waiter smiled. "No, that's the name of our company: One Perfect Day in June."

Avivah spread jam on her croissant. "What if you cater a wedding in October?"

He finished pouring with a wrist flick that prevented coffee from dripping on the tablecloth. "Then we become One Perfect Day in October. We're a movable feast."

Everyone groaned. The young man looked pleased. "Oh good,

a sense of humor. You have no idea how often that joke falls flat. My name is Simon, and I'll be your liaison today. First rule: *Simon-says* jokes are out. There isn't one I haven't heard, and I'll be too busy to laugh.

"My goal is to help you relax and enjoy this day. We recognize that family and friends are essential to a perfect wedding, but are often forgotten in the shuffle. That's why we provide a refreshment area—under those trees—with coffee, tea, cold beverages, light snacks, as well as aspirin, antacids, tissues, ice packs, a sewing kit and other essentials. In return, we ask that you avoid the kitchen and tent areas where we are working. Second rule: If you need anything, ask any of our employees to find me, and I will do my best to make today perfect for you."

Simon had no real grasp of what would make today perfect. Avivah asked, "Are any of your employees Irish or Irish-Americans?"

Saul, Darby and Pepper all stopped, eating implements in various poses.

A cloud moved across Simon's face. "I don't think so. No, I'm sure not. Is that a problem?"

"Not really. I was just asking."

People resumed chewing, cutting and spooning. Simon made a little bow that clearly said he'd seen it all before, the customer was always right, and no oddball question at breakfast was going to ruin *his* perfect day. He started back toward the back door. After a few steps he pivoted neatly on his heel. "We do have a book of inoffensive jokes and toasts appropriate for all occasions. There are some Irish toasts in there, if that's what you're looking for."

"Yes, that would be fine."

Simon's cloud lifted. "I'll see that it's on your table with the other essentials."

He disappeared into the kitchen.

Around a mouthful of scrambled eggs, Darby said, "Simon seems to have G-1 well in hand."

Saul's eyebrows bent into a V. He looked at Avivah, who said, "General Staff One: responsible for personnel and administration. The guys who keep a military unit functioning smoothly."

"Guys and gals," Pepper said, as she nicked a strawberry from Darby's plate. He put his hand around her wrist and squeezed on the pressure points. Pepper struggled to hold on to the fruit, but it dropped neatly into Darby's outstretched other hand. They grinned at one another. Pepper and Darby were usually so well behaved, but here they were flirting in public. Avivah scanned the sky for flying pigs.

Pepper wiped her fingers on a napkin. "Saul, you get to be responsible for communications."

He looked puppy-bright. "Do I get a G number, too?"

"G-6," the other three said in unison.

"What exactly does a G-6 do?"

Pepper laid her hand casually on Darby's back. "Today, mostly deal with the wedding photographer. He's due at Lorraine's at ten o'clock for a series of candid, before-wedding shots. Then the bed-and-breakfast to photograph the groom's party, then back here by twelve-fifteen, at the latest. Oh, and if anyone asks, wedding gifts go in Frannie's studio."

Avivah wasn't about to ask Pepper if she'd submitted a formal request, in writing, to Sandra for the use of the studio. The presents posed other problems. Could she require that all boxes be opened and inspected? Not likely. They weren't even through breakfast and the security nightmare had already begun.

Darby laid his fork and knife precisely across his plate. "I'm G-5, civil affairs. Translation, parking attendant. I'll be directing people to the Baptist church's parking lot up the road. Lorraine's brother-in-law and a couple of Benny's friends will run a shuttle service for those who can't or don't want to walk back the half mile."

Pepper looked at her watch. "Right now the wedding party and both families are at seven o'clock Mass in Hot Springs. They're scheduled to be back at the bed-and-breakfast by eight-thirty. Everyone picks up a boxed breakfast from Mrs. Somerset, and then the party splits up, with Lorraine and her attendants returning to her trailer, and Benny and his party remaining at the bed-and-breakfast. One of Lorraine's friends will corral all of the older children for games and activities until twelve-thirty.

"We have no idea when the guests will start to arrive, but hopefully, not before eleven. The Baptist Church's nursery, staffed by teenagers from the congregation, will open at eleven-thirty for infants and small children. The caterer is already here, the florist due to arrive in half an hour, and Father Fred, the celebrant, arrives at noon, God willing. Wedding is at one, reception immediately following. Supper dance starts at five. Bride and groom make their getaway by ten, we all turn into pumpkins, collapse and get our lives back."

Trust Pepper to assign herself to both operations and logistics.

"Avivah, I assume you have security in hand?"

G-2: Intelligence and security. Over Pepper's shoulder, Avivah saw Nate's car pull up into the gravel parking area. She laid her napkin beside her plate. "Actually, security may have gone to hell in a handbasket. I'll be right back. I think you'll want to hear what Detective Alexander has to say."

She walked across the lawn to meet him. Nate wore an off-white linen suit, white shirt, Panama hat, and snazzy red polka-dotted tie and matching pocket handkerchief. Today he looked more like an escapee from a Tennessee Williams play than a fifties television cop. He handed Avivah an oblong package, wrapped in silver paper and tied with a silver-and-white bow. It was heavier than she expected and she almost dropped it.

"It's a pressed-glass pickle dish and pickle forks. They don't have one already, do they?"

Avivah had no clue. "I'm sure they don't."

"I hate shopping for presents. My wife always did it."

Past tense. Was he no longer married or had he just not wanted to wake his wife before dawn to ask her opinion on pressed-glass pickle dishes? They'd decided only last night that Nate would be a presence at the wedding, and it was now early morning. The only place he could have bought the gift was an all-night drugstore. Maybe, for all Avivah knew, at the same place where Mrs. Nibb bought her candy dish.

She put the package on a lawn chair and hoped she would remember to take it to Frannie's studio before someone sat on it. "Have you had breakfast?"

"Coffee and an egg sandwich. Takeout."

"Come over and meet everyone."

By the time they arrived at the table, a fifth chair, an additional cup of coffee and a fresh croissant were already in place. Simon was no slouch. Avivah made introductions, and sat down again. "We were just talking about security."

Nate added sugar and cream to his coffee. "The Sheriff can give us one deputy, plainclothes so as not to alarm the guests. As a precaution, Avivah and I will be discreetly armed, though I, personally, think that's overkill."

Avivah suddenly had the impression of being surrounded by a pack of beagles. Give Darby and Pepper one whiff of excitement and their ears almost stood on end. Saul had a nose for news, and it was quivering. "I hadn't gotten as far as being armed."

"How far had you gotten?"

"I'd said that security might have gone to hell in a handbasket."

"Of course, that was before I arrived."

"Right. We're secure now."

Avivah composed herself and looked at the others at the table. "We have a problem."

On the road to the bed-and-breakfast, Pepper saw the car carrying Lorraine and her parents approach from the opposite way. She raised her fingers from the steering wheel and inclined her head back, giving a Madison County neighbor's greeting, which Lorraine's father returned. He was an orchard-man in Oregon. Maybe all farmers knew the country signal for *Hi,* like some secret fraternity.

Tank sat in a rocker on the front porch, with a white cardboard box balanced on his lap. In a summer shirt and pair of tan slacks, he looked as relaxed as a Secret Service agent at a Lyndon Johnson barbecue. He'd had a haircut since the last time Pepper saw him, and his scalp showed white along the sides of his head.

As Pepper approached, he stood, cradling the box, and barred the door. "Sorry, Pepper. Only wedding party in or out. Benny and his folks have enough on their minds today without visitors."

She sat in a rocking chair. "The honor is all yours. I came to see you."

He held out the breakfast box to her. "I have a bad feeling I'm not going to like being honored."

In spite of her just-finished breakfast, the homemade ham biscuits did look good. She resisted, limiting herself to a thin slice of melon. "We have a problem."

She talked and Tank ate. Unlike Benny, the thought of action didn't seem to dampen Tank's appetite. When she'd finished laying out the situation, Tank put down his now-empty box. He picked up a green walkie-talkie from beside his chair. It squawked as he pressed the button. "Wedding One, to all stations. We are condition yellow. Repeat, condition yellow. I will rendezvous at your individual positions within ten minutes with details."

Pepper's heart melted a little. It was so refreshing to be back in the land of instant preparedness. "You were expecting something?"

Tank's face turned red. "No, but habit is habit." He pulled his rocker in front of the front door. "Sit right here, don't move, while I go bring everyone up to speed. I think we need radio silence. The drill will be 'No one in, no one out of this house, including the wedding party, until I give the go-ahead.' Based on what you've told me, we don't want anyone wandering around the grounds unattended."

She took the walkie-talkie. "Okay, I get to keep your walkie-talkie. Just in case I see anything, of course."

He grinned. "Of course," meaning if she wanted to play soldier, fine with him.

"What are the codes?"

"You're Wedding One, Jeff is Wedding Two, Warren is Wedding Three, and The Saint is Avenging Angel." He held up his hands, palms out. "Not my fault. He chose it."

A soldier without black humor was in a lot of trouble. Pepper sat in the rocker and rocked it with her foot. Simon's Perfect Day had become even more luscious, with not only brighter colors, but also more of them. She was seeing greens she'd never noticed before.

Adrenalin, that's all it was. Tomorrow, maybe tonight, she'd crash like a rocket, but that was in the future. For now she had lovely colors and . . .

A smidgen of movement in the side garden attracted her. Bother, she should have asked if anyone was already outside the perimeter, because Joseph Kirkpatrick clearly was. He'd come up a side path. Pepper watched him sit on a stone bench, bend over, and bury his face in his hands. Pepper had just enough time to think that she'd rarely seen a more dejected figure before a second man appeared behind Joseph.

Pepper had never met Kevin McCormick, but the man in the trousers and sports coat certainly looked like the description Nate Alexander had given them at breakfast. In one movement he grasped Joseph's hair, pulled his head back, and put his finger, like a knife, along the edge of Joseph's throat.

She was close enough to hear Kevin say, "See how easy it is, boy-o? Did you like the stink bomb and razor blades? It just as easily could have been a real bomb. None of your family is safe."

Pepper's heart pounded. She jammed down the walkie-talkie button. "Wedding One to all stations. Side garden. Two men, one unfriendly. Take them both down."

When the going got tough, a good Army nurse knew to get out of the way and prepare to pick up the pieces. Pepper pushed her chair aside and went inside, putting the screen door between herself and what was going to happen. Not that a screen door provided much protection, but it was all she had. For a moment, she longed for the good old days of flak jackets and metal helmets.

She never heard or saw a thing until four men erupted out of the trees. Strangely enough, it was Joseph who was the wildcat. It took three men to subdue him, one to subdue McCormick. Of course, Tank was the one on McCormick.

When they had both men on the ground, Pepper ran to the garden. The screen door flapped behind her.

Joseph had his head twisted in her direction. He screamed, "Get your Nazis off of me!"

Jeff bent double so that his face was down, next to Joseph's. "At Fort Bragg, we eat punks like you for breakfast."

Pepper's private Army pulled the two men to their feet.

Pepper asked the stranger, "Are you Kevin McCormick?"

Only then did it dawn on her, God help them if he wasn't.

"Who the hell are you?"

"Elizabeth Pepperhawk."

"Well, Elizabeth Pepperhawk, you'd better have a warrant and a badge or I'm going to sue the pants off the lot of you." Over his shoulder, he commanded Tank, "Take your fucking hands off of me."

Tank let him go. The other three let Joseph go. McCormick collapsed on the bench and took something out of his pants pocket. "Medicine," he gasped. "I have to take some medicine."

Pepper considered the possibility he was about to slip himself a cyanide capsule, like in spy movies, but decided that what McCormick held looked more like nitroglycerine. Maybe he had a heart condition. She certainly didn't want to be responsible for a heart patient kicking off, but she did watch intently as McCormick squeezed a few drops of liquid under his tongue.

Joseph straightened his clothes and brushed himself. "What is going on here?"

McCormick wasn't strangling and turning blue, so maybe he hadn't taken cyanide after all.

Pepper said, "Hamilton thinks some of your IRA buddies, through McCormick here, plan to wreck Benny's wedding, as a payback for Hamilton not contributing to their cause. The police have had a be-on-the-lookout order out for Mr. McCormick since yesterday."

"How the hell is Hamilton involved in this?"

McCormick put the medicine back in his pocket. "I met your jerk brother once in Chicago."

"My brother is not a jerk."

"Every one of you Kirkpatricks is solid-gold trouble. I should never have agreed to meet you."

Pepper asked, "Why *are* you two meeting?"

Joseph sat down on the bench beside McCormick, who

moved away as far as he could. Joseph said, "I set this up weeks ago, from Ireland. I thought with everyone busy with the wedding, no one would notice if I snuck away this morning."

"That's how, not why."

"I wanted to persuade McCormick to introduce me to his cousins in Omagh."

"Why can't you introduce yourself to them?"

"Because they refuse to be in the same room with us."

"Who are *us*?"

"Peace Through Art. Artists and performers, from both sides of the border, who are trying to negotiate common ground through music, drama, and art."

McCormick spat on the flagstone walk at Joseph's feet. "Common ground? I told you in Ireland: not with you, not with anyone."

Joseph rounded on McCormick. "*Sienn Fein.* Ourselves alone. Trying to be more Irish than the Irish, are you? It's bull-headed attitudes like that that keep the killing going."

"In case you haven't checked lately, boy-o, you're an American too, with no authority to stick your nose into something that's none of your business."

Pepper's Army divided themselves two-on-one, ready to pull the men apart if they made a move toward one another. She asked Joseph, "This other Joseph Kirkpatrick, is he part of your peace group?"

"No, he's a hard-liner, but at least he's willing to talk to us, which is more than I can say for McCormick's family."

"Mr. McCormick, will you come with me to talk to Detective Alexander?"

"I don't suppose I have a fucking choice, do I?"

"Sure you do. Come with me, or have the Sheriff pick you up. You may not be familiar with this part of Madison County: one road, and two places to end up. The Sheriff can have both ends of the road blocked in five minutes."

Except that the Sheriff could do no such thing. The distances were too great. Pepper hoped Kevin McCormick didn't know Madison County geography as well as she did.

"All right. I'll talk to your detective."

Pepper relaxed. The colors weren't so bright anymore. She hadn't planned on feeling this tired until after Benny and Lorraine drove off. She'd have to dig deep to find the energy to get through the rest of the day.

They walked back to the house. Joseph was about to open the door for Pepper when the sound of footsteps came barreling down the staircase. Hamilton, carrying two suitcases, flung the screen door open from the inside, pushing Joseph out of the way. He didn't seem to notice any of the other people crowded around on the porch.

Joseph yelled, "Hamilton!"

Hamilton unlocked his rental car, got in, and spun his wheels as he pulled out. Pepper had only caught a glimpse of his face, but she could swear that he had been crying. She turned to Joseph, "What's wrong?"

"We had a family meeting a little while ago. Hamilton got some very disturbing news."

After keeping her secret all these years, why had Grace told Hamilton who his real father was only hours before Benny's wedding?

Chapter 27

What had been the larger bedroom in the old house was now Frannie's classroom. Soothing wallpaper with wide vertical stripes of muted sea green and pale blue covered the walls. A green chalkboard hung on one wall and a line of floor-recessed electrical outlets, with round brass covers, ran down the middle of the room. Nate—or maybe the ever-perfect Simon—had produced a folding table and several chairs. White tablecloths hung, pleated and pinned, over both windows. That was definitely Simon's work.

Muted guest noises penetrated even the closed windows. Occasionally, the noise level rose and fell as someone came into the studio to leave another gift. Nate had stationed the Madison County Sheriff's deputy outside the studio. His job was to watch for anyone acting suspicious as they delivered a package. It wasn't perfect security, but short of asking each person to unwrap their gift, it was all they could do.

From one corner of the closed room, an electric fan circulated hot air and new construction smells. Better heat and vapors than someone walking by an open window and overhearing their interrogation. With two men in the room, Avivah didn't dare pull her dress away from her sweaty skin and blow cooling air into the V made by her bra.

She had discovered that a silk dress didn't accommodate a service revolver. The pockets were too small and her thin belt wouldn't support the weight. A purse was out. Better to be unarmed than try to do a quick draw from a purse. If anything went down, she would just have to cope with being unarmed.

Nate's coat hung on a rack behind the fan. He had his tie off, and his shirtsleeves rolled up, looking for all the world like a twenties Southern politician stumping for reelection. He sat with his legs crossed at the knee, swinging one leg impatiently, waiting for McCormick to complete his medical *toilette*.

Whatever means Pepper had used at the bed-and-breakfast to convince McCormick to come for an interview, he was spooked good and proper. He measured, mixed, drank, dripped his Rescue Remedy under his tongue, and applied creams and ointments to his wrists and temples. His hands trembled. Avivah had known Pepper to have that effect on several people.

McCormick zipped his case closed, took a deep breath and folded his hands on the table in front of him. "I understand you've been looking for me."

Nate uncrossed his legs. "You threatened Joseph Kirkpatrick by pretending to hold a knife at his throat."

"It was my finger, not a knife."

"You implied that you were responsible for the smoke bomb and razor blades in the tin whistle bag, and stated that none of his family was safe."

"His kind think they can end the Troubles by singing together, writing a play and painting pictures. I wanted to teach him a lesson. He and his artsy friends have no idea how much danger they are in. If they don't stop messing with things they don't understand, none of them will be alive this time next year."

Avivah had seen too much unexpected death in Viet Nam to dismiss Kevin's prediction. Joseph Kirkpatrick could well be living on borrowed time. There wasn't a damn thing she could do about it. Turning away from the things she couldn't change, she asked, "Where have you been since yesterday afternoon?"

"Asking for help and guidance from our—that is, Peter's—generous supporters."

"The two people you share a house with are dead, and you're out soliciting charitable contributions? Hard-hearted, don't you think?"

"I only boarded with Peter and Tallulah. I wasn't a business partner, and I don't have access to their funds. I can't afford to ship two bodies back to Tennessee, much less pay for two funerals. Fortunately, one of our contributors agreed to co-sign a loan. All I want to do is go home and put this horrible week behind me."

"Will you be staying at the farm?"

"I can't. Tallulah owned the farm and she must have a relative somewhere, no matter how distant. If she doesn't, the county will sell the property for taxes."

Poetic justice. If Peter had been running his usual scam, he would already have the deed to Mrs. Nibb's property. Maybe he did, not that it would do McCormick much good.

Nate leaned forward. "Information has come forward that suggests that you were part of a blackmail scheme, coming out of Northern Ireland, to raise money for political causes."

"All I did was to help set up charitable collections in Chicago for humanitarian relief."

"For a ten-percent cut."

"Expenses."

"What's your connection to Northern Ireland?"

"My dad's relatives live there. I visited them once."

"When?"

"December 1971. I stayed on into January, four weeks in all."

"Is that where you met Joseph Kirkpatrick?"

"Yes."

Avivah asked, "Which Joseph Kirkpatrick?"

"Two of them. The man I had an appointment with this

morning, and a second, older man."

"Did the man you met this morning put you in touch with his brother, Hamilton?"

"No."

"But you did meet Hamilton Kirkpatrick in Chicago?"

"That was, as they say, luck of the Irish. I moved to Chicago for a while after I retired from the Air Force. In a pub one night, this bloke and I start talking at the bar, you know, *crac*—conversation—over a couple of beers."

"Did you tell him you'd met Joey in Ireland?"

"Why should I? Where I'd been or who I'd met was none of his business."

"But you figured out that the two men were related?"

"I saw a family resemblance."

Got you. Joseph looked like Quinn; Hamilton looked like Grace, or maybe, now that Avivah knew the truth, the tiniest bit like Peter Taft. No way Kevin could have seen a resemblance between the two brothers.

"When Joseph arranged this morning's meeting with you, he told you where he was staying?"

"I was there this morning, wasn't I?"

"When did you plant the stink bomb and razors in the tin whistle bag?"

"Earlier."

"Children could have cut their fingers to the bone."

McCormick looked at Avivah, "What children?"

The problem with con men was that Avivah could never trust when one was telling the truth. Maybe McCormick hadn't known the whistles were intended for children, just that a stink bomb and razor blades would create havoc whenever the bag was opened.

Nate described the memorial Mass card. He stressed the *memorial* part. "Are you familiar with those?"

"Vaguely."

"Did any one in your family in Ireland, or their associates, send such a card to Hamilton Kirkpatrick?"

"You'd have to ask them."

Nate leaned forward on both hands. "Granted that you've only been in Ireland once, and that you don't want to speak for anyone else, let me ask you for your best guess. You're not committing yourself, you understand, I'm just asking for information. Is it even remotely possible that someone in Northern Ireland sent such a card to Hamilton as a threat?"

McCormick shifted uneasily. "It's possible."

"What would you do if you received such a card?"

"I'd make myself scarce." He looked down and picked a piece of lint from his trousers. "I've never had a stomach for the really hard stuff, and to tell you the truth, I was glad to put the Atlantic Ocean between me and my cousins. That's why I wanted to warn Joey. He's a naive kid who *will* end up dead if he keeps pushing the wrong people."

"You're a real humanitarian."

"I'm a guy who's trying to get by, and thought maybe he could do someone a favor. Is that all? Can I go now?"

"No, you cannot go. I have several hours more of questions for you about your relationship with Peter Taft, and Tallulah Nibb, your relationship to several possible confidence games and your exact movements on the night Taft died. Unfortunately, I don't have several hours to give you right now. Since this is Madison County, I have no jurisdiction. The deputy outside will take you to the Sheriff's office, and hold you there until I can find those hours."

Kevin clutched his leather case to his chest. "They won't take this away from me, will they?"

For a moment, Avivah felt sorry for him. Maybe the story about lung cancer was true. He certainly looked like a drowning man clinging to a piece of driftwood. She had watched Nate go over every square inch of the case. There were no hidden compartments, and whatever McCormick was drinking, breathing and applying didn't appear to have done him any harm.

"They will have to take it into their custody, but I'll ask them to allow you to use it under their supervision."

Avivah escorted McCormick through the studio. The number of wedding gifts had quadrupled in the time she'd been in the interview.

She handed McCormick over to the deputy, making sure to instruct him about his need for his medicine case. McCormick looked pathetically grateful.

Avivah watched the two men walk to the officer's unmarked car. McCormick stopped suddenly and the deputy almost ran into him. It was a blip, a little movement she might have missed, but for the first time, Avivah saw real fear in McCormick's face.

She turned in the direction he had been looking. All she saw were dozens of people, some she knew and some she didn't, milling around in small groups.

She hurried back inside. Nate was retying his tie.

"Someone out there scares McCormick. He spotted someone and went white as a sheet. Do you want me to call him back?"

"Won't do any good. He won't tell us, and the longer we are in here, the less security there is out there, especially with the deputy gone." He put his gun back into his shoulder holster and slipped on his coat. "I'm going to phone Ollie and see if he's doing anything this afternoon. We could use another pair of eyes." They walked into the studio.

Avivah said, "At least McCormick told us one thing."

"What?"

"We don't have to worry about wedding presents. He sailed through here without a second glance. It was only after he got outside that someone spooked him."

They walked out into the yard and surveyed the orderly confusion. A wedding party. A perfect catering company. Two families. A hundred and fifty guests. One person with a grudge. As odds went, it was the pits.

Pepper stood in the middle of her backyard, closed her eyes, and reveled in the sounds of happy people having a good time that washed over her. As did the sounds of two unhappy people.

"You said you wouldn't come."

"No, you said I shouldn't come. I said I'd think about it. I thought about it; I came."

She opened her eyes. It took a minute to spot the arguing pair, who stood at the yard's edge, near where the woods began.

A purple dress, probably hand-painted silk, flowed around Frannie, but she did not look like a woman going with the flow. She moved a heavy-looking box from one hip to another. Cody Doan, dressed in a summer sports coat and dress pants, reached over and took it from her. "Give me that." He grunted. "What did you get them, a cast iron toaster?"

"This isn't from us. I gave them our present a few days ago. I told Sandra I'd put this in the gift room."

Cody pointed a finger at Frannie as well as he could, encumbered with the box. "*Us.* You said *us,* and *our.* You gave them a present from both of us, didn't you?"

Pepper snagged a passing waiter. "Simon says come with me." She pulled the hapless man by the hand. The more she tried to hurry, the more her heels sank into the grass, and she finally had to slow her pace.

"All right, I did. Big deal."

"What did *we* give them?"

"A silver scrying ball and a gift certificate toward landscaping their garden."

"I approve."

Pepper hefted the box out of Cody's arms and handed it to the waiter. "This goes in the gift room." She turned back to Cody, "Why are you here?"

He tapped his coat pocket. "You sent me an invitation."

"Frannie said you weren't coming."

"Frannie's been wrong about a lot of things."

Frannie turned toward the gate, but Cody reached for her and put a hand on each of her arms. "I know there's a difference in our ages. I know we've both got hang-ups about my drug history, but I never realized how much I'd miss you. I called my folks and yours and all of them said do it."

"Do what?"

He jiggled her arms. "Don't run off, promise?"

"Be quick about it. I have a wedding to go to."

He took a small, blue box from his pocket. From the box, he took a diamond ring, picked up Frannie's left hand and slid the ring on her finger. "You certainly do. Marry me."

Frannie started to jerk off the ring, but Pepper reached over and put her hand over her friend's fingers. "If you fling that away, we'll never find it in these trees. If you must take that off—I think you're a fool if you do—at least hand it to me."

Frannie worked her hand free, balled it into a fist, then spread her fingers and looked at the ring. "All right, I won't take it off, but that doesn't mean I'm saying yes."

"But you're not saying no, either, right?"

"I'm saying we have to talk, and this is the worst possible place to do that."

Pepper turned them both around so they faced the yard. The crowd had stopped milling and was parting like the Red Sea to make space for Simon and another waiter who carried the wedding cake toward the reception tent on what resembled a small, white stretcher. Pepper whispered. "I promise you no one will notice if you two slip off. I'll even save you some wedding cake."

Pepper followed the cake procession into the reception tent, veered off and snuck through into the wedding tent. It was more a wedding canopy now. Since no clouds had materialized, Simon's perfect employees had removed the tent sides, leaving only the white roof to act as a sun shield. Some of the older guests had already taken seats. They sat talking and fanning themselves with paper fans.

Pepper ducked behind the white partition that hid the groom's waiting area from the guests. The Saint was in conversation with Father Fred, who was dressed in gold and white vestments. She was prepared to meet any opposition from Tank or the others, but Tank looked at her, nodded and the groom's party melted away.

Benny leaned against one of the tent poles, his head bent, and his arms wrapped around his stomach. Pepper sidled up to him and slid her arm around his waist. "You holding up?"

He turned the side-by-side hug into a full, almost bone-crushing one. Pepper was careful not to mush the white carnation in his lapel. "Scared shitless," he whispered in her ear. "Has Hamilton shown up?"

"I haven't seen him. Am I right that your mom gave him unexpected news this morning?"

"Mom and Da told all of us. Said we needed to hear it as a family." He moved her away to arm's length. "How long have you known?"

"Wednesday? Thursday? The past week runs together. Whatever possessed your parents to tell Hamilton this morning?"

"Last chance for all of us to be together. Lorraine and I are taking off from here. The whole family had been to Mass, taken communion and had breakfast. I guess Mom and Da figured we were fortified physically and spiritually, but if you ask me it was piss-poor timing."

"The pissiest."

On the other side of the panel the organist played a few experimental arpeggios. Benny quivered. "I didn't think there could be anything more frightening than being ordered to defend an A-camp that was under siege. I was wrong."

Pepper gave him a peck on the cheek. "This, too, shall pass."

CHAPTER 28

When the question of seating had come up, Pepper had suggested that since she and Avivah were friends of both bride and groom that they place their chairs in the aisle and let the wedding party walk around them. Instead, they flipped for it, so that when the usher asked, "Bride or groom?" Avivah responded with some pride, "Family of the groom." The usher led her and Saul to the second row of the right-side seats.

Saul whispered in her ear, "It's backward."

At Jewish weddings, the groom's side was on the left. Avivah whispered back, "Pretend you are Earth's ambassador at a diplomatic wedding on an alien world. Ours is not to question why."

"Do you have any idea what we do during the ceremony?"

"We follow everyone else's lead."

Saul eyed the two kneeling benches at the front. "I hope it doesn't get too Popish."

Avivah ran her hand over his back in sympathy.

The parents and families came up the aisle, Benny's father escorting Lorraine's mother, one of Lorraine's brothers escorting Grace, and various pairings of siblings. Darby escorted Pepper to the bride's side. When they had sorted themselves out on proper sides of the aisle, Avivah noticed that Hamilton wasn't with the rest of Benny's family. Before she could ask Saul if Hamilton had been inserted into the wedding party at the last minute, a man's voice said from the back, "All stand."

They stood.

Randy, dressed in a red cassock and white surplice, headed the procession, carrying a gold cross atop a wooden pole. Avivah knew the words for his clothes only because Randy had scrupulously explained them to her. Behind him walked two of Lorraine's nephews, similarly attired. One of them carried a book with a white leather cover, and the second boy carried a tall candle, the flame of which he carefully protected by cupping his left hand around it.

Then came Father Fred, Benny and Lorraine's parish priest, dressed in white and gold, with a funny-looking four-cornered hat, topped with a large white pom-pom. He walked with his hands hidden under his garments, like a Chinese mandarin, and nodded to people as he walked up the aisle.

The procession reached the front. Randy set his cross in a holder. Father Fred took off his hat and handed it to one of the other altar boys, while the boy with the candle lit a dozen other candles set on stands in front of the tall flower baskets. Everyone sat down again.

The groomsmen processed by height—Warren, Jeff, then The Saint. The height dipped to accommodate Tank and finally Benny, who came down the aisle with his arm on Mark's shoulder. Mark held both hands high, carrying a silk pillow covered in gold-and-white embroidery. Two wedding rings were tied to the pillow with gold and white ribbons.

Where *was* Hamilton?

Avivah sensed a stir on the bride's side as the men passed. At first, she assumed it was a reaction to The Saint's bald head and tattoo, but when the men lined up at the front of the pavilion, she saw that all of the wedding party, except Mark and Benny, wore diamond studs in their left ears.

She leaned over again to Saul. "How many ears got pierced Thursday night?"

"More than one. Benny's gift to his groomsmen: diamond ear studs. Can also double as tie pins, for the squeamish."

The pavilion became quiet, the silence broken only by shuffling feet and an occasional, last-chance cough.

Avivah caught movement on the bride's side, near the front of the pavilion. Hamilton Kirkpatrick snuck in quickly, sat down beside Pepper, and grasped her hand. He leaned over and said something to Darby, followed by Pepper whispering in Darby's ear. Darby nodded, then Hamilton and Pepper got up, still hand-in-hand, and walked outside the pavilion. Once they were outside, where most of the guests couldn't see them, Pepper held up her and Hamilton's clasped hands, and with the other hand waved frantically toward the groom's party. Tank saw them. He tapped Benny and pointed. Benny looked in the direction Tank pointed, grinned and gave a thumbs-up salute, which Hamilton returned. Then Hamilton and Pepper disappeared around the side, reemerged at the back of the pavilion and took seats in the very last row.

That was going to take some explanation.

There was a long chord, and the organist played music that Avivah thought she might be able to name, if she weren't so excited she couldn't hold two thoughts together. Lorraine's three bridesmaids entered, one by one, with a decorous interval between. The first one wore a slim, pale pink dress, with V-neck and little shoulder caps of gauzy material. Her summer hat was the exact shade of pink as her dress. Gold and white ribbons and tiny gold baubles on stems covered the hat; the gold baubles nodded as the woman walked down the aisle. The second and third bridesmaids wore identical hats and dresses, the second one in a medium rose, and the last in a dark rose. The matron of honor, Lorraine's sister, wore a flower wreath instead of a hat, and a sleeker version of the dress in green, tied in an empire style with a white bow.

At least Avivah could identify Lohengrin's *The Bridal Chorus.* The congregation stood, in waves, as Lorraine walked down the aisle on her father's arm. A bouquet of green, white, and pale yellow calla lilies, orchids, and lady's slippers cascaded in front of the off-white lace and tulle dress. Hers had a V-neck as well, with tulle rising between the V and the lace collar around Lorraine's neck. Where her attendants' dresses were almost sleeveless, she had long tulle sleeves, which ended at her wrists in wide lace cuffs. Instead of a veil, she wore an elaborate headdress of white and gold flowers, with a short length of netting trailing down her neck. With her blond hair and fair skin, she looked like a Nordic princess.

Lorraine and her father reached the front. Father Fred stepped forward, with one of the altar boys holding the white, leather-covered book so he could read it. "Who gives this woman to be married?"

Lorraine's father took a step forward. "Her mother and I do." He kissed Lorraine, and then took his seat beside his wife.

Lorraine handed her bouquet to her matron of honor. She and Benny knelt side by side.

Father Fred held both hands up to the sky. "Let us give thanks that we have an opportunity to come together today to witness this joyous union between Lorraine and Benjamin." He led everyone in a short prayer before they sat down.

Each of the four parents took turns reading from the Bible. Avivah recognized the Old Testament reading that Lorraine's father did, and the Psalm that Grace Kirkpatrick read, but the other two were unfamiliar to her and she supposed they came from the New Testament.

When the parents had taken their seats again, Father Fred said, "The bride and groom chose to have their wedding Mass this morning, with their families and attendants. So, you can relax because I've already delivered my wedding sermon."

There were titters throughout the crowd. Apparently this was an inside Catholic joke.

He spoke briefly about how Lorraine and Benny had persevered in their faith through hard times. He charged them to make faith the center of their home, not only for their own sakes, but for that of their children as well. He finished with, "If anyone knows a reason that this man and woman should not be joined in holy matrimony, let him speak now, or forever hold his peace."

Avivah had a brief nightmare of Randall Fulford, dressed in bloody fatigues, suddenly rising up from the middle of the congregation and objecting, but when she looked around at the dresses and suits, at the pleased, expectant faces, the vision faded. There wasn't a single military thing here today, not even an American-flag pin. She said a silent Kaddish for Randall. Saul's lips were moving, too. Tears began to flow down Avivah's cheeks.

"Benjamin James, have you come here of your own free will to give yourself to Lorraine Hannah in marriage?

"I have."

"Lorraine Hannah, have you come here of your own free will to give yourself to Benjamin James in marriage?"

"I have."

Father Fred held his hands over their heads. "Will you honor and love one another as husband and wife for the rest of your lives, and accept children from God lovingly, and bring them up according to the law of Christ and His Church?"

The "I will"s sounded one beat apart.

"Please join your right hands. Benjamin James, do you take Lorraine Hannah for your wife, to have and to hold, from this day forward, for better, for worse, for richer, for poorer, in sickness and in health, until death do you part?"

"I do."

"Lorraine Hannah, do you take Benjamin James for your husband, to have and to hold, from this day forward, for better, for worse, for richer, for poorer, in sickness and in health, until death do you part?"

"I do."

The priest turned to Mark. "May I have the rings please, Mark?"

Mark stood open-mouthed, the pillow held rigidly in front of him. Tank gave him a little push and Mark walked forward. Father Fred blessed the rings, untied the first ribbon, and took Lorraine's ring, which he handed to Benny.

"With . . . With . . ."

Father Fred prompted, in a tone that said, come on, you've practiced this, "With this ring I thee wed, and pledge thee my troth."

"With this ring I thee wed, and pledge thee my troth."

Lorraine managed to slip Benny's ring on his hand without prompting.

"By the power vested in me by the Church and by the state of North Carolina, I now pronounce you man and wife." He made a sign of the cross over their heads. "May the Lord in His goodness strengthen your consent, and fill you both with His blessings. What God has joined together, let no man put asunder. You may kiss the bride."

For this, Benny needed no prompting. A few minutes later, the couple walked down the aisle, arm in arm to a boisterous rendition of Mendelssohn's *Wedding March,* leaving the rest of the wedding party to trail behind them like wisps of pink-and-green clouds.

For a few minutes Avivah had forgotten that everyone here might still be in mortal danger.

Chapter 29

Pepper shook blood back into her left hand. When Hamilton appeared at her side, he'd clutched her hand and whispered, "The only way I will get through this is if I sit in the back, where no one can see me, and hang on to you."

Pepper had leaned over and whispered one word to Darby. "Dustoff." It was the only word she could think of that conveyed the situation's urgency.

He'd nodded. Who was he to deny Hamilton emergency medical evacuation?

Hamilton had held her hand in a vice-grip for the entire ceremony. Now he'd gathered enough courage to join the receiving line, though Pepper noticed he positioned himself at the very end, where he could escape if he had to.

Avivah crossed the lawn, carrying two champagne glasses. She handed one to Pepper. "What was that with Hamilton just before the ceremony?"

"Emotional CPR. This morning, Grace and Quinn told him who his father was."

"Why this morning of all times?"

"They didn't want any more family secrets, and they'd run out of time to have the whole family together to hear what they had to say. Benny and Lorraine will be on their honeymoon the instant they can get away from here. Hamilton needed a buddy in the worst way. I've no idea why he chose me."

"Don't you?"

Pepper took a swallow of champagne and promptly spit it out again. "This is ginger ale. I thought it was champagne." She put her hand to her mouth. "Oh, God, I forgot. I could have picked this up off a tray, and drunk it without thinking. Thank you, Avivah."

Her pact with Darby and Benny was very specific. One alcoholic drink, and they were out of her life forever. They'd honor no lapses from abstinence, even at a wedding. They knew as well as she did that she could never stop at only one drink.

"Calm down. We're all on edge. If it's any consolation, there's ginger ale in my glass, too."

"You still think there's going to be trouble?"

"Every minute that slides by, I figure we're one minute closer to a showdown. I thought we'd be okay once we got our prime suspect in custody, but he recognized someone here, and it scared the living daylights out of him."

"Who did he recognize?"

Avivah looked around. "I don't know and it's driving me crazy."

"Any clues about who to look for?"

"Someone evil."

"Big help."

Pepper walked through the crowd looking at friends and strangers. Who knew what evil looked like? She paused, looked around, walked through the tent, but couldn't find the person she wanted.

Simon and his minions were busy converting what had been the wedding tent to what would be the dinner/dance tent. As the day wore on Simon looked less like the perfect host and more like a stevedore. His face had taken on a permanent sheen, and his spotless white shirt wasn't quite so spotless.

"Simon?"

He paused in the middle of setting up a table and assumed

his perfect-day face. Even the face looked a little shop-worn. "Yes, ma'am?"

"I'm looking for one of the wedding party: the tall man, with the shaved head. Have you seen him?"

"He was hungry, so we fed him. Try the necessities table."

A wooden folding screen, bearing a sign that read *Family and Wedding Party Only,* separated the necessities table from the rest of the gathering. Pepper found The Saint, sitting on a folding chair, blowing soap bubbles from a child's bubble bottle. He capped the bottle when he saw Pepper, and put it back in a plastic box filled with crayons, drawing paper, and small toys.

"Sorry. Bubbles and marbles. I never could resist either of them as a child." He picked up a plate containing the last few bites of a roast beef sandwich. "Wasn't it Napoleon who said a wedding party traveled on its stomach? Or was that an Army? A man my size can't sustain himself all afternoon on tea sandwiches."

"I need spiritual counseling."

The Saint leaned back in his chair, took a deep breath and set the food aside. "I don't think I'm the right person."

"You *are* a chaplain."

He patted the empty folding chair beside him. "Sit down."

She did.

The Saint sighed, looked at the crowd without appearing to see them, and sighed again. "Pepper, I'm a priest. For now at least. Father Thomas Clarke Devoy."

Bother. In spite of the way she felt about Darby, The Saint had stirred thoughts in her, thoughts that were she still a practicing Catholic, she would eventually have to bring to the confessional. "Why didn't you tell me?"

"Benny said that you, being a lapsed Catholic, had reservations about priests. I figured you and I might get along better if you weren't wondering about genuflecting and calling me *Father* every two minutes."

So much for even a tiny slice of a fantasy life. "What did you mean by being a priest for now?"

"The Church and I are, you might say, in negotiations."

"A crisis of conscience?"

"My third tour in Viet Nam. Too many last rites administered to parts of bodies. You know what they say, three times and you're out."

"If you part ways with the Catholic Church, won't the Army be up shit creek without a paddle?"

"That's one way of putting it."

"The Church can't revoke your priesthood, can it? 'The Lord has sworn an oath and will not change his mind. You are a priest forever after the order of Melchizedek.' "

"Ah, someone who has studied the Psalms. What the Church can do is prevent me from publicly practicing my priesthood, and they can excommunicate me. I have no plans to resign my commission. That would leave the Army with a Catholic chaplain who wasn't a Catholic anymore."

"Tricky. Does your commanding officer know about this?"

"Yes."

"He must be jumping through himself."

"That is putting it mildly. So you see, I'm not the best person to consult on spiritual matters."

What better person than someone who was facing a spiritual crisis? She bet Father Devoy—that sounded so strange—had done a lot of thinking about right and wrong lately. "I need to talk to someone about evil."

"Ordinary, everyday evil or evil-evil?"

"The kind of evil that puts innocent people, strangers, children at risk for the sake of a sick practical joke."

"The tin whistles?"

"The tin whistles escalated. Something happening here,

today, just for the sake of meanness."

Devoy rubbed his hand over his chin. "Ditch meanness as a motive. It's not strong enough. Real evil comes out of a darker place: revenge; pure, unadulterated anger; or an old grievance that's festered for so long it's eaten the person away inside. You're looking for someone who has no charity left, no tenderness, no ability to give or be thankful, no hope. That's where you'll find real darkness. Is that any help?"

"I don't know yet." She leaned over and kissed him on the cheek. "Let me know how it goes?"

"You mean the unholy trinity, me, the Army and the Church?"

"I mean you. The Army and the Church have survived for a long time, and I suspect they will continue to survive."

Sunlight glinted off his diamond stud as he cocked his head. "How old were you when you started bringing home birds with broken wings?"

"Five, maybe six."

"That's what I figured. The best advice I can give you is to look at people's faces. Get them to look at you. When you find someone who can't reflect your own humanity back at you, chances are pretty good you've found the person you're looking for."

Great advice, but fraught with complications. After a couple of close encounters with people who didn't appreciate Pepper checking them for reflected humanity, she decided to find Avivah and tell her what The Saint had said. Let Avivah stare at people for a while.

No ability to give. Give. Gift. Present. Something she'd seen today suddenly made no sense. She went to Frannie's studio and nodded to several people who were perusing the mountains of gifts set out on every available space. She found the package immediately. It was overwrapped with a heavy, flocked paper, tied with masses of ribbon and topped with a veritable forest of bows. When Pepper lifted the box, it was heavy. Cut glass, she thought, or an entire silverware service for twelve. Something that heavy had to be ostentatious and terribly expensive.

Ignoring the stares, she took the package to the classroom and locked the door behind her. There was no gift tag. If she hadn't heard Frannie say this was from Sandra, she would have had no way of knowing who the giver was.

In the South, proper gift giving was a minefield, fraught with opportunities for any possible social *faux-pas*. The importance of the right gift, at the right time, wrapped the right way, with the right card was something Pepper had absorbed from child-hood, and she bet Sandra had, too. Some things were just not done, and one of them was that Sandra Waine—essentially Fran-nie's hired help—had gotten beyond herself to give Benny and Lorraine, people she hardly knew, an elaborate, expensive present.

Pepper put her ear to the box. It wasn't ticking, so likely it wasn't a bomb. Were there ways of setting off a bomb without a ticking timer? Benny would know, he'd been cross-trained in demolitions, but there was no way she was going to interrupt his wedding day to ask him.

She thought of soaking the box in water. That's what they always did in the movies with a suspicious package. Either that, or toss it out of a window. Neither sounded like a good idea.

Pepper used her fingernail to carefully slit the tape on one end, and peeled the paper back enough to see a canned peaches carton from a supermarket. Big time *faux-pas*. A wedding present demanded a pristine gift box. She removed the paper. It was an ordinary canned peaches carton, taped shut with industrial-strength tape.

There wasn't a thing in the room she could use to slit the tape. Using one of the wire coat hangers from the coat rack, she finally managed to pry the box open. Inside, lying on its side, was a scuffed home movie projector, a take-up reel and a reel of movie film. Pepper lifted the projector and set it upright. She plugged it in and turned it on. A square of linty white light was projected on the green chalkboard.

She held up the reel and unwound a few inches of film, but the frames were too small and dark to see what was there. It took her a few minutes to figure out how to thread the machine. Finally the take-up reel bit onto the film's end; film began to move through the machine with a clacky sound.

At first Pepper thought it was someone's home movie of a safari, poorly done, at that. There was a bamboo cage, about the right size for a lion, set in some dense foliage. A small man, wearing black pants, an overshirt and a pyramid-shaped woven hat moved into the frame. His back was to the camera and Pepper couldn't see his face, but she recognized the clothes all too well. Almost every Vietnamese man she'd seen wore the same thing.

The man poked in the cage with a stick. He unlocked the cage and stepped aside. A man crawled out. He was skinny, filthy, with long hair and a beard. He wore rags and Ho-Chi-Minh sandals. He had to use the bars of the cage to pull himself to a standing position.

Pepper bent her head, screwed her eyes shut and clapped her hands over her ears to stop the clacking sounds of the projector. She didn't need to see this. She couldn't bear to see it.

Something cold touched her neck. Pepper jumped and turned around. Sandra Waine held a small, silver revolver in her right hand.

Her heart pounding, Pepper backed up until she stood in front of the lens. Images of moving figures covered her body, until looking at the projector's light blinded her. "How did you get in here? I locked the door."

"Internal door. Doesn't even need a key. Just insert something long into the knob's hole. The sound of the movie projector covered the sound as the lock popped."

Pepper moved away from the projector. Her vision gradually returned, but it was blurry.

Sandra's left arm cradled a large glass jar, with what Pepper first thought was a paintbrush. What in the world was Sandra doing painting today of all days?

Sandra said, "Tears. How touching."

As Pepper's eyes cleared, the object in the glass jar resolved into a sixty cc syringe, topped by a large needle, the kind used to draw blood. White cake frosting coated the needle.

Sandra held out the jar. "Want to lick it? I wouldn't if I were you. Lye. Liquid drain cleaner. One of the things I learned working for ChemCover was how many lethal chemicals are found around the house."

"There are children out there."

"They won't get any cake. I *enhanced* only the top layer, the one the bride and groom share with one another. One delicious bite shared between them, burning away the linings of their esophagus all the way down. If they survive, they'll have to be fed with stomach tubes for the rest of their lives. Or maybe they'll cough, and suck it into their lungs. It dissolves bronchial trees, too."

"Why are you doing this?"

"The friend of my enemy is my enemy, too. Or is it the other way around. I can never get that straight."

"Benny and Lorraine never did anything to you."

"Not Benny, his stupid mother. Kevin, Peter and I were doing okay with our little MIA gig, until Peter realized who Lorraine's future mother-in-law was. How's that for bad luck? We picked a mark who was going to be related by marriage to a woman Peter knew—in the Biblical sense—thirty years ago. They must have had some hot stuff going. Soon as Peter figured out who Lorraine's future mother-in-law was, he unraveled. He was going to fess up, tell his long-lost love everything. Then where would we have been?"

Sandra set the glass jar on the table. "They're about to cut the cake. Let's go watch the fun, shall we?" She put her hand holding the gun inside her jacket pocket. "Don't let the small size fool you. In the right place, the bullet makes an adequate hole, and I am a very good shot. My firearms instructor was a bit anal-retentive, but Second Lieutenant Baxter insisted I learn to shoot, without reference, and without error. It's a skill I've kept up over the years. Something to honor him, you might say."

Pepper went first. The gift room was empty. Of course, no guest wanted to miss the cake cutting. She looked at the piles of presents. Darby always said a weapon was anything you had to hand. If only she knew what the boxes held. Bopping Sandra with towels or a set of sofa pillows would likely get her killed.

She spotted the oblong package Nate had handed to Avivah that morning. It was heavy; Avivah had almost dropped it. As they walked past it, Pepper reached out, grabbed the package and spun in a full arc. The package connected with the side of Sandra's head with a satisfying *thunk*. Sandra went sprawling into a pile of gaily wrapped packages. As she raced for the door, Pepper heard the sound of glass tinkling.

The door was locked. Her sweaty hand slipped on the doorknob. She finally unlocked it, and ran, only to have her heels sink their full length into the soft dirt. She abandoned her shoes and ran barefoot across the lawn, ripping the soles of her stockings as she ran.

Halfway across the lawn, she saw flashes of light in the reception tent, the rapid kind of multiple shots a photographer did to make sure he got a good picture of cutting the cake.

She spotted Avivah and screamed, "The cake is poisoned."

Benny and Lorraine each had a huge piece of cake on the ends of silver forks. The forks moved toward open mouths.

Pepper and Avivah converged from opposite sides of the tent, knocking over chairs as they went. Benny and Lorraine looked toward the sound of the confusion. Both women threw themselves at the small cake table. Avivah pushed at Benny's and Lorraine's arms. Forks and cake went flying. Pepper's momentum carried her into the cake table, which broke under her weight. Cake, flowers, silverware and plates crashed to the floor.

Cake oozed down Pepper's dress. The fabric began to smoke. Her skin burned. Her gaze met Darby's. "Lye," she said, holding up her cake-encrusted left hand. "Burns like hell."

Darby grabbed one punch bowl and Tank grabbed the other. Pink punch cascaded down Pepper's dress. Her left hand was sloshed in green punch. Grace Kirkpatrick came running at Pepper with a garden hose turned full on. The cold water hit Pepper's chest as the world dissolved to black.

CHAPTER 30

The dinner tent was polka-dotted with empty tables. Avivah surmised that some guests had decided their nerves couldn't take any more, and had left early. Benny and Lorraine had paid for more food than the remaining guests would eat. Avivah wondered if she and Pepper could rent an extra freezer to hold all of the leftovers until the Kirkpatricks got back from their honeymoon.

Ollie pushed away a plate with only bones left on it. "A lesser man would have crumbled."

Nate mashed a last bite of potato into chicken gravy and corralled it on his fork. "I'm going to be a long time forgetting Simon standing on a chair in the middle of complete chaos, yelling, 'Roll the ice cream trucks.' I keep seeing John Wayne in *The Sands of Iwo Jima.*"

Avivah twisted open two chocolate cookies and licked white icing from the middle. "All the ice cream sundaes and cookies you can eat. Who cares if there was no wedding cake? I've got such a sugar buzz that I won't come down for a week."

Ollie started on his strawberry shortcake. "I especially liked Benny and Lorraine, dressed in sweatshirts and jeans, feeding each other animal crackers. Those kids have spunk."

"They waited a long time for today. Benny said he'd be damned if he'd let his guests go home before they'd had a real party."

Nate looked at the head table where a mercifully intact wedding party sat. "They got lucky."

Avivah looked across the tent to the table where Pepper, with her left arm in a sling, sat in a wheelchair, her head nestled against Darby's shoulder. "A lot of people got lucky."

Nate asked, "Anyone do a final damage tally yet?"

"Everything Pepper had on, my dress, Lorraine's wedding dress, Benny's rented tux, a cake table, table linens, the cake, several gallons of punch, and lots of cake plates. We'll be digging china fragments out of the lawn for the rest of the summer. Simon says he has an Act of God policy for all of his stuff. I have a feeling, though, that Kirkpatrick *et. al* are on his *never-again* list."

Ollie tapped his spoon on the dish holding Avivah's strawberry shortcake. She passed it to him. He waved his spoon. "Don't forget the wedding presents. What a mess. All those crushed packages and cards strewn over the floor. Someone is going to be sorting out who gave what for a long time."

"Any word on Sandra?"

Nate stretched and sat back in his folding chair. "Floating in and out of consciousness, but the doctors say she'll recover. Your friend packs a wallop with a pickle dish."

Avivah raised her water glass in Pepper's direction. "My friend packs a wallop in life. You should have seen how she ran an orthopedic ward at Fort Bragg."

Nate said, "We screwed up when we decided that McCormick and Mrs. Nibb had only one car between them. We missed the possibility that McCormick had a ride—Sandra—waiting for him outside the Bible camp. My guess is that Mrs. Nibb saw McCormick leave the tent revival and followed him."

He said it without guilt, as if eventually getting it right made up for occasionally screwing up on the way there. Avivah had forgotten what tough cop-hide looked like. She liked being reminded that cops didn't have to be perfect to be good. She said, "We screwed up twice. We kept seeing Frannie and missing her little shadow, Sandra. McCormick, of course, says the whole MIA scam, and Sandra insinuating herself with Frannie to collect information about Lorraine and Randall, was Sandra's idea. Anyone want to bet that when Sandra regains consciousness, she says the whole thing was McCormick's idea?"

"No takers," Ollie said, as he polished off Avivah's dessert.

While McCormick was willing to talk about meeting Sandra in Chicago, how she had cooked up the MIA scheme and hired university drama students to make the fake POW movie, he was completely closed-mouthed about what had happened the night Peter Taft died. Avivah had already made herself dizzy with a list of possible permutations for that night, depending on how many of the players had been in Taft's motel room that Friday night, and whether or not Peter Taft had injected the fatal drugs himself. With both Taft and Mrs. Nibb dead, she doubted they would ever be certain exactly what had happened.

Nate said, "Monday morning we should phone ChemCover, and ask if they have a pharmaceutical division. I'm betting they do. I want the pathologist to take a hard look at exactly what chemicals Mrs. Nibb had in her body when she died, and I think the Houston police are going to want to take a closer look at Sandra's friend's supposed *suicide*."

Ollie asked, "What about John Taft? Was he or was he not Peter Taft's son?"

Avivah made a mental note to phone Taft's next-of-kin in Alaska. "The right age, both men from Alaska. Likely he was."

The big Juvenile sergeant shook his head. "What kind of man builds a confidence game on the memory of a dead son?"

Avivah said, "Both Frannie and Grace said Taft always had a rough streak in him. I guess he figured that since the boy was dead, nothing would hurt him."

Ollie reached into his coat pocket and took out an unsealed

345

envelope, which he laid in front of Avivah. "Some time Monday this is going to be all over the station house, so I wanted you to be the first to know."

She took out the single sheet and read it. "You're resigning?"

"Davie needs grandparents, even in the Azores. Madge and I want to watch our grandchild grow up."

Avivah folded the paper and put it back in the envelope. "Why not take a leave of absence? You'll be back in two or three years. When you come back to the force, you'll have lost all seniority."

"I've done twenty-seven years with the city police. I can retire with a pension. It's time to do something more positive for kids. Recreation director, maybe: hang out with normal, healthy kids, shoot a few baskets, and plan Friday-night sock hops."

"Nobody does sock hops anymore."

"Maybe they should. The point is that Juvenile is going to need a new Sergeant. The chief would appoint you in a minute."

Avivah felt her stomach tighten, a bad idea, considering all the cookies and ice cream it held. "Because I'm a woman, and women are good with kids, and it would be great public relations?"

"All of that, but you also have a degree in sociology, and policing experience."

Avivah looked at Nate, who wasn't looking at her. She'd seen the same expression on a boy in eleventh grade when she'd told him she'd picked another boy to go with to the junior prom. If she remembered correctly, prom night had been a disaster. "Tell me about your daughter."

Nate folded and unfolded the tiny square of paper that his dinner mint had come in. "What's to tell?"

He looked at Ollie, who gave him the slightest encouraging nod.

"Tash was a pistol. Smart, funny, graduated sixth in her class at Carolina Law, first woman to article with the top criminal law firm in Raleigh."

Might as well cut to the chase, strike while the iron was hot, all of those clichés her brain was using to conceal that she was scared to ask the next question. "How did she die?"

"Stroke. She stood up to present closing defense arguments in a grand theft trial, passed out, and in an hour was on life support. The doctors said she was brain-dead. It took me six weeks to work up the courage to tell them to turn off the machines. I didn't know she'd gone on the pill. Her mother did. Tash believed that the only way a woman could rise to the top of the legal profession was to make sure she didn't get pregnant."

"Where's your wife?"

"Chapel Hill. Failing first-year pre-law. She wanted to continue what Tash started. My wife graduated from high school in 1940. She hasn't been inside a classroom since, and she thinks she can hack law school."

Maybe she could, with Nate's support, but Avivah would have to get to know him a lot better before she told him that.

Avivah handed the envelope back. "Sorry, Ollie, but Nate asked me first." She folded her arms on the table and leaned forward toward Nate. "Let's be sensible about this. It's not fair to replace your driver on a whim. Tell him he's got six months to decide what he wants next in his policing career. That will give me time to take some graduate classes in criminology. First of next year, I come to work with you as a detective; that is, if you two good ole boys think you can swing an Affirmative Action appointment from the Chief by then."

Hours later, Saul and Avivah danced under a mirror globe that rolled colored lights over them. She'd been waiting for the right song, and it wasn't going to get any better than this slow waltz. She put her head on his shoulder, and realized how nice it was to dance with a man taller than she was.

"I can't go with you to New York. It's not that Nate needs me, but we need each other. I know NYPD would have me in a second, but I don't want to be a big-city cop. I like it here. I like living on the homestead, I like being close to Pepper and Benny. If you promise not to tell my mother, I'll tell you a secret."

He tightened his arms around her and led her in a turn. "Promise."

"I like grits."

"I wish you'd told me earlier. What man would ever think grits could stack up against New York City?"

They jerked to a stop, and Avivah looked at Saul's face. For a man who had just been jilted for a Southern corn product, he looked remarkably calm. "You don't sound disappointed?"

He nodded his head in beat with the music and picked up the dance again. "This afternoon, while Simon was commanding the ice cream forces, I phoned my friend at the *New Yorker* and said, thank you very much, but not right now."

Avivah's heart skipped a beat. "What are you going to do?"

"First thing tomorrow morning, I'm moving my bed into a real bedroom, one with a door I can close. Sleeping in the living room is like sleeping on a flyway. I have a lot more sympathy for geese now."

Suddenly the tent, with a cool evening breeze flowing through it, felt too warm. Maybe it was a side effect of her sugar high, or maybe not. "What about a job?"

"I'll freelance. I'd like to write a book. You should have heard some of those stories Benny's friends told Thursday night. People need to hear those stories. Pepper gave me a line on a Catholic priest who is caught between his crisis of faith and his commissioning oath. My friend at the *New Yorker* is already interested in that story. The way I figure, if I hang around you people long enough, I'm a shoe-in for a Pulitzer or a jail term. I can't wait to see which one it will be."

They danced away, out the side of the pavilion, and into the soft, Carolina night.

The music stopped. At the head table, Benny stood at the microphone and tapped his water glass with a spoon. Everyone stopped talking.

Pepper pushed herself blearily into a sitting position. The hospital had pumped her full of antibiotics, a tetanus shot, and painkillers. Some time soon, she should probably go to bed, but she was having too much fun—in the moments she was conscious—to leave yet.

"Lorraine and I hoped we could make it until ten o'clock, but we're calling it a night. I hope no one minds if we scoot out early. The band is booked to midnight, and I understand from Simon that there's food left, if anyone is still hungry."

There were groans all around the pavilion.

"Thank you so much for coming. I can't tell you what it means to me—" He looked down at Lorraine and took her hand, "To both of us, for you not only to be here today, but to stick it out through everything. My father and mother tell me they have one last thing to say, then Lorraine and I are out of here."

He sat down, still holding on to Lorraine's hand. Grace and Quinn made their way to the microphone. Quinn took papers from his tuxedo pocket. "We hadn't planned to do this publicly, but well, this week hasn't been exactly the week we planned."

No shit, Pepper thought.

Quinn leaned and looked down to the far end of the groom's side of the table, where Ginny Mae sat. "Virginia Maeve, will you come here?"

Hamilton raised his eyebrows. "Virginia Maeve. They only call you that when you're in real trouble."

Ginny Mae swatted at him playfully as she passed behind his chair.

Quinn leaned into the microphone again. "This is Benny's sister, Virginia. She has a birthday a week from today. She'll be twenty."

Scattered, polite applause moved through the crowd. Ginny looked embarrassed.

"I know it's customary to mark the twenty-first birthday celebration with something special, but we couldn't wait. When Virginia was six, she saw on television that stores had midnight-madness sales. One night she took my keys, snuck out of the house, opened up our hardware store, made posters and held a midnight-madness sale of her own. Until the patrolling policeman shut her down and brought her home."

This time laughter rolled across the spectators.

Ginny blushed. "Da!"

"It's all right, honey. That's when her mother and I realized that it would be our daughter, not one of our sons, who inherited the business. In talking to people here today, I've discovered some of you are farmers. You know that small farm towns are having a tough time of it. We wanted Virginia to have more of a future than we saw for her at home."

He stood aside and Grace moved to the microphone. "I was born and raised in Alaska. My parents still live there; all of our sons were born there, but Virginia was born in Missouri, and she has told us, vociferously, frequently, that she felt cheated not being able to call herself a *sourdough*."

Quinn held up a photograph. "I know you can't see this, so I'll pass it around in a few minutes. This is a picture of Grace's parents, standing in front of a building in Anchorage, Alaska. They're pointing to the sign they just hung on the building. It says

V.M. Kirkpatrick and Family Hardware
Serving Alaska since 1974
"If we don't have it, why would you be needing it?"

A chill moved down Pepper's spine.

Quinn handed his daughter an envelope. "The deed to the store. Happy Birthday, honey."

Virginia Mae clutched the envelope, her mouth opening and closing soundlessly, like a fish. Everyone at the head table was on his or her feet, hugging Ginny and kissing her, while the pavilion rocked with applause. It took a while before Ginny came to the microphone again. She held her hand tight against her chest.

"I don't know what to say. I'm speechless."

"A first," Joseph Kirkpatrick said, grinning.

Grace leaned into the microphone. "We want you to say one thing. While you're considered an adult in Alaska, which means you can legally sign contracts, please don't sign anything without consulting me or your father. This is still a *family* business, and your Da and I have a lot of experience that we'd hate to see go to waste. Promise?"

"I promise."

Quinn handed his daughter five envelopes. "Here's your ticket to Alaska, and if you would pass the others down the row to Randy, Mark, Joseph and Hamilton. Since we get together so infrequently as a family, and since Grace's parents' health didn't allow them to travel to the wedding, we decided to move the party to Anchorage tomorrow."

Quinn hesitated and ran his finger over the microphone stand. His voice wavered. "Grace and I have a little business to conclude here in Asheville first."

Yeah, like a charge for concealing a death, which could still put Quinn in jail for several years.

Quinn took a deep breath. "But I'm sure that will work out,

and after we do, Grace and I are moving back to Alaska. We've bought a secondhand fishing boat and a house, right down the street from our hardware store."

Normal people retired to Florida. Kirkpatricks retired to Alaska. It figured.

Benny leaned over and softly beat his head against the table. Darby laughed.

Pepper asked, "What's wrong with Benny?"

"You asked me to wheedle out of him where he was going on his honeymoon, you know, guy-to-guy. He's taking Lorraine on a romantic cruise up the Inside Passage. Five days from tomorrow, their ship docks in Anchorage."

"And all of his family will be at the dock to meet them."

"Looks that way."

Pepper laughed, but somewhere in the middle of the laughter, she began sobbing, and couldn't stop. People at the tables around them looked concerned.

Darby stood, and guided her wheelchair. "You, pretty lady, are going to bed."

CHAPTER 31

Pepper let out a slow, even breath, trying to imitate sleep. Good. No ragged sobbing. When she cried lying flat on her back, tears ran into her ears. She didn't dare move for fear of waking Darby.

His hand moved in a soft, sleepy circle around her belly button. He untangled himself from her, turned over, looked at his lit wristwatch dial, and snuggled back in place. His voice sounded muzzy. "It's four-forty-seven. You want another pain pill?"

As long as she stayed still and warm nothing much hurt, except her heart. "No."

"Glass of water, anything?"

She felt tears rising in her throat again. "I don't want scars. Benny's scars itch, he can't wear certain kinds of clothes, and he has to be careful about not getting sunburned. I don't want that hassle."

Darby fumbled for her unbandaged hand and pressed it into his shoulder, with her fingertips in the middle of the crater formed by an AK-47 round. "People cope." Grace Kirkpatrick coping with being raped had almost destroyed her family. Frannie had coped with being an abused wife, married to a drug addict. She'd almost lost Cody because of how well she'd coped. Hamilton assumed money could buy coping. Father Tom Devoy had hoped faith could. If Benny and Lorraine hadn't coped so patiently, they could have been married years ago. "I don't want to cope. I want to yell and scream, and throw things, and get

Sharon Wildwind

my share of the world! I want you to take off those damned gold eagles and marry me. I am tired of being alone."

He moved her hand away from his scar. They lay in darkness, hand-in-hand, side-to-side, not sleeping.

"I have an engagement ring for you."

"I thought you might."

"Bad timing?"

"The worst."

"When would be a good time?"

"The day that you come knocking on my door as a civilian. No matter how I twist it, or slice it, or try to fool myself, I would make the world's worst general's wife. Pretending otherwise wouldn't be fair to either of us."

"Four years, two months, and twenty-two days from today."

"What's that?"

"If I give up any idea of being promoted to general, the length of time until I can retire with a full pension. August 31, 1978."

"I can't wait. I have to get on with my life—as a civilian. I want to quit the Veterans' Administration and find a real, civilian nursing job. Benny and Lorraine have moved on. Avivah is moving on. I want to go with them."

"Can you wait three weeks?"

"Why three weeks?"

"Long enough for me to get Nancy out of Hanoi. I didn't do right by her when we were married. I owe her. Give me a chance to settle that debt."

"You wouldn't have really taken me with you, would you? To Hanoi, I mean? That day in the recruiting station, that was talk to placate me, wasn't it?"

"The moment you suggested it, I got caught up in possibilities. Later, common sense set in. If I had six months to train you, if I had even a month I would take you, but a rescue mission as on-the-job training would get both of us killed."

354

"I don't want you to go away, even for three weeks. I want you to stay forever."

He loomed over her, bent his face to hers, and kissed her on each eyelid. "Forever is going to come soon enough. Hang on to that thought."

If she moved slowly, and took her pain pills, Pepper discovered she could supervise quite a lot.

Simon and his minions managed to fit all the leftover food into Pepper's freezer, though when they finished there wasn't a square inch to spare. With Saul's appetite, Pepper figured space would open up soon enough.

The rental company carted off the bar from the fairy grove, and their pavilions, leaving two large squares of trampled grass and one yellow spot of dead grass where the cake table had been. It was only the beginning of June. There would be plenty of time before fall for reseeding.

Sunday afternoon, while Saul and Avivah moved Saul's bed into Benny's old bedroom, and put the living room in order, Pepper calculated that there were one million, eight hundred and fourteen thousand, four hundred seconds in three weeks, which was a heck of a lot better than how many seconds there were in four years, two months, and twenty-two days. When she tried to calculate that number of seconds, she tangled herself in an incomprehensible morass of zeros.

By late Sunday evening, most of the Kirkpatricks were winging their way north to Alaska. Pepper hoped Quinn and Grace were hunkered down at the bed-and-breakfast, cuddled up hard together.

Frannie and Cody had yet to surface. Pepper wondered how long it would be before she could think *wedding* without cringing. She had a feeling Frannie might ask her to be in her wedding party.

Darby was—somewhere—an amorphous place between the homestead and Hanoi. Twenty-five thousand and two hundred seconds had passed since the last time she calculated.

Pepper sat on her couch, alone in her dark house, cradling an unopened fifth of bourbon she'd found wedged in the V of a tree down at the fairy grove.

When she'd stood in front of the projector, facing Sandra, images had seeped into her bones. She saw Randall in that cage, and, but for the grace of God, Darby and Benny, and men she hadn't thought about in years. Viet Nam had put them all in a cage.

Benny and Lorraine had helped each other break free. Maybe Saul and Nate Alexander would do the same for Avivah.

Pepper went to her kitchen, not bothering to turn on a light. The paper collar around the bottle tore as she twisted the cap. She set a jelly glass on the counter and poured until there was bourbon behind every one of the flowers printed on the glass. An aphrodisiac odor, like the smell of a lover's skin, surrounded her.

She stared at the glass for a long time, then dipped her finger in the liquid and ran her finger around the rim until it squeaked. Who had she been kidding? Benny and Lorraine could move on. Avivah might. She and Darby couldn't.

Abraham Lincoln's words at Gettysburg came back to her. ". . . from these honored dead we take increased devotion to that cause for which they gave the last full measure of devotion . . . that we here highly resolve that these dead shall not have died in vain."

She and Darby had been civilians once, but they'd gotten over it.

He wasn't going to resign his commission in three weeks, and she wasn't going to make him. Whatever solution they would find together had to last a lot longer than four years, two months, and twenty-two days. A general was good for thirty years' service, maybe thirty-five if Darby did it right. He'd never know who he truly could be until he made those imaginary stars on his shoulders real. After what she'd done to him, gotten under his skin, loved him, helped him discover that he could love her in return, he wouldn't get his stars without her. She was going to have to grow up and learn how to be a general's wife, only she didn't have the courage to face that prospect sober.

In the dark, she dialed a number she'd memorized months ago, on the off-chance she'd ever need it. Not that she ever would.

"AA. My name is Jonathan."

Pepper took a deep breath. "Do I have to give you my name?"

"Not if you don't want to."

"I don't think I do."

"That's fine. What's on your mind tonight?"

"I've got a glass of bourbon in front of me that I don't want to drink, but I don't think I can stop myself. Help me prove to myself that I don't need it."

ABOUT THE AUTHOR

Sharon Wildwind was born and raised in Louisiana. She was twenty-three when she went to Viet Nam as a nurse with the U.S. Army Nurse Corps, and a lot older when she finally made sense of the experience. She has lived in North Carolina and Canada.

Missing, Presumed Wed is her fourth Elizabeth Pepperhawk/ Avivah Rosen mystery. She is currently at work on the fifth (and last) mystery in this series. In addition to being a mystery writer, Sharon is a nonfiction writer, keeps an extensive personal journal, and teaches workshops in both journal-keeping and writing. You are invited to visit her web site at www.wildwind author.com.